The Return of Philo T. McGiffin

DAVID POYER
The Return of Philo T. McGiffin

BLUEJACKET BOOKS

NAVAL INSTITUTE PRESS
Annapolis, Maryland

This book is a comic novel.
"Comic" means that it laughs, where it could choose otherwise.
"Novel" means that it is fiction; it is made up, a story.
The uninitiated reader should know that it is not all true.
Those who have been there will know that, for the most part, it is.

Originally published by St. Martin's Press
First Bluejacket Books printing, 1997

Library of Congress Cataloging-in-Publication Data

Poyer, David.
  The return of Philo T. McGiffin / David Poyer.
    p.   cm.
    ISBN 1-55750-689-2 (alk. paper)
    1. Universities and colleges—Maryland—Annapolis—Fiction.
  2. United States Naval Academy—Fiction.   3.   Annapolis
  (Md.)—Fiction.   I.   Title.
PS3566.O978R4   1997
813'.54—dc21   97-46

Printed in the United States of America on acid-free paper ∞

09 08 07 06 05 04 03 02   8 7 6 5 4

To develop midshipmen morally, mentally, and physically, and to imbue them with the highest ideals of duty, honor, and loyalty in order to provide graduates who are dedicated to a career in the naval service and have potential for future development in mind and character to assume the highest responsibilities of command, citizenship, and government.
> —"Mission of the United States Naval Academy"

We don't want intelligent men at Annapolis; we want men we can make naval officers out of.
> —Admiral J. Paul Stern, 1911

Fake it till you make it.
> —Found carved on an airplane-wing Sleep-Eze desk on the top deck of Melville Hall; date unknown

The Return of Philo T. McGiffin

PROLOGUE

They both agreed, as the game was ending, that it was one hopping hell of a Homecoming game.

For a full three hours the two men—not young, not yet quite old—had cheered and shouted from the fifty-yard line. When the Cannoneers fired for the last time, throwing a wreath of smoke out over the Navy stands, they shook hands, smiling in the clear late sunlight of October. Then, coming to attention, they faced front. Below them on the field four thousand midshipmen, the Brigade, stood at attention with them as they all, together, sang "Navy Blue and Gold":

> Four years together by the Bay
> Where Severn joins the tide,
> Then by the Service called away
> We've scattered far and wide;
> But still where two or three shall meet
> And old tales be retold,
> From low to highest in the Fleet
> Will pledge the Blue and Gold.

And now it was evening. They sat, the two of them, at a table in the basement of Alumni Hall, on King George Street. In front of the man in civilian clothes was a martini. In front of the man in service dress, his chest stiff with fading ribbons, was a double shot of Anchor bourbon. Around them in the taproom other men, young and old, fresh-minted ensigns and long-retired admirals so ancient they could barely sit erect in their wheelchairs, argued and drank beneath the paintings of vanished ships and the seals of classes gone from living memory. Behind the bar three Filipino stewards stood impassively, watching it all.

"Quite a game," said the uniformed man again. He grinned and swallowed half his bourbon. Above the ribbons he had a long, ugly face, crushed together at the sides, a wide smiling mouth, and a nose like the bow of a cruiser. His skin was dark, pitted, and leathered, as if he had spent years squinting into an open flame.

The civilian nodded silently, intent on relighting his pipe. He was shorter than the officer, stocky in a blue blazer, blond, with a close-trimmed, graying beard. His eyes, small and set deeply in a network of wrinkles, looked out skeptically, warily, but with a kind of suspicious humor.

Both of them—like everyone else in the room—wore massive gold rings, as much a part of their left hands as their thumbs.

"Sure was," he said at last, taking the pipe out of his mouth. "That last quarter was close, though. I thought the defense might lose it for us."

"Never happen at a Homecoming. Remember our youngster year, when Truck nabbed the ball on the forty, in the last ten minutes—"

The double clang of a ship's bell interrupted him. At the door a fortyish man, built like a weightlifter, was taking his cap off, too late to avoid the penalty. He looked around, smiling a little sheepishly, and as the room filled with shouts of "Double here!" and "Thanks for the free drink, Bill!" he shrugged and reached for his wallet. He wore the uniform of a Marine colonel.

"You know him?"

"Him? That's Bill Tabor. Played fieldball with him when we were segundoes. Eighth company, I think. He's with CINCLANT now."

"That's right. I remember him," said the civilian. He glanced at his pipe and saw that he had to relight it. Instead he laid it down. "So. How have things been for you, classmate?"

"Not that bad. You know what it's like. Retired on three-quarters of what you couldn't live on before."

"How's Kath? And the kids?"

"Great. Great. Jack got his appointment for next year."

"That's fine."

"How's your business going? Consulting, wasn't it?"

"That's right. It's going well, thanks."

They sat together silent for a time then, watching their drinks.

"You know," said the civilian at last, "It's damned funny, the way we all turned out."

The officer—he was a full commander, the three gold stripes on his sleeves tarnished with age and the sea—looked up from his empty glass. "Funny? What do you mean?"

"Just . . . strange. When you think about who we were—and how we've ended up. J.J. dead out in the Pacific. Truck Cross the chairman of—what is it—General Dynamics. Remember how he used to sweat over his shoes? Len Ind a senator, the Wop a high-powered Ph.D. You and Rollo and the rest staying in, getting all we used to dream about—battles, rank, medals, command."

"Command," repeated the officer. He wiggled his nose a little. "And don't forget the others. Like Norforms. He's probably still in jail in Turkey. Think he's learned any Dago by now?"

"He always used to say—you rate what you can get away with."

They laughed together.

"And Tony Castigliano."

"Good old Wop," said the commander softly. "Remember the time Lunchbags had him under the sink, with the doors closed, smoking that foot-long stinker he brought back from Cuba? And to make it more entertaining he ran the hot water the whole time."

"Lunchbags wasn't the most squared away guy I ever knew," said the civilian. "I heard that when he went up for his nuclear power interview Rickover asked him: 'What do you think of the Jewish race, Mr. Baylor?' And he clutches for a minute and then comes out with, 'I don't know, Admiral—who are they racing this year?'"

"And Snorkel," said the commander, leaning back in his chair. "Leadership by example—what a joke. Remember the night he caught us at the Beehive, chugging pitchers inside the Limit? We were all in civvies, too. We'd have been marching extra duty till June Week—only the lieutenant happened to be dragging somebody else's wife that night."

"A conspiracy of silence," said the civilian.

The new drinks came. They raised them, nodding thanks toward the Marine, and looked at each other over the rims for a long moment.

"To Mother Bancroft," said the civilian.

"To the Brigade."

"Yes. They looked good out there today."

"The women too?"

"Them too," said the civilian. "Why not? All of them. Poor bastards."

"Poor bastards," agreed the commander. They drank, then sat looking into their glasses.

"And the Mouse."

They both smiled suddenly, simultaneously. "God," said the civilian, "the Mouse. It's been years since I've heard anyone say that. It's been a while, hasn't it? And remember how we used to think, when we were plebes, that climbing Herndon would be the end of the world." He noticed his pipe again and picked it up, and then said suddenly, "Herndon—the Chapel, that night—"

"The sword trick he pulled at Army—"

"The buns on Breen's balcony—"

"The time he and Do-Dirty Dan went over the Wall, and Black Bart was waiting for them—"

"The night he was going for the Virgin Guns, and took White Lightning out instead—"

They both laughed hard, forgetting themselves. "Christ, he was something, the Mouse," said the commander, his face reddening. He unbuttoned his uniform blouse. "It sure would be nice seeing him here tonight, wouldn't it?"

"It sure would," said the civilian. He pulled his tie loose. "Getting a little tight . . . you know, on Black Thursday I weighed a hundred and fifty pounds. By Hundredth Night I weighed one-twenty-five."

"That was a long time ago."

"Yes, it was."

"But then," said the commander, his eyes going far off, as if estimating a target angle on a distant ship, "It doesn't seem that long . . . not today. Not here."

"I know what you mean," said the civilian. "It's as if time doesn't really exist here, doesn't pass; as if nothing changes, the way it does on the outside. It's hard to tell even what year it is, here in the Yard."

At the tables around them the old men reminisced. The young

men, single stripes gleaming new, drank furtively, not looking around, abashed by the brass that showed up on this one evening out of the year.

"Yes," said the civilian again, pulling on his pipe. It was well lit now, drawing solid deep down in the bowl. It would smoke for a long time. The night was early, only a little after eight bells by the brass chronometer behind the bar. "A long time. I remember it all, though. It doesn't leave you, it doesn't fade. Stays with you—like Keyes used to say about the mess hall pancakes."

"Uh huh," said the officer. He smiled a little with his ugly mouth. "I guess we'll remember it forever, all of us. June twenty-eighth, Black Thursday. When it all started."

"The day," said the civilian, taking a deep draw and then watching the smoke ebb outward, dissolving, slowly becoming one with the already hazy air of the taproom, "the day we first met Philo T. McGiffin."

CHAPTER ONE

TDSY WUX RE ROME NY
TO: MUNICIPAL HOME
RAYMONDSVILLE PA

202115Z FINAL RECORD RECEIVED AND IS
ACCEPTABLE. YOU ARE AUTHORIZED TO
REPORT NAVAL ACADEMY THURS 28 JUNE 0900.
ALL PAPERS MAILED TO YOU FROM BUREAU
NAVAL PERSONNEL 5 MAY. SUPERINTENDENT
US NAVAL ACADEMY ANNAPOLIS MD SENDS =

Midshipman (n): A young man with great opportunities
behind him.
                    —Graffito found in seaward head, 5-2

The Yard was green and hot and lovely that late June afternoon. It was green and quiet, green and shaded between the granite buildings, the old trees, the marble monuments; and a sea wind from the Chesapeake rustled in the elms above Stribling Walk and the Macedonian monument and the Chapel. The faded red brick walks were empty. The Brigade was away; at sea, on leave, in Pensacola for flight training, out with the Fleet for summer cruise. The bronze doors of the Rotunda were closed, and in Dewey Basin the knockabouts nodded gently to their dolphins.

Only in back of the gray stone pile of Bancroft Hall was any activity apparent.

The Class—though it was not a class yet, in any sense but the potential—was standing there in line. They stood in quiet, apprehensive groups between the chain-link fences of the tennis courts. They wore sport coats, suits, dress whites, loud shirts, expensive loafers, farm boots with mud still in the crevices. They carried tennis racquets and golf clubs, sea bags and guitars, and suitcases full of books and brand-new razors. They stood uneasily in the heat, a thousand of them, with a thousand photographs of young, anonymous girls, most of whom they would never kiss again, in their wallets.

At the edge of one of the groups, standing a hundred yards back from the head of the line, a short, dark-haired boy of seventeen shifted from foot to foot, sweating silently. His face was narrow and his complexion poor. He was thin, stood with his shoulders hunched, and wore a hunted expression, a worn black suit coat a couple of sizes too large, a white shirt, a black tie, and cheap new black shoes. His hands were sunk deep in the pockets of brown corduroy pants.

Jeez, it's hot, thought Philo McGiffin.

That morning he had come in by bus. It was a long trip, twenty-eight hours, with connections in Pittsburgh and Scranton. He'd gotten off up on West Street, with about fifty others, and along with most of them headed straight for the station restroom. Waiting for a urinal, his eyes drifting over the scrawled comments on the walls, he realized suddenly that he was really, finally here—in Annapolis.

USNA: Marking time for four years in the P-rade of Life.

All personnel desiring to put clamps to T. Doyle sign up with respective battalion adjutants by taps tonight

What has eight wings, three hundred and sixty heads, and sucks?

Along with the others, none of them speaking much, he walked the long downhill mile through the cobblestoned streets, between the shuttered storefronts, the old white clapboard and brick colonial homes. Few of them, burdened with bags and gear, knew where they were going; they simply followed the crowd, down Main to Market House Circle, and then down Randall to Gate One. At the circle, looking up as he made the last turn, he saw something gleaming and sparkling in the sun, beyond the gray buildings: the Chesapeake.

Salt water, he thought, stopping as he caught the smell of it on the wind. It was the first time he had ever seen it. From his uncle's sea stories, from the books he had devoured, he had expected a deep clear blue, but the bay was gray-green.

He swung the suitcase to his shoulder and went through the gate without looking back.

In the line now they talked in subdued voices, passing time. The sun beat down on them and the wind gradually died. Some took their jackets off. Most stood silently, thinking about what they had left behind, or what was to come. They looked about them, at the athletic fields, at the bay, at the copper-green mansard upper works of the building that filled the whole western sky.

"Where you from, pal?"

"Tulsa."

"Boca Raton."

"Bolivia."

"Oahu."

"Chi."

"From all over. I'm an Air Force junior."

"Air Force? Aren't you at the wrong academy?"

"Didn't have enough teeth for Colorado Springs."

The line shuffled forward. "Where you from?" someone asked the thin boy.

"Raymondsville. That's in Pennsylvania."

"I'm from Severna Park. Right here in Maryland. Isn't that crazy?"

"Yeah," said Philo, looking away. Out beyond the tennis courts, beyond the flat green of the playing fields, he could see the white sails of a boat far off on the horizon. He wondered where it was going. He put his hand in his jacket to check that the papers, the telegram, were still there. The line shuffled forward. At its head, two men in white uniforms and military caps stood with clipboards. If he strained his ears he could hear them.

"Name?"

"Sam Cross."

"He on your list?"

"You from Huntsville, Alabama, Mister Cross?"

"Yeah. Here's my—"

"Hold on to them. Go on in. You'll be in Lima Company this summer. Get in line under L."

The line moved forward. The thin boy dragged sweat from his forehead and moved his suitcase a few feet on. The sun was intense. Heat shimmered up from the tennis courts, making the sea and the buildings and the distant sails dance and flicker. He had never felt heat like this before. He moved up. The two men in short-sleeved whites looked crisp, hard, virile; their voices were rapid and assured. Then, suddenly, he found himself at the head of the line and they were looking down on him as he went through the wrong pockets for his papers.

"What's your name, stud?"

"Philo McGiffin."

Above his head the two men exchanged looks. "Knock off the bullshit," said the bigger one. "This ain't the place for it. What's your name, mister?"

The way he said *mister* chilled Philo's heart.

"It's, uh, McGiffin," he said. He found the papers. The two men stared down at him. He dropped the papers, retrieved them, and held them out, the damp pages trembling. After a moment one of them took them, holding them by the corner. From under the low-pulled, gleaming black visor of his cap he looked them over, and his expression changed subtly.

"That's what his orders say."

"They say McGiffin?"

"They say Philo T. McGiffin."

"No shit?"

"No shit, Sherlock."

"He's not on the list."

"Friggin' joke, probably . . . some smartass in Main Office." The bigger man handed him back the papers and jerked his head to one side. "We'll check you out later, stud. Wait over there. Come on, move!"

He stood to the side of the line for two hours, till the last man was through. He was limp with sweat and heat. He was afraid even to sit on his suitcase. He looked away from the line, toward the playing fields. A brown and black mongrel lay there, watching them with its head between its paws. It had an odd look of belonging. Beyond it was the bay. He watched as the sailboat grew smaller and smaller and at last was gone. Birds circled overhead, gray and white in the sunlight, and with a little shock he realized that he was seeing his first seagulls.

When the last civilian was through one of the men in white went inside. The other leaned slightly against the side of the building. He looked as crisp and neat in the starched uniform, white cap, black shoulderboards striped with gold, as he had when he started. He tucked the clipboard under his arm, narrowed his eyes to the sun, and finally looked over to where McGiffin was standing. Phil straightened nervously. The man looked at him for several seconds. Philo tried to smile but the only thing that happened was that sweat slid saltily into his mouth. The other did not smile back.

"Your name really Philo McGiffin?"

"Yeah. It is."

"You better start saying 'sir,' stud. From here on."

"Yessir."

"*Sir.*"

"Yes, *sir.*"

"You know who I am, Mister McGiffin?"

"Your name tag thing there says Corpen."

"Sir."

"Sir. Your name thing there says Corpen, sir." He laughed, intending it to be friendly, but it came out as a squeaky giggle. Corpen stared at him, disgust gradually overtaking his features. The second officer (Were they officers? Or what?) came out.

"He's on the master list all right. Jimzo thought it was a joke so he left him off ours."

"Holy hell," said Corpen, looking at Philo with distaste. "It's really Philo McGiffin?"

"That's right. Wait. It gets better. He's assigned to 34th."

"Sweet *Christ*," said Corpen, the distaste growing sharper until it seemed his upper lip would split. "Of all the . . . and a lousy sand-blower, too. Get in the line for Lima, boot. *McGiffin!*"

"Yes, *sir.*"

The afternoon began too fast and grew progressively out of hand. Lost in the granite immensities, the endless green-tiled corridors of Bancroft Hall, he wandered with a thousand other lost souls, each with a checkoff list and a smudged, unreadable map in hand. He found sick bay, and his arms bled from flinching during a series of shots that suggested the plebe class was destined for an invasion of New Guinea. He found the barber shop and came out a pound lighter, with an odd, clear feeling of space impinging on his near-nude scalp. At noon there was a quick meal in a dark, immense cavern called the mess hall, and there he heard his first 1MC announcement echo through the corridors: *"Personnel to be sworn in as midshipmen, United States Navy, assemble in T-court at this time."*

"Where's tea court?"

"Everybody's going that way."

"I hope whoever's up front knows what he's doing."

A thousand shaven-headed civilians, encircled and overawed by granite and flapping flags, stood in a vast space of yellow brick. Blinking in the bright June sunlight, his arm trembling as he held it aloft, he repeated in unison with a thousand others: "I, Philo T. McGiffin, having been appointed a midshipman in the United States Navy, do solemnly swear that I will support and defend the Constitution of the United States against all enemies, foreign and domestic; that I will bear true faith and allegiance to the same; that I take this obligation freely . . . and that I will well and faithfully discharge the duties of the office on which I am about to enter; so help me God."

The sense of dedication, the glow, was allowed to last for about four minutes. After the swearing-in the assembly line began again. He crept to the mid store and was issued soap and toilet articles; to the bookstore, for a stack of books two feet high, and a slide rule (an ominous engine—he was afraid of mathematics); back to sick bay, for yellow fever, which they'd run out of the first time he'd been there.

At three o'clock he stood in the corridor in what he hoped was the

second wing, third deck, and studied his list again. All he had left
was the uniform issue.

"Shoe size!"

"Seven, sir."

"Doan' need to call me sir, boy."

"Yes, sir."

"White works. Say, how short *are* you, kid?"

"Five three and a half, sir."

"Chart only goes down to five four. That's minimum."

"Then I'm five four, sir."

"Well, take these. You'll grow."

"Neckerchiefs, two."

"Hats, blue rim, two."

"Socks, athletic, six pair. Black, twelve pair. White, six pair. Sign
here."

"Undershirts, small, twelve."

"Drawers."

"Neckties."

"Gloves."

"Belts."

He passed from civilian to military somewhere along a line of
scuffed folding tables, his arms wilting as the pile grew higher.

"Net bags."

"Sweat gear. Gonna be your best friend, buddy."

"Athletic shoes."

"Rain gear."

"Reindeer, sir?"

"Boonies."

"Bath sandals."

"Stencil kit. You got to mark all this gear."

He panted. Faces blurred in front of him. With a pile higher than
his head, holding more under his arms, dragging two more bags
bump-bump behind him, he toiled up six flights of stairs to the room
that was pencilled on one of the pieces of paper. He dropped it all
on a naked mattress, flopped into a chair, and looked around the
empty room, seeing it with the same sudden terrible clarity with
which he had seen everything that day.

Room 2230 was for three men; at least, he saw three beds. Three bare gray-striped mattresses. Two full-length mirrors in wooden frames. Beige walls, without decoration. Two metal desks. Three sturdy-looking metal chairs. Green tile floor, rather dusty. Three built-in light wood closets, with lots of removable shelves. Near the door were a sink, a shower stall, and a closet with a hanging bar and what looked like book racks, though they were oddly arranged. It smelled of floor wax and closed-in heat, and aside from the furniture it was as bare as if no one had ever inhabited it. As he was investigating it someone backed into him, coming through the door. They both turned, startled, and faced each other. To Philo the big guy looked vaguely familiar. "Hi," he said, then saw the uniform and said, "sir—"

"It's okay," said the big guy. "I'm former enlisted. Same as you now. J.J. Fayaway. Who're you?"

"Phil McGiffin."

"Good to meet ya, Phil. Guess we're wives."

"What?"

"Roomies." They shook hands. Phil felt the power; Fayaway's hand was twice the size of his. They looked each other over. The sailor was enormous, in a chunky way; his face was square and open; his short hair was the color of chewed gum. He looked to be twenty, twenty-one. His air was calm and unhurried. He heaved his gear onto one of the beds and looked around the room. "Who else we got, Phil?"

"Me," said someone from the corridor. A high voice, rather pissed off. "This twenty-two-thirty?"

"That's what it says on the door," said Philo.

The third occupant was taller than Fayaway. He was thin, though, thinner even than Philo, and incredibly bony. His cheekbones arched high on an eroded face and his nose jutted like the gnomon of a sundial. Black greasy-looking hair fell across his forehead. He stared at them, too-long arms wrapped around two enormous bundles of clothes, like an ant caught in the act of plunder. There was a wild, focussed, glassy look in his eyes.

"I'm Howard Zeard," he said. "And I'm taking that upper bunk."

"You got it," said Philo. "I'm afraid of heights."

Zeard circled around Fayaway as if he feared he might explode. The sailor turned to follow him around, his mouth open a little. "Hey," he said. "You missed your haircut."

"Screw that."

"Hey—"

"I got a infection," said Zeard, cutting off any further speculation on the subject. He let his bundles thump to the floor and slammed open one of the lockers. "Shit," he mumbled.

"Plebe ho," someone shouted in the corridor. They turned to look at the door. *"Plebe ho!* Everybody out here. Get hot!"

In the corridor, twenty feet wide, ten high, and some hundred yards long, stood two men. One of them Philo recognized instantly as Corpen. He stood rocking on his heels, still in the incredibly crisp white uniform, his thumbs inserted lightly under his white uniform belt, under the brass buckle that gleamed like gold. His cap was shoved back, and he stood watching the recent civilians, half in mufti and half in uniform, come hesitantly out of their rooms. The other man, compact, dark, and scowling, stood with his bare hairy legs wide apart. He wore blue shorts with a gold stripe and a gray USNA T-shirt, and he carried a lacrosse stick, tossing a ball up occasionally and catching it with a cradling motion.

"Everybody out!" Corpen shouted again. He paced past a couple of the rooms, looking in to see that they were empty. Plebes stood awkwardly about in the corridor. His eyes fixed on Philo for a long second, then moved on, roving over the others. His mouth narrowed in what looked like angry nausea. Abruptly, he pointed to the wall. "All right, studs, hit that bulkhead."

They looked where he pointed.

"Hit it!" Corpen screamed suddenly. "Get your asses up there!"

"The wall," Fayaway whispered. He pushed Zeard and Philo toward the side of the corridor. The others began to move too, scared, half comprehending.

"Up against the bulkhead!" Corpen screamed, stalking along the rough line of plebes that formed, facing one another's paling faces, across the width of the hallway. He walked like a Doberman barely held in leash; his eyes flicked over them contemptuously. "Get those guts in. Hands at your sides. I want you pussies at *attention.*"

Behind him, silent, the other upperclassman tossed the ball up and caught it; tossed it up and caught it.

"I'm Midshipman Second Class Corpen," said Corpen, his voice dropping suddenly to a nearly normal tone. "You will call me Mister Corpen, sir. This gentleman in gym gear is Midshipman Second Class Stamper. You will call him Mister Stamper, sir. Do you understand?"

When they had shouted *yes sir* four times, each time louder, till the tile walls of the corridor rang and their ears rang, he paced the length of the line and turned back. His spotless white suede shoes, rubber-soled, whispered on the gleaming floor. Except for that the silence was complete.

"Mister Stamper and I," he resumed, "are your first set plebe summer squad leaders, gentlemen. We would like to take this opportunity of first meeting you to welcome you to the Trade School, to the Chesapeake University of Naval Technology, to Crabtown Finishing School, to the Annapolis Yacht Club, to Ernie Flagg's Hotel Bancroft. I venture to say, gentlemen, that you will remember it, and most particularly us, after many other things have grown dim."

He paced the length of the line again, shoes whispering uninterpretable secrets, and thirty pairs of eyes followed him as he turned.

"Gentlemen, you are now in the Navy. Midshipmen fourth class, and—God help us—the future backbone of the Fleet. You are now at Annapolis. *This is not a college.* This is your first duty assignment in the Navy. USNA, Lima Company, Thirty-fourth Platoon."

He paused, and paced again. "So who are we? Mister Stamper and I are not your teachers. We are not your wet nurses. We were ordered here. It is our unenviable and perhaps ultimately hopeless task to transform a sloppy lot of ill-assorted pussies, maggots, whimps, baggers, and pukes—yourselves, gentlemen—into something halfway ready to meet the Brigade when, in nine short but never-to-be-forgotten weeks, it comes back to the Hall. We expect your full cooperation in this mission, important as it is to the national security of the United States and the preservation of the Free World."

He glanced at Stamper. The other second class stood juggling the ball, staring off toward the end of the corridor, where late afternoon sunlight streamed in to lie in squared-off golden ranks along the deck.

"In doing this," Corpen continued, pacing again, "you'll have to know one another, help one another. No one ever got through this place alone. You're classmates now, God help you. You'll depend on one another. You never bilge a classmate. You never let a classmate down. So you'd better start getting acquainted." He pointed to a sleepy-looking kid at the end of one line. "You. Sound off, stud. Name and nickname."

"Uh, Anthony Castigliano. Tony, sir."

"Knock off the sir for now. You're talking to your classmates. Next."

"Stan Mitchell. Stan—or Butch."

"Moishe Kaufman. Mick."

"Richard Gray the third. Dick."

"Fayaway, John. J.J."

"Robert Engel. Bob, I guess. My sister calls me—"

Stamper pivoted suddenly. There was a moving blur and then a flat *splat* as the ball rebounded from where Engel's head had been. White-faced, he straightened slowly.

"Just what you're asked," Corpen said softly. "We don't go for excess bullshit here, Engel. Remember that. Next."

"Uh . . . Roger Darrin. Rog."

The names went on. Philo tried to concentrate on them, tried to link names to faces. But all the faces were the same. Shaven. Scared. Young. Only the single black plebe was at all distinguishable from the rest. With something like insight he realized that, except for height, all of them looked alike. The sole clue to individuation was the black-and-yellow name tags that some had already pinned on their white cotton jumpers.

"Ash, John. John's okay."

"Sherman Shubrick. Sherm."

"Sam Cross. Truck."

"Zeard, Howard."

"No nickname?"

"Nope," said Zeard. There was something indefinable in his voice. It was not respect.

"Wait a minute," said Stamper. It was the first time the dark upperclass had spoken and they heard his voice with a collective thrill
of horror. He crossed to Zeard and stood in front of him for a while,
fondling the ball in the thonged pocket of the stick. "You. Zeard.
Wasn't there a haircut on your checkoff list, mister?"

"I have a scalp infection," said Zeard. "Sir."

"Let's see your chit."

Zeard produced a crumpled half-sheet of paper. Corpen came
over and the two second class examined it with interest. "Who's
this?" said Corpen. "This scribble?"

"That's my dad's signature," said Zeard.

"You got to be shitting me," said Stamper. His mouth had come
open a little.

"He's a doctor," said Zeard. He was taller than either second class
and his lids drooped in his ruined, old-looking face as he looked
down at them.

"Drop," said Corpen.

"What?"

"I said *drop*, shithead. Give me ten. Ten pushups." Corpen
pointed to the floor. "That's a deck, *Mister* Zeard. I strongly suggest
you hit it. Now. And count."

"One."

"Sir, Zeard. Say sir."

"Two, sir."

"You missed one. Start over, stud."

"One, sir. Two, sir. Three, sir. Four, sir. Five, sir. Six, sir.
Seven, sir. Eight, sir. Nine, sir. Ten, sir." He started to get up.
Corpen's white shoe on his back stopped him.

"How about one to beat Army, Mister Zeard?"

"One to what?"

"To beat Army, hot dog. An extra pushup to beat Army. Clean
the shit out of your ears, Weird."

"One to beat Army." Philo could see that the last pushup hurt,
but Zeard finished it. "*Sir.*"

"Good. No, don't get up. You can just stay like that till we secure . . . this position, by the way, is what we call 'leaning rest.'
Now, gentlemen; proceed."

"Charles Hartford. Chuck."

"Philo McGiffin. Phi—"

Splat.

Shaken, Philo straightened. Still filling his sight was the black circle of Stamper's lacrosse ball, aimed straight at his face. "Whoa, Snatch," said Corpen. "That's really his name."

"You're shitting me," said Stamper, staring at him. "Philo McGiffin?"

"Yes, sir."

"Gimme ten," said Stamper, cradling the ball.

"Sir? What did I—"

"Make that twenty," said Corpen, "And pipe down. We got a lot to get through this afternoon. You can count under your breath.

"Now. You fourteen on that side: my squad. You men: Mister Stamper's squad."

"Welcome aboard," said Stamper ominously.

"Mr. Stamper and I wish to extend to you, once again, the warmest of welcomes to plebe summer. But now our pleasure ends. It's time for official business." He handed papers to one of the fourth class. "Pass these out, boot . . . you are now being issued the following, one per each: locker stowage diagram for wings one through six, stenciling instructions, uniform table, basic daily routine, Plebe Summer training schedule, room assignments for summer classes, and a copy of COMDTMIDN Instruction 1531.2, Professional Development of the Fourth Class, Procedures for."

The plebe with the papers stopped beside Phil, who was still at "leaning rest," his arms beginning to ache. Finally he laid them beside him on the deck.

"Tonight, after I dismiss you, you will proceed to your rooms in a timely manner. You will not visit other rooms tonight except for the head. You will occupy yourselves with checking your uniforms and gear against the list on page 14–2 of your reg book to ensure that you have a complete issue. You will try on your uniforms for fit, preparing yourselves for inspection in White Works Charlie tomorrow morning. You will stencil each item as per instructions. You will read the U.S. Naval Academy Reg Book, one copy of which will be issued to the ICOR in each room. You will read your Reef Points, the little blue book, completely through, preparing to memorize it."

Philo glanced at Mister Stamper, who was staring, quiescent once again, out the window. Blue sky was visible beyond him, dimming toward evening. He snapped his eyes back to Corpen. "Lights out will go tonight at twenty-two-hundred. That's ten o'clock; better get used to the twenty-four-hour system. After that you will be free to visit between rooms until twenty-two-fifteen, at which time all hands will be in bed with room lights out. Reveille will be at zero-six-fifteen. You will know it is reveille because a bell will ring very loudly. At reveille one man from each room will appear at the door before the bell stops and will make the report, 'All hands on deck.' This means everyone in the room is out of the rack, covers turned back to air, room lights on. Don't let us catch you touching that sack after that except to make it after morning meal. Any time. Got that? Good. Snatch?"

"Nothin' to add," said Stamper, looking out the window.

"Any questions, maggots?" said Corpen. He waited, pushing his cap forward and settling its bill an inch over his nose, so that he had to tilt his head back slightly to see them. There were none. "Good. If you have questions later, or if any of you have realized yet you've made a terrible mistake, Mister Stamper and I will be in room twenty-oh-five. That is the squad leaders' room and platoon office. Mister Zeard, report to us there when your classmates secure."

"I'd like to see this character, too," said Stamper, looking at Philo. "You hear me, cowboy? Let's make it right now."

"All right, sir," said Philo.

"Okay, turkeys—fall out," said Corpen. No one moved. "Fall out! Secure! Assholes and elbows—clear this passageway. Too fucking slow, shitheads! *Move!*"

The corridor was suddenly filled with running, colliding bodies.

When Philo got back to his room, still shaking a little, Fayaway looked up from one of the desks. Spread on it before him were stacks of new uniforms, a fitted-together stencil, and a pad of gooey black ink.

"How'd it go, uh, Phil?"

"Not too great."

"They don't seem to like you."

"Maybe it'll pass." He took a deep breath, smelling the ink and the fresh cotton of the clothes, and looked at the bags of things on his bed. His "rack." "It's something about my name, I think."

"I was in the Fleet for a while," said Fayaway. "And then at NAPS . . . but I don't know anything that would be funny about your name. Anyway . . . where's Zeard?"

"Corpen's giving him a haircut."

"Oh."

Philo took the first piece of clothing off his pile and unfolded it. It was a heavy white cotton blouse, with a deep V neck and a square flap collar in back. He tried it on. It was too big. When he looked down he could see his shoes between it and his chest, and the sleeves came down over his thumbs. He pulled it off and decided to stencil it anyway. He didn't feel like taking it to Mister Corpen, or, even less, to Mister Stamper. He stood by the desk holding it and watched Fayaway mark his gear, swiftly, efficiently, humming to himself. The stenciling instructions Corpen had given out lay open in front of him. Philo took out his own copy. The "jumper, white works," that must be it, was to be stenciled inside the neck, at the rear. He opened the kit and began fitting the letters together, still looking at the paper. When it was ready he tried it on the jumper and was rewarded with a smeared DOOR W. T. "How's that?" He asked Fayaway, holding it up.

"Who's that?"

"Who's what?"

"Who is 'Door, W. T.'?"

Philo looked at the jumper, then at the paper. A little light went on in the recesses of his tired brain. "Oh," he said.

"It must be sort of like John Doe, around here," said J.J. "I guess just line it out, and put your name below it."

His second try came out smeared too, but at least it was MCGIFFIN P. T.

Presently their roommate came back, bald, looking more remote than ever. The three of them made up an assembly line then and got everything marked—blouses, trou, leggings, underwear, towels, sheets, pillowcases ("fartsacks," Fayaway called them), the funny blue-rimmed sailor hats called "dixie cups." Philo saw that each article had to be folded in a certain way and stowed in a specified place in the locker. Skivvy shirts, for example, were stenciled at the neck and folded starting face down, right side over, sleeve turned back, left side over, sleeve turned back, bottom turned up, smoothed and squared with the flat of the hand. Then each went into a neat stack in Fayaway's locker. "Like boot camp," the big plebe said. "And they showed us a lot of this at NAPS."

"What's NAPS?"

"Naval Academy Prep . . . they send guys from the Fleet there, get us up to speed to take on you collegeprep hotshots. It's a crazy place. But fun."

They worked away. Philo liked the sense of working with the others, part of a team, but also friends. There hadn't been much of that at the Home.

"How you guys doing?"

"Wow," said Philo. "You're dressed already. Looks swell."

The boy at the door did look nice. The white duck blouse fit him and his bell-bottoms broke clean just above the new black shoes. The dixie cup was tilted jauntily on his shaven head, above a self-conscious grin, and the black neckerchief was rolled loosely and tied in a Windsor.

"What do you think, guys?"

"Uh," said Zeard.

"What are you doing here?" said Fayaway. "We're supposed to stay in our rooms and turn to. You heard the man."

"Oh, come on."

"Come on, hell. You better get back to your room."

"But what do you think of this uniform?"

"I think it's unsat," said Fayaway. "You've kind of got the idea, but . . . here, let's get you squared away, uh, classmate. Your name tag's on the wrong side, and it's got to be parallel to the deck. The cover goes tilted forward, like this." He adjusted the boy's cap.

"It's too loose. It won't stay on that way."

"They'll shrink after they're washed a couple of times. And you'll get some hair back later . . . now, the neckerchief. That's all wrong." He pulled it loose and rolled it tight and tied it around his classmate's neck with a quick flip. "Use a reef knot. You don't tie it like a necktie."

"What's a reef knot?"

"Sorry. A square knot."

"What's a square knot?"

"Oh, shit," said Fayaway. "Go on, get out of here before one of the squad leaders sees you."

McGiffin went on folding and stowing, looking carefully at the diagram. Even the socks had to be rolled a certain way and neatly stacked, segregated by colors, on a designated shelf. He couldn't quite believe it. But when it was done his locker looked rather nice, in a neurotically over-regimented way. "There. What's next?"

"Reg books," said Tony Castigliano, from the door. He had a stack of gray-green pubs under his arm. "Mister Stamper said for the ICOR to sign this paper."

"What's an ICOR?"

They looked at each other and then at Castigliano. He was large and friendly looking, a little moon-faced. He shrugged. "I don't know."

"Why didn't you ask him?"

"I just wanted to get *out* of there."

"Oh, I'll sign it," said Zeard. "Way they were talking when I was in there, McGiffin, you better not put your name on anything you don't have to."

"Why? What did they say?"

"I didn't get it all. Something about practical jokes."

"I don't do jokes," said Philo. "As a matter of fact, I never felt less like making a joke in my whole life."

"Where you from, buddy?" said Castigliano.

"P.A. How about you?"

"Paramus. You're Philo—and J.J.—and—"

"Howie."

"Hi." They shook hands around. "Well, see you later, men. I got to get these Navy Bibles around to the troops."

"So long, Tony. Swing low."

"Yeah."

Outside the window, unnoticed as they worked, night had come. Philo took a moment from reading to look out. Below them was a wide redbrick terrace, roofed with Egyptian-looking pillars and porticos, and beyond that were more buildings, dark now, of the same granite as Bancroft, massively cut. Lights glowed here and there about the grounds, throwing shadows from bushes, a few parked cars, trophy cannons. Beyond the buildings was a dark expanse of water, and then, far off, a scattering of distant lights, like a town. That dark expanse . . . the Severn? Through the opened window the sweet smells of magnolia, wisteria, drugging to his northern senses, came in on the wind. He couldn't smell the sea from here, at least that he could tell. When he looked back into the room both his roommates were reading, Fayaway the regulation book, Zeard a new copy of *Mad Magazine*. He sat at the desk and opened the little blue book someone had shoved at him sometime during the day.

. . . it is by no means enough that an officer of the Navy should be a capable mariner. He must be that, of course, but also a great deal more. He should be as well a gentleman of liberal education, refined manners, punctilious courtesy, and the nicest sense of personal honor. . . .

There are 489 panes of glass in the skylight of Memorial Hall.

When the first substitute is flown from the starboard main yardarm, the officer whose flag or pennant is flown by the vessel is not on board. When the second substitute is flown from the port main yardarm, the Chief of Staff is not on board; when the third substitute is flown from the port main yardarm (destroyers at fore yardarm) the Captain is not on board.

Crew—Coach, Jim Swartz; Captain, Sterett Turner IV.

The Plebe will never allow his behavior to be such as to subject his classmates or anyone else to a reprimand or conduct report.

It went on and on. What had Corpen said—that they would have to *memorize* this? It buzzed in his head already. Perhaps he was getting a fever from the shots. He laid down Reef Points as Fayaway finished the reg book, and he switched to that.

0402.1 . . . any attempt to commit an offense will be treated as if the offense was actually committed.

0401.1 . . . Midshipmen shall conduct themselves properly at all times, observing the customs and traditions of the naval service.

0432.1 . . . Public display of affection by midshipmen in uniform is prohibited.

0506.10h . . . Only small plants, in good taste, may be kept in midshipman rooms; no more than three (3) plants to a room.

. . . rooms shall be kept in Condition A, ready, for inspection, between the hours of 0800 and 1530. . . .

"Hey," he said aloud. Fayaway and Zeard looked up. "ICOR: In Charge Of Room. That's what it means."
"Sounds like a red-ass to me."
"What's a red-ass, J.J.?"
"It means a Navy True Blue Good Deal, Phil. A banana in the ear. Being top man on the shit list. Guest of honor at a blanket party. Sucking left hind titty on a two-titted sow."
"But if there's only two tits, then how—"
"You got it, boy. You got it."

When, later that night (the things Corpen had assigned only half done or not done at all, because there just was not enough time before lights out), he lay between crisp unfamiliar-smelling sheets, he could not sleep. He lay and listened to the night. Fayaway's slow unconcerned breathing; Zeard's quick, nervous snore, like a jigsaw whining through plastic. Lying there, staring at the ribbons of light the blinds left on the ceiling—the *overhead*—he thought for the first time that day about where he was; where he had come from; where he hoped to go. He was desperately tired and his arms ached from shots and pushups, yet he stared upward for what seemed to be hours, unable to resign his consciousness to the dark.

It frightened him, being here; but he could not go back. There was nothing for Phil McGiffin any longer in Raymondsville. No parents; he had never known his father, and his mother left town one day when he was twelve, and never came back. His uncle Will had taken him in for a while, till he lost his job with Thunder Oil. Then it was the Home. He had to admit they hadn't treated him badly. When the news of his appointment came, the city had even loaned him the hundred dollars for his entrance fee.

But beyond that debt, there was nothing more he owed them. Raymondsville cared nothing for him now that he was of age. There was no money for college. He had to make it here, no matter how strange, how unfamiliar, how frightening. To make it through Annapolis . . . his uncle had told him about the sea, but it was more than that he wanted. Respect, belonging; to *be* somebody.

Phil McGiffin had never thought of himself as large, or brave, or very smart. He knew he was small, rather timorous, and his passing of the entrance exam for the Academy still impressed him with a sense of the profound mystery in life. But he had passed and been appointed, and now here he was; among a thousand strangers, yet already, in some undefinable way, friends—his classmates.

Tomorrow, he promised the darkness, I'll hit it hard. I'll be up early . . . first one at the door, to report all turned out. I'll study hard. I'll find out what the rules are here, and obey them to the letter. That was all he had to do—what he was told.

It was plain that things were going to be rough. So plain that, hidden in his rack, he shivered and was unable to close his eyes. There were so many things he didn't understand. The very language—bulkhead, deck, reg, reveille. This odd business about his name. But I'll learn, he promised himself. I'll learn it all.

He would, too.

CHAPTER TWO

*. . . plebe summer is an intensive program of training
designed to facilitate the transition of young men from
their status as enlisted or civilian candidates to a new
status as junior members of a highly disciplined
organization . . . this difficult and demanding
experience provides the fourth class midshipman an
intensive opportunity to confront and overcome
challenges and to develop physical and mental stamina.*
  —COMDTMIDN INST. 1531.2, para. 0201, "Fourth
  Class Summer Indoctrination: Objectives"

*The Naval Academy is like a Japanese bath. Once
you're in, you realize it's not as hot as you thought.*
  —Found in margin of page 113, reissued
  copy, *Principles of Thermodynamics*

As the fourteen new fourth class in Midshipman Second Class
David Corpen's summer squad woke, made their first reveille
reports, showered, and shaved the next morning, there were many
things they but dimly grasped.

One, of course, was what they were in for.

Another was the size and complexity of the plant, the environ-
ment, in which they were housed and fed and would be taught and
run and indoctrinated over the next eleven months; and in which, if
they made it—and one out of three of them would not—they would
spend the next four years.

In that year the United States Naval Academy at Annapolis consisted of 302 acres in, but not of, the state of Maryland. It was bordered on the east by Chesapeake Bay and on the north by the Severn River, one of many brackish estuaries of the bay. Its four thousand midshipmen all lived in Bancroft Hall, the largest dormitory in the world, an immense, eight-winged granite fortress dating from 1902 and containing over two thousand rooms, three barber shops, stores, snack bars, tailor shop, post office, express office, bowling alleys, firing ranges, and, certainly not least appreciated, 360 restrooms, or heads. Included in the Bancroft complex were Memorial Hall, Macdonough Hall (the gym and pool), and Dahlgren Hall (the armory), as well as the world's biggest dining room, seating all four thousand men at once.

At 0630, dressed in brand-new white works, the new plebes gathered in a loose formation in the corridor, were mustered, and led through the labyrinth to the first event of the day, morning meal. They devoured stacks of pancakes, scrambled eggs, cereal, milk, juice, and a big, stainless steel bowl of ice cream that Corpen assured them was from U.S. Navy cows. "Stuff yourselves, turkeys," he said, looking on. "Cram it down. Eat till you're full and jump up and down a couple times and take some more. Pork yourselves, studs. You're going to need it."

The second event took place out on the red-tiled portico Philo had looked down on the night before. Arranged by Mister Stamper in ranks and files, they were instructed in standing at attention, facing left, facing right, facing about, coming to parade rest, and saluting. He corrected each man individually, poking at protruding guts, straightening arms and heads, tilting their chins up or down as if they were mannequins. "You!" he would shout suddenly, making them all flinch in unison. "You there on the right! Can't you keep your eyes in the boat? Why are you starin' at me? Got a hankerin' for my trop white ass—is that it?"

"Ah, no, sir."

"Eyes front, blivots. I'll tell you all you need to know. Christ, what a bunch of pussies on parade. This is the Naval Academy, not the Barnum and Bailey Clown College. But we'll shape you up—or ship you out."

Finally he formed them up in marching order and led them

around the portico, calling cadence and then commands. Philo found it hard to do it all at once: keep step, keep distance and "dress," listen to Stamper's exasperated bellow and try to figure out in the half second between order and execution which way to go and which foot to turn on. At last he called "To the rearrr . . . *barch*," and half of them tried to turn, and the other half kept going, confused, and the platoon collapsed in a welter of sprawling bodies. Stamper had to go behind one of the pillars. When he reemerged his face was straight and appropriately vicious again. "Okay, enough drill for today," he said. "Get back to your rooms, don athletic gear, and be back here, in formation by height, in ten minutes. We'll take a little jog around the Yard, show you the place."

The tour, done at double time, took an hour and a half. From time to time Stamper would slow them to a walk and point out a building, a monument, a bronze plaque set into a walkway.

"This is the Macedonian monument. That figurehead, and those guns, were captured from a British frigate in 1812 by Captain Stephen Decatur."

"This is the Chapel." They tilted their heads back, panting; another mass of granite and white brick, but this one not squat, but soaring; domed with age-greened copper and capped with a golden needle, glinting high above the trees . . . under there somewhere was the crypt of a Scottish refugee, a Russian admiral, a Parisian pauper—John Paul Jones. "The baddest ass in the Yard," Stamper told them, grinning. "Takes a church to hold him down, two Marines to keep him quiet, and he still spends all of his time pickled."

They jogged on, Philo keeping up easily. He liked to run. Past the old academic complex; Maury Hall, where the few liberal arts courses were taught; Mahan, with a library, a lecture hall, and a stage; Sampson Hall, science. Back of them were Griffin and Isherwood and Melville, the engineering buildings, where they peered up in awe at a full-sized destroyer boiler plant, engine, and reduction gears. Back of Isherwood they crossed a rickety old wooden pier bridge—Stamper shouting back at them to break step, or they'd shake it down—and trotted steadily around Hospital Point and along winding paths through the cemetery and down to Lover's Lane.

Philo was keeping up, but he found himself sweating beyond anything he had ever felt. The moist, clammy heat was terrific. Still,
they weren't running all that hard—a fast jog, no more—and he was
able to stay near the stocky upperclass without exhausting himself,
unlike some of the plebes, who hung back, puffing and red-faced
even on the downhills. He felt a small prick of pride and sprinted
ahead of Fayaway jauntily.

Crossing College Creek again, they passed Dewey Field and
jogged sweating along the quiet green Severn toward the bay.
Stamper pointed out the YPs to them, miniature destroyers for prac-
ticing tactics and shiphandling; the wood of the seawall was splin-
tered from decades of abortive approaches. At the northeastern
corner of the Yard a basin cradled dozens of sturdy-looking sail-
boats.

As they panted along, sucking air, Stamper talked almost without
pause, running backward at times to shout back at them. The whole
Academy, he explained, was surrounded by a ten-foot wall, with
three main gates, all locked and guarded at night. It was indepen-
dent of the town of Annapolis, or "Crabtown," as he called it, with
its own steam heat, power, laundry, food supplies, homes for staff
and officers, and even its own water.

He told them much more; but for the final mile, from the fore-
mast of the *Maine* down Farragut to the Field House and back, he
did not talk at all; only ran, full out. Philo took the challenge and
sprinted out. He couldn't catch the upperclass—he ran like a deer—
but he finished within a hundred feet. The others did less well.
When they stumbled to a halt at last, strung out behind him for
three hundred yards, Stamper stood and watched them straggle in
with a strange expression, half contemptuous, half proprietary.

"Any questions on your tour, studs?"

There were none. They were all too busy grabbing air, and several were retching quietly into the grass.

"That's all right. We'll build you pussies up. Chow and exercise,
eat and sweat. By the time the Brigade gets back you'll be able to
sleep at double time."

A shower and a uniform change, and they mustered for noon
meal. This formation was a little sharper; they tried to line up on

each other, tried to stand at something resembling attention. After chow they fell in again and were marched about the Hall for a couple of hours, through corridors of whose debouches they were ignorant, to places the location of which they did not know, where they were issued gear they did not recognize.

A five-minute rest, then "Plebe ho!" sounded in the corridor. Corpen took them for an hour and showed them how to tie neckerchiefs, assemble combination caps, fix leggings, and give military shirt tucks to each other. Then he drilled them in saluting again until Philo could no longer lift his right arm. At 1700 they fell in with the rest of their class on Tecumseh Court, where they had been sworn in, and marched by platoons down Stribling Walk to Maury for welcoming addresses by the Commandant of Midshipmen, the Dean, and the Summer Set Brigade Commander. They didn't follow much of what was said, but by this time they were glad just to nap in a padded chair for an hour. A band struck up outside as they formed to march back, and suddenly, in the midst of his classmates, though their step was ragged and their alignment shaky, he felt, for the first time, *military*.

At evening meal the two second class urged them again to "load up." To Philo, the food was fantastic: New York cut steaks, all they wanted; vegetables, baked potatoes, fresh bread, blueberry pie. To get seconds you just held up the empty tray and a steward would bring you a full one. After the limited rations of the Home it was like a dream. He watched Stamper's glee as Zeard ate four pieces of pie. At meals, without his lacrosse stick, the saturnine squad leader seemed almost human.

That evening it got even better. After fifteen minutes' rest—he spent it trying on his combination cap in the mirror and reading "A Message to Garcia" and the Bancroft Hall fire bill—they all reported to the squad leaders' room with their Navy Songbooks. Sitting around on the deck, they sang "Anchors Aweigh," "Army Mule," "Whiskey Johnny," "Abdul Abulbul Amir," a round dozen of fight songs, "The Marines' Hymn," and four verses of "Fifteen Men on a Dead Man's Chest." Stamper had a hoarse voice, perhaps due to shouting all day, but Corpen turned out a clear tenor, and some of the plebes sang decently, though the emphasis was on volume over

quality. As they sang Philo glanced around at his classmates, shaven
and scared-looking in their too-large uniforms.

Already, he realized, he could put name to a lot of them, and in
spite of their uniformity could even link personalities to some of the
faces. John Ash, the peppy little cherub-faced guy with almost
white hair. Len Ind, the black mid he had noticed before, who said
little and saw much. Richard Gray, Dick, a handsome smaller guy
with quick movements and a confident air. Mick Kaufman, tubby,
with a surprisingly rich laugh. Castigliano, the New Jerseyan, even
this early an unmistakable non-sweat. Darrin . . . Engel . . .
Linowicz . . . Cross . . . Porter . . . and of course Howie and J.J.,
his own roomies. . . .

"Last song," Corpen announced. "We'll finish off with one you'll
need Sunday in Chapel. Page fifty-six."

> *Eternal Father, strong to save,*
> *Whose arm hath bound the restless wave,*
> *Who bidds't the mighty ocean deep*
> *Its own appointed limits keep;*
> *Oh, hear us when we cry to thee,*
> *For those in peril on the sea.*

Corpen shut his book. Stamper had never opened his; he had
them all by heart. A few of the plebes started to talk.

"Cut the chippin', back there," growled Stamper.

"Listen up," said Corpen. "Okay. Good sing, guys. You'll have to
know this songbook cold by September 6. That's when the Brigade
gets back—and you better believe that's when the shit is going to hit
the fan.

"That's what I want to talk about now—among other things.

"You guys"—he looked around, his dark eyebrows arched—
"have got a lot to learn this summer, and fast. You'll be getting
some class time. Computers, seamanship, math. We'll be having infantry drill daily out on Faggot. That's *Farragut* Field. There'll be a
lot of P.E. over in Macdonough. Boxing, judo, and especially swim-
ming. The Navy's not going to put fifty thousand bucks into you
and not have it insured. We'll be doing some sailing, and later on

we'll field some company teams. Mister Stamper will lead Lima
Company's lacrosse jocks. I'd suggest that sport as particularly career enhancing, gentlemen."

"Yeah," said Stamper.

"Later on, in August, you'll have two full weeks of range time—
one week rifle, one week pistol. All personnel in Thirty-fourth Platoon will shoot expert." He aimed a finger at Philo. "Right,
McGiffin?"

"Right, sir."

"Now, what you've all been waiting for—the gouge on the plebe
system."

Stamper grinned at the deck as Corpen paused.

"They don't say much about the system in the catalog—you
know, the one you looked at in your high school library, with all the
pretty pictures. But I'll bet you've heard a lot of stories about hazing, and all that shit. Well, remember this: there's none of that here.
Ever."

Stamper's grin expanded. The plebes glanced at him uneasily.

"There's no hazing because it's a dismissal offense. See? That's
straight poop. One of you clowns turns an upperclass in, his ass is
going to fry. And his classmates aren't going to like you after that.
Hazing is a word you better think twice before you use. You'll learn
what goes and what doesn't pretty quick. Nobody can hit you, for
instance. Sick stuff is out. Hurting people permanently is out. If
anything like that happens, let people know—your squad leader,
your company officer when ac year starts. But it won't. You won't
get 'hazed' here. What you *will* get is indoctrinated."

His smile now matched Stamper's downward-directed grin. "And
that indoctrination includes running your asses off morning, noon,
and night; making meals living breathing hell; tearing your mind
down to animal reflexes, and building it back up again, the Navy
way. There'll be times when you feel like killing people, and times
when you'll be so scared to go out of your room that you'll crap in
the shower and beat it down the drain with your shoes. It's meant to
be hairy. We don't want people here who can't hack the worst and
still produce. The plebe system—and plebe year—is something
you'll remember all your lives. That, Mister Stamper and I guaran-

tee. It lasts for eleven months. If you can gut it out, if you can hack it, anything that happens for the rest of your life will be strawberry pie.

"We'll start the summer plebe system in two weeks. You'll be in the grooves here by then. Study your Reef Points, listen up, get in shape, stay with the program." He paused, and his eyes sharpened. "Resolve right now to give it all you've got—*the best you have*—and you just may make it.

"Well—you got a lot to do tonight. Remember, you're responsible for knowing officer, enlisted, and midshipman rank insignia tomorrow, as well as the other stuff I gave you. Okay. Snatch?"

"Nothin' to add."

"Okay, clowns. What's the best kind of cure?"

"See-cure!"

They knew that already.

"What do you think, J.J.?" he asked Fayaway, back in their room. The big mustang looked up from his shoe polishing and blinked.

"What about, Phil?"

"All this plebe stuff."

"Well, just what he said, I guess. Like boot camp, only for a year. Keep your mouth shut, your head down, and a poker up your ass. That academic stuff worries me, though. Looks like they expect some brainwork here."

"How'd you do in high school, J.J.?"

"Never went. Got my G.E.D. in the Fleet. That's why—oh—we'll see."

Philo sat down on his side of the desk and pulled out his Reef Points. His shoes needed work too, but he figured he could get to that later in the evening. Let's see, he thought, flipping pages. Yard Gouge, Famous Quotations, Table Salt . . . ranks. He began to study. Ensign, Lt (jg), Lcdr, Cdr. . . .

Zeard slouched in. He flopped into his chair and reached for a stick of gum. Tilting his head back, he chewed with an expression of utter weariness.

"What's new, Howie?"

"Well, did you hear about what happened at rifle issue today?"

"No. What?" Fayaway polished on, listening; Philo looked up from his book.

"One of our classmates, from Bravo Company. They toss him an M–one and he gives it back. He won't touch the sign-out card. 'What's the story, stud?' the squad leader asks him. 'I won't carry an aggressive weapon,' he says. 'I didn't sign up to be a killer.'"

"What? For real?"

"Jeez," said Philo. "What'd he come here for?"

"Maybe to learn bootblacking," said Zeard, watching Fayaway. "Anyway, pretty soon there's this little knot of second class around him, and then they take him off to Main Office. And that's all she wrote."

"We won't see his name tag around here any more," said J.J., licking his rag and taking up a bit of Kiwi with a practised, circular motion. "'I didn't sign up to be a killer.' I like that. Guy had balls."

"But no smarts."

"Maybe."

Zeard looked at Philo. "Studying?"

"Uh huh."

"Hit me."

"Okay." Philo flipped the pages. "Famous naval sayings."

"You may fire when ready, Philo."

"'Don't cheer, boys; the poor devils are dying.'"

"Captain John Phillips, USS *Texas*, Santiago, 1898."

"Right. 'Damn the torpedoes; four bells'—"

"—'Captain Drayton. Go ahead, Jouett, full speed.' Admiral Farragut, Battle of Mobile Bay."

"Uh, yeah." Philo flipped more pages. Fayaway, fingers still moving against the gleaming toe of his shoe, was no longer looking at it, but at Zeard. "Here's one. 'The first vessel—'"

"'The first vessel of note in the Navy was the *Ranger*; the first man-of-war and the first warship with the propelling machinery below the waterline was the *Princeton*; the first iron-clad, the *Monitor*; and the first submarine, the *Holland*. USS *Michigan* was our first dreadnought, *Langley*, our first aircraft carrier, and *Nautilus*, our first nuclear submarine.'"

"That's good," said Philo. "Word perfect, in fact."

"Wait a minute," said Fayaway. He opened the reg book, which lay, as per instructions, on the corner of their desk. "Howie. Page 12–10."

"What paragraph?"

"Article 0303, paragraph two."

"'Formations. Fourth class will consider themselves in ranks when in the passageways of Bancroft Hall. They will march at the position of attention in the center of all passageways, chin in, eyes in the boat, squaring all corners smartly and not speaking unless spoken to by an officer or upperclass. Fourth class will march at double time from six-forty-five to twenty hundred, unless—'"

"Okay. Wait. Bluejacket's Manual, page 520. Start at the top."

"'. . . the white range lights to be shown. Miscellaneous vessels called barges or scows may properly show in Inland Waters special white lights, with or without the usual red and green side lights. Sound signals. When ships are subject to the inland rules, they use long blasts—'"

Fayaway and McGiffin both stared at him. "Son of a bitch," said J.J. at last. "It's like you were reading it."

"I can see the page in my head," said Zeard. He shrugged. "Look—just don't tell the upperclass. I don't care if you guys know. But why get them riled up?"

"Sure," said Philo. "But, jeez, Howie—you've got it made here."

"Memorizing isn't everything," said Fayaway, but he sounded anything but certain of it.

"Well, I got to get to work," said Zeard. He pulled off his blouse and went to the sink; they heard the sound of running water.

Ten minutes later the taps bell rang. Unable to believe it, Philo looked at his watch. "That should be free corridor," said Zeard. "We can go out in our b-robes now—right?"

"Should be," said J.J. absently.

Surveying his desk, Philo felt sick. He was far behind. He hadn't touched his shoes yet, hadn't broken his uniforms out for reveille, hadn't even finished the reading Stamper and Corpen had assigned. And now he had to shower, brush his teeth, write a letter sometime soon to the Home, explaining how he would pay off the loan . . . when would they get paid here? He moved about the room erratically, unable to decide what to do first. Lieutenant—two broad stripes, or two silver bars. Silver bird, colonel in the Marines. Oak leaves . . . what were oak leaves. . . .

There was a clicking of paws at the open door, and a black and brown animal trotted into the room and stopped, rolling its eyes up at them. "Hey," said Fayaway. "It's a mutt."

"I saw him before," said Philo, holding out his hand. "He was out watching us check in yesterday. Here, boy. C'mere."

The dog stood still in the center of the room, its tongue out, and watched them.

"What the hell?" said Fayaway.

"All secure here?" said Corpen, coming in the door. Fayaway jumped up. The second class looked down at the dog and then at Philo. "Well, McGiffin?"

"I guess so, sir."

"Pop to, maggot!"

He got the idea, too late, and came to attention. He was eye to eye with the second class, except that he was shorter, and he could smell sweat and toothpaste and Brasso.

"Fayaway!"

"Sir."

"You come to attention for upperclass?"

"Yes sir."

"You weren't at attention when I came in here."

"Sir?"

"Dodo, dumbhead. Midshipman Dog, Second Class. Why didn't you pop to for him?"

"No excuse, sir," said Fayaway, his face blank.

"That's right, there's no excuse. Dodo's been here a lot longer than you nerds have, and he *rates. You!* McGiffin!"

"Sir."

"What's the matter? Am I ugly, boy?"

"Well, no, sir. I guess you're all right, sir."

"Then why can't you keep your eyes in the boat?"

"Well, I, was just looking at the, uh—"

"What's the matter, McGiffin? Don't you subscribe to Reef Points? There's only five responses to a question here, doofus. Yes sir. No sir. Aye aye, sir. I'll find out, sir. No excuse, sir. Think you can master that?"

"Yes sir."

"Let's try it again. You negat, that's not attention. Get those thumbs along the seams of your trou. Get those shoulders back. Look at your roomie here. That's a proper stance of attention. Now. What about my looks?"

"No excuse, sir."

There was a choking sound from Fayaway. Corpen whirled, and in seconds the big plebe, face red, was cranking off pushups beside the dog, which followed him up and down calmly with its eyes. The second class shoved his face close to McGiffin's. He had small black bristles on the end of his chin. "All right, nerd. Everybody loves ass. Nobody loves a smart ass. *Copy me, boy?*"

"I didn't mean—"

"*Yes! No! Aye aye! I'll find out!*"

"No sir," Philo said. He felt his legs trembling, his hands curling tight. It was suddenly very real: the bright, clean room, the angry face of a man who as far as he could see had absolute power over them all, the watching dog, the wheezing from Fayaway—he was counting in the twenties now. "No, sir," he said again, into the blazing eyes.

"Are you scared of me, McGiffin?" whispered Corpen, centimeters away now, so softly that not even Fayaway could have heard. "Are you? You look scared to me. No, don't answer. This is free advice. I'd wipe that look off my face right now, maggot, and never let it back on, or you aren't going to last long at this institution at all."

Philo felt his eyes widen, his lips and then his legs begin to tremble before that glare; but just then the door banged open and Zeard came in, whistling. "I hear the squad leader—" he started to say, then saw Corpen. He came to a rather sloppy attention.

"Hit it, Whistler's Mother," shouted Corpen, turning away from Philo. "Another wise ass. Bopping around the corridors, whistling like a college kid. And that was a cute trick with that note from your daddy, Weird. You bagger. I'm going to be keeping my eye on this room, gentlemen. Be assured of that."

"Thirty, sir," groaned Fayaway, from the deck.

"You secure. Zeard, you do ten more. You're too thin, you need it."

"Dave?"

"In here," he called. "Be right out, Snatch."

"And you, stud." He tapped the cotton of Philo's skivvy shirt where it stretched taut over his chest. "You better watch your fucking step, cowboy. You got a lot to learn, and that name tag isn't going to make things any easier when the Brigade gets back. You copy me, McGiffin?"

Philo swallowed. He felt tears blur the corners of his eyes.

"McGiffin!"

"Aye aye, sir."

Corpen left. The dog looked them over once more and then trotted out after him. Fayaway relaxed the instant his tail cleared the door. Zeard did his last few pushups and came aboard, coughing. They both looked at Philo. "Hey," said Fayaway. "You okay, big fella?"

"He don't look too good," said Zeard.

"I'm all right." He sat shakily at the desk as the lights went out in the corridor, and rubbed his eyes with his hands. "Look—I'm sorry, J.J., Howie. I guess something about me makes him mad."

"Forget it," said Zeard, turning away.

"Hey, it's all right," said Fayaway, still looking down at him. He rubbed his chin. "Say, look, Phil, you got to get used to getting your ass chewed once in a while. It shouldn't make you . . . well, we got a saying at NAPS, *'Illegitimitandi nil nisi carborundum.'*"

"What's that mean?"

"'Don't let the bastards grind you down.'"

Philo laughed; suddenly it was better. But as he picked up his shoes he saw that his hands were still trembling.

The weekend passed quickly. Saturday was a working day but Sunday was free, except for mandatory Chapel. The fourth class had Yard liberty Sunday afternoon. Most of them put it into shoe polishing and study.

On Monday classes started. From the first day it was hot and

heavy. Along with what was now a routine of musters and inspections, marching drill each day and plebe hos in the corridor each
evening on fourth class rates and naval customs and the honor system, they had academic work. In the mornings it was desk stuff; trig
and analytic geometry, naval orientation, basic engineering, com-
puter programming. In the afternoons they progressed from marlinespike seamanship to sailing in the eighteen-foot knockabouts
("Chinese fire drills on the Severn," Zeard called them, after falling
overboard three times in one afternoon), and then to more complex
evolutions in the Academy's fleet of racing yawls. Three days a
week they studied personal combat under Captain Schich, a six-foot
four-inch Marine with the build of a Cummins diesel and a head the
size and shape of a battle lantern; he considered a match successful
only when he saw blood. It was Kaufman, El Rollo as he was now
universally known, who first smuggled catsup out of the mess hall,
and got in consequence the only A Schich gave that summer.

And a week after that, the summer athletic season started.
McGiffin, along with most of the others in 34th Platoon, went out
for lacrosse. He was small but fast and Stamper put him in at midfield. For most of practice he was in constant motion, following
the ball back and forth across Faggot Field, shouting and dodging
and being run over. Except for that—the contact—he liked it.
For one thing, he could run, though he was clumsy at first with
the ball and stick. For another, on the field the fourth class and the
second were equal, and there was considerable satisfaction for them
all in seeing Mister Leeper, the Juliet Company segundo, being
sprawled and smashed by three big plebes halfway through their
first real game.

In mid-July, Corpen told them, the summer set plebe system
would start. In the meantime, they began to get some idea of what
being a plebe would mean.

The plebe never spoke unless spoken to first. In the corridors of
Bancroft he moved always at double time, with his eyes straight
ahead and his chin "rigged in"—pulled back into his neck until he
looked like a pop-eyed rat. At meals he "braced up," sitting rigidly
on the forward two inches of his chair, chin in, eyes ahead, and ate a
"square meal"—moving his spoon or fork in right-angled courses to

and from his plate. At all times the plebe carried his Reef Points. Inside it, for the convenience of upperclass, he also carried a "plebe kit," with matches, needle and thread, a dime for the phone, two aspirin, and a blank report chit with a stub of pencil.

The plebe was expected to do more than look like a plebe. He had to know things, too. His "rates" included the number of days remaining to the Army game, Christmas leave, the Ring Dance, Graduation; the names and companies of the officers of the day; the menu, for three meals in advance; the movies being shown in the Yard and in town; upcoming athletic events, and the scores of those just played. All of these changed daily. Permanent knowledge, to be gotten verbatim and retained ready for instant playback on demand, included the Oath of Office, the Mission of the Naval Academy, the Code of Conduct, the Songbook, the Chain of Command, the coaches and captains for all fall sports, the Laws of the Navy, and pages and pages of Reef Points, the little bluebound book full of such gems as the answer to the question "What time is it?"—

Sir, I am greatly embarrassed and deeply humiliated that due to unforeseen circumstances beyond my control, the inner workings and hidden mechanisms of my chronometer are in such inaccord with the great sidereal movement with which time is generally reckoned that I cannot with any degree of accuracy state the correct time, sir. But without fear of being too greatly in error, I will state that it is about — minutes, — seconds, and — ticks past — bells.

And "How's the cow?"

Sir, she walks, she talks, she's full of chalk. The lacteal fluid extracted from the female of the bovine species is highly prolific to the nth degree.

And "Why didn't you say 'sir'?"

Sir, sir is a subservient word surviving from the surly days in old Serbia when certain serfs, too ignorant to remember their

lords' names, yet too servile to blaspheme them, circumvented
the situation by surrogating the subservient word *sir*, by which
I now belatedly address a certain senior cirriped, who correctly
surmised that I was syrupy enough to say sir after every word I
said, sir.

—along with a couple of hundred assorted bits of professional
data; what a CVA was, and a CAG, a BB, an AGC and an APD, an
LSD and an MHC and an AVS, an SST and an SS(B)N; an SH–3,
an F–8, an A–4, an S–2C; the max and the effective ranges of six-
inch, eight-inch, sixteen-inch, and various types of five-inch guns,
with weight of shell and types of ammunition for each; and suchlike
trivia, which increased in mass whenever something new was mentioned in class or at the table or at one of the professional lectures
they attended every night.

And all this, Corpen told them, was only their "basic rates"—the
bare scratchy minimum they would need to know, cold, the first day
the Brigade came back and their education would *really* begin. Plebe
summer, they were told, was only to get them warmed up. The
miles they ran each day before dawn were only to toughen them for
that not-so-distant apocalypse when the *first class* would come back
from the Fleet, and doom and destruction would descend on the
heads of all baggers and hot dogs, whimps, slackers, pussies, raters,
sea lawyers, and other dickheads—categories, they were assured, to
which all of them each and severally belonged. They listened silently, believing everything they heard, desperate for each scrap of
forewarning; yet even so they did not understand half of it. It was
hard for them to believe that anyone could do any more, deprive
them of any more, than they had lost already in the transition from
coddled civilians to fourth class dip-shits, USN.

The day summer system started, Philo's name came up on the
watch bill for the first time. He drew duty at Main Office, the show-
place of Bancroft Hall. Still he had to eat morning meal. It was
unmitigated horror. First off, there was no room on his regular
table. He was bumped, and had to run at a brace down the middle
of the mess hall, feeling like shark bait, until he spotted an empty
seat in totally foreign territory. He chopped up, requested permis-

sion to come aboard, and had already perched on his two inches when he realized with a start of horror that the second class at its head was no other than the same Mister Leeper that Lima had wiped out on the lacrosse field.

"Where you from, sandblower?"

"Pennsylvania, sir."

"I mean what company, maggot."

"Sir . . . Lima Company, sir."

The table froze; the fourth class paused in their task of handing along food; ten forks halted halfway along their right-angled routes to the maws of hungry plebes. Philo caught the horrified pitying eyes of his rigid classmates across the table, and felt sweat leap to his own forehead.

"Lima," Leeper's voice repeated softly. "You wouldn't be one of Mister Stamper's lacrosse jocks, would you?"

There was the tiniest temptation to say, no sir, I'm on the cross-country team; but he remembered the honor lectures: *A midshipman will not lie, cheat, or steal, nor will he mislead or deceive anyone as to known facts.* "Yes, sir," he whispered.

He got nothing to eat that morning, and by the time dismissal bell rang had accumulated three comearounds to Leeper; one for not knowing Navy's squash schedule that year, one for making the excuse that no one had told him he had to know it, and one for not shaking his neckerchief fast enough in a little "stow neckerchiefs" drill Leeper, apparently, had invented. Also he did not like the way he had shaved, and Philo was directed to report to his squad leader that he had been bagging it at another company's tables.

"Aye aye, sir," said Philo.

"And wipe that crybaby look off your face, shithead!"

"Aye aye, sir."

At noon meal he was back on his regular table, and for once glad to be there. The platoon was braced up "tight as an eight-year-old virgin's bunghole," as Mister Stamper described it, but rotation had taken him to the far end of the table and he was left, for the moment, alone. The upperclass tended to concentrate their fire on the plebes in range, though occasional long shots would burst around the head of any young charger who looked too relaxed.

The next day was Sunday, and intensely hot. The temperature hovered just over a hundred, and the bricks in T-court seemed to glow. In the afternoon the MOOW, the Midshipman Officer of the Watch, gave him a special job: delivering the mail around the hall. He went at it with a will. It was his first taste of Responsibility.

He was fried twice, once for losing the tuck in his blouse, and once for failing to say "sir" to two second class in civvies—he was so dizzy from running up ladders in the heat that he had forgotten himself for a moment.

But that, he consoled himself, was only bad luck.

When at last the MOOW called "Fall out, the offgoing watch," he lingered in the head on 1–1 for a moment, unwilling to face the corridors again, and the everlasting brace; then took a deep breath, and pushed back through the swinging doors, into plebe summer once again.

In the room, Fayaway and Zeard were sitting barechested with the windows wide open, dripping sweat, polishing shoes like men possessed. From down on the terrace the tramp of boots drifted up as the extra duty squad pounded the bricks. There was not a breath of air in Bancroft. He dropped onto his rack without thinking and groaned aloud.

"Phil."

"What?"

"If somebody comes in—"

"Oh, shit, yeah." He got up and smoothed the spread and tightened the corners again till it was ready to bounce the five-franc piece Stamper tested racks with.

"How was watch?" asked Zeard.

"Not too hot. What did you guys do last night?"

"Had a plebe ho after evening meal. We had all our shoes out in the hall. Corpie wiped them out. Said they were all unsat."

"Unsat?" Philo couldn't believe it. They put in at least an hour a day polishing them.

"Spitshines," said Fayaway succinctly. He spat on his rag, a new skivvy shirt, and scraped more Kiwi out of the tin. "He says he wants to see his face in them."

"A noble ambition," said Zeard.

"But those are your boonies! What good's a spit shine on those if we march around Faggot in 'em three times a week?"

Both Fayaway and Zeard looked at him. "Okay, okay," he said, and reached for his own boondockers. "J.J., would you—"

"Let's see . . . the upper layer of polish is cracking. You got too much on, but it's not sticking right. You got to take it down, start over."

"Oh, Christ. How do you do that?"

"Kerosene works good. I got some Zippo fluid here'll do it."

"Thanks, J.J. Jeez, it's hot."

"That's what I like about you, Philo," muttered Zeard, his face bent close above the toe of his gleaming boonie. "That almost intuitive grasp of the obvious."

A few days later small arms training started. Lima Company, composed of plebes destined for the 34th, 35th, and 36th Companies, was the first group out. The range was across the Severn, reached each day by motor launch from Dewey Basin and then a mile of double-time along a dirt road. In the heat the running, in heavy dungaree blues, left them gasping and staggering and covered with dust when they reached the pits. The range was humid and hot as the inside of a boiler. The grass was brown and crisp and lifeless and the targets shimmered like bad dreams as the heavy M-ones bruised their shoulders. The instructors were enlisted Marine marksmen whose teaching methods consisted of kicking the prone plebes until their slings were tight and their holds correct. But they knew their stuff, and everyone in the squad qualified except Philo. This earned him a high rank on Corpen's shit list for a week. He decided he was afraid of guns.

Meanwhile, back in Bancroft, he was piling up demerits: Irish pennants on his uniform, failing room inspections, screwing up in drill, clutching on his rates. He got one meal of carry-on, for a long lob into the goal during a close-fought game with Charlie Company.

When small-arms qualifications were over the physical conditioning began in earnest. The temperature held steady at ninety-five to a hundred, and the humidity, despite an occasional breeze off the bay, was nearly unbearable. Mornings began with forty-five-minute runs, followed by pushups, chins, leg-raisers, and insane relay races up and down the corridors, varied, when men collapsed, with periods of being braced up and shouted at. Classes were followed by two hours of sports and then another long comearound just before evening meal. They began to feel like machines; they *were* machines; they burned chow, water, and salt tablets, and produced sweat and miles.

And still the squad leaders assured them that all this was merely preliminary. Stamper enlarged on this theme one evening at the table. "Let's get that turkey around, Engel," he said. "You'll have to move a lot smarter than that when the Brigade gets back, or you'll spend your plebe year shoved out."

Ten plebes, staring straight ahead around the table, balanced on the very edges of their chairs, wondered what "shoved out" meant; but none of them cared to become the first to demonstrate it by asking.

"Mister Cross," said Corpen politely, "may I trouble you for the twins?"

Truck passed salt and pepper to his left.

"Permission to send out for more broccoli, sir?"

"Hell no," said Stamper.

"Oh, let 'em," said Corpen. "We got to bulk these boys up, Snatch. Go ahead, Kaufman."

"Rollo's too fat as it is."

"He'll make weight in September," Corpen predicted confidently. "The firsties will take that suet off him. Believe me, maggots, along about October you'll be longing for the rosy days of plebe summer, when you spent your day loafing, ate all you wanted, and had Mister Stamper and me to look after your every need and whim."

"No shit," grunted Stamper, jaw-deep in turkey. "Hey, McGiffin. Aren't you forgetting something?"

"Sir?"

"My goddamned *tea*, McGiffin. Why is my glass half empty? I ought to clamp you on."

"Not now, Snatch. Lieutenant Duke's over on Kilo Company tables."

"Pukey Dukey . . . shall we send a wild man after him?"

"After the OOD?"

"Just jokin' . . . McGiffin! You know the man overboard drill?"

Philo hesitated, his spoon halfway to his mouth. He'd memorized it from Reef Points, but . . . he decided to chance it. "Yes, sir."

"Let's give it a shot. Rollo!" He pointed his fork at Kaufman. "You're sharkbait. Porter, you be the shark. McGiffin's Officer of the Deck. Weird, you're bosun's mate. Got it? Gray, you're lookout. Hit it."

"Man overboard, port side," said Gray.

"What the hell! Knock 'em together!" said Corpen, leaning forward. "This is a man overboard drill, not teatime conversation. You're out at sea, you're on watch, you've just seen a guy hit the water. Put a little blue into it, Gray!"

"Man overboard! Port side!" Gray yelled.

The two upperclass looked expectantly at Philo. For an instant his memory faltered; then he had it. "Man overboard, port side," he screamed, upsetting his chair. "Port engine stop. Right full rudder! Sound six blasts on the ship's whistle! Break the OSCAR flag! Bosun's mate—where's the bosun's mate?"

"Bosun's mate aye," said Zeard instantly.

"Take charge!"

"Man number two lifeboat. Stand by the falls! Lower away together. Stand by to let fall. Let go the after fall! Let go the forward fall! Coxswain, take charge!" He looked at Truck Cross.

"Stand by your oars—"

"Goddamnit, Porter," said Corpen, "You're the goddamned shark, aren't you? Rollo's in the water, isn't he? Chase him!" The two plebes started up from their chairs. At the tables nearby, conversation had stopped; the second class were watching, grinning, and the fourth class were drawing up with the rectilinear rapidity of sausage-stuffing machines.

"Out oars!"

"Have 'em use their forks."

"Stroke! Stroke! Stroke!"

They were catching on. The whole table surged into motion. Four plebes on each side, faces intent, muscles straining, rowed vigorously with their forks. Kaufman, puffing, completed his fifth circuit of the table, with Porter, his teeth bared, immediately behind. Zeard caught his arm on the sixth lap and hauled him bodily aboard. The plebes on the starboard side fought a ravenous Porter off with their oars. McGiffin sneaked a look at the second class. That was all there was to the drill; he had remembered every word.

Corpen, he saw, was smiling. "Pretty good," he said, "for a first time. One and a half minutes since he hit the water."

"Pretty good?" growled Stamper. "Yeah—except the guy's dead. *McGiffin!*"

"Sir!"

"Kaufman went over to port. You put the rudder right. Know what that does? Swings the stern right over him. He got sucked right into your screws."

The plebes were silent. Kaufman and Porter resumed their seats. Philo swallowed a couple of times, fighting a wave of self-pity. I ran the whole drill right, he thought, except for one little mistake. The book didn't even say anything about that. The whole thing had been fun, until Stamper ruined it.

Why weren't they ever satisfied? If Gray had been doing it, now. . . .

"Dave, I'm going over to talk to Jimzo," said Stamper.

"Sure. Say—that wasn't too bad. The drill. I'm going to give them a taste of carry-on."

"Don't get them used to it."

"They won't," said Corpen.

Stamper left. Corpen flashed them the two-finger carry-on sign and the plebes relaxed warily, glancing at one another. They slid back on their chairs and worked their jaws and began to eat normally, crowding their plates.

Philo, on the hot seat next to Corpen, topped off the squad leader's glass, then filled his own, Academy-style: half white milk, half chocolate, two ice cubes. He glanced at the second class. His square, dark face, heavy eyebrows, were bent over apple pie with ice cream. Corpen, at least, had smiled during the man overboard drill. He had even given them carry-on. Was this the time to ask his question? It's probably the best time yet this summer, he thought, and mustered his courage.

"Mister Corpen, sir?"

"What?"

"Permission to ask question, sir."

"Go."

"Sir, the first day—when we were checking in—you, uh, said something about my name. What, ah, what did you mean, sir?"

"Don't stammer, McGiffin."

"No, sir. I mean, aye aye, sir."

"Your name? You haven't figured that out yet?"

"No sir."

"No one's told you?"

"No sir."

"Jesus," said Corpen thoughtfully. "Well, pour me a moke of that java there and I'll fill you in."

The other fourth class looked up, interested. Philo poured coffee carefully from the heavy pewter pitcher into the white-and-blue cup at Corpen's elbow and added cow and lighthouse. It smelled good, but fourth class rated coffee only on Sunday mornings, right after Chapel.

"The real Philo McGiffin," said Corpen, sipping at the cup, "is sort of a legend around this place. He *is* a legend. Not like W. T. Door or Joe Gish. Those are just nicknames for the average mid. McGiffin is different. He was real." He held out the cup. "More White Death."

He added sugar, and his squad leader went on. "Philo McGiffin . . . well, I'll just tell you what I've heard from my upperclass. I can't vouch for how much of it's true and how much is just scuttlebutt, just sea stories.

"See, Philo McGiffin was a mid here around 1880, 1883. His specialty was practical jokes. He used to roll cannonballs down the ladders at the officers of the deck. He blew flour all over the watch squad from an upper deck, when they were mustering for inspection in dress blues. Once, they say, he climbed up the old chapel and left his cap on top of the steeple. Ever since, tradition is that if any plebe does it, the whole class gets permanent carry-on. But nobody could, the new Chapel is so much higher.

"Maybe his best one was . . . you guys know the two guns in

front of the Rotunda? The old French cannons with the faces cast into them?"

"Yes, sir."

"Those are called the Virgin Guns. Legend is that they'll go off if a real virgin ever walks between 'em with a mid. Well, they say McGiffin got sent out to the old station ship to restrict after he got class A'd for the flour deal. He used to climb out the sideports and swim ashore and go drinking in Crabtown. Well, while he was there, he cumshawed some black powder and some fuzes from one of the gunner's mates. When he got out he fixed the Virgin Guns one night to fire when he pulled a cord.

"He waited and waited . . . and then let them go the next day, just as the Superintendent and his wife came up the steps."

Corpen grinned too as they all laughed. "Well, that nearly got him thrown out. But he finally graduated. Only in those days they could only afford to commission about half the firsties who finished. The rest of 'em got paid off and went back to civvieland. But McGiffin wanted to be a naval officer in the worst way.

"So one day he hears about an opening in China. He takes his mustering-out pay and heads for Canton. In no time he's an admiral in the Chinese Navy. He commanded a fleet, I think, in some battle out there and got wounded all to hell."

Corpen paused; Philo looked down the table; the other plebes had stopped chewing and were listening, staring at the squad leader, and at him. "So," said Corpen again, "That's about it. There are lots of other stories about him, but like I say, I don't know how true they all are. It's just what I heard when I was a plebe. It's been passed down from class to class. But he's a legend, all right.

"That answer your question, McGiffin?"

"Yes, sir," said Philo. At least he knew now why the upperclass did double-takes at his name tag.

The remaining weeks of summer passed rapidly. The plebes were run and fed and drilled and run again. They memorized, polished, marched, studied like men inspired, and they were. By good old-fashioned military fear.

And then one day the Brigade came back from sea.

CHAPTER THREE

01664 D McGiffin Philo Norton B-Pa A-Pa Honorably discharged 30 Jun 1884 under act of Congress 05 Aug '82 NAVCDT Died Feb 11 1897 NY
>—U.S. Naval Academy Alumni Association
>Register of Alumni; 95th edition

Don't piss into the wind.
>—The Second Law of the Salt Mines

The fourth deck, eighth wing, 34th Company's permanent home, was filled all that morning with upperclass. They dragged B–4s and AWOL bags, duffels and suitcases, slamming open doors and shouting to each other across the corridors about their sea tours, their flight training; about liberty in Marseilles and Newport News and Yokosuka; about the Campfire Girls, who offered themselves by trash fires in the Neapolitan night; about Whisper Street; about Olongopo, where at the Pit you could buy a live duck for a peso and throw it to the alligator.

The plebes sat silently in their strange new rooms, glancing at one another, watching *them* pass, and wondered if they could ever hope to be so salty, so swaggering, so incredibly yet casually squared away.

The night before, sick of studying and polishing shoes, Philo had taken his half hour before study time began, and gone across Bancroft to the Rotunda. It was about the only place in the Hall a plebe could go without bracing up, except the head, and there was only so much time you could waste taking a dump. Feeling immea-

surably tired, depressed, and scared, he had slowly climbed the
marble steps up into Memorial Hall, hoping to find a place just to sit
for a moment and be alone.

The great room was empty and dim. The parquet floors were
vacant and the smell of wax lingered in the air. His steps echoed
from marble and bronze as he slowly crossed the room, under the
immense English chandeliers, the murals of sea battles of the age of
sail, toward the tall windows that looked out on the bay.

Halfway there, he stopped. From the shadows, from one of the
arched niches, someone was watching him. He stiffened slightly,
opened his mouth to sound off, and then shook his head. The light
had fooled him. It was only a statue. Some old admiral or other.
Probably he should recognize him, but he didn't. He walked closer.

> *. . . dedicated by his classmates in loving memory. . . .*

He paced along the walls, reading. Shipwrecks. Insurrections.
Battles. Men drowning in the surf, dying in flaming turrets, in
prison camps . . . he read the old chiseled script, the cast brass and
bronze. And suddenly he understood the hush, the dim light.

This was a graveyard . . . except that there were no bodies. There
had been nothing to bury. The sea did not yield up her dead.

He crossed the parquet floor again, feeling the old wood creak
under his polished shoes. Between the tall windows, blue-gray now
this close to night, the only lights in the room glowed before a
thirty-foot slab of bronze.

The Roll of Honor.

The lights glowed softly over the ranks of names. Academy graduates who had fallen in battle. 1863. 1898. 1917. 1928. 1942. And
the new names, the vacant spaces, that someday would be filled,
perhaps by men he knew.

After a long while his eyes rose. Atop the bronze, high above
him, hung a swatch of faded blue bunting, with clumsily-cut letters
stitched onto it.

DON'T GIVE UP THE SHIP

Lawrence's dying words; Perry's flag of conquest on Lake Erie. He looked up at it for a long time, and slowly his thoughts made their circle and he came back to himself.

Two months out of eleven. That was the score. Nine more months of plebehood. The worst nine, of course. He felt scared even thinking about what would begin the next morning.

But I made it this far, he thought, looking still at the tattered old banner; and he lifted his head a little, unconsciously. I made it this far. And I'll make it all the way.

He was thinking of that flag now, as he stared at his fingers trembling on his desk, as upperclass beyond counting thronged the corridor just outside their open door. In the move from 2–2 they had swapped roommates, and he sat now in a four-man room with Kaufman, Zeard, and Gray. They sat apprehensively at their desks, glancing at each other, waiting for the inevitable.

It came. Khaki filled the door. "Attention on deck!" shouted Gray, and they all four popped to attention, chins rigged in as far as they could and still breathe.

"What are these?"

"Our new fourth estate, it appears."

Worn-looking shoulderboards with a single vertical strand of gold moved into Philo's peripheral vision. First classmen! He hardly dared to breathe. He felt dizzy. His legs began to tremble as he felt their eyes crawling over him, heard them moving about the room.

"Look at this shrimp. He about comes up to your belt buckle."

"You. The funny looking one. Sound off, charger."

"Midshipman fourth class Zeard, sir."

"What? I didn't quite catch that."

"Midshipman fourth class Zeard, sir."

"Where's your name tag, beanpole?"

"Here, sir. I was putting it on, sir."

"What do they call you, Zeard?"

"Howard, sir."

"No. They can't call you that. With a nose like that you got to have something better than that."

"Some of the second class call me Weird, sir."

"That fits."

"Hey! Look at this, Muff! Look at this guy's name tag!"

Oh, Christ, thought Philo.

When they were done with him for the moment, and he and Zeard stood rigging their M-ones at arm's length, the firsties began to prowl about the room. "Totally unsat," said one, looking into the shower.

"A shithole," agreed the other. They began pulling clothes from the lockers and tossing them casually to the deck. Caps followed, then socks, bouncing about the tiles like soft handballs, scarves, underwear, whites, the new issues of Working Uniform Blue. Philo's eyes flicked to his roommates. Gray, his handsome face without expression, did not remove his eyes from the boat; he was waiting, suspended, encapsulated in an attitude of rigid attention.

"Thirty-fourth Company! Plebe ho!" sounded in the corridor, repeated by strange voices, echoing away down the shaft.

"Permission to shove off, sir?" said Gray crisply, coming to life.

"Go."

Eighth wing, fourth deck, was different from the rest of the Hall. The seventh and eighth wings had been built later than the rest of Bancroft, without the frills of mock French Renaissance; the copper guttering was unadorned, the granite unchiselled into writhing dolphins and tridents. On 8–4, the topmost deck of the eighth wing, the corridor was narrow and the overhead almost low enough to touch. The mansard windows were so small that the corridor itself was almost dark when lights were off during the day. In this slightly subterranean dimness the fourth class quickly arranged themselves along the cool tiles of the bulkhead, bodies taut in a brace, chins in and eyes straight ahead. They stood motionless, waiting.

"Have them carry on, Mister Breen."

"Aye sir. Fourth class, carry on. Listen up to the Thirty-fourth Company officer."

Philo allowed himself to relax a little. Shooting a glance sideways, he saw a round little man in his mid-twenties, in a wrinkled, too-tightly-fitting tropical khaki uniform, with the bottom button undone. The silver bar of a lieutenant junior grade gleamed at his collar. On his chest was the double dolphin insignia of a submariner. His face was soft-looking, squeezed into an expression of benevolent command.

"I'm your new company officer, Lieutenant Portley," he began.

His voice, too, was soft. "Along with you gentlemen, I'm a new arrival here. As company officer, anyway—I spent a few years here as a mid, a while back. Mother B hasn't changed much. I guess plebe summer hasn't either, has it?"

They gave him the titter he appeared to want.

"Seriously, men, I hope you've had a good summer. Studied hard, played strenuously, got yourselves ahead of the power curve for ac year. I know that the summer squad leaders, fine men, have put a lot of work into shaping you up.

"I won't take a great deal of your limited time this morning. You should, however, know who I am." He nodded, chins wobbling. "As part of the Executive Department, and as your senior officer in the Navy chain of command, I am responsible for your performance and your welfare. I want you to know that I take the chain of command concept very seriously. I'll be interviewing each of you individually over the next few weeks. We'll get to know each other better then. Be aware, however, that I'll be in the Company Office most weekday mornings. If you have problems of a personal or confidential nature, see the company commander, Midshipman Lieutenant Breen, for an appointment with me; or, if it's short fuze, simply knock and enter. Of course, a problem of a less serious nature should be handled through the midshipman striper organization."

Portley smiled and looked up at the overhead. "I understand they call this deck the Ghetto—or at least they did when I was a mid. You fourth classmen are new here, but I know you'll enjoy it. Give your upperclass your respect and confidence, work hard, play clean, and this will be a year you'll look back on with good feelings when you're out in the Fleet.

"Again, welcome. Mister Breen—care to add a few words?"

"Just to welcome them aboard, sir. And you've done that very well."

"Thank you. I guess that's all, then."

As if Portley had timed it—and perhaps he had—the bell rang for noon meal formation. Although the weather was fine, the first formation of the academic year would be inside. With considerable confusion and cursing, the hundred-odd men of 34th Company fell into ranks in the narrow corridor. In each squad of twelve the fourth class rubbed shoulders with third, second, and first classmen; from a ratio of fifteen to one, the plebes were now outnumbered by the upperclass one to three. They felt gawky and uncomfortable. Philo and Gray and Kaufman and Fayaway found themselves in Midshipman Ensign Singleterry's squad. He was blond and tall and haughty-looking, with a fine nose, and he wore his uniform with a lounging but impeccable elegance that made them feel like ragged beggars. The other first classs in the squad was Mister Kim, a Korean. Stamper was in their squad, as were two other second class, a Mister Schochet and a Mister Reefer. That left slots for three third class, the sophomores. Four short months before they had been plebes themselves.

"Thirty-fourth Company: a-ten-*but!*"

Lieutenant (junior grade) Portley stood silently to one side, watching, as the firsties took command.

"Ree-*port.*"

"First platoon, all present or accounted for."

"Second platoon ditto."

"Third aye."

"Sir, Thirty-fourth Company all present or accounted for, sir," said the company commander, turning to Portley with a practiced, offhand salute. He, Philo saw, was a broadshouldered man of above average height, with a wide, coldly masculine face and a solid chin. Portley returned the salute gravely. "Very well, Mister Breen," he said.

Breen handed the muster report to a waiting mate, who double-timed off. "Stand at ease; attention to word," he said, his voice carrying easily over the ranks. "All personnel will sign up for fall sports in front of the company office before eighteen-hundred today. Class cards will be delivered via the mailbox during the afternoon. Laundry will go out tommorrow morning. Tailor shop schedule for fourth class is posted on the bulletin board." He paused and looked at the leaders of the three platoons. "Anything else?"

"*Luftgekuhlte,*" said someone.

"Yeah. The Famous Slack Thirty-fourth Air-Cooled Devils will meet in the Rathole tonight for rally scheduling. That all? Hope you guys all had a good summer. Okay. Company! A-ten-*hut!* Lelft-*hace!* Forward . . . *harch.*"

They filed down eight flights of steps and out the big double doors between the sixth wing and the mess hall. It took quite a while. Philo could see that the very remoteness of 8–4 would add up to a lot of hours of travel during the year. In Smoke Park the familiar sweetness of jasmine hit him like a body block and he sucked in his breath as he entered the mess hall and tucked his chin and chopped through the strolling upperclass to table 251. The plebes stood tautly braced behind their chairs as the upperclass arrived, talking among themselves, glancing from time to time at the already sweating plebes.

I've got to remember it all now, Philo was thinking, viciously, desperately, in a pleading incantation to his own memory. This is it. The Brigade. I can't clutch now. Movies in town. Evening meal: salisbury steak, o'brien potatoes, peas and carrots, chocolate cake, coffee and milk. Eighty-two days to Army, ninety-one to Christmas leave, 159 to first class graduation, 155 till second class Ring Dance. Stephen Decatur, "Sir, I cannot receive the sword of a man who has—"

"McGiffin," said a voice close to him. "I heard about you. You know your rates, ploob?"

"Yes sir." God I hope so.

"Take a strain, damn it! Chins! You call that a brace?"

"Aye aye, sir." He pulled his chin in till it felt like he was gnawing his backbone.

"Let's hear the football schedule."

"Yes, sir. Boston College, September 16; Penn State, September 23; William and Mary, September 30; Princeton, October 7; Air Force, Octo—"

"Air Farce, boy. We say that *Air Farce* around here."

"Air Farce, October 14; Villanova, October 21; Washington, October 28; Notre Dame, November 7; Syracuse, November 11; Georgia Tech, November 18; Army, December 2." He paused for breath. "Sir."

"Mister Gray, you look uncomfortable. Is that right?"

"Sir," said Gray, "request permission not to bilge a classmate."

Oh shit, Philo thought. What did I do wrong? It was just like Gray to bilge him. It was already plain that the slim, handsome plebe lusted after high grease.

"Bilge him."

"One of the dates was incorrect, sir," said Gray humbly, as if he regretted showing his roommate up. "The Notre Dame game is on November 4."

"I thought you said you knew your rates, McGiffin?" said a large youngster. Philo's peripheral vision, which was growing quite good, gave him the single anchor at his collar that denoted a third classman, told him also that his interrogator was sloppy, bulgy amidships, and fat-faced. His name tag said Dubus.

"I . . . yes, sir, I did."

"And you don't? That's a falsehood in my book, boy."

"You mind, Danny? I'm talking to him now," said the second classman.

Dubus subsided, looking closely, however, at McGiffin. The Brigade was called to attention from the central podium, addressed by the Brigade Commander and the Commandant—during both of whose speeches the upperclass fidgeted, whispered, and played with their chairs and silverware—and subjected to grace by the Chaplain. Then they were seated.

"Foo-*bar*."

"Just like old times."

"Bring on the chow. Hey steward! Over here!"

The plebes busied themselves serving iced tea and passing around food and condiments. As they had been told, the firsties were served first, then the segundoes, at the foot; then the youngsters, who sat opposite the plebes, along the other side of the twelve-man table. After that, if there was anything left in the serving trays, they were free to draw up for themselves. Zeard was on the hot seat today, but Philo, next to him, tried to keep an eye on the firsties' plates too; Howard had a tendency toward absentmindedness that had earned them all a few crap rations that summer. But he did all right today, and after some rather easy questions, where each was from, that sort of thing, Singleterry and Kim left them alone, directing them, however, to come around that evening to "get acquainted." They began to talk about the upcoming semester. The second class were busy eating. Philo could see, from the corners of his fixed eyes, Dubus' gaze on them.

"Gray," he said.

"Sir?"

"What are you famous for, stud?"

"Sir, I was the forward lookout on the Titanic, sir."

"That's an old one."

"Yes sir," said Gray. "I'll work up some better ones, Mister Dubus, sir."

"Zeard. What are you famous for?"

"Sir, I fried Samson for his haircut, sir."

"That's not bad," said Dubus. "How's the cow?"

"Sir, she walks, she talks, she's full of chalk." Zeard reached out to shake the milk carton. "The lacteal fluid of the female of the bovine species is prolific to the fifth degree, sir."

"Fayaway," said Dubus. "What kind of a pussy handle is that?"

"Turkish, sir," said Fayaway. His voice was very quiet.

"Where you from, Fayaway?" asked one of the other youngsters.

"L.A., sir; previous enlisted."

"That so. I'm from Redondo Beach."

"Inglewood, sir."

"Hey, McGiffin," said Dubus, his voice cutting into his classmate's. "How big is your girl's podunk?"

"Sir?"

"*Sir*," mimicked Dubus. "I said—you even got a girl, McGiffin? Let's have a cap check."

The four plebes reached under their chairs for their caps. Corpen had told them they'd better have a picture of a girl in each of their caps by the time the Brigade got back. He had to cut one out of a magazine. He thought about the one girl, Barb Spenser, he had dated at Raymondsville High. She was not really his girl. Still you could not explain all that. It had to be yes or no. And what was her podunk?

"Yes sir," he said at last.

"Well? How big is her podunk?"

"I . . . she never let me see her podunk, sir."

The youngsters laughed. "A podunk is a home town, McGiffin," said someone.

"You a virgin, McGiffin?" asked Dubus, belching.

"Dan," said one of the other youngsters.

"Hell, I'm just asking him . . . hey, I got one . . . where do you caulk off, Gray?"

"Cock off, sir?"

"Yeah, caulk off. Don't tell me you haven't caulked off this summer."

"No sir."

"Well, where did you caulk off, then? Answer up."

"I . . . in the shower, sir. Twice."

"That's funny. Most people caulk off in their racks." All the youngsters laughed.

"Let's get those veggies around," Singleterry's languid voice interrupted. "All gone? Send out for more. Don't wait for permission on my table. When something is gone, send out."

Philo held up the heavy tray for one of the stewards to refill from steaming carts that roved the center aisles. Dessert arrived: small pie shells filled with cherries and piled with whipped cream. His mouth watered as he passed them toward Singleterry and Kim. He'd had time for only a few bites of lunch between the barrage of questions and his duties. In spite of himself his eyes followed the pastries. Singleterry took one; Kim one; Stamper one; Schochet two; Reefer one; Weibels two; Dubus two; Barch one. That left one for the fourth class.

"Permission to shake for dessert, sir?"

"Do it."

"Leave me out," said Fayaway in a low voice. "I don't want any."

Zeard, Gray, and Philo held out clenched fists. "Hup, hup, *ho*," murmured Gray. They counted fingers, added them, then counted around. Philo won. The battered tart, smallest one of the trayful, came to rest on his plate.

The dismissal bell rang. He swallowed hard—he could taste the cool sweetness of jellied cherries, the smooth creaminess of the topping—and pushed back his chair. As he turned to chop off he saw Dubus scrape the tart off his plate. Fourth class weren't allowed to take food from the mess hall. Neither were upperclass, but obviously they did. He swallowed his disappointment along with a mouthful of saliva and turned his mind, as he walked across the brightness of Smoke Park, to his room, to the thousand things he had to do and prepare and memorize and fold that afternoon, and still find a little time to study the advance lessons for his first classes.

The afternoon passed swiftly. Other upperclass came in from time to time to size them up. Sports had not yet started so at 1600, in place of practice, he suited up and went out running with Zeard and Len Ind. The black fourth class, he discovered, was one hell of a middle-distance runner. But Philo, after a summer at midfield, was no slowpoke either. They finished three laps of Farragut with a quarter-mile neck-risking sprint along the big canted blocks of the seawall. He finished about four yards behind Ind. They flopped down, panting and wiping sweat, by the two AA guns that looked toward Greenbury Point. They lay full length, Ind prone, Philo supine, looking out over the sun-tinselled waters of the bay. From the Crabtown dock an oyster dredger was putting out, the put-put of its one-lunger engine throbbing clearly across the flat water, the flat rocks. "Hey," said Ind, "nice running. You really pushed me. You going out for cross-country this fall?"

"Thought about it. I'm getting out of lacrosse. They're too rough for a guy my size. How about you?"

"B-ball, I guess,"said Ind, yawning. "If I stay."

Philo glanced over at him, surprised. It was the first time he had heard anyone say he might not stay, although they all knew about attrition, they all knew about the guys in first platoon who had quit, and the two plebes in Charlie Company their classmates had caught in a compromising position. But no one talked aloud about leaving. Ind saw his surprise and shrugged.

"It ain't worth it, Phil. I had a scholarship offer from Alabama, to play ball. And my grades are good. I don't have to take the crap they're putting out. There's no reason for it."

Zeard arrived, finally, long and awkward-legged as a crippled spider. A fat bruise purpled his knee and he let go a few good salty curses as he sagged to the grass between Philo and Len. "Friggin' rocks," he wheezed, finishing up. "Why'd you guys go so fast?"

"It felt good," said Philo.

They lay in the sunlight. The grass of the little plot was cut short, and its sweet wild smell mingled with the salt breeze from bayward. The sun was bright and hot in a cloudless sky and it sparkled from the waves the trawler left in its wake and from zircon flecks of quartz in the granite of the seawall. From inland, behind them, came the distant shouts of an impromptu kickball scrimmage and the dull hypnotic clang of sailboat rigging in the basin. It was altogether peaceful and pleasant, hot and almost timeless, unscheduled, unseen, free of the twin tyrannies of upperclass and bells.

"I wonder if we're allowed to lie here," he said.

"Don't worry," said Zeard, stretching. "Somebody'll let us know if we aren't. Jeez, my leg hurts."

"You fell?" said Ind. Zeard nodded. "Better have it looked at. Misery Hall should be open."

"Ah, later," said Zeard lazily. His long, ugly, marked face was relaxed, his eyes closed; he lay open to the sun, one with the grass. "I'm just enjoying rigging my chin out for a change."

"You said it."

"No lie."

Philo worked his T-shirt over his head and lay half naked in the sun. The heat felt good. "You know," he said, "this is the first time since we got here that I feel halfway normal. It's rougher than I expected, that's for sure."

"Too true," said Ind.

"It's got to be rough," murmured Zeard.

"What?"

"Got to be. Otherwise it wouldn't work."

Philo raised himself on an elbow, stared at him for a moment, and then let his body sag back against the warm soil. "What do you mean?" he said. "Wouldn't work for what?"

"You know what. What they're doing to us."

"Indoctrination?" said Philo.

"Fuckin' us over?" said Ind.

"No. Neither one. It's a mold, that's all."

They waited, feeling drowsy.

"It's like a process," Zeard went on, after a moment. "See? For four years they screw down this mold on you. It's a hundred and fifty years of tradition, unmarred by progress. First they soften you up—run you day and night, no sleep, not enough to eat, under pressure all the time. We're not that mature yet; we can't resist even if we wanted to. They challenge every habit, every idea. There's a Navy way to do everything."

"Fold your skivvies."

"Open a cereal box."

"Take a shower. Lots of soap—squeegee with your hands—"

"—Exactly. Different vocabulary, different clothes, a certain way to talk and think; only certain things you can say. And they're the same for everybody. The mold comes down and they turn the heat on and if you don't fit it you start changing yourself until you do. If you don't make the tolerances they got a quality control system that pulls you out and rejects you. Not inferior, exactly, but just that you're not ring-knocker Academy officer material."

"Where'd you memorize all that horseshit, Howie?"

"I didn't *memorize* it. It's pretty obvious that's the purpose of all this plebe year stuff."

"Sounds pretty bad when you say it that way," said Philo. "Like brainwashing."

"Call it what you want. As long as you realize what's happening to you. I don't think realizing it can stop it or make it any different; but the way I figure, it's better to know what's going on, even if knowing doesn't do you any real good."

Philo rolled over and looked again at his roommate, closely this time. It was a new side of the Zeard he had always seen as gawky, ugly, letter-perfect on his verbal rates, but prone to clutching solid at the table. The guy had a brain. "Well," he said stubbornly, "whatever you call it, I'm staying. I'm going to make it through here."

"I hope you do, Phil. I wish we all could. But we won't. Guys like Truck Cross will make it—jocks. Gray will make it—squared away, a little of the brown-noser already about him. Guys like J.J. will probably squeak through—hard workers, regular guys without a lot of imagination to scare themselves with. But it isn't a place for intellectuals, or people wrapped up in themselves, or—" He paused.

"Or what?" said Ind. "Or blacks?"

"No," said Zeard, his eyes squeezed shut in the sun. "I was going to say—guys without—"

"Without what?" said Philo, sitting up.

"I can't think of a nice way to say it," Zeard mumbled. "C'mon, let's jog on in."

"Wait a minute. Finish what you were going to say, Howie."

"You'll get pissed."

"No I won't. We're roommates, aren't we?"

"Okay. Here it comes. Philo, you don't come across as a very—gutsy—kind of guy."

"What do you mean by that?"

"I think you probably know," said Zeard. His eyes opened and they looked steadily at each other across a yard or two of sunlit grass. "Look, the last thing I mean is to insult you. I know you've got balls. And maybe the whole thing is none of my business, except that you're my roommate and my classmate. But those balls don't show, Phil. You look so scared sometimes. In a place like this that's one of the most dangerous things you can do. I've seen you at lacrosse, avoiding contact out there, flinching aside when one of the big guys comes at you."

Philo looked at him. A rush of feelings—anger, shame, denial—hit him, so suddenly that he couldn't think of anything to say. He opened his mouth, but it all stopped halfway down, somewhere in his stomach.

"Phil?" said Ind. His voice had an odd, tense quality.

"What, Len?"

"You hear Howie?"

"Yeah. Yeah, I heard him."

"Look, maybe I shouldn't even of mentioned it," said Zeard. He rolled over. "Forget it, Phil. All right? I was probably wrong anyway. Hey! Look at that yawl."

Philo and Ind lifted their heads. One of the Luders yawls was heading in from the Chesapeake, hugging the point under full sail. The spread of white dacron luffed, full-bellied to catch the whisper of breeze. The slim blue hull swayed gently, passing so close they could hear plainly the splash of cloven water under her forefoot.

"Hey . . . isn't that a woman?"

"Where?"

"Just forward of midships. Lying down under the boom."

"Bikini!"

"Blonde!"

The mainsail sagged suddenly and began its slide downward. The ratcheting of the winch came over the water to them, and they watched the woman wordlessly, hungrily, as she stood and gathered in the flapping folds as they descended around and over her, finally hiding her from their view.

Zeard got up. "Well," he said, uncertainly, "see you guys later. I'm going over to have this leg looked at."

Philo looked after him as he jogged off toward Macdonough.

"Shit, McGiffin," said Ind suddenly.

"What?"

"I don't believe you, man." The black mid sat up. "You sit there. Just sit there and let your own classmate shit on you, call you a pussy."

"I said I wouldn't get pissed," said Philo.

"There's times you got to get pissed," said Ind. "Or else I feel sorry for you, man. Because he's right."

Philo looked at him. Ind stared right back, and after a while he looked away, out to where another yacht was passing, bound up to Baltimore, or Washington, or maybe to the wide blue boundlessness of the open sea.

"We better be getting back," he said.

It hurt too much for him to say any more.

They reported to Singleterry's room, as ordered, at 1800, dressed in the standard comearound uniform: gray Navy sweat shirts and pants over gym shorts and USNA T-shirts, white athletic socks, rubber-soled gym shoes. And jock straps, of course, underneath it all; Stamper had warned them during the summer never to forget those. Their squad leader wasn't there, so they waited in the corridor, braced up in a line, backs against the wall, staring at nothing. They were well content. Philo rehearsed his rates in his head. Passing upperclass eyed them curiously but did not interfere. At 1805

Singleterry arrived. Twenty seconds later they were "warming up" by crab-racing down the corridor. After two or three heats of this, crawling on all fours but belly up, their arms felt ready to drop off. The first class watched them, casually leaning against his door jamb, an unlit Camel filter in a bamboo holder drooping from his pale aristocratically planed face. Fayaway, the winner, got leaning rest while the three remaining plebes did three laps duck-walking, with their hands under their arms, waddling along in a squat. Zeard won this one by a hair, his long ungainly legs eating up the length of the corridor. He too drew leaning rest beside Fayaway. That left Philo and Gray head to head. The next race, Singleterry intimated languidly, would be a salamander. "Get ready," he said, the cigarette holder bobbing and shedding tobacco as he spoke.

"Permission to ask question, sir," said Gray, gasping for breath.

"What?"

"We don't—we haven't done that yet, sir."

"Never done a salamander race?"

"No sir."

"Well—how about a greyhound?"

"No sir," said Philo.

"Good heavens," said Singleterry. "What is this? You can do a dead horse surely?"

They looked at him blankly.

"Clamp on? Carrier landings? Green bench? Know how to swim to Baltimore?"

"No sir," said Gray. Behind them there was a *thud* as Zeard's arms collapsed and he hit the deck.

"You, Zeard," said Singleterry, pointing down the corridor with the Camel. "Go get me Mister Stamper. Say, 'Sir, Mister Singleterry sends his regards, and requests the honor of your presence in his room.' Got that? *Go.*"

Zeard showed elbows and assholes, skidded around the corner, and disappeared. Singleterry looked over the remaining three of them. "Come aboard, Mister Fayaway," he said. "You gentlemen can go get your rifles. There are some little drills with those they probably left out this summer too."

When Mister Stamper came by, in his shower shoes and the gray

Army b-robe decorated with his three N stars for lacrosse, the three of them were rigging thirty pounds of M-ones out at arm's length, their arms already beginning to sag below their bleached faces. "What's up?" Stamper asked Philo.

"Fidelity is . . . up, sir. Obedience is . . . down"—the Reef Points response.

"No. I mean, what's the trouble?"

"Snatch," said Singleterry, coming out, patting on Aqua Velva, its smell cutting through sweat and gun oil, "What did you do with these boys all summer? They don't know a God-damned thing."

"You clutch on the football team again, McGiffin?" Stamper asked Philo.

"No . . . sir." The rifle dipped. He brought it up again, groaning through his teeth. His arms felt as if they had died some hours before.

"Then what's the trouble?"

Singleterry explained. Stamper looked at the plebes. "Look," he said. "You got to watch that shit. You know that stuff is out. And we were on 2–2 all summer, two minutes' walk from the OOD shack. It was by the book all the way."

"They're in the Ghetto now," said Singleterry. "There's a lot goes up here that don't go on 2–2. Or 6–2 for that matter."

Stamper paused, shrugged his shoulders inside the gray flannel of the b-robe, and then turned and walked quickly down the corridor. Halfway down it he turned again. "You're their squad leader," he said. "Just don't get your balls caught in a crack."

"I won't," said Singleterry. "I learned from the masters. You," he went on, pointing at Gray, "you look the most squared away out of this sorry bunch. You've got the OOD watch. Post yourself at the head of the ladder there. You see an officer coming up, even if it's only the Snorkel, you better get here before he does, or your ass is grass. Got it?"

"Aye aye, sir," said Gray.

"And now, gentlemen," said Singleterry, smiling, turning to the three of them as the rifles dipped and swayed, "Welcome to plebe year."

CHAPTER FOUR

"I have not yet begun to fight."
> —Commodore John Paul Jones, aboard USS
> *Bonhomme Richard*, 1779

*When they make it too tough for everyone else, they
make it just right for me.*
> —Seen on a cork board in vicinity of 6–3

The room was hot and long and very old. Dull green paint, the color of pennies that have lain for years in wet drains, arched over ranks of V-shaped wooden desks layered with graffiti so deep that long study was necessary to make out what each one said. From the front of the room a droning voice seeped out over the nodding heads of sixty midshipmen. From time to time the air of hushed stasis was interrupted as the small figure gestured with a pointer or drew a weary line on the diagram that had grown on the board over the first half of the fifty-minute period. The only other motion in the room, lightfilled and warm and airless, was the slow sagging and sudden jerking upright of one or another of the rows of close-cropped heads.

". . . For this solution we will utilize the first set of equations, taking components of all forces along horizontal and vertical axes. Again we assume that all forces are concurrent and coplanar. If our load at point S-sub-one is fourteen thousand kilos, then the horizontal component acting along segment SN will be found to be dependent on. . . ."

In the next row from the back the distant buzzing, the close air, enfolded Philo McGiffin like warm hands. His breathing was long

and slow. His eyes, fixed on the white coat a hundred feet away at the
front of the room, blinked at twenty-second intervals. His Statics
book lay open by his left elbow, and a notepad, a pencil across the
blank page, lay by his right.

He had slept for three and a half hours the night before. The rest
of the time between taps and turnout had all been undercover work,
memorizing major league football lineups and scores and schedules
by the beam of a non-reg flashlight. The silent Mister Kim had
turned out to be a sports fanatic. That morning at comearound, find-
ing that Philo didn't know what soccer was, he had appointed him
goalie for a day, standing in front of the open corridor window on
8-4 while Fayaway and Gray sailed dixie cups past him and down
into the parking lot. Now he knew what soccer was. He also knew
the first-string lineup of the Washington Redskins and the complete
life history of Joe Bellino.

But right now no one was running him, and it was warm, and six
brownies with nuts from a care package Gray's mother had sent
were relaxing in his stomach . . . and he was remembering that one
date he had in high school and how Barb Spenser had moved when
they danced, and what might happen if he met someone like that
blonde on the yawl, or. . . .

Beside him Rollo Kaufman saw his head drift forward and extended his pencil, eraser first. Philo jerked, grunted, and sat up
again.

". . . the first step in solution of the problem is to plot the polygon of external forces, both loads and reactions. We see now, with
the clarification provided by this notation, that as the forces act ver-
tically, the sides of the polygon fall in the line BK. No special construction for their derivation is necessary at this point. The next
step. . . ."

The first four weeks of academics had been a shock. He was carrying twenty hours this semester, and it would get heavier every
year. He had five class hours of calculus, four of chemistry, with
another hour of lab; three engineering, three of language, an hour of
P.E., and then the English and history—along with the professional
stuff: seamanship, marching, and so on. It was the same for everyone. Every mid took the same courses, carried the same books to

class, took the same tests as his classmates. The Lockstep, they called it. It was rough, too. The instructors were mostly officers, though there were a few civilian profs, and they moved fast. They covered the material and never went back. If you lost the bubble you were supposed to go in for extra instruction during your "free" periods. But somehow there was never time to go in, to sit watching the prof sketching diagrams, equations, staring at you in growing awe at your obtuseness until you said at last, "Yes sir, I see it now," just to get away, to go memorize something useful that would please the upperclass. But whether you understood it or not, there had to be time for homework. If you didn't have that ready, even if it was wrong, they didn't bother to chew you out. They just told you to put yourself on report. Though there were a few profs who would cut you some slack. A few. . . .

Something dug into his ribs again and he jerked upright. "I was awake," he hissed at Kaufman. "Stop poking me with that god-damned pencil."

"You were zonked," whispered El Rollo. "Another minute and you'd have knocked yourself out on your desk."

"Up your afterburner, Rollo."

"Screw you, Philo."

He liked Rollo. He was short and chubby and harmless, but he never gave up. He smiled gamely as he dropped rifles and puffed his way through relay races. He suffered at the tables and made up for it with interprandial trips to the Steerage for boxes of fat pills, milk shakes, Twinkies, chocolate chip cookies. He got bagels in the mail and shared them with his classmates, most of whom had never seen them before and considered them a species of stale doughnut, but who wolfed them down nonetheless. Dubus caught him once hand-ing them out in the head after taps and made him wham-o three of them into his mouth one after the other. Yet the Academy was changing El Rollo. In nine weeks of plebe summer and four of aca-demic year weight had dropped from him like tallow from a melting candle. Under the buzzing fluorescents of Melville Hall, dark stains were visible under his eyes. He blinked frequently, anxiously, try-ing to keep his eyes open, and from time to time he reached up from scribbling load diagrams to rub at the loose skin of his cheeks.

"You don't look too hot, Rollo."

"Maybe I'll take a couple of weeks off, get a place out on the Island."

"You getting anything out of this class?"

"Sure. Stress, tension, and I'm thinking of getting a truss."

"Who's chipping back there?" said the lieutenant-commander loudly, rapping the board with his pointer. Heads jerked awake. Philo and Kaufman looked sadly at each other and raised their hands.

"See me after class, gentlemen."

"Aye aye, sir."

"Oh, it's Mister McGiffin. Perhaps you'd feel more awake at the board. You've been following our analysis, haven't you? Given that the force applied at G is thirty-three thousand, five hundred pounds, and the chord of the entire structure is sixty feet, work out the compressive forces in each of these five base members. Explain as you go, please."

After class, walking rapidly along Decatur Road, past the bulk of Maury Hall and the supercilious observation of the bell tower, waiting to disgorge its smug reminder that time, the ever-present, ever-precious, was hurrying on with or without his notice, favor or even acquiescence, Philo nervously patted the report chit tucked inside his blouse. The prof had fried him for "inattention." That wasn't too bad, though it wouldn't help his conduct grade any. But if he lost the slip it could be a class A—forty demerits or more. As he passed Sampson Hall a full commander in blues came out and Philo saluted him automatically, shifting his books to his left hand and his right arm coming up straight, halting just above his eyebrow, fingers extended, thumb under; not with either the casual flip of the Reserve or the quivering rigidity of the Marines, but the Academy salute, up straight and steady, held till it was returned or till you were past, and then quickly back down again. The commander stood patiently by the door, saluting a steady stream of at least forty passing mids before he got into the clear in the direction of the Officers' Club. Philo glanced at his watch. He had four minutes to get to the last class of the day. It was Saturday, and this afternoon was the first game Navy played at home, against William and Mary. He hurried along the straight brick walks. There were shortcuts, but they were reserved for upperclass use. He noticed vaguely that there were a lot of tourists around the Yard, older men for the most part, standing in groups watching the mids, but he ignored them; unless they wore uniforms they did not really exist.

"Hey, Phil. How's it going?"

It was "First Sub" Perry, a youngster on his batt cross-country team, who had spooned him, shaken hands and recognized him as a friend, when Phil beat him in the last hundred feet of the Hospital Point course. "Hey. All right, Sub," he said. "How're you?"

"Okay. Going to Calc?"

"Uh huh."

"Me too . . . I don't know why they bother with me any more. I forgot everything I learned plebe year over summer cruise."

"Where'd you go?"

"The Med. Greece, Italy, that routine. I was on the *Springfield.*"

"Fun?"

"Not the word for it. Wait till you go."

"If I make it."

Perry slapped his shoulder; they paused near a fountain, beside a metal track where Michelson, Class of 1873, had measured the speed of light. "Hey! I don't want to hear any whining. Look at me. If I could make it you sure can. Don't pussy out on old Sub. What do you weigh?"

"Uh, about one-thirty, last time I looked."

"When things get rough say to yourself: a hundred and thirty pounds of twisted steel and sex appeal. As the missionary said to the cannibal, you can't keep a good man down."

Philo tried to grin, but it didn't feel too convincing. Perry glanced toward the math building, but hung back. "Look. In a couple of years you'll be pushing plebes. Think you'll treat 'em like they're doing to you now?"

"No. I'll treat them like human beings."

"Hell you will. You'll run their flabby little asses into the ground." Perry turned. "See ya at practice Monday."

The youngster disappeared through the doors. Philo looked back over the Yard, wondering, Is he right? Will I be just like Single-terry—or Dubus?

He stood absentmindedly for a moment, balancing his books on his hip, looking out over the green, over the red brick, across the elms to where the copper-green dome, the gilt needle of the Chapel rose bulbous and then sharp over the roofs of the town beyond. And suddenly, tired as he was—or perhaps being sleepless, deprived of food and rest for so long was part of it—he seemed to see the sunlight, the colors, the few midshipmen who strolled back along the walks toward the Hall, all of the sunflooded Yard itself as new and beautiful, golden, verdant, *alive;* as *significant.* The place so many great men had walked as scared boys. It was the same thing he had felt, dimly, standing in Memorial Hall, surrounded by captured flags and dead heroism and self-sacrifice; a feeling of continuity; of being not just an individual but a man in ranks, no, a part of a chain, a living tradition, no . . . all of the above; and yet something more, something even all that was just a part of, something that he felt he could put into words, or into feelings, if he just had time, a little more *time.* . . .

Bong, bong. Bong, bong. Bong, bong.

Six bells. And in Room 102, the class leader would be looking at his empty seat.

He turned from the glowing Yard and hurried inside to class.

At 1159 Philo, in his new double-breasted blue uniform, heavy as horse blankets, took his station at the end of the corridor, at attention, facing the clock. Some past devotee of the absurd had decorated it with a cartoon of Mickey Mouse wearing a white cap and striper's sword. As Mickey's gloved hand clicked over to 1200 his voice, a little shrill, began with a hundred others in every deck and corridor of the granite mountain to bellow out chow call.

"Sir! You now have ten minutes until noon meal formation. The uniform for noon meal is service dress blue with white gloves. Formation is outside. The menu for noon meal is: bacon lettuce and tomato sandwiches, shoestring potatoes, mixed fruit cup, iced tea, white and chocolate milk. Sir, the officers of the watch are, the Officer of the Watch is, Lieutenant Commander Harrow, Second Battalion Officer. The Assistant Officer of the Watch is Lieutenant Loosh, Fifteenth Company. The Midshipman Officer of the Watch is Midshipman Lieutenant Commander Fogarty, Nineteenth Company. The Assistant Midshipman Officer of the Watch is Midshipman Lieutenant Crane, Nineteenth Company."

He took a breath and went on with the chow call. The whole thing—time, menu, officers, movies, days—took about a minute to spit out, shouting at top speed with his mind in automatic. ". . . major events in the Yard today are: varsity football, Navy-Marine Corps Stadium, William and Mary, fourteen-hundred; Plebe and JV soccer against Prince George, Dewey Field, sixteen-hundred. This morning varsity cross-country beat Fordham University. Ten minutes, *sir!*"

As he inhaled Philo could hear, behind him, the same litany bellowed from other companies and other decks. He chopped toward his room, checking each of the upperclass in his squad to be sure he was awake, squared the corner smartly, and sagged into his chair for a moment. Gray was at the sink, shaving for the second time that day, though as far as Philo could see any application of a blade to his smooth skin was pure affectation. "Hey, buds," said his roommate, catching his image in the mirror, "got a sec? Brush me off, okay?"

As he whisk-broomed imaginary lint from Gray's uniform Philo took a quick look at himself. Noon formation on Saturday was the tightest inspection of the week. His cap was sharp, with no "smile" visible above the black band, the visor polished with Pledge to a slightly wavy mirror, like the bay by night, and all brushed spotless. His gold anchors were set precisely on his lapels, measured with homemade plastic cutouts. His blues were freshly pressed. His trousers were cleaned, creased sharp as the edge of a bayonet, and under the coat, out of sight, his belt buckle gleamed like new gold; the protective varnish had been stripped off with boiling water and it had been Brassoed front and back, top and bottom, and touched afterward only with gloves lest a fingerprint discolor it. His grease shoes, representing as much investment of time as a three-hour course, gleamed so beautifully that they reproduced the entire interior of the room, himself, Gray, the mirror, in two tiny spherically-distorted black universes. He decided he looked all right. He finished Gray's brushoff and hung up the broom, seeing, as he did so, his roomie's eyes sharp on him in the mirror.

"Where are your gloves, Philo?"

"Oh, shit, I forgot . . . they're all out in the laundry! Oh, jeez!"

"Don't *panic*, buds. Here." Gray went to his locker and tossed a pair to him. They were still in the plastic mid store wrapper. "I bought some extras."

"Hey, thanks, Dick."

"Just don't tell anybody. You know we aren't supposed to lend items of uniform."

"I appreciate your breaking the regs for me, Dick."

Back at his post, braced up, he fixed his eyes on the clock again. Mickey sneered down at him. His arm quivered, then clicked over to 1205.

"Sir, you now have *five minutes* till noon meal formation. . . ."

He continued the topspeed incantation of the chow call, staring straight ahead now, into the clear blue sunlight of the open window. Across the intervening space between the wings he could see the back of a plebe on 6–4, chanting the same words, the same cadence. He forced his mind back. He couldn't stop, couldn't clutch. Not now. The corridor was filling with upperclass, sauntering toward the ladder in casual groups. His classmates swept by him, eyes front, running awkwardly on their heels to avoid cracking their shines. Behind him he could hear them shouting "Beat William, fuck Mary, sir!" at each turn as they went down the stairwell. He returned his eyes to the clock, sweating in the heavy uniform. He had to stay till the one-minute call, which practically guaranteed that he would be late for formation. He gave the four-minute call. Breen came by, wide-shouldered, chin high, carrying his white gloves tucked into his cap. A sword jingled at his belt. "What's the good word, McGiffin?" he said.

"Beat William and Mary, sir!"

Zeard and Ind chopped by him, faces impassive, chins in. More upperclass. Two youngsters came out of their rooms and walked toward him. One of them, he saw, was Dubus.

"Got the dutes, McGiff?"

"Yes sir."

"How'd you do on that applied strength test?"

"Got a three-six, sir."

"You're shitting me," said Dubus, stopping. He looked too big for his uniform. He must, Philo thought, have gained a lot over one summer. He couldn't have been that fat as a plebe.

"No sir."

"I only got a two-two."

His eyes went to the clock. Ten more seconds.

"Come on, Dan," said Wiebels, the other youngster.

"Why don't you give me ten," said Dubus. "Seeing as how you're such a fucking physical wonder, pizza-face."

Philo waited for a bare second, but there was no trace of humor in the youngster's eyes. He dropped and began. "One, sir." At the fifth rep his cap fell off and rolled lazily around the deck. When he got up the two youngsters were gone.

At the two-minute call the last firsties left their rooms, moving fast. Then the corridors were deserted. He stood rooted, every muscle twitching to run. At last the clock clicked over. "Sir!" he shouted to the empty hallways. "You-now-have-*one minute*-to-noon-meal-formation — All-hands-are-reminded-to-turn-off-all-lights-running-water - and - electrical - appliances - lock - all - confidential - lockers - and - open-all-doors — Sir-time-tide-and-formation-wait-for-no-man— I-am-now-shoving-off—One-minute—*Sir!*"

He scooped his cap from the deck and bolted.

When he came out into the LA area, panting from a four-deck sprint, it was filled with sunlight and with the Brigade. Rank on rank, perfectly spaced, here and on T-court four thousand young men stood in thirty-six companies, six battalions, two regiments— the Brigade of Midshipmen. On the far side of the Hall the band was playing "Up with the Navy." Inside the Rotunda the High Stripers waited at parade rest. As he crossed the court he felt hundreds of eyes following him—the chow caller from the Ghetto, and from 7–4 on the other side of the hall, were always last to formations—and he wiped his forehead quickly and slid into ranks beside Jack Ash, the shortest man in the company except for him.

"Company. Atten-*hut!*"

Inspection began. A strange firstie, a four-striper—must be the

battalion commander, Midshipman Lieutenant-Commander Ruehlmann. As the inspection party moved through the squads Philo
flexed his knees, straightened his back, riveted his eyes straight
ahead. He heard a murmur to his left, in front of Zeard. Faint but
clear he could hear the band playing "Eyes of the Fleet." Above the
men in front of him, high on the ornate balconies of 6–4, painted
sheets flapped bloodthirsty football slogans in the sunlight.

The batt commander stepped sidewise into view in front of him.
His eyes, almost a foot above Philo's, were blue and remote as the
sky. He steadied his gaze at the level of the striper's tie. The dimple,
he noted, was perfect. The eyes flicked up and down him. "Tie's too
loose," Ruehlmann said. "His lapel wings stick out. And look at the
top of that cap cover. Filthy. Unsat."

Oh, shit, thought Philo.

The blue eyes moved on one pace and Breen appeared in his
place. His eyes were green flecked with quartz and even colder than
the battalion commander's. None of them spoke to him; they only
looked and remarked, as if, he thought, he was something dispos-
able, a used toothbrush they were thinking of throwing away.
"McGiffin: totally unsat," Breen was saying to Singleterry, who was
third.

"You want a form deuce on him?"

"That's up to you. You're his damn squad leader. Just get him
squared away. Check out that cap—looks like he's been playing
kickball with it."

Singleterry moved in front of him, staring down like the rest, his
pale eyebrows lifted slightly. He looked terminally bored. Philo kept
his own eyes fixed and his face straight, though he could feel fluid
trickling under his armpits and at the small of his back. Suddenly he
felt his squad leader's glance harden. "McGiffin. What's this expression for?"

"Sir?"

"This hurt little pissed-off expression of yours, doofus. Are you
pissed off?"

"No sir."

"Do you rate being pissed off?"

"No sir."

"That's right, McGiffin. Plebes like you get pissed on, not pissed off. Got that?"

"Yes sir."

"Your cap cover is gross, McGiffin. I've decided to put you on the pad for it. Any comments?"

"No sir."

"Smile, McGiffin."

"Aye aye, sir."

He grinned on, feeling his face start to hurt, and at last the inspection party moved on and he wiggled his locked knees back and forth a few millimeters so the blood wouldn't pool. Another form two. And why? He looked better than any of the third class. And they never got chewed out. Only the plebes. And of all the plebes, him. He stared ahead, grinning, envisioning himself as put-upon martyr.

That damn Dubus, he thought.

With a blare of trumpets and a flash of swords, the Brigade came to attention.

Third from the end, wagging the Brigade's tail, Slack 34th swung along past the Chapel, blue and gold guidon fluttering, the sun warm on their shoulders.

"Sound off!"

"One, two."

"Hear it again!"

"Three, four."

"Bring it on down."

"One, two, three, four, one, two—three four!"

"My mother was home when I *left*," came Corpen's clear tenor, soaring above the shuffle and stamp of the march, the sigh of wind in the elms, the fine simultaneous crash of a hundred heels on the bricks at once.

"You're right," a hundred voices bellowed.

"My father was home when I left."

"You're right."

"My girl was home when I left."

"You're right."

"And that's why I left."

"*You're right.*"
"Sound off!"
"*One, two.*"
"Hear it again."
"*Three, four.*"
"Bring it on down."
"*One, two, three, four, one, two—three four!*"

Two hundred arms swung as one, two hundred feet rang on the pink bricks, swished through crisp fallen leaves. Behind them the marching band fell in at the end of the long line of blue, silent for the moment save for the heartlike thud, thud, thud-thud-thud of the drum. Later they would strike up; for now, each company provided its own music, its own cadence. Dubus' beery-sounding voice was the next thing the 34th heard.

"Got a girl, her name is Jill."
"*Got a girl, her name is Jill,*"
"She won't screw, but her sister will."
"*She won't screw, but her sister will.*"
"Sound . . . off!"
"*One, two.*"

There was no real order to it. First one and then another of the upperclass would sing or roar out a couple of lines, each repeated by the hundred throats; then the company would sing out the count. As they passed under Gate Three, past the brick guardhouses that were the oldest buildings in the Yard, Philo, bringing up the rear with the rest of the sandblowers, heard Rollo Kaufman, beside him, clear his throat; and into the next silence heard him shout, too shrill, but loudly:

"Hark the herald angels sing."
"*Hark the herald angels sing,*"
"Three more years till I get my ring."
"*Three more years till I get my ring.*"
"Sound off."

As they counted down faces turned to look back at them; he saw Wiebels smiling, Stamper craning back from the fourth rank. When the count was over he heard the chubby plebe take another deep breath.

"Hark the herald angels shout."
"Hark the herald angels shout,"
"Four more years till I get out."
"Four more years till I get out," screamed all the plebes, caught on
by now, drowning the laughter of the upperclassmen.

"You turkey," whispered Philo, beside him, grinning. "That was
all right." But inwardly he was asking himself, Why didn't I do
that?

He could think of no ready answer.

Outside the walls, marching north along King George Street, past
the green sloping lawns and crumbling brick of St. John's College,
they passed in a straight blue line, white gloves flashing up and
across their chests in a long horizontal, dressing and covering instinctively as they came abreast of the civilian students lining the
sidewalks. Behind them the band struck up "Sons of Slum and
Gravy." The Johnnies, dressed in their best tattered jeans, jeered
from the sidelines and threw beer cans into the passing ranks. The
mids grabbed for them eagerly and then shouted insults, fired them
back; they were empty. Past that Crabtown petered out quickly.
They broke step obediently on a steel bridge and turned left on
Route 450, past Gate Eight, and relaxed the tautness of the march a
bit as they climbed a short hill. The Doorknob to the World, the
Academy water tower, loomed up as they descended Taylor Avenue, and the stadium, glittering in the distance with thousands of
windshields, came into view. They slowed to close ranks. Company
by company the Brigade marched onto the field for the form-up, for
the cap tricks they had rehearsed for weary weeks, and then at last
broke ranks with a yell for the stands.

Football was still a new game to Philo. He'd been too small to
play high school ball and had only seen a couple of games in Raymondsville, coming away with a confused impression of crashing
bodies, but not really understanding the fine points.

This Mister Kim and the other upperclass had soon remedied.
With the coming of the season the Academy went abruptly football
mad. Everyone from the Supe on down, the officers, the upperclass,
the wires profs, the Brazilian exchange officer who taught Por-

tuguese, talked statistics, point spreads, lineups, passing games. The sports pages of the *Washington Post* and *The New York Times* went from hand to eager hand, read by upperclass, memorized by plebes to be repeated on demand. From the Rathole, the first class wardroom where no plebe ever trod, the sounds of televised games blared out on Sunday afternoons. In short order Philo became an instant expert, ready with the latest scores, the current lineups, the most respected opinions on the chances for the Big Blue to crush their miserable opponents the next weekend.

The plebes hit the stands running, and were about to relax into decent seats on the forty-five yard line when they heard it: "Funnel!" Cursing, they scrambled for the field again, where they joined hands in a chute as the Mule Maulers came trotting out. Their final seats were cramped together low down near the thirty, looking out over the end of the Navy bench. The goat was out there; Dodo was out there, wearing his little blue blanket that said BITE ARMY. They weren't playing Army that day, but all the mids understood the little mongrel's sentiments.

The game opened well. Navy won the toss and kicked off. A few minutes later, to a plebe-generated wave of sound that filled the stadium, the score was 7–0. Philo was on his feet. All the plebes were on their feet. They were looking at the William and Mary cheerleaders.

Women—yes, women. As the game went on Philo found his eyes wandering from the field to the faces around him in the crowd, the upperclass drags sitting patiently outside the compact mass of blue, waiting for the game to be over; the cheerleaders; even the ancient women, well, some of them not so ancient, who sat with the flask-wielding Old Grads in the sections around the mids. With something like horror he realized he was missing an entire segment, an entire integral major irreplaceable chunk of his life.

Something was happening on the field. Without giving it his full attention he screamed with the mass of plebes around him so loud that an echo of it rolled back, a sound like an angry sea, from the stands opposite; from the steel overhang, gray like the hull of a carrier, set with the names of other games the Navy and the Marine Corps had played and won: Peleliu, Savo Island, Belleau Wood, Inchon. But even jumping, even screaming with his mouth open to the sky, his eyes kept moving from aisle to aisle, from face to face.

Women. There, profile to him, a caryatid; darkish blond hair, short, small pointed chin, almost double, almost pouting, fine nose, her cheeks flushed above a blue and yellow scarf; some upperclassman's drag, some captain's daughter, maybe both . . . beyond her a woman of about thirty, but still attractive despite her superannuation, her look a little tired, a little haggard; she brushing back hair the color of varnished walnut with a pale hand; a child beside her, face a slightly chubby, slightly off adumbration of her own, its hair a paler shade of hers . . . girls, women, with long hair, short, with narrow faces, faces heart-shaped, oval, round, young with promise, heavy with flesh, old with experience, closed with passion, intent, pulled out of themselves; faces with eyes roving, eyes intent on the field, eyes turned to talk or kiss, mouths pursed for love, for reproach, for demand, for a can of Schlitz, glances yearning and glances satisfied . . . for a moment a glimpse of hair bright as fire, like the scarlet heart of a hot flame. . . .

"Ah, hell!" screamed Ash, almost in his ear, so that he winced and jerked his attention back to the field. Rowe, the William and Mary quarterback, had fired a forty-yard pass that connected at the Navy ten-yard line, and a knot of blue jerseys and white had tortoised over the limed line into the end zone, with the man almost hidden underneath, but still, it seemed, on his feet . . . touchdown. A moment later the ball cut the goal posts and the big NAVY:VISITOR scoreboard winked, blanked out, then flickered on again; a solid extra point.

At halftime the score was still tied 7–7.

At the end of the third quarter it was 12–7, visitors leading, and he was so hoarse with screaming that the air hurt in his throat when he breathed. He had forgotten about women, forgotten about the Hall, forgotten about himself or that he existed. His whole being was down there on the field, in the crush of exhausted bodies, the wobbling flight of a ball lofted with the last strength of despair and its snatching disappearance in a welter of men, the deadly flash of a flag against churned-up green and the trampled brown of dirt. It was no longer a game and he was no longer just a spectator. It was a battle and he was in it; no longer himself, one, but part of the Brigade, lifted on its mighty tide, one with its roaring hundreds; fused with the crowd in a continuous minutes-long roar that grew and grew as the clock ticked down and the ball, Navy's ball, was bulled and fought closer and closer to the enemy's end zone. . . .

Then in the middle of it all a gun boomed and the roar of the mids changed to amazement, incredulity, and stopped.

The final score was William and Mary 18, Navy 10. After the Alma Mater a long silence poisoned the Navy stands. People moved aimlessly about; no one seemed eager to leave; no one seemed to have anywhere to go. Kaufman pushed his way through the other plebes to Ash and McGiffin. His eyes were reddened. They looked at each other and then at the floor of the stands, scuffed, littered with butts, crumpled pop cups, and candy bar wrappings.

"The excrement's going to impact the ventilator now, guys," said Kaufman.

Philo nodded. He knew El Rollo was right. The brigade took its resentment at defeat out on the nearest targets of opportunity: the fourth class. It was their fault the team had lost; they hadn't had the spirit, hadn't shouted loud enough, pep rallied enough, and so something had to be done . . . it made the coming six days till the next game a melancholy prospect.

"You going into town, Rollo?"

"I don't know. Are you and Jack going? There's not much out there."

"I think I'll hit the books," said Ash. "Liberty in Crabtown is sort of like having seasickness and lockjaw at the same time . . . say, did you hear about the lady who woke up in the morning and found an elephant in her bed?"

"Not yet," said Philo.

"She rolls over and sees the elephant and says, 'Jeez—I really must have been tight last night.' And the elephant looks over and says, 'Not really.'"

"Let's go into town," said Kaufman, holding his stomach.

The stands were clearing. They began jumping down from seat to seat.

"I got fried this morning," said Philo. "Twice, I think."

"What for this time?"

"Offie gave me five for inattention, and I got burned at noon inspection." He told Rollo about Dubus and his cap. "I just didn't have time to clean it. Hell, I didn't even notice that it was dirty—just grabbed for it and cut in the afterburner for T-court."

"That sucks. You really think Singleterry will pap you?"

"I'm sure of it. Just by the way he sort of sneers at me when he inspects. I'll probably have to march it off next week, so this could be my last libs for a while."

"I see why you want to get some town time, then."

Except for the rankle of defeat, it was a pleasant walk back into Annapolis. The upperclass had joined up with their girls and took no notice of the two plebes walking side by side. They stuck to the wide four-lane of Bladen Street, the State House spiring slowly ahead of them, and left it to port and went around Church Circle and down Main Street. They discussed and dismissed the idea of a movie at the Star; the few hours of liberty were too precious to spend in the dark. Philo wanted to savor each minute out here, outside the walls, savor the sense of being transiently and under a kind of false pretense back in the lost land of civilianhood. The very sun looked different outside the Yard, freer; and the air tasted lighter than the fear-laden gas they respired inside the Hall. Philo looked down at the old bricks of the walks, admiring how each one was different, individual, unique, and yet they all fit together in the pattern, each one conforming a bit to the oddities of its fellows. Unconsciously he and Kaufman moved along at a marching pace, rapidly and in step.

"How about some ice cream?"

"Look at all those upperclass in there."

"And girls."

"Upperclass' girls. Nah—we can get sundaes in the Steerage cheaper."

As they descended Robber's Row, the shabby shops and storefronts crowded close together, Philo found himself remembering with nostalgia the day he had walked toward the bay from the bus station, his suitcase heavy, his heart full of joy and fear; he had walked these very bricks, this very—

"Hey," he said.

"What?"

Ahead of them, not a hundred feet away and coming up the
street, was a brilliant tangle of flame-red hair. Unmistakably the
same shade. It was, it had to be, the girl he had glimpsed at the
stadium. Now, though, he could see her head on, threading her way
confidently through the crowds of mids flowing down toward Market Square. And then he saw why: on each arm was a big grinning
second class. Philo and Kaufman stepped off the curb to let them
sweep by three abreast. The segundoes did not give an inch or even
look at them. Philo stood stock-still, looking up the hill.

"She's nice," he said.

"Who?"

"That redhead."

Kaufman turned to look, as if he had missed her when she passed
five feet from him, but Phil found he could retrieve her face perfectly in memory: the smooth freckled cheeks, small nose, full too-
wide mouth, open in laughter at something one of the upperclass
had said. Oddly, under the cascade of almost orange hair the eyebrows had been dark, yet the hair looked entirely natural.

"Awful tall," said Kaufman, turning back. "You like that?"

"She can stick one of those in my eye any time."

"You're getting as foulmouthed as everybody else around here,
McGiffin . . . anyway, think about next year. We'll be youngsters.
Riding in cars, dragging on weekends . . . the works. Want to stop
in here for a minute?"

"Peerless? We can't buy civvies."

"I just wanted to look," said Kaufman. "My uncle's a tailor."

"You serious?"

"Sure."

"Well, all right . . . but it's a hell of a way to spend an afternoon."

As they went in he paused for a moment, looking up the street
again; but she was gone; and though the sidewalks of Annapolis
were full of mids and their drags, blonde and brunette, white, black,
yellow, he had a sudden and strange sense of loss.

They faced that Monday morning's comearounds with dread, and
the dread was justified. For the first time Mister Kim, who had

taken the loss to William and Mary hard, took a hand running them. The South Korean did not go in for races, as Singleterry did. He preferred stationary exercises.

"Shove out!" he told them proudly.

"Sir?" said Gray.

"You sit down there."

Zeard made a motion toward a chair; Kim negated it with a wave. "No. No. Don't use the furniture."

"Sir?"

"Sir, sir, sir, you sound like Japanese. Sit down. Only don't use chair. That is shoving out."

Philo got the idea first and squatted down. "Like this, sir?"

"Sit farther back. Farther back. Let arms hang down."

Zeard, Gray, and Philo sat in a row on the air. For the first few seconds Philo fought an impulse to laugh: they looked ridiculous. Then their legs began to tremble.

"Sit back, gentlemen. Be comfortable."

Philo straightened his backbone; he rocked back on his heels and almost went sprawling. You had to balance . . . no, it wasn't possible. The center of gravity had to be over the heels. But with the back straight, in the sitting posture, that meant you were holding the whole weight of the trunk with the muscles of the calves and thighs. It was an impossible position to maintain. After a full minute of it his legs began to cramp. Zeard gave in first, sinking slowly downward, fighting it all the way in lip-biting silence. Philo felt his own eyes begin to protrude.

"This is 'shoving out,' gentlemen. You know when I was plebe it was for real. I had one firstie made me shove out over his bayonet."

Philo didn't even like to think about it.

By the time the Korean was done they could barely hobble out of the room.

At breakfast not one of them got a single bite to eat.

Perhaps it was that, the ache in his thighs that lasted for hours, that made him forget. Or maybe it was just stupidity. But it was that morning, studying in his room during his free third period, that he forgot to wake up Dubus for his fourth-period class. He did not think of it until he was sitting in Maury Hall. *Oh, shit*, he told himself. It had to be Dubus, too. And on this worst of all possible days.

The third classman was waiting as he came back from class. His uniform was rumpled and he had a slip of paper in his hand. He stood in the center of the corridor and Philo, completely terrified, came to a rigidly braced halt in front of him.

"Hi, McGiffin," said Dubus.

"Sir, I'm *sorry*—"

"Fifteen big ones," said the big youngster, unfolding the chit. "Second time I missed that class. I woke up myself at eleven-twenty and ran all the way to Leahy. Came in in the middle of class—and then I see I forgot to put on my tie. I'm in line for an F now. Thanks, McGiffin. You really put one over on me this time." He nodded slowly, wonderingly.

"Sir, permission to make statement."

He was going to say that it was purely accidental; that he hadn't meant to put anything over; that he had simply forgotten. But Dubus shook his head sadly. "No, McGiffin. No excuses. Because tonight you're coming around."

"I owe Mister Kim tonight's comearound, sir, for pussying out on the Green Bench."

"Not any more," said Dubus. "I talked to Kim. You can work that one off later. If you survive. See you at eighteen-hundred, you piece of ratey mung."

"Yes sir," said Philo.

"What?"

"Aye aye, sir."

"Get out of my sight."

"Aye aye, sir." He chopped off down the corridor. As he pushed open the door to his room he stopped.

Every article of clothing he owned was strewn over the room, across the deck. Socks lay in the sink, soaking wet. Blue uniforms, freshly pressed, had been torn out of the lockers and apparently walked on. His grease cap lay mashed flat on the shower floor. Zeard sat at the desk, his long face immersed in a calculus book. His side of the room was untouched.

"Hey," he said, looking up suddenly. "Dirty Dan was here, about three minutes ago. He's somewhat pissed at you."

"No shit," said Philo. He picked up a tie and looked at it. A dusty footprint was clearly outlined on the black wool.

"What'd you do?" asked Zeard, his nose back in the book.

"Forgot his wakeup call. He got fried."

"Big?"

"Fifteen."

"That's big," said Zeard, etching a curve onto graph paper with a blue pencil. "For him. I hear he's piled up a lot of fraps this year already. And I think he almost got booted plebe year too. He's kind of a bad actor."

"I'm going around to him tonight."

"Well, I guess you rate it," said his roommate. "Say, you looked at this homework yet?"

"I guess so," said Philo. "I guess. But he thinks I did it on purpose."

"This is a bear . . . they keep leaving the proofs to the student. I can memorize it okay, but I don't understand the words."

"Anyway it can't be worse than Mister Kim."

"There's a guy in my class does imitations of old Todds. 'Gentlemen, this is a thirty-minute quiz; you have ten minutes to work it. I'll give you one hint: they're all trick questions.'"

"Hell," said Phil. He started hanging things up. His WUBAs were ruined. He would have to go through the whole hassle of getting them drycleaned again. "It can't be worse than Kim," he said again, more to himself than to the oblivious Zeard.

He kept telling himself that through noon meal, during which he got to eat half of a toasted cheese and ham sandwich; the rest of his time was taken up with doing the can-can between the tables, in line with three other plebes, and getting extra french fries from the carts for the second class. He told himself that through the afternoon classes, learning nothing but at least staying awake with worry, and all through a battalion cross-country meet in which he took fifth. When at 1800 sharp he reported around to the youngster's room in fresh sweat gear he almost believed it.

When he got back to the room Kaufman was at the sink, putting a final gloss on his shoes with cotton wool soaked in rubbing alcohol. He looked up from the shoes and his face went blank, then concerned. "Phil?"

"Nothing," said Philo, wiping his face dry with the back of his hand. He wanted to turn away, to hide, but there was nowhere to hide. Nowhere to be alone even for a moment. He went to sit down but outside, in the hall, Darrin's voice began to bellow the five-minute call. He began blindly to strip off the sweat gear, the blue and gold gym shorts, the issue jockstrap—

"Hey," said Zeard.

Gray turned, but said nothing. His eyes widened a little.

All of them stared at the livid purple-red weals. There was a little silence in the room, interrupted by the brief rattle of the shower. Almost as soon as it went on it stopped—you had to shower after comearound, but no one said how long—and they saw their roommate step out, his eyes terrible and remote, and begin to towel himself off. Rollo, still standing by the sink, reached out to grip his arm.

"Phil, what happened? Was it Kim?"

"Dubus."

"That asshole!"

"What did he hit you with?"

"I don't know. A swab handle I think." He swallowed, crossed the room, and groped for his clothes.

"Sir! You now have four minutes till evening meal formation—"

"He hit you?" said Gray. "He can't do that. That's against regs."

"You can't let him get away with that shit," said Zeard. "None of us can. It'll be us next."

"He's an upperclass," said McGiffin. His voice, even to him, sounded odd, choked, distant. He flipped his tie over his head and tightened it with a savage jerk. "He can do anything he wants. What can you do? Turn him in? You know how long I'd last here after that."

"You can't just take it."

"What else can I do?" he said. "What else can I do?"

And a terrible silence hummed in the room, broken only by a half-choked sob.

CHAPTER FIVE

If that fellow wants a fight, we won't disappoint him.
—Captain Isaac Hull, USS *Constitution*, 1800

If you want to wake up with a smile on your face here, try sleeping with a spiffy in your mouth.
—The Log

"Only one thing you can do, man," said Len Ind, leaning forward on the desk, his fists clenched till the dark knuckles went pale. "You got to kick ass, Phil. That's all there is."

The murmur of approbation that followed came from all corners of the room. There were twenty-four plebes in it, it was just before taps, and it was Jack Ash's room. It was their first meeting alone as a class; and in the center of the room sat Philo.

"I can't. He's a youngster."

Again the murmur, the shaking of heads, this time negative, disagreeing, from his classmates where they sat on radiators, on the deck, perched on the sink top, leaning against the bulkheads. "No, it ain't that way, Phil," said Castigliano. "I talked to Weaver about it."

For some reason Weaver, a turned-back second class, had spooned Castigliano when the plebe had the mate's watch and he came in drunk. "He said it's the only way to settle it—go over to Macdonough and put on the gloves."

"Gloves, shit," said Ind. "In Philly—"

"We aren't in Philly, Len," said Gray. "But he's got no right to beat on one of us. It's there in black and white in the cook book and he ought to go down big. I think, Phil, you ought to consider taking it upstairs. See Mister Breen. Or maybe go right to the lieutenant."

"To Snorkel?"

"No way, Dick."

"Hell no."

"You can't bilge the guy."

"But look what he did to Philo," said Kaufman.

"He didn't *bilge* him. He wiped out his room—hardass, but it was Phil's fault he got fried, right? The ass-whipping was nonreg. That's hazing. But if Philo turns him in, with his conduct record, it's the shitcan for him and three years as a whitehat." Zeard pointed his nose around the room. "You guys want that? Philo, you want *that?*"

He shook his head.

The room was quiet, for about thirty seconds. They all saw that Zeard was right. You couldn't turn another mid in. There was something deep that prevented that. But it was equally unthinkable that he should get away with beating on one of them. Their silence was broken by the door banging open.

It was Stamper, in his Army b-robe. He stared around the room. "What the hell is going on here? A mutiny? No, don't all of you shout at me—carry on." He flashed them two fingers. "Now—what is this?"

"A fourth class meeting, sir," said Gray.

"Oh. I wanted someone for a coke run—I'll buy if they'll fly—but never mind, I'll get it myself." He started to leave, then hesitated; turned back into the room, and eased the door closed again. "Wait a minute. Is this about Do-Dirty Dan?"

News moves fast, Philo thought. But no one answered Stamper. The second class' eyes found McGiffin, noted the pillow he sat on.

"It *was* Dubus."

"Yes sir," said Fayaway, standing up. "And we were talking about what to do. Let it go by—turn him in, or—"

"Or?"

"Or have Philo fight him—sir."

"Fight him," said Stamper to Philo. "And I hope you beat some of that surly shit out of him. When he was a plebe he was a fat nerd and now that he's a youngster he's a corpulent dickhead. I wish it was me up against him."

He left. "Well," said Fayaway, after a couple of moments, "I guess that settles it."

People began to get up, looking relieved.

"Wait a minute," said Philo, and his classmates stopped, looking at him, there in the middle. "I can't fight him, I said."

"Why not? Mister Stamper just said the second class will back us up."

"He's not even popular with the other youngsters," said Zeard.

"But—but he's twice my *size*, damn it."

That did not sound, even as he said it, quite right. "Huh?" said Ind. "What'd he say?"

"He's way bigger than I am. He'll tear me apart."

"Show us something, McGiffin," said a voice from the back of the room. "Don't act like a goddamned pussy."

"Look, Phil," said Gray, "we'll back you up, whatever you do. We're your classmates, right? But you're the guy he did it to. You've got to decide."

As they looked at him the last bell rang. Immediately there was a rush for the door; the second class would be starting room checks any minute. Philo looked at Ash, who stood wordless, staring back at him; and then realized that it was Ash's room, not his, and he too ran out into the darkened corridor after the rest, fleeing ghosts whose shower slippers filled the hall with applause. It's crazy, he thought, ducking into his room and colliding with Zeard. I'm not going to fight him. He'd stomp me like a cupcake.

"Room eighty-four twenty-three."

"All present, sir."

"Get that light out."

"Aye aye, sir."

After taps sounded, the bugle echoing distant and lonely out in the court, they lay in silent darkness for a time. Philo realized he still had his klax on under the sheets and pulled them off and tossed them to the deck.

"What was that noise?" said Zeard.

"Me. Took my klax off," he whispered.

"Phil."

"Yeah, Rollo?"

"What were you going to say there when the bell went? What did you decide?"

"I've got to think about it. I don't know yet."

And then there was the sound only of a body turning over, seeking its rest; and after that, though he lay awake for a long time in the darkness, none of his roommates spoke to him again.

The next morning, according to his comearound log, he belonged to Mister Singleterry, for serving him chocolate milk without ice. But when he reported around, stepping in smartly and sounding off, the squad leader simply looked at him meaningfully and asked if there was not perhaps some other upperclass he would rather talk to.

"Sir?"

"I mean a certain youngster, Mister McGiffin. I understand you have something to say to him. Is that right?"

It had gotten out. Faster than the beam of light old Michelson had timed flashing across the Yard did scuttlebutt travel in the sealed world of Bancroft. As he realized what Singleterry meant he felt his normal and by now customary morning comearound fear escalate to something more like panic. If Singleterry knew, then all the firsties knew. And the segundoes. And the youngsters. . . .

"You break my transmission yet, McGiffin?"

"Uh, yes, sir."

"Why don't you go see him right now? He's probably waiting for you."

And then there was nothing left to do but say "Aye aye, sir" and face about smartly and chop out into the corridor. As he neared Dubus' room, running as slowly as he could and still be at double-time, he saw with a sinking heart the knot of upperclass around the fat third class' room. As he approached it, going even more slowly until he was almost walking, they began to drift apart casually, leaving the door clear. "Here he comes," someone said.

"McGiffin."

"Get out of his way, man."

One of them, as he neared the group, was Corpen. His summer squad leader grabbed his arm as he chopped up, swung him to a halt, and punched him lightly in the stomach. "Get that head up, boy," he said softly. "What's your name?"

"Philo T. McGiffin, sir."

"And don't you forget it. Give him hell. Youngsters don't rate what he's getting away with."

The door loomed and, that suddenly, he was through it, and coming to attention. Sounding off. "Midshipman Fourth Class McGiffin, sir."

There was no answer for a moment, and he looked around.

"Get those eyes in the boat, dorf," said Dubus.

The youngster's sloppily uniformed bulk was sprawled over his rack, an act that, between reveille and morning formation, was just as irregular for a youngster as a plebe. A tattered girlie magazine peeped from under his pillow, where he had thrust it as the door opened. He squinted up at Philo. "McGiffin," he said. "You didn't have to come around this morning too. Last night was enough. We're even, doofus."

"Yes sir," said Philo, feeling a vast wave of relief. He about faced, to find the doorway solid with watching upperclass. For a long moment he stared at them, and they stared back. Then he faced about again, swallowing.

"Go on," said Dubus, rolling over. "Shove off, or shove out."

And Philo stood stock still, trembling a little as he realized too late that he had spoken in formulas for so long—yes sir, no sir, I'll find out sir—that to *say* something, to express a thought not prescribed, not previously memorized, a voluntary statement that came from *him*, seemed unthinkable, appalling, like fainting in formation, or farting in Chapel.

"Shove off," said Dubus again. "Go take a message to Garcia or something, turd."

"Sir."

"Shove off."

"You hit me last night, sir."

"You rated it, mung-breath. Get out. That's an order."

How did you ask an upperclass to fight? If he had the words he could do it. He wasn't sure about the fight yet, that he could stand and do it. But he could say the words. If he only knew them. Then, to the top of a mind bubbling like molten lead, came the ancient dross of some old book he had read years and years before.

"Mister Dubus, sir," he blurted out, hearing his voice quiver. "I w-w-would like to settle this man to man."

"He's challenging you, Dan," said someone from behind him, from the door. "Whaddya say?"

"He can't challenge me. He hasn't said—"

"I challenge you, sir," said Philo, grasping the formula instantly. He was rewarded by some nasty laughter behind him—aimed at Dubus, he felt sure—and by Corpen's voice: "Bravo Zulu, McGiffin. You catch on quick."

"Get out of here, McGiffin."

"Aye aye, sir. I'll see you in the ring," said Philo. He did as snappy an about face as his rubbery legs would permit, hearing another burst of laughter as those in front passed his last remark to those out in the corridor, and headed out. The upperclass parted once again for him and as he passed through them he felt hands slapping his back. An odd, hot feeling ignited in his chest. Not knowing where to go, and seeing he still had most of the come-around period left, he headed back to Singleterry's room.

"Did you do it?"

"Yes sir."

"Good man. Couple of guys had money that you would pussy out. You know your rates?"

"Yes, sir."

"Even better. See that shower?"

"Your shower, sir?"

"Get in it."

He got in and stood waiting.

"Close the curtain, doofus."

He stayed in the shower stall for the rest of the comearound period. Doing nothing; just standing there with the curtain drawn. After a little while he even squatted down. It was intensely private and refreshing.

For some unperceived reason all his classes that morning seemed delightfully simple, and even the walks between them were beautiful and all too short. The days were cooler now and the wind felt fresh and clean. Perhaps part of it was the unaccustomed full stomach he had inherited at breakfast. He had been asked only the briefest of rates, and for the first time in his Academy career had made it through a meal without adding to his long list of comearounds. Dubus sat silently eating, ignored by everybody; it was as if he were not at the table at all.

By the third period he had realized one of the primary philosophical lessons of military life. If something good happens, or if they let you alone for a while (the two are synonymous for all practical purposes), it was no good thinking about it, or worrying about the future. Just enjoy it, the present, with everything you are. In his Statics class, when the professor called on him to recite, it seemed to him that the dry little officer even smiled at him, and corrected his error—he was applying compressive force to a rope—without his wonted sarcasm. In fourth period, when he stood at the board groping for a tense, one of his classmates, working next to him, reached over when the prof's back was turned and stroked in an accent mark, showing him instantly what was wrong. In T-court, on the way back from class, he paused for a moment in front of Tecumseh, the bronze figurehead of the *Delaware* that had been the Academy symbol for a hundred years. It was true, he saw. On certain very good days the grim visage of the Indian *did* wear a fleeting smile.

When he got back to his room there was a note on his desk. Mister Stamper wanted to see him ASAP. He left his books in the room and chopped around.

"Ah, McGiffin. Take two. Sit down."

He sat down uneasily, but the second class was smiling.

"It's all arranged. We let the company commander know, and Breen said he hadn't heard a word I said. Tonight's out, though. Rubber Heels has got the watch. Too risky—they say he was a night crawler as a mid; he knows all the places to check. Is Wednesday night okay?"

"Uh—for what, sir?"

"For your fight, McGiffin. Where's your mind today? On leave?"

Philo looked at him blankly.

It was all set, Stamper went on. He spoke with something approaching relish. They would meet, with seconds, at 2100 Wednes-

day night, in the ring under Macdonough Hall. The first class
would cover their absence from study hour. Was that, he wanted to
know, all right with Philo?

He said it was, and left. As he stood in formation at noon, conscious of Dubus' protruding stomach a couple of places to his left, he
felt the first groundswell of anxiety. What had he let himself in for?
What the Reg Book called "challenge to personal combat" was, in
Mister Singleterry's precious phrase, a "no-no." He was still unsure
how it had come about. He felt carried on the crest of events, felt
like a reactant in a process the end products of which he could not
predict. His stomach began to knot, but he breathed deep, fighting
it down. Nine tomorrow night—that was a long time away. An
enormous time, on the scale a plebe grew accustomed to think in.

If I play my cards right, he thought, facing left at Breen's shouted
command, I can get in five full meals before then.

He jerked awake suddenly in the darkness the next morning, to
find his alarm cranking out noise and Zeard moaning. He grabbed
for it hastily and stared at the dial, groggy. 0240. But it's set for
0530, he thought. Isn't it? Half an hour before reveille gave them
unscheduled time, a few precious minutes stolen from sleep to polish
brass and shoes, to skim a few paragraphs at least of the reading for
English Comp, to memorize the headlines in the *Pest*. It was against
regs of course but all the upperclass had done it when they were
plebes, expected it, and anyway none of them would bother now to
get up before reveille to catch them. But no, the dial plainly said
0240, and it was set to ring now, too. Then he remembered. It was
the first day of window closing detail.

Wonderful. He rolled out of his rack, automatically turning back
his sheets to air bedding, and got his b-robe from the locker. Zeard
groaned once more; then the room was quiet again. He shuffled out
into the hall.

The corridor of 8–4 looked different at night—wholly different.
Deserted. Peaceful. He shuffled sleepily, yawning, hands in pockets, where glancing sideways or rigging his chin out for a moment
would earn him, in daylight, twenty or forty instant pushups and an
invitation to come around. Across the moke-polished green tiles of

the deck long squares of light lay from outside, and long parallelo-
grams of it slanted along the overhead. Halfway down the passageway a single blue light burned near the mate's desk, over the coiled
hose of the fire station.

He strolled down the hall, yawning, conscious of a sudden and
wholly unaccustomed sense of freedom. It was almost worth missing
sleep. He felt that he could do anything he liked so long as it was
quiet. Passing the door of the Rathole he hesitated. No plebe was
allowed in the company wardroom. He pressed it open silently with
his shoulder and looked in with the sense of trespassing on a holy
place. It smelled of tobacco smoke and popcorn. The television,
dead, crouched in its seaward corner. The shadowed trash can was
heaped with discharged coke cans. A Playmate of the Month center-
fold hung from above the coffee machine; three steel darts transfixed
her at erotic points. As he stared at her implausible breasts, a hand
touched his arm and he came to attention, squeaking faintly.

"It's only me, man," said Ind. "You got this horse's-ass detail
too?"

"Yeah."

"How you wanna cut it?"

"How about if I take one side of the hall and you take the other."

"Okay. You got the wakeup bill?"

"Yeah. Right here."

Thirteen upperclass had signed up to have their windows closed.
Most, though not all, were firsties. At the head of his list was the
company commander. As Ind padded off in the other direction Philo
stepped out of his klax in front of Breen's room.

In his bare feet, moving with infinite care, he eased the door open
and slipped within. It was black dark and he stood for a moment,
smelling the sleeping men, letting his eyes adapt till vague shadows
resolved themselves into desk, chair, windows, racks. Then he
moved forward, feeling his way with his toes. It was so quiet in the
room he could hear the shallow breathing of the sleeping firsties, the
low, sixty-hertz hum of their electric clock. He envied the clock.
Plebes rated only wind-ups. The soles of his feet made sticky noises
on the deck. At last he reached the windows, mercifully without
tripping over anything, and contemplated the problem.

The sash was lifted, cracked about six inches. A steady flow of cool outside air washed against his face. The venetian blinds were at half-mast, as per room regulations. He, the window-closer, had as his mission to close both windows without sound, without waking the room's occupants, so that at reveille fresh-air-loving upperclass would be spared emerging from warm racks into a cold room. He tried it. The blinds were tricky; if he brushed them accidentally they could wake the dead, let alone a first classman, who could caulk off during every free period. When both windows were secured he looked once more on the sleeping firsties and then crept out. With the door safely shut behind him he exhaled noisily. One down; five more to go.

As it turned out, only in the last room did he have any trouble. They had left their sound system on, playing a Washington all-night FM station softly, and under the aural cover he became a little care-less. The sleeve of his b-robe fouled something as he passed the desk and it fell over with a little clatter, a skitter of small metallic-sound-ing objects. One of the sleepers stirred. Philo froze, willing even his heart to stop beating, breathing with his mouth wide open, until two long, ticking minutes had passed. The music played on, softly, softly. He stared at the green luminescence of the tuning dial. The man who had moved breathed regularly again. He waited an addi-tional minute, then drew down the windows with the tender care of a man closing his mother's eyes for the last time, and sneaked out. Ind was waiting for him outside. "You done?" he whispered.

"Yep."

"Night, then. Oh—and hey, Phil. You goin' to pound that son of a bitch today, right?"

"Oh, hell," said Philo.

"What's the matter?"

"I forgot all about that."

"Oh." Ind looked at him oddly. "Better grab some Zs, man."

"Okay, Len. Night."

"Night."

It was 0340. He could get in another hour and twenty minutes of much-needed sleep. He wanted it desperately. Yet to be up like this, wandering the corridor, unwatched, unnoticed, was so novel and pleasant that he grudged going back to his rack, to wake at 0530 into another interminable day of hyperactivity, disciplined thought and speech, a progression of minutes each of which screamed its own urgent and unpostponable demands. And now, damn it, Ind had reminded him that a fight lay at the end of it. He hadn't thought about it once since waking up for the detail.

I'll hit the head before I turn in, he thought. That's what I'll do.

The head was darker and marble-cold. He left the door of his stall open and squatted on the smooth porcelain, thinking of the radio. To have a radio in one's room, to play it all night long . . . it seemed suddenly infinitely desirable to him, a thing of unreachable privilege and luxury. That green eye glowing steadily, the distant thrum of guitars, the tiny voice of a woman singing in your cool, night-darkened room, and you asleep, unconscious of it, yet lying with it all there, all yours. A privilege to have it, a luxury to waste it. It was beautiful. It seemed a symbol, the end and goal of life.

As he squatted there, thinking of the radio for a while, and then after a time not thinking of anything at all, the sounds of bells gradually penetrated his consciousness—faraway bells, ringing on the cool wind that breathed sea-dank in through the windows of the fourth deck head. He finished his duty and pulled up the PJ bottoms that only plebes wore and tied his b-robe closed and went over to the window to look out and down.

Far below, five decks down, spread the night-lighted grounds of the Academy. Directly below him were the tennis courts, still lit, and a few parked cars: MGs, Vettes, Jags; the firsties' cars. The 34th's first class specialized in air-cooled sports machines, headed by the company commander's shining white Porsche. Beyond the gleaming hoods were the Field House and the bleachers of the running track. They were empty. The wide expanse of Faggot Field—all that, he had been told, had been once part of the bay—was empty, dark. Beyond that was an even profounder blackness, the Chesapeake itself, wide and nightfilled, cloaked with the wind.

Yet it was *not* silent; still, from out there somewhere, swelled and rang the bells, clanging and calling in the dark. Their sound grew and waned with the wind that came through the window, cooling his cheeks.

Then he understood, and smiled to himself. There were no bells.

Those were the knockabouts, moored in their docile rows along Santee Basin. The solemn clanging was the halyard fittings, slatting and banging against the masts with the sway of the hulls.

Yet he lingered by the window still. The sound; the darkness; the distant lights low on the horizon, far out on the bay; the cool steady wind. It *meant* something, he felt. Something deep, something mysterious and enduring; something that evoked or even reflected the loneliness and passion in his own heart. The distant, sad ringing was the call of the sea, that vast, chained darkness of ocean, calling plaintively to the chained earth; as if all of it, all of them, were doomed to serve a billion years of imprisonment for some reason only dimly remembered, or dimly suspected once again, on dark mornings.

And standing there in the head, tired, hungry, afraid, he knew and understood this: that he was alive. He was here, and what he did, succeed or fail, mattered. He too was chained, but he was free.

He was one with the wind, and the sea, and the darkness.

"Fall in there at the end! First platoon! Hurry up, damn it!"

Wednesday afternoon is Brigade Dress Parade.

Feeling ridiculous and martial at the same time, you hurry down the outside steps toward the parking lot, where the 34th forms up for march-on. You are in full dress blue: the short monkey jacket, padded in front with foam rubber like a pigeon's breast, with a double row of big gold buttons and high choke collar with anchors. Hooked over the second button from the bottom is your white bayonet belt, bleached with Clorox and scrubbed with Ajax and a nailbrush until it glows white in the sun. The big, oval, pewter buckle, probably seventy years old, brands you with FIDELITY and OBEDIENCE. The high-waisted trousers, of the same blue cloth as the jacket, break clean six inches above your white leggings and polished boondockers. You carry your freshly oiled and waxed M-one at port arms.

"Fall in! Let's get this show on the road!" bawls Breen's voice.

You fall in. From the rear of Singleterry's squad, first platoon, at parade rest, you look upward from under your cap brim at a sky as blue and clear as an untroubled soul. It is surprisingly warm for fall. From over the Field House the sun delegates floods of golden heat.

From your right, off in the direction of T-court and the Chapel bandstand, comes the distant but very clear *thud . . . thud . . . thud, thud, thud* of drums. The last few firsties come down the steps, ambling toward their positions in the ranks. Ahead of them, facing the company, paces Midshipman Lieutenant Breen, resplendent today in three-striper full dress and sword. Beside him stands Kim, the battalion CPO, holding the brass-ringed guidon negligently aloft, where the sun blazes from time to time off its polished spear point.

"Thirty-fourth Company . . . ten-*hut!* Report."

The platoon leaders report, saluting Breen. The mate scampers off with the muster lists. Breen fondles the pommel of his sword, but does not draw it. He glances toward T-court.

"Thirty-fourth Company . . . riiiight . . . *hace.*"

You and a hundred others pivot instantly on your toes.

"Thirty-fourth Company," Breen calls, his voice going sharp in command, echoing from the granite walls of Dahlgren, "Riiight shoul-der . . . *arms!*"

Up with the heavy rifle, *slap, slap*, salute, *snap*. The company stands in perfect alignment, facing northwest, caps level, eyes elevated to the guidon, weapons welded to their right shoulders.

"Forwarrrd—"

The guidon lifts—

"*Hartch.*"

As the pennant drops, on the first *thud*, you and a hundred others step out. To the song of the drums the company gathers way, following the Gungy 33rd under the Dahlgren portico, and swings right with a crisply sung "Column riiight . . . hartch!" to join on at the tail of the companies that formed on T-court itself. The sun blazes down. Eyes front, you nevertheless can see along Stribling Walk the knots of women, officers, tourists, and you stiffen yourself a little more and strike out smartly, imagining you can hear your step in the crash of a thousand others at the same second. Beside you two of the youngsters are talking in ranks.

"See *that?*"

"Look at those forward mounts!"

"Major caliber."

"Wonder whose grease girl she is."

You ignore them. You are marching. The rifle is snug and massive against your padded shoulder, its butt solid in the cup of your right hand, settled in, moving with you. You check the men ahead. Gray has his barrel canted inward just a trifle, swaying it out of the line of steel of those ahead in his file. "Dick," you say softly, not moving your lips. "Butt left."

The weapon moves a fraction, back into line. You wonder if your own is aligned. There is no one back of you to say. That's one of the problems with being short, a sandblower, relegated forever to the rear rank, unless someday, as a firstie, you should rate stripes.

And somehow, on this bright day of drums, even that does not seem impossibly far away.

"Column lelllf . . . *hartch!*"

As you clear the winged mass of Maury, the sound of the band bursts over you. Sousa, "The Golden Jubilee March." Leaning into the blast of music, you file past the marble frosting of the Tripoli monument. Then there is a halt, marching in place, a bottleneck ahead somewhere. From the front rank comes Breen's voice, distinct even through the trumpets, shouting something at the 33rd Company commander. And then you are moving again, too fast, and the eddy movement leaves you and the other short-legged guys in the rear double-timing to catch up. Around you the youngsters curse.

"Thirty-fourth Companyyyy! Half-lelllf . . . *hartch!*"

And then, suddenly, as you leave the road, come for the first time onto the trampled hay-smelling grass of Worden Field itself, the whole green expanse of it opens to your view. You can flick your eyes a little, hidden in the moving ranks, and see the first ten companies flung wide over the cropped grass, flags snapping over rigid blue and glitter, the slight wavering of the moving companies behind them, guiding on the blocks, halting, dressing, snapping to parade rest. And beyond them, the ruddy brick and white pillars of Captain's Row, and the stands solid with spectators, officers, parents, girls. The sun gleams and flashes from white, gold, deep-hued blue, and from under your feet the grass smell comes up, and the shafts of sunlight click on and off between the spaced moving bodies, filled with the whirling of golden dust. The band plays "Anchors Aweigh."

The 34th swings into position, guiding on the 33rd, sixth battalion, second regiment, and moves forward. Kim is out to the side, watching the ground for the blocks. You see Breen's head turn, gauging his position, ready to halt even if the Korean misses the small, bronze markers that space the companies evenly over the field. Once, you have heard, someone stole them the night before the last parade of June Week, and the Brigade weaved about the field like drunken clowns in front of the Chief of Naval Operations and eight foreign ambassadors. Now they're screwed in so deep it would take blasting to get them out of the ground.

"Thirty-fourth Companyyyy . . ." *Thud, thud.* "*Halt.*"

You stop, swaying forward slightly. Your dust swirls forward with you for a few feet and then begins to settle. There are small movements, an inch back, an inch to one side, as the company corrects its instantaneous spacing at the halt.

"Orderrrr . . . arms!"

Undirected by conscious thought, a hundred heavy rifles tip forward from a hundred right shoulders, pivot in the air, and are received by left gloves as they fall *slap*, right arms up to the sling swivel *slap*, butts to the deck *thud*, left hands back to position *snap*.

"Thirty-fourth Company. PUH-rade . . . rest."

Behind you, borne on a Severn breeze, sound faint commands as the last companies take their intervals and halt. The thirty companies already in place stand motionless as spaced ranks of toy soldiers, perfect as the ranks of Chin's buried army. Waiting for the 35th and 36th to dress and cover, you're glad you aren't in First Company, doomed to stand an extra quarter hour twice a week for four years, waiting for the others to march on.

Then, finally, the music stops, suddenly, in mid-beat, and there is utter silence across the field; the eyes of four thousand men meet on the distant stand where an officer steps up and the PA system crackles and then booms out.

"Ladies and gentlemen, the Brigade of Midshipmen."

A scattering of applause from the stands; the men stand motionless, waiting. The officer speaks on, but to the left there is a mutter of laughter in the ranks, and your ear tunes to that instead of the ceremony. It's Dubus. "Before you on historic Worden Field stands the Brigade of Midshipmen," he mutters loudly. "Composed of forty-two hundred undistinguishable units, snatched from real life in fifty states and several foreign countries. Today's parade will be highlighted by the presentation of a medal to a superior unit, who functioned properly under conditions of stress beyond design requirements. . . ."

The introduction ends. There is more clapping, a distant whistle or two. The midshipmen lock and unlock their knees surreptitiously.

"Ree-*port!*"

There is a long, hot pause. Something is going on up front. The high stripers pace and salute before the reviewing stand. Swords flash in the sunlight. The midshipmen stand rigidly bored. Presently it will end, but meanwhile there are Marines with binoculars and clipboards on top of the grading stand, on the bandstand, all around the field. In the ranks no one moves. The random explorations of bees in the trampled grass are watched with apprehension. The company is being graded. Screw up, slap at a biting fly, faint, drop a cap or (worst of all) a rifle, and your ass will suffer its fate. Then at last the muster is over.

"Brigade attention."

"Firrrst Regiment! Atten—*hut!*"

"Seconnn' Regiment! Attain—*hub!*"

"Preee-sen' *harms.*"

And up suddenly comes the rifle in one swift lift from the ground, arrested and suspended with the left hand high on the stock, the other just below the trigger guard at the crook; the sling swivel floats at eye level, and you stare out over the gray steel as the crowd rises from the stands and the colors dip and the company guidon falls in salute.

The national anthem mingles with the snap of flags above the picked men of the color guard. Dogs bark far off. A radio is playing somewhere near, seemingly in the ranks. The sweet smell of grass, the smells of polish, hot wool, hot foam rubber, sweat, the feel of it trickling down your back. The whine of a wasp. The rifle floats in front of your nose, gathering to itself the weight of a body, of a car, of the earth. You promise yourself that next p-rade you will take out the operating rod, the springs, the oiler, the follower, anything to lighten it. It begins to shake. Your muscles squeak audibly, like cheap toys.

. . . and the home of the brave. The band brasses to a halt and the quiet vibrates for a long instant, hovering over thousands of trembling arms. To the right a man goes down. His cap rolls on the grass.

". . . *harms.*"

Crash go four thousand butts into the soil, shaking the air.

The manual of arms begins. Simple movements, but done crisply, with military simultaneity: it must be impressive, seen from the stands. It's different standing here, doing it.

"Present arms!"

"Right shoulder arms."

"Port . . . arms!"

"Left shoulder arms."

"Or-derrr . . . ahms."

A barely audible sigh sweeps the field; that's over . . . the easiest part to screw up. With thousands of arms and rifles moving at the same instant a mistake stands out. Now there is more palavering up front; and finally that too is over and present arms again and you wait, tensing yourself.

And then the first gun goes off behind you, a heart-stopping concussion that brings screams from the stands and a flinch even though you were ready. Boom. Boom. You count them. The rifle, suspended, begins its exponential gain in weight again. The powder smoke drifts forward through the ranks, obscuring the trees, glowing in the sunlight. Seagulls whirl through it and ascend screaming. Rifles jerk as men sneeze. At last you flinch but there is no explosion, just silence for a while, then ground arms; and then come the words every mid on the field has been waiting an hour to hear.

"Paaa-a-a-a-ss in review!"

With a renewed blare the band strikes up for the last time. You wait, scared but ready, watching the sky, the sun, the company next to you poising and then swinging suddenly into movement, then the next, and finally Breen's voice comes faint over the music—

"Thirty-fourth Company! For-waaaard . . . *harch!*"

"Column reigh . . . *harch!*"

Around the turn, into it; don't swing wide, watch the interval . . . past the elms, spectators on Rodgers Road, old homes, captains watching from porches . . . then another column left, the last, and this is it, the last stretch, and you match cadence and dress and cover, and the dust comes up in sunlit streamers, your piece solid with your shoulder, bayonets glittering, the reviewing stand ahead, and then the band hits those slow brassy bars of "The Stars and Stripes Forever" and the hair goes up on your neck and chills stiffen your spine and you watch the guidon now because no one could hear a command, and then it swoops, hangs poised, and dips and eyes *right*. Your head snaps a quarter turn, and along a long rank of chests, a long line of white gloves that rise and swing and stop in perfect synchrony, the slightly stooped figure of the old man, the Superintendent, is taking the salute. That's him, gold up to his elbow, and you can never hope to be that old, that noble; and at the same time you know that once he was a mid, like you; once he marched too, on this soil, like Mahan and Dewey and Cushing, and Michelson and Fiske, King and Halsey and Spruance, Nimitz and Burke and Rickover.

And there, for that moment at eyes right, the band playing full and clear, you realize that *you are in ranks with them*, the men who in war and peace conquered the enemy and themselves, the thousands who led and died, and you are no longer just a scared plebe but part of something glorious that stretches back into a past echoing with the sounds of guns and the clash of bloody steel. And then, just as you feel it, just as it is almost real, graspable, so that in one more moment you can hold it and carry it with you forever as part of yourself, the guidon goes up and eyes *front* and you step out and then your boonies are ringing on concrete again, the grass is gone, and column *lelft* and the moment breaks as you turn. Upperclass begin to talk around you. The rifles sway from perfect alignment to the sloppy cant of men carrying things, and you are off the field and instead of the last in a file of heroes you are . . . Philo McGiffin . . . Midshipman Fourth Class . . . Sir.

And ahead of you a wide face turns, grinning, and Do-Dirty Dan Dubus says, "McGiffin . . . you still got that wild hair up your ass?"

"Yes sir."

Heads turn toward you. Dubus, incredibly, has stretched out his hand. You look at it. To take it means that you're spooned; first names; no more rates between the two of you; means buddies.

"Hey. Come on, Philo. I made a mistake. Okay?"

You do not take the hand. Both of you are surprised. The youngster's mouth hardens then. "All right, dipshit," he says. "I'll see you tonight."

Gray looks back at you, eyes wide. He seems about to say something, but a command from one of the firsties snaps his head around again. You march on. The music fades behind you.

And with horror you ask yourself suddenly, coming out of the music, What have I done?

It was intensely, gloomily, carbon-black dark outside Macdonough Hall. They were grateful for it. At 2100 they should all have been in rooms, studying. Instead they had crossed the immense stone pile of the Hall underground, through the pipe-ceilinged warren of the 00 level, and come out of Bancroft past the closed mid store at the third wing. As Stamper went ahead to check for jimmylegs, Philo and Fayaway, his second, stood in the shadows. Philo's stomach felt weird. The upperclass had stuffed him with pasta fazool and cannonballs for evening meal, saying he needed his strength, and even two hours later the food lay in his gut like lead ballast. He rubbed his knuckles on his gym gear nervously.

A low whistle came from the side door of the natatorium. They ducked across the roadway and crossed the cavern of the olympic-size pool, shimmering darkly under the night lights, and descended into the lowest level of the athletics building. The ring was brightly lit, mercuries humming over the scuffed-buff canvas. No one else was there. Stamper motioned them in.

"Hey, McGiffin, you feel okay?"

"I guess so . . . sir."

"I talked to Doc. He's in Misery Hall there. He won't come out unless we call him."

"Yes sir," said Fayaway.

Someone was coming down the main ladder from the gym deck.

They all froze, looking toward it. It was Dubus. Wiebels was with him, looking annoyed. They looked even more displeased when they saw Stamper. "Hi, Dan," said the second class easily. "Thought I'd referee. You guys ready?"

"Sure, if les ploobs are."

"Suit up, then."

Philo remembered from summer boxing, theoretically at least, what he had to do. He pulled sixteen-ounce gloves and headgear from the long rows pegged on the bulkhead. The leather stank with generations of sweat and blood. He buckled the headgear on while Dubus selected his, and held out his hands for Fayaway to tie the gloves. They felt heavier than they had that summer. Wiebels was doing the same for Dubus. With his white works blouse off the youngster looked enormous.

"He's bigger than you are, Phil," J.J. was saying. "But remember, he's a tub of lard; you're little and fast. You play midfield, you run cross-country. He's just a gedunk sailor. Fake him out. Keep moving. Fast footwork. Duck his punches and jab. Gut it out if you take a hit. You feel all right?"

"Why does everyone keep asking me that?"

"Well, you look kind of weird."

"I'm scared."

"No you're not."

"No. I'm not."

"You're not scared."

"Yes. I mean, no."

"Get in the ring, Philo," said Fayaway.

The ropes vibrated behind him. The canvas was bright and hard under his gym shoes. Stamper waited in the center of the ring. Philo remembered from somewhere that Tunney and Dempsey had fought in this ring, this one, purchased later by the Navy. In the other corner Dubus smacked his gloves together. Fayaway hung on the ropes, a towel on his shoulder. The light overhead hummed. Everything was suddenly brighter and he realized several more bulbs had flared into life.

Stamper looked at his watch. "One minute rounds," he said, "till a knockdown, towel, or blood. Ready, guys?"

Guys, Philo thought, looking at the lights overhead. One of the guys. He nodded, the heavy gear making his head bob.

"Standby—*mark*."

Stamper stepped clear. Dubus walked forward. He looked gigantic. Philo moved out in a curve, dancing on the balls of his feet, as he had been taught. Dubus danced a little too, as if reminded of it. Under his stained T-shirt his pecs jiggled like Shivering Liz in the mess hall.

"Jab him!" Fayaway said, in a kind of hushed yell. Philo sidestepped, advanced a little, danced, moved forward. Dubus stood there, his hands up. Philo rattled him on the side of his headgear with a left jab. He had to reach up to do it. Dubus swung and missed. Philo jabbed him again.

Bam! Something like a laundry truck impacted his chest. He bent with the shock, forgetting to cover up or move back. *Bam!* Again, this time in the side. He twisted away and scampered for the far corner, breathing hard. His ribs hurt.

"Get back out there!" said Fayaway, almost into his ear. "Cover up."

He turned. Dubus had lumbered forward a couple of steps. Philo shook his head and moved in a circle, shuffling his feet on the canvas. They made a dry sound. Dubus moved forward. Philo tried a right but the youngster brushed it off and let go with a swing. He blocked it, or anyway most of it, but the glove grazed his headgear, twisting it half over his eyes. It was too big. He was trying to right it so that he could see when a glove came from nowhere and burst like a contact-fuzed five-inch on his nose, scattering reddish fragments into a bloom of yellow light.

"Time," said Stamper's voice, very remote.

"C'mon, Phil," said Fayaway. The towel felt cold on his face. He felt clumsily for his nose, the gloves and the headgear both in his way. "It's okay, just a trickle," said J.J., pulling the laces tight. "Damn it, you got to go in and hit him some! Quit running around. Stand there and toss a couple into his gut. He'll go down like a Norfolk whore."

"I see blood," said Stamper. "Do you want—"

"He's okay, sir. He's okay."

Up and weaving, recovered some with the wet towel, Philo still felt the stitch in his side from the punch, or maybe it was from breathing so fast. He felt dizzy. Bob and weave. He—

Bam! For a second it was the world weaving instead of him. He ducked his head and moved back instinctively, whimpering a little.

"Hit him, damn it!"

"Quit backpedaling!"

"He's running him right around the ring," he heard Wiebels say.

"Come on," Dubus grunted through the mask. First words he had said. "You challenged. Now fight me, you little pussy."

Stung, Philo stepped forward and unleashed his left. It bounced off Dubus' headgear. The youngster kept coming. He threw another jab, then remembered, the *gut*, and tried a combination, left-right-left, just like in class, to chest and body. Under the T-shirt the gloves hit fat. For maybe an inch. Then the big third class was as solid as Tecumseh. He ducked a slow right, thank God he could see now, and moved back. Sweat burned his eyes and he wiped them quickly with the back of the glove. Dubus moved forward. He jogged back.

"Damn mouse," said the third class. "Look, you guys. Look at him run backward." He feinted, and Philo jumped back, hitting the ropes. Wiebels and Stamper laughed.

"Time," said Stamper, looking at his watch as if he had forgotten. "Hey. You boys had enough yet?"

"Just getting warmed up," said Dubus.

"McGiffin?"

Philo stood in his corner, letting Fayaway knead his shoulders. He couldn't think of anything to say. "He's still in the fight," said J.J. after a moment. "He's just getting his second wind."

"Getting his wind up?" said Dubus. The upperclass laughed.

"Okay," said Stamper. "Round three. McGiffin, you ought to mix it up a little. This isn't foxtrot training in Memorial Hall. Standby . . . *mark.*"

But as soon as he stepped out he found himself dancing again. He forced his legs to steady and walked toward Dubus, his guard up.

Bam!

Something pungent and nasty crowded his nose. It stung. He

coughed and came up swinging. The Misery Hall corpsman pushed him back down to the canvas. "Fight's over, boy," he said, dabbing something at his nose. "For five-six minutes now. You feelin' all right?"

He sat up. His ears rang and buzzed. The light was too bright and his mouth felt loose and salty. He saw the faces over the corpsman's shoulder. "Hey," he said weakly. "How'd I do?"

"He all right?" said Stamper.

"Guess so," said the corpsman, screwing the cap back onto a bottle. He looked down at Philo. "You can get up now, son. Listen. Tonight, next couple days, you get any headaches, nausea, somethin' funny with your eyes, you come back an' see me—or go down to sick bay if I ain't here. Got that?"

"Yeah," he said. He reached for the ropes and got up. The other faces drifted back. Fayaway, eyes remote, handed him back his blouse without speaking.

"That's it then," said Stamper. "Let's get back to the Ghetto. They can't cover for us all night."

"What happened, J.J.?" he asked when they were out in the night again. He felt his nose cautiously and discovered it was packed with cotton.

"He knocked you out."

"Oh. How—how did I do?"

Fayaway didn't answer for a minute. Then he said, "You looked like you were running a marathon in there."

"What do you mean? I hit him."

"Twice. A couple of jabs. The rest of the time you were double-timing to the rear."

"I didn't think it was that bad."

"Damn it, man—the whole *point* was to get in there and try to lay 'em on him. Nobody expected you to win. He had forty, fifty pounds on you, and six inches reach."

"So why—"

"Because, you dummy, if you hadn't pussied out Snatch and the Weebs would have made him spoon you afterwards. But you blew it. You let him use you like a brasso rag! You were scampering around that ring and whimpering! I was so damn ashamed—"

The click of heels came from a side corridor. Wiebels signalled, and the five of them faded behind a laundry cart. Philo caught a glimpse of dull green; two pair of glassy shoes; the heavy jingle of a saber. They held their breaths. The footsteps faded off down the corridor. "It's Black Bart," Stamper whispered. "And his little mate, with a pad of personalized form twos and a sharp pencil. Nobody but him would be down here . . . okay . . . fast break . . . *go.*" They sprinted across the corridor on tiptoe. A hundred feet away, heading toward the third wing, the Marine major did not look back.

No one else spoke to Philo all the way back to the rooms. He felt angry; he felt confused; he still felt afraid. His nose began to hurt. He felt like shouting at them—explaining that it was a lucky punch, that he was just warming up, that he wanted a rematch—that it was all a mistake.

But he knew deep down that none of that was true. He had whimpered. He had pussied out.

The next day all the upperclass began to call him Mouse.

CHAPTER SIX

*The new Fourth Classmen at the Academies each year
are young men from all walks of life. Many . . . directly
out of high school, may not have had the opportunity of
learning what to do at formal dances, or how to greet
those in the receiving line. . . .*
          —*Service Etiquette*, U.S. Naval Institute, 1963

—How long have you been in the Navy?
*—All me bloomin' life, sir! Me mother was a mermaid,
me father was King Neptune. I was born on the crest of
a wave and rocked in the cradle of the deep. Seaweed
and barnacles are me clothes. Every tooth in me head is
a marlinespike; the hair on me head is hemp. Every
bone in me body is a spar, and when I spits, I spits tar!
I'se hard, I is, I am, I are!*
                              —*Reef Points*

"**M**ister McGiffin," said the voice, cutting into his dreams with a kind of weary emphasis. "Are we boring you?"

"Uh . . . no sir."

"Resting your eyes, no doubt."

"Uh—"

"You should take this class a little more seriously," the civilian professor said, without a great deal of conviction; he had been teaching plebe calculus at Navy for a long time. "Section leader. Could you and . . . McGiffin here stay for a moment after class, please."

Jeez, thought the Mouse. Sleeping in class was a big fifteen demos. And he'd been inspecting his eyelids, all right. He sat up straighter

and rubbed his face. As he lowered his hand there was a jabbing
pain at his collarbone, so sharp he almost cried out. Gingerly, he
worked the spiffy free of his skin. He'd set the points of the wire
collar-stiffener to gouge him if his head sagged. And even that
hadn't worked.

Jeez, he thought again. Why does it all have to come in a lump?

Two long weeks had gone by since his bout with Dubus; two
weeks of straight unadulterated downhill shitfits. He stared glumly
at the old prof's back as he drew wavy lines and divided them into
little blocks, meditating on his own problems. In two weeks he had
piled up eighty demerits, frying like an egg for his haircut, for gear
adrift, a gross shirt tuck, sleeping in Chapel, failing to salute the Air
Farce exchange officer, and for trying to kick Dodo (he missed, but
went down for "Abuse of a Public Animal" nonetheless). The laundry had lost four of his white works blouses. All the upperclass were
on his case at tables. And just yesterday, at dental quarters, they
had told him his wisdom teeth would have to come out.

There was, he thought bitterly, only one good side to it: it kept
him from worrying. Any lower in grades and the Academic Board
would heave his ass over the wall. He was dead last in grease; even
his own classmates had him typed as a shit magnet now. Having
him on the table was the next best thing to carry-on. And thanks to
Kim, he had more time on the green bench than the whole Navy
second string.

Sitting there, blinking vacantly at the board, he thought that he
could actually feel his memory going. Everything from that morning
meal back was a blank, a dim chaos of comearound after comearound, endless running in early morning darkness, incessant, hammering questions at table; nodding in classes over the abyss of sleep,
clutching on the simplest rates from pure fatigue, living in exhaustion and habitual, nervous fear. His hands trembled so that he cut
himself nearly every morning as he shaved. At times he felt like
laughing at nothing; at times, standing over Singleterry or Corpen or
Dubus as he closed their windows, like grabbing his bayonet and
reconning from room to room, leaving a steaming trail of red. He
weighed a hundred and twenty-five and had a demerit for every
pound.

It could be worse, he thought, catching himself nodding again. He had peed down his pants leg once at comearound but he'd been sweating so hard no one noticed. That would have been forty more easy.

Chalk screeched on the board, and a little ripple of wakefulness moved over the class. This prof did that a lot, probably on purpose. Philo rubbed at his face wearily. I have to admit it some time, he thought. *I'm not going to make it.*

The reluctant articulation of the thought left him feeling empty. Not depressed, not angry—simply numb. He strongly suspected that weariness was the only emotional response he had left.

It would be fruit, leaving. Whether it was the Ac Board that bilged him first, for grades, or the Executive Department for conduct, or the Supe for aptitude. It won't cause me any pain to leave this Mickey Mouse happy horse-shit parade, he told himself.

There was only one thing wrong with that; it wasn't true.

First off, where would he go? The bilging process was a little unclear to him. He knew that under certain circumstances you had to serve out the time you'd promised to the Academy in the Fleet. Being a white hat, he was sure, was no picnic, though anything had to be better than plebe year. But still, after that he'd be out, twentysome years old, still with no money and no degree and no skill. And if they didn't send him to the fleet it could be even worse walking out Bilger's Gate and up Maryland Avenue with nowhere in the world to go, nowhere and no one he belonged with. And there was more to it than that.

Damn it, he thought, I don't want to go. I can hack it here.

He could; he felt it instinctively. He could lick skinny, and steam, and even calculus, if he had the time to study. Dago and bull were a snap to him, though he knew that most of the mids liked languages and English only a little more than Water Survival. He was good at athletics; he had a 3.4 in P.E. and was turning in consistent seconds and thirds in batt cross-country. Already they'd asked him about the track team in the spring.

If only he could get *some kind of break*. . . .

It was what Zeard called the Halo Effect. If you had a halo everybody thought you were a saint. He, on the other hand, was little, so

they'd begun by perceiving him as a whimp. Then Dubus had nick-
named him "Mouse," and that had sealed his fate. They all, even his
own classmates now, expected him to act like a pussy, so everything
he did turned out that way. He never got a chance. They always put
him down. . . .

He sat there feeling sorry for himself. Presently paper rustled at
his elbow. He started, took one, and passed the rest on, smelling the
alcohol curling up off the mimeographed sheets, and tuned in again
to the voice. ". . . so, to perk you all up a little, here's a pop half-
hour p-work. You've got ten minutes to finish. Should be an easy A
if you've been listening up."

Jeez, he thought again. He looked at the paper fearfully. Only the
curlicue curves of the integral signs looked vaguely familiar, as if he
had memorized them out of the sports section sometime in the early
hours before morning comearound. . . .

"Oh happy day," crooned Zeard. The room door banged shut
behind him. "A six-N day, but lacking something; I know; no
p-rade. . . ." His eye fell on his roommate's slumped form. "Hey,
Mou . . . Philo, you asleep?"

"No."

"Way you got your head down on your desk like that, it's taking a
risk . . . hey, you okay?"

"Yeah."

"Aren't you going to run this afternoon?"

"Not today. Got a meet with second batt tomorrow. No practice
today."

"No rest for me," said Zeard gaily. He hung up his WUBA trou
carefully and reached for sweat gear. He dressed quickly, humming.
Today was his first day with the company fieldball team. He'd already tried plebe fencing and batt b-ball, and been shit-canned from
both. But nobody ever got dropped from fieldball, sport of last re-
sort for the fat firsties who majored in popcorn and TV . . . he was
heading for the door when he noticed his roomie's head was on the
blotter again.

"Phil."

"What, dammit, Howie?"

"Hey! It's me! Old Weird Zeard, man of scrap steel, white hunter, fig plucker. What's up? Need a cigar? A No-Doz? A fat pill? A kick in the tail? What's eatin' you, pal?"

"Nothing," said Philo. "Go on, shove off, Howie. Go play basketball."

"Fieldball. Well—okay." He paused again, by the door. "But you better snap out of it by nineteen-hundred, cowboy."

"Why?"

"Tea fight."

"Oh, no! Not *tonight!*"

"A firm titty on your last. This very post meridian."

"I thought it was next week!"

"Then chin up; it's tonight. Packing houses from D.C. to Richmond have been scoured so that you, Philo McSqueegee, can hold within your arms your very own fourteen-year-old, subpubertal, acne-enhanced *femme fatale*, with more braces than a courthouse porch in Arkansas. Damn!"

"Hey, Howie. This isn't the normal Weird Zeard. What are you on?"

"Sir?"

"Why did you say sir?"

"Oh no you don't."

"What are you so up in the air about?" said Philo, grinning in spite of himself.

Zeard folded himself into the chair opposite. His long face contracted around his nose in what could only have been meant as a wink. "Confidential NOFORN?" he asked.

"You got it."

"Mary Jo's coming in tonight."

"You're kidding. To the pig push?"

"Roger that."

"All the way from Chicago?"

"Didah. Didit dah dit. Didit dah dit. Didit. Didahdit. Dahdah."

"But how will you . . . what if somebody else draws her?"

"No sweat. We're allowed to cut in on anybody in a tea fight. Then she just tells the other guy she knows me and we swap dates."

Philo thought about it for a moment. "Well . . . it's a swell idea. You got balls, all right. I wish you luck, Howie."

"Thanks, old man. Well, I'm off. See you this evening. Who you going around to?"

"I'll have to check my appointment calendar."

"Never mind. Bye—and one other thing." Zeard leaned closer over the desk. "I don't know what's got its teeth in you, but get that chin up. A lot of the crap you take you attract to yourself."

"I know. The halo effect."

"With you it's more like horns. You go around looking hangdog and you're gonna get dumped on. Look at Dick Gray. He's no smarter than you are. But he goes around with his eager puppydog look, keeps smiling that big shit-eating grin, and he rates top grease. That's true in here, it's true outside. Look around." He got up. "Well, I'm off. Future fieldball champ, Turkey Bowl contender, iron man Zeard takes to the field to mutilate firsties till his true love appears."

Philo looked after him as the door banged shut.

"No caps, sir?"

"You don't dance with caps on, nerds. Check 'em here."

"Aye aye, sir."

Philo and Jack Ash and Len Ind stood together at the entrance to Dahlgren Hall. Inside—they could see a little through the partially opened double doors—the murmur of conversations, the sound of a band surged back and forth beneath an arched castiron overhead, under the glow of colored lights. "Man," groaned Ind, "I don't want to go to this thing."

"We got to," said Ash. His cherubic face, normally ruddy, was white. "It's a scheduled evolution. They take a muster."

"How they gonna take muster at a *dance?*"

"They've had a hundred years to figure it out, sailor."

"Greetings, fellow revelers," said Zeard, joining them.

"My, you look gay," said Ash.

"Watch it, pal . . . what are you waiting here for? Printed invitations? The social director assures us the girls of our dreams are here."

Too apprehensive to joke further, they followed Zeard in. From the balcony, lined with racks of M-ones, they could see the whole dance floor at a glance. But only for a moment: a second class usher, fourragere gleaming on his shoulder, moved them along. They went down the curving ladders to the main deck, walked past a stationary 5"/38 twin mount and a rack of torpedoes, and found themselves in a blind file. Plebes ahead of them, plebes around them, more plebes coming down the ladder behind them. Nothing but plebes, natty in service dress blue and black bow ties and little medals. The line of them was blocked on either side by white canvas curtains, like, Philo thought suddenly, the ones nurses pushed around beds in the movies when someone was dying.

"Hey," said Zeard. "It's just like the stockyards."

"Moo," said Ind.

"Moo," said Ash.

"Ma-a-a-aw," lowed Philo. His was best; there had been a dairy not far from the Home.

In seconds the whole fourth class was bawling and grunting like a herd of longhorns on their way to the corned beef machines. They ran to and fro and butted each other. In the stampede someone rammed the curtains, trying to knock them down. Under the edge they could see a line of womens' ankles and the sight excited them like the smell of water after a long drive.

When they got tired, about the time the second class ushers had threatened themselves hoarse, the line moved on again, to a table with two segundoes at it.

"Names, studs?"

"Ash, sir. John."

"Ind, Leonard, sir."

"McGiffin, Philo T., sir."

"What?"

"I heard of him," said the other man. "He's in sixth batt. He's for real."

"Go on, then. Remember, you turkeys, you're supposed to be gentlemen. Congress says so."

Ind said something.

"What's that, mister?"

"Just clearing my throat, sir."

"You. McGiffin. You guys got carry-on for this dance. You can rig your chin out."

"My chin *is* rigged out, sir."

Ash and Ind clutched their sides and turned away. "It's not *that* funny," said Philo. "You mother-torquers."

"Anyway, we passed muster," said Zeard. "Now let's have a good time. I hear they serve punch at these things."

"Maybe it's spiked."

"With what? JP-5?"

"Shut up, you guys. We're almost there."

"Next," said the second class at the head of the line, where the two canvas cattle chutes intersected. "You, the black guy. Get up here, stud. Miss, you in back, there—"

"Oh, mother," they heard Ind say. "Hel *lo,* foxy lady."

"Look at that," said Ash, awed.

"My God. Why don't they issue me one of those."

"Move on up! You, with the white hair—get up here."

Jack drew a Swedish battlewagon. He grimaced back at them desperately, then disappeared in the direction of the punch bowl.

"You—Tecumseh! You're next!"

Zeard drew someone skinny and small. Philo couldn't see her face, but Howie's gaiety seemed strained. He stepped to the front of the line.

"Sweet Jesus," he said.

"Yeah. Let's get some punch, right? Before they suck it all up. It goes right fast at these things."

The punch bowl was wide and crystal, but contained nothing but ginger ale and grapefruit juice, with hemispherical lumps of Naval Academy ice cream floating in it, slowly melting into goo. Across it, as she dipped her glass, he finally got a good look at her. She was tall, taller than he was by three, four inches. From her height your eyes went next to the hair, the striking red of it, glossy. Her face was freckled and smooth and round. More freckles on her shoulders, right down to the low top of her blouse. Tall as she was, she had a shape that would sail close to the wind and leave a wide wake.

"Beg pardon?" he said.

"I said, I'm Tawdry Doyle. What's your name?"

"Philo McGiffin. It really is."

"Oh, I believe you. Want some punch?"

"Okay, thanks."

"You know, I'm glad to meet you."

"Oh yeah?"

"Yeah. Most of the ushers know me. They match me up with some real losers sometimes."

"What did you say your first name was?"

"Tawdry. It's really St. Audrey. But people call me Tawdry for short."

"Oh. Yeah."

"This same goddamned ginger ale punch . . . you want to dance?"

"Okay."

They did a couple of fast dances. Philo could not keep from staring at her. She danced like a woman in a trance, head back and eyes closed, that rounded, healthy body moving in oiled grooves. When he was able to look away he saw that the NA-10 was playing, the upperclass dance band. He saw Len Ind and his partner move by them, doing some kind of fast step, something they hadn't taught at Memorial Hall dance class. He didn't see anyone else he knew, though the floor was crowded with plebes and girls, and it came to him how few of his nine hundred classmates he really knew, or ever really would know.

The band stopped, and then a slow dance started. "Want to dance this?" she said, opening her eyes and stepping up close to him.

"Uh, sure."

They stepped together. His chin went just under her collarbone and he felt something soft against his neck. Her hair smelled like soap and flowers, pricking at his cheek.

"You gonna dance, or just stand here and quiver, Philo?"

"Oh. Dance."

"Good."

They went around a couple of times. It was a lot better than waltzing with Fayaway on the parquet in Memorial. He did the box step for a while, then tried a couple of turns, and was pleased with how well they worked. He was getting ready for a dip when he felt a hand on his shoulder. "Cut, please."

"What?"

"It's me, Howie. I'm cutting in."

"The hell you are, Howie. I'm dancing."

But really they were stopped, there in the middle of the floor, because Zeard had hold of his arm. Philo tried to pull away. "What the hell?" said Tawdry. "Who is this creep?"

"This is my roommate. Tawdry, this is Howie. Howie, this is Tawdry."

"Hi, Maude," said Zeard.

"Tawdry."

"Howie, let go."

"I rate cutting in. You got to let me cut in."

"What?" Philo stared around; their classmates were looking in their direction as they danced by. "Who says?"

Zeard's eyes clicked distant. "*Service Etiquette*, page 60, bottom, 'Cutting In. During any hop, program or otherwise, unless the tune being played has been designated a "no break," you may cut in on another couple if you are already acquainted with the young lady—'"

"I never seen this turkey before in my life," said Tawdry, waving at someone on the balcony.

"'—*Or* are such a close personal friend of her partner that you can expect to be introduced.'"

"Get lost, Howie. Where's your date—Mary Jo?"

"Never mind. Come on, Philo, just one dance."

"I don't like this guy," said Tawdry.

"What's the trubs?" said a deeper voice, and suddenly there was a clear space around them. They turned to face a first class with sword and armband: the CMOOW.

"Nothing, sir."

"This guy annoying you?"

"No sir," said Philo. "He's my roommate, sir. I was just introducing him to Miss Doyle here."

"To who?"

"St. Audrey Doyle," said Tawdry, lifting her head.

The CMOOW gave her an odd look. "Come on," he said to the mate, who had been standing behind him, pad of report chits open in his gloved hands. "If you aren't going to dance, get off the floor, stud," he said to Zeard.

"Aye aye, sir."

"What was all that about?" she asked, after they had stepped together again, and he felt the same shock at her warmth, her convexity, the close entangling wonder of her hair.

"I don't know. Howie's a little weird sometimes."

"You all are."

"Who?"

"Swabbies."

"What are those?"

"It's what we call midshipmen out in town."

"Out in what town?"

"Crabtown is what you call it. Annapolis."

"Oh," said Philo. He missed a step and tried to retrieve it and almost fell, did a clumsy save, as if he was trying a takedown in reverse. "You, uh, you go to school out there?"

"I went to St. Mary's High, yeah . . . hey, Philo."

"Yes—Tawdry?"

"You know the difference between dancing and marching?"

"No, what?"

"I didn't think so . . . let's sit down for a while, okay?"

They found a seat underneath one of the missiles that hung from the arched overhead, and watched the crowd for a while, not talking much. The last of the plebes were through the chute, without girls; they wandered through the dancers like bees through a field, like free electrons through a semiconductor. He saw Zeard, alone, walking as if stunned, trying to cut in on people and being rebuffed. He saw the receiving line at the opposite end, some battalion officer and his wife, the social director, some second class and his girl. "Hey," he said, turning to Tawdry. "We ought to go through the receiving line."

"You really want to?"

"We're supposed to."

"They won't miss us," she said airily, sipping at the punch. It was her fourth glass.

The lights behind her shone through her hair, casting a strange reddish glow over her face. Close to her now, he saw that she was not really beautiful. Her mouth was too wide, her eyes too far apart, her face too broad for that. Her nose was wide and short with an Irish turn to it, as if its point had been planed off. But she was striking. That was a better word for her. Her bare arms and shoulders were all ovals, all curved, rounded, as if barely containing an internal pressure.

"Well," she said. "I pass inspection?"

"You sure do."

"You're a funny guy."

"You said we were all weird."

"What do they call you, Philo?"

"Who?"

"The guys. Don't you have a nickname or anything?"

Shit, he thought. "I guess I do. I don't like it much. Some of the upperclass call me Mouse."

"*Mouse?* That sucks."

"It sure does. Why don't you just call me Phil?"

"Okay." She dug her fist into his side. "Don't let names get to you, Phil. I been called some nasty ones myself."

"What?"

"Never mind. I'm not going to repeat them."

"Oh."

Ash came over. He was alone. He nodded to Tawdry. "Hi. Hi, Phil. Looks like you got lucky."

"Thanks. Where's your girl?"

"The big one? She got mad."

"Why?"

"Well, as soon as we got out on the floor I asked her, 'Who's afraid of the big bad wolf?', you know, leering, kind of. She says, 'Oh, *I'm* not.' I said, 'That's funny, the other two pigs were.' She got mad and went off looking for somebody to complain to."

"You're gonna gnaw the big pickle, pulling crap like that. She's probably some captain's daughter."

"She'll never recognize me. I didn't smile once."

"Tawdry, this is Jack Ash, classmate of mine."

"Hi."

"Hi. Well, I'm off. We're allowed to smoke outside, aren't we?"

"I don't know," said Philo.

"Yes, you are," said Tawdry.

Ash left. "You seem to know a lot about the Academy," said Philo.

"I come to a lot of these tea fights, and hops, and stuff."

He was about to say, and football games too; remembering her flaming hair and her head tilted back in laughter with two second class, down on Robber's Row; but he didn't. Instead he said, "What do you say we go get some air?"

"Okay." She smiled and got up quickly. It was her first smile at him and he found he liked it a lot.

As they passed under the balcony, somebody, one of the upper-class who came to watch the tea fights, like Romans watching a spectacle, leaned over to shout at them.

"Hey—Barnacle Lips!"

Philo looked up, but Tawdry dragged him on outside. She was surprisingly strong.

Outside, in the park between Ward Hall and the second wing, it was a little chilly; a few lights had been rigged on poles, but it was still dark. They got a bench to themselves beside one of the Long Lance torpedoes. The music was muted behind them. Beyond the last light the stars were out over the swelling dome of the Chapel. Philo looked at Tawdry's white freckled shoulders, at the top of her dress, and then back at the dome.

"Smoke, Phil?"

"No thanks. I'm in training."

"I couldn't live without 'em." She lit a long filter and sucked on it angrily. The smoke blew slowly past him, rising past the lights to become invisible. He watched her hand; it was rubbing the blunt nose of the torpedo, slowly, nervously. "Well, tell me about yourself," she said suddenly, turning to face him. "Where are you from? Up North I bet."

"P.A."

"Navy family?"

"Oh, hell, no."

"What are you doing here then?"

"I don't know."

"Do you have a girl back there?"

"Not really."

"What's that mean, 'not really'?"

He explained how he had dated Barb Spenser once, how they had walked to the movies, how he had kissed her afterward. "That was it. I don't know who she's dating now."

"You don't write to her?"

"No."

"That's bad," she said, though she didn't sound as if it was. He watched her hand moving on the nose of the torpedo, stroking it. "Everybody ought to have somebody. Especially here. To help you get through the time. Don't you think?"

"Yeah. You're right."

"Come here," she said.

When she let him go he licked his lips. He could still feel her tongue, like a hot little animal foraging in his mouth. It was the first time he had ever kissed somebody, been kissed, like that, and suddenly all the back-row dreaming in calculus wasn't just dreaming any more.

"Do that to me again, you degenerate," she whispered.

He was on his third or maybe his fourth helping when he felt a hand on his shoulder. He turned, angry, thinking it was Zeard again, but then he saw the armband and started to jump up.

"It's just me," said the plebe mate, looking back toward the lights of Dahlgren. "The Man's inside. But he said he was going to check out here next. If he sees this action it's PDA for sure."

"Thanks, buds," said Philo. "We can't kiss out here," he said to Tawdry. She was looking at herself in a compact, powdering a freckle on her nose.

"I know."

"Then why'd you do it?"

"I figured you needed it."

"I did, I did."

"And that's probably not all you need."

"What?" said Philo.

"Come on," she said, getting up from the bench.

"Where are we going?"

"It's too cold out here. Let's go in the coat room."

"The coat room?"

"Yeah. After the girls check their coats they mostly leave them alone till they're ready to leave . . . come on. You ever messed around standing up before? We're about the right height."

"Oh, God," said Philo, but he kept it under his breath. He followed her inside, seeing the CMOOW, the mate who had warned them beside him now and one step back, as per regulations, heading out the other door. He followed her into the check room. As she had said, there was no one there. Near the back, where the coat racks came together, there was a sort of muffled alcove up against the brick walls. She wriggled between the masses of coats, wool and fur-trimmed, and when he followed her they swung closed behind them and they were in a long dim cave, smelling of the furs and the wool and a mingling of perfumes. When they were well concealed she turned, and her skirt was already up, and he saw the white body of Tawdry Doyle, his first and only love.

In the 8–4 head that evening, in the fifteen minutes free before lights out, the plebes gathered to recount their luck and bemoan their fate. Ind, by mass agreement, had made out the best. "Her name's Debra," he said, "And she comes fully equipped. She's got the moves, the bod, and brains too. Goes to George Washington, in D.C. I'll be seein' her again."

"You know about Battleship Brenda," said Ash, making a face. "I saw her later, with Mrs. M. in tow, doing a sector search for me. They were both after blood. But I was safe. Fell in with this little brunette. Got her number. A possibility."

Mitchell had been bricked, he admitted. A little townie with stringy hair and breath straight out of a dog kennel. "And a pair of coke bottles as powerful as seven by fifties," he added.

"I like glasses on girls," said Darrin. "You can breathe on 'em, and then they can't see what you're doing."

"How did you and Mary Jo get along?" Kaufman asked Zeard, who had up to now hung at the edges of the group, wiping his nose and saying nothing. "I saw you cruising around alone."

"That wasn't all he was doing alone," said Philo.

"I don't want to talk about it."

"How do you mean?"

"I didn't get to see her."

"I thought you had it all figured out," said Ash. "What happened—wouldn't the guy she drew give her up?"

"I don't know if he would have or not," said Zeard. He looked haggard, shaken, like a man whose sense of the rightness of the world has been shattered. "One of the ushers got her. A guy named Reiver."

"Bill Reiver? The second class?"

"The right guard?"

"You got it. The ball player."

They all looked at the slimy tiles of the head. They understood. There was no way Zeard could have cut in on an upperclass without giving away his scam. And the fact that his drag hadn't done it for him meant only one thing: another fourth class was due for a Dear John letter. They all avoided looking at Zeard.

"How'd you do, Phil? Didn't see you out on the floor at all."

"I was there."

"How'd you make out?"

"Okay, I guess."

"Good looking?"

"All right."

"College girl?"

"I don't think so. She said she was a crab."

"Oh," said Kaufman. "Well, they say there's only two kinds of girls in Crabtown."

"What's that?"

"The kind you wouldn't want to meet in a dark alley; and the kind that wouldn't fit."

"Yeah, tough luck, Philo," said Ind. "But there'll be more tea fights."

"Hooray for that," said Zeard bitterly.

One of the second class came into the head. After study period corridor rates were off till taps, and of course they were always off in the head, but they still felt uncomfortable talking with an upper-class there and they stood and started to drift out. In the darkened hallway Philo felt Rollo's arm on his back. "You can't fool me, Phil. You met somebody. Got her number?"

He stopped dead in the corridor. The coats . . . the near panic and then the wonder of the first time. "No," he said. "Damn it, I forgot."

Mister Corpen came down the hallway, carrying his towel. He wore a Greyhound bus driver's cap with his b-robe. "Better get to your rooms, guys," he said. "Rumor committee has it Black Bart's planning a strike tonight."

"He wouldn't raid the Ghetto, would he, sir?"

"Never underestimate a short Marine. And we *are* in his battalion. But you guys need your sleep anyway. Gonna be a big buildup for Army this year."

"We're ready, sir," said Philo absently, still cursing himself for his stupidity. Well, maybe he could find her in the phone book. . . .

"You just think you are, McGiffin. You'll never see a buildup the way the Rathole does buildups."

Corpen went on, his klax flopping. Rollo and Philo looked at each other and had no more words; and they wended their ways to the blue trampoline.

CHAPTER SEVEN

*The relationship between first and fourth class is a
professional one, based on the normal tenets of human
dignity and mutual respect. There must be intelligent
deference by the junior; but there must also be
patience, understanding, and a feeling of responsibility
on the part of the senior. Any act that may tend to
degrade or humiliate a midshipman is in violation of
these principles.*
—COMDTMIDNINST 1531.2, paragraph 0205

Dream on.
—Common Bancroft Hall expression

And gradually, almost unnoticed amid the crowded days, they
found time passing. The heat of autumn waned to a noontime
warmth and the first frost came. On the bay, on the knockabouts
and YPs, they found that already they needed gloves and the heavy
melton peacoats called reefers. For the upper classes life settled into
the grind: study, recite, watch the Big Blue bite the big pickle every
Saturday. For the lowest class, the plebes, time seemed at once endless and incredibly swift. The past did not exist; it slipped back
second by second into the inchoate hell called yesterday, forgotten
even as it happened, for once past it meant nothing compared to that
far more orderly and personal hell they called today.

In early November the sets changed, and everyone drew new
squads. On table 249 there were three fourth class now, Philo, Castigliano, and Engel. Cross was assigned to 249 too, on paper, but he
usually ate on training tables; he was making a name for himself in

plebe ball, and most of the upperclass treated him like a youngster (jg). There were four third class. Corpen and a Mister Laird were the segundoes; and for firsties, Mister Keyes, Philo's new squad leader, and Breen, who was now the assistant company commander. That left one open space on the table, which would be filled with roamers. The plebes had looked forward to second set for days, hoping, with the desperate optimism of the oppressed, that any change might loosen things up; and they sprinted for their new seats with a by-now-intimately-familiar mixture of fear and anticipation, hope and dread. They braced rigidly behind their chairs while the upperclass leaned against theirs, waiting for "seats." Breen toyed with his silverware, idly trying to flip his spoon into his water glass by dropping the glass on it. Philo furtively studied the square profile of his jaw, the heavy, handsome forehead, the dark, smooth hair. Along with being the highest-greased man in the company, Breen looked like the hero of a nineteenth-century boys' novel.

"Castigliano," said the firstie, dropping his glass and watching the spoon flip and miss once again.

"Sir."

"Know any cheers?"

"Yes sir."

"We'll do some later; get you guys up for Army. Know your rates?"

"Yes, sir," said Castigliano. Philo could tell from his voice that he was trying to sound serious, but this, for the Wop, was always a doomed effort.

"How many panes of glass in the skylight of Memorial Hall, Wop?"

"Sir, there are four hundred and eighty-nine panes, sir."

"Bet your ass?"

"Cover you and raise you one cheek, sir."

Somehow when Tony said things, they were funny. Philo wondered why. Now, if *he* had said something like that. . . .

"You count 'em, Wop? Or did someone tell you that?"

"They had to tell me, sir. I can't count that high."

"How long have you been in the Navy, Castigliano?"

"Since Moby Dick was a minnow, sir."

The upperclass laughed, and Philo felt a flush of anger. It wasn't the Reef Points response at all, and yet they accepted it. If I'd said that, he thought, they'd have me doing pushups in a flash.

Keyes was talking; his new squad leader. Slight, blond, quick, Philo knew little about him, other than that he was a fanatic for cleanliness; rumor had it that he and Breen, his roommate, scrubbed the little balcony outside their room, a locale that nobody else cleaned or even used, with a nailbrush, just so they wouldn't have to look out at the seagull scat. "Funny," Keyes was saying, "but you can't hug center stage all day, Wop. You got to give some of your classmates a chance."

"Yes sir."

"Engel. That a Jewish name, stud?"

"Yes sir."

"Name some famous Jews for us, Engel."

"David Ben-Gurion, sir; Albert Einstein, sir; the—"

"Not politicians, Engel. Not scientists. I mean *famous*."

"Yes, sir. Sir, there's Admiral Rickover, sir; Commodore Uriah Phillips Levy, sir; Rear Admiral Morris Smellow, sir."

"Who's Admiral Smellow?"

"Class of '23, sir, he graduated with Arleigh Burke."

"With *who*, Engel?"

"*Admiral* Arleigh Burke, sir."

"Well, I guess that counts . . . that's pretty good, Engel."

Something green was moving among the tables, just outside Philo's narrow line of vision. He was too intent on Breen's voice, waiting for his turn to be quizzed, to wonder what it was.

"McGiffin. What are our chances this year against—"

"Excuse me," said someone. Breen turned, annoyed, then came to attention. Facing him now Philo saw a small man in Marine service dress, with the long curved mameluke sword belted at his waist. He was looking at Breen's collar. "A striper," he said thoughtfully. "A man of your rank in the Brigade should set a good example for the troops—don't you think?"

"Yes sir," said Breen.

"You're aware of the regs concerning conduct in the mess hall?"

"Yes sir," said Breen again, sounding just a little puzzled.

"I'm going to have to place you on report, Mister Breen, for handling table materials before 'seats' is given. Article oh-seven-oh-four. Mate, take his name."

"Yes sir," said Breen, his voice again perfectly respectful. The mate, looking sorry and at the same time gleeful, stepped up with his pad. Breen gave him his name and company. When the Marine left Breen looked down at the spoon, which had fallen, unnoticed by anyone, into the glass at last. "Well, bite my ass," he said.

"Black Bart strikes again," said Keyes. "That's ten and two as I call it. I hear last night he got a second class at watch squad inspection for not polishing his zipper. But this was a clean score. I guess that'll teach you a lesson, you blot on the blue and gold, you."

Keyes' tone was so dry, the spectacle of a firstie being papped out of the blue so unexpected, that Philo, unaware, let himself smile. One of the third class, standing opposite him, tried to signal, but he didn't notice.

"Brigade . . . seats."

"McGiffin!" said Keyes suddenly, as they sat down, the plebes scrambling to hit their chairs before the upperclass. "What's so goddamned funny?"

"Uh, nothing, sir."

"I think our boy here was laughing at you, Brad."

"Are you laughing at me, Mouse?"

"No sir."

"You were laughing at Mister Keyes."

"No sir."

"Were you laughing at Major Bartranger?"

"No sir."

"Then what the hell were you grinning at, McGiffin?" shouted Breen, making conversation stop all over that part of the mess hall.

"Nothing, sir," said Philo. Already, braced up as he was, he could feel sweat beginning to gather at the point of his nose.

"That's grounds for a section eight, isn't it?" said Keyes, regarding Philo as if he was a seagull. "Laughing at nothing?"

"Are you striking for a section eight, McGiffin?"

"I'll find out, sir."

"What do you mean, you'll find out? Don't you know what a section eight is?"

"No sir," said Philo desperately. "Sir, would you like some cow, sir?"

"If I want any of your friggin' cow I'll ask for it!"

"Yes sir."

"Mouse," said Keyes gently, "you think you're a right smart little sea lawyer, don't you?"

"No sir."

"You think Mister Breen and I are right out of the comics, don't you?"

"No sir."

"Well, what *do* you think of us, then, McGiffin?"

Philo sat silent, sweating steadily now, like a spring. Even with his eyes straight ahead he could feel the firsties staring at him. He could not think of any acceptable answer.

"Well?" screamed Breen.

"I'll find out, sir."

"My God, Mouse, don't you even know what you think? What kind of farce are we staging here?"

"I think we have a little problem at this table, Brad," said Keyes. "And it starts with M-C-G and ends with F-I-N."

The food came: salisbury steaks. Philo got the tray and poured the hot grease off into his coffee cup and passed it down for Engel to hold while Breen and Keyes selected the biggest. "Elephant turds again," muttered Keyes. "Mouse, what's the main course tomorrow night?"

He spoke automatically, passing the mashed potatoes and the gravy boat. It scorched his fingers but he didn't feel it. "Sir, the main course for evening meal tomorrow is—"

Then nothing. Suddenly his brain was empty. He felt utter terror, and stuttered, holding the hot gravy boat as he tried to concentrate. "Sir—"

"Knock 'em together! I said, what are we eating? Tomorrow night?"

A tray of peas and carrots bumped at his arm. He passed the gravy on and turned, and heard at the same instant Castigliano's subvocal whisper, a single word: *"Jooze."*

"Roast prime rib of beef *au jus*, sir," he said.

"That's some better," said Keyes. "How about dessert."

Thank God, the menus were standard. "Cookies and ice cream, sir."

A minute or two passed. At the far end of the table someone began to tell a story about a guy who joined the Foreign Legion. "So he says, 'What do you do around here for girls?' And the sergeant says, 'You go out back of the mess tent, and you'll see this *camel.*'" Philo, half-listening, reached for his fork and knife and slashed the elephant turd into inch-square pieces. With his chin in it was hard to chew, but he got the first chunk halfway down his throat, where it stuck. As he began to cough a rising clamor came from the far end of the mess hall, almost a quarter mile away.

"So the next evening he's hard up, and he goes out behind the mess tent."

"McGiffin," said Breen, his mouth full.

"Yes sir."

"You don't like it here much, do you?"

"Yes sir."

"You do like it here? Where assholes like us abuse you all the time?"

"Yes sir."

"And there's two camels standing there. One of them is old and ugly and all caked with camel shit."

"Do *you* like it in Slack Thirty-four, Castigliano?" said Keyes.

"Yes sir, I love it here, sir."

"Why, Wop?"

"Because all my friends are here, like you and Mister Breen, sir."

"The second camel is young and pretty, with long eyelashes, and has a beautiful Persian carpet over her humps."

"We're not your friends, Wop!"

"Horseshit!"

The clamor grew closer. Now they could see successive tables standing up and shouting. The cheer was traveling toward them like a wave. Then it was on them and the plebes at the next table were on their feet shouting: "Deck the Halls!"

"With Army Balls!" screamed Philo, Castigliano, and Engel, primally, as loud as they could. They sat down again. Philo felt a little better.

"So he's working away with his pants down and the sergeant comes around the side of the tent. Next thing he knows he's up to his neck in sand and the ants are picking his nose for him."

"Why isn't your chin in, Mouse?"

"Aye aye, sir."

"What?"

"No excuse, sir."

"Stand by for a broadside! Starboard side! In batteryyyy—"

The three plebes stuck their jaws out and waggled them.

"Fire!"

"Boom, sir!" they screamed as their jaws went in.

"And he says to the sergeant, 'What the hell? You told me if I got horny to go out back and screw the camel, didn't you?'"

"You think we're pricks, don't you, Mouse?" said Keyes.

"No sir."

"Go on. Tell the truth."

"And the sergeant says, 'Yeah, you idiot, but *you were fucking the officers' camel.*'"

"Yeah," said Breen around a mouthful of potatoes. "Verbal carry-on, Mouse. Ten seconds. Unload that suffering candy-ass little soul of yours."

Philo took a breath. A certain facility of speech was expected in verbal carry-ons. "Breen," he began, "I think you're the biggest dickhead in the Brigade. You're as squared away as a bowling ball and as good looking as a pile of Pekingese shit. Your girl gives blow jobs to mokes and you're too dumb to be in the Marine Corps, *sir!*"

The second class broke up; even the third class felt free to snicker. None of the plebes moved a muscle of their faces. Philo wound his fists into balls under the table and waited for the firsties' reaction.

"McGiffin."

"Yes sir."

"That hurt my feelings. About the Marine Corps, I mean."

"Yes sir."

A drumming clamor from Kim's table broke out, twelve men hammering on the wood with cups and dishes and fists and empty pitchers, and then as the din reached its peak jumped up and unleashed another cheer.

"Rip 'em up!"

"Tear 'em up!"

"Give 'em hell!" came from the next table to theirs; and then they were rising, screaming:

"*Laundry!*"

Phil and the other plebes resumed their seats and their braces. Breen, though, ignored the interruption. "So for hurting my feelings, why don't you clamp on for a while."

"You gave him verbal carry-on, Brad," said Keyes.

"And now I'm clamping him on. You got a problem with that?"

"No," said Keyes.

"McGiffin! What are you waiting for? A letter from home?"

"Aye aye, sir."

Clamped on, supporting himself on the edge of the table with his elbows and knees, free of the chair and the floor, Philo stared ahead. From beside him he could hear Castigliano and Engel chewing. The sweat began to drip into his eyes, but he couldn't spare a hand to wipe it away.

"McGiffin," said Breen, "You and I are going to be spending some time together. I don't mean just on the table. You better start checking your comearound log, breaking free a few periods. I don't know what Mister Singleterry's been doing with you, but whatever it is, it wasn't enough."

"Aye aye, sir."

"You better get squared away, McGiffin. Squared away, and fast. There's no slack in my company. No place for whimpy crybabies. You haven't got much longer to get wise. McGiffin. You understand me?"

"Yes sir," said Philo. He watched the drops plop between his elbows, forming a dark spot on the tablecloth.

He hated Breen, he realized. But what good was that?

*   *   *

"How's your new table?" asked Gray, when they were back in
their room that evening.

"The usual—unsat. How's yours?"

"Not too bad. I think the worst of it's over."

"For you, maybe."

"Maybe," Gray smiled. "You seen the first set grease list?"

"Aptitude? No."

"It's on the bulkhead by the company office. I did all right."

"That's good, Dick. I'm glad you got good grease."

"Oh, there's a message for you on the desk. The mate brought it
around." Gray glanced at the door. "It's from the Snorkel."

"Thanks."

Lieutenant (jg) Portley wanted to see him in the company office at
1930. Philo glanced at his watch. Ten minutes. He stripped off the
sweatsoaked uniform and shirt and showered and put on fresh working blues, brushed off his tie, bent a new spiffy. At 1929:55 he
knocked on the closed door and entered. Two paces, come to attention, remove cap, sound off. "Midshipman Fourth Class McGiffin,
sir."

"Relax, Mister McGiffin," said Portley. "Sit down."

He sat. He had never been in the company office before. It was
more luxurious than the midshipmen's rooms, with a dark walnut-
grain desk, green drapes, a slightly darker green carpet, and heavy
vinyl-covered green armchairs. A Naval Institute print of the
Monitor-Virginia battle hung on one wall and a large color photograph of a surfaced submarine at speed on the other. A bowl of
small colored spheres sat on Portley's desk, on the blotter, in front of
the marble and brass pen set with his name on it.

"Do you smoke?" said the lieutenant.

"No, sir."

"Care for some Trix?" He held out the bowl. Philo looked at it
and then took a few. Two of them, one yellow and one reddish-
orange, fell to the carpet. He bent to pick them up and then held
them, feeling them grow wet in his hand, knowing he couldn't eat
them in front of Portley once they had fallen on the floor, but not
knowing where to put them. At last he unbuttoned his shirt pocket
and slipped them in and buttoned the flap again.

"Mister McGiffin, I understand you've been doing some running for the battalion team. Track, is it?"

"Cross-country, sir. Track is a spring sport."

Portley looked displeased, but went on. "That's very good. Very good. Sports are an important part of character building here. My company, the Eighth, was fieldball champs for our battalion my first class year. We had some good times."

Philo said nothing; it was not a question. He wondered what the lieutenant wanted. He ate the last three Trix, mashing them in a dry mouth.

"Mister McGiffin . . . Philo?"

"Yes sir."

"Philo, I wanted to talk to you about your career here. In some ways you're doing well. Sports, P.E., more than adequate. Your grades aren't quite so outstanding, but with some luck on your finals you'll be sat your first semester. Pretty good for plebe year, after all." Portley tipped his hands and studied him over them, smiling.

"Yes sir," said Philo. Portley's steady smile made him aware that he was sitting on the last two inches of the armchair. He tried to relax, sliding himself back and letting his spine curve. He thought of crossing his legs, but that might be disrespectful. He looked down at his shoes.

"But everything isn't rosy," said Portley. "Primarily we have two problems. Do you know what they might be?"

"Ah . . . conduct? Sir?"

"That's one of them. You've built up a lot of demerits. Forty or fifty more this semester will get you in real trouble. But that's not the worst thing." Portley tossed back a few more Trix and smiled. "Lots of guys have conduct trouble. You know that Marc Mitscher bilged out and his dad had to get him reappointed. Chester Nimitz used to have beer parties on the roof of the second wing and throw the bottles down into T-court. Cushing resigned to avoid getting thrown out, and of course your—namesake—was no saint."

Philo laughed dutifully.

"So conduct is a problem, yes. But I hope you're learning what not to do." Portley looked expectant.

"Yes sir. I think I'm learning, sir."

"Good. But the second problem we have is a little bigger. It's aptitude. That's a different thing entirely."

"Sir?"

"Philo, have you seen the grease list—I mean the professional aptitude ladder?"

"Not yet, sir. I understood it was up but I haven't looked at it yet."

"Well, I'd hoped you'd seen it already—but I'll be blunt. You're rated last in the company. Very bad marks from your upperclass, and even your peer grease, from your own classmates, is twenty-sixth out of twenty-six."

Philo looked at the rug.

"In view of that, I thought I'd give you some advice. Have you in here early and look at what you can expect your fifty-four A to look like."

"Yes sir." He got up to look at the paper Portley slid across the desktop. He read it, looked at the check marks neat in their boxes. Goal setting and achievement: marginal. Subordinate management and development: not applicable. Working relations: bottom 30%. Professional knowledge: typically effective. USNA support and loyalty: typically effective. Application/Industry: typically effective.

"You can see," said Portley. "We're giving you a break on most of those top ones. You try hard; everybody can see that."

Philo turned the page. Judgment: bottom 10%. Personal behavior: marginal. Moral courage: marginal. Maturity: bottom 10%. Imagination: bottom 30%. Forcefulness: bottom 1%. Analytical ability: marginal. Reliability: marginal. Growth potential: unknown.

And the last, biggest block: overall ranking. He already knew what that would be: bottom one percent. He read the "remarks" section, beginning to feel sick. Phrases jumped out at him, stopping his eye for a moment until the awful curiosity that leads one to explore an open wound pushed him on to the next. "During plebe summer, performance at an acceptable level, bearing poor . . . lacking in properly forceful, confident attitude . . .inadequate application to conditions of midshipman life . . . poor relations with upperclass . . . could conceivably serve adequately on a staff, but severe deficiencies in command presence would handicap him as a line officer."

Portley was looking at him. He put the paper back on the desk. "What do you think, Philo?"

"I don't . . . I don't think it's quite fair, sir. I've been giving it all I've got."

"I don't doubt that a bit. And that counts in your favor, believe me. Someone average who tries hard often gets the nod over the talented man who doesn't really care about what he's doing." Portley scraped the 54-A back and forth across his blotter. "But let's see . . . is it *fair?* I think it is. Let me read you one of the inputs. Here it is . . . an evaluation report from the P.E. department, one of the swim coaches. You've got a good overall grade in P.E., so that's why I'm picking this report out. It's about your performance on the Water Entry."

The Water Entry: just the phrase made him cold and dizzy. Looking down at the green carpet he saw again the smooth, rippled blue-green of the natatorium, sixty feet straight down from the platform just under the skylight. The class had warmed up with a few sputtering laps around the pool, and then the coach, a young guy with the vast shoulders and shaven body of a former Olympic contender, had showed them how to climb the swaying Jacob's ladder that led straight up from the water, up, up, till he stood far and foreshortened and small above them, the sunlight pouring down around him, his voice falling faint toward the shivering swimmers. "You'll step up to the edge. Cross your arms over your chest, like this: that'll be over your Mae West if you ever have to do this for real. If there's any seas up you wait for the roll. Time your step-off so the hull's rolling away from you as you drop. Lot of guys broke their backs in the war 'cause they forgot that. Then—as you drop—tilt your head back. Be sure and cross your legs or you'll be singin' soprano for a while. Drop straight, come up, swim to the side—like this." And he took a breath, stepped off, dropped, dropped, coming down through the sunlight, drifting down, legs crossing themselves at the last moment, and hit and came up and took three strokes and pulled himself out, water beading on the smooth bunched muscles of his arms. "Okay—first section, into the water. Up that ladder! No waiting at the top—just step up and step off. Let's go!"

And he remembered how he'd followed the rest up the ladder, closing his eyes from time to time as they got higher and higher, and how the water dropped away below them and the pool got smaller, and the light brighter, more golden, around them as they ascended; and the way his classmates joked nervously as they hung on the ladder waiting; and then over the steel rail to the platform, metal decking, perforated so you could see right through, all the way down. *All the way down.* And as he stared down the man ahead stepped off and disappeared and sailed down, and he saw the white bloom of foam and then the man came up and shook his head and swam off and someone nudged him from behind and then he stood there, toes over the edge, hands locked on the rail, looking down.

"Come on," shouted the coach. "Jump."

The faces below turned up. "I can't take heights," he whispered.

"What?" said Portley.

"I said, I'm afraid of heights, sir."

"So it seems. According to this report it took the coach and your classmates half an hour to talk you into jumping. And when you did you forgot to cross your legs."

Philo nodded. "Hey," said Portley, his voice changing. "Hey. I didn't get you in here to upset you. Hey."

"I'm all right," he said, enraged at himself. "Sir."

"Look," said Portley. "I know it gets rough sometimes. Not everybody can do it. Have you thought about getting out? There's nothing wrong with it, if you've given it a fair shot. And you have."

"I'm not getting out."

"You've thought that over?"

"Every night, sir."

"All right. Good. I'm glad to hear you say that, Philo. I *personally* think that with some work you can turn this around. Study and application of the proper leadership techniques—that's what's needed here. I've got some books I'd like you to look over."

"Thank you, sir."

Portley assumed a solemn look. "And another thing—something you've probably considered already: you've got a *name.* Philo McGiffin. Right? You've got to live up to that. Can you do it? I'm sure you can."

"Yes sir," said Philo.

*   *   *

When he left Portley's office at last he felt drained, used, like the fender on a YP that has been bashed against the pier so often its resilience is gone. He chopped into the head and washed his face. Wiping it with a paper towel, looking at himself in the mirror, he felt rage and fear and disgust with himself. *Christ!* he thought. Why did you have to cry? That's really the way to impress Snorkel with your self-control. When his eyes looked more normal he chopped back down the corridor and into his room. Zeard and Gray were deep in study; neither did more than glance up as he came in.

"Carry on, guys," he said.

"Uh," said Zeard to his *Principles of Naval Engineering*. "Anything important?"

"What?"

"Portley."

"Oh. No," said Philo. "Nothing important." But as he dropped into his chair and flipped open his own assignment he reflected suddenly that it was these people, his own classmates, his own roommates perhaps, who had greased him at the bottom of the whole company, and he felt a surge of bitterness. Before he could think much about it, though, there was a quick double knock at the door. A youngster came in in white works. In one hand he carried an AWOL bag. "Shh," he said quickly, before they could react or sound off. "Carry on, guys. Want to buy a sandwich?"

"Sir?"

"Got PBAJ, baloney, ham; chips, cokes, Snickers bars. Cheap and fresh. What d'you need?"

Zeard got a sandwich; Gray settled for a bar of gedunk. Philo was hungry but almost broke: he was still paying off his loan. "No, thanks," he said.

"Phil, you want something?" said Gray. "I'll lend you a buck."

"No thanks."

"You sure? You won't get much to eat down at the tables."

"I said no."

"Okay, okay. Just trying to help out."

"I don't need your help!"

They all, including the youngster, looked at him a little strangely, but no one said anything more. The third class counted out Gray's change, stuck his head out to scan the corridor, and then was gone, swinging his bag of illicit goodies behind him. Philo looked at Zeard, wolfing down his sandwich single-mindedly; at Gray, the high greaser, eating his candy with a pious expression; and suddenly he had to get out of that room, at least for a while, or he would hit the window screaming. He got up and put on his hat and reefer. "Where you off to?" said Zeard, around a mouthful of ham.

"I'm going to sign out to the library. Be back at taps."

"Better be," said Gray.

"I said I would, goddamn it, Dick!"

Gray looked up at him in surprise; perhaps—or was he only imagining it, hoping for it—with surprised respect as well. He grabbed a couple of books at random and went out. He signed out at the mate's station and ran down five flights to the 0 deck.

Outside Bancroft Hall the November air tasted like fresh cider and the stars and the wind felt clean and new. He walked slowly across the pavement toward the library. They had study carrels there. Maybe for a while he could be alone. Just study and forget it all. But when at last he sat in the little soundproof box, staring at the lines of print and figures in the chemistry book, he found he couldn't keep his mind on more than four words at a time.

He got up and strolled aimlessly through the library. Mids—upperclass, for the most part—sat sprawled at study tables, at carrels, absorbed in their work. A few wore earphones and nodded their heads slightly as they read to music.

I don't know what to do, he thought.

Live up to your name, Snorkel had said. Granted that anything Portley came out with was by definition worthless, an axiom widely accepted in the 34th and indeed through the Sixth Battalion, the advice sounded as if there was something there. His name . . . his damn name. It wasn't even his, somebody had made it up for him. If it wasn't for the viciousness of coincidence, he could have kept a low profile; sneaked through; had a chance to bag it once in a while. His name made him as visible here as a red ant in a black nest. And they told him to "live up" to it!

Damn it all anyway, he thought. What was all this about McGiffin? He gave up all thought of studying and went back to the

reference desk and when the librarian looked up from her copy of
Cosmo asked her about it.

A few minutes later he was back in the carrel, with a couple of
books and a copy of the Naval Institute *Proceedings*. One of the books
was quite old, by someone called Richard Harding Davis. He looked
through them, reading carefully for about a half hour, and then
leaned back in his chair and thought.

The stories tallied—some of them. There seemed to be a lot of
conflict between the "legend," as Corpen had told it at the tables
plebe summer, and what the books said were the facts; and some of
them disagreed with each other. What was the truth? It was hard to
tell.

The original McGiffin, Class of 1882, was a Philo N., not Philo
T. He was from Pennsylvania—*like me*, he thought vaguely, flipping
the pages. As Sweetman's history of the Academy said:

> Another who did not make the cut was Philo N. McGiffin, the
> wild man of the Class of 1882, whose legendary exploits live
> on in the collective memory of the brigade of midshipmen. In
> the words of his boyhood friend Richard Harding Davis: "To
> him discipline was extremely irksome. He could maintain it
> among others, but when it applied to himself it bored him."
> One of McGiffin's most noted misdeeds involved a decorative
> pyramid of cannon balls from the War of 1812 which stood on
> the landing of his floor in the New Quarters. To amuse himself
> one evening he rolled them down the stairs one at a time, with
> predictably ruinous effects on the steps, banisters, and walls
> encountered in their descent. For this he was confined on
> board the *Santee*, where he talked the old salt who kept the
> brig into giving him six powder charges. Upon his release, he
> used them to fire a midnight salute from the antique cannons
> flanking the Mexican Monument. McGiffin's daring was not
> demonstrated only in pranks, however. On another occasion he
> rescued two children from a burning house, an act for which he
> was commended by the secretary of the navy.

Prevented from following a naval career under his own flag,
McGiffin offered his services to the Imperial Chinese Navy.

DAVID POYER

Although the mandarins who interviewed him made it clear
that they considered the twenty-four-year-old applicant a pre-
sumptuous boy, he did so well in the professional examinations
they gave him that he was appointed professor of seamanship
and gunnery at the Chinese Naval Academy at Tientsin. In a
few years he was a commander. Classmates in the U.S. Asiatic
Squadron, none of whom had reached the rank of lieutenant,
visited his palatial quarters and wondered who had really had
the luck. But McGiffin lived for the day when he would be
readmitted to the U.S. Navy. In 1894, he resigned his commission and had arranged passage home when war broke out between China and Japan. It was not McGiffin's fight but he
believed that honor obliged him to see it through.

"The library will be closing in twenty minutes. Twenty minutes.
Thank you."

The morning of September 17, 1894, found McGiffin serving
as adviser to the captain of the battleship *Chen Yuen*, one of
two new capital ships in a Chinese squadron lying off the
mouth of the Yalu River. The approach of a Japanese squadron
precipitated the first major sea fight of the battleship era. With
twelve vessels each, the opposing forces were numerically
equal, but the better-armed and better-handled Japanese
squadron soon gained the upper hand. McGiffin assumed command of the *Chen Yuen* when her captain fled the bridge early
in the engagement, in the course of which the ship took more
than 150 hits. When the battered *Chen Yuen* reached port, she
had only three shells left for her big guns. McGiffin was badly
wounded. Threatened with blindness and in constant pain, he
shot himself in a New York hospital in 1897.

Philo leaned back and thought. It was quite a story; sort of funny,
and sort of brave, and sort of tragic, near the end; blowing his brains
out after leaving a last joking note pinned to the pillow: "Look alive
that the bed is not set on fire by my shot. My compliments and

adieus to all. I regret that my destination must remain to you unknown, but you may guess. Apologies for the row."

But so what? Philo T. McGiffin thought. It was an entertaining
story, sure. He would have liked to meet old Philo N., Class of '82.
But it really didn't have anything to do with him, almost a hundred
years later. He was nothing like that, could never be like that. The
fact that their names were the same . . . that was just an unfortunate
coincidence.

He sat for a while longer, then got up and drank some water at
the scuttlebutt to try to forget his hunger. He stared for a while at a
painting of the *Olympia* at Manila and then went back to the carrel.
He studied the picture in the old book of McGiffin after the battle of
the Yalu. The tall man with the elegant handlebar moustache stood
jauntily, one hand tucked in his pistol belt, his bare legs showing
through great tears in his white uniform trou. A stain of blood
showed at his thigh. Around his head and over one eye was wound
white bandage. He must, Philo thought, have been in pain even
then, and the fleet he had trained for ten years was at the bottom of
the China Sea.

Yet he stood *jauntily.* . . .

What was Philo N. trying to tell him?

When he looked at the bulkhead clock it was ten minutes to taps.
He got up hurriedly and checked out the Davis book, intending to
read the rest of it later.

When he got back to the room he found Zeard and Gray and
Kaufman dressing. Zeard was in sweatgear, boondockers, and white
bayonet belt. Gray was wearing his highcollared white service
blouse with dungaree trousers and his fencing mask. Kaufman had
on his PJs and a white beret made out of a cap cover.

"What the hell's going on here?"

"Got to dress out," said Zeard. "Word is there's a spontaneous
pep rally sked for right after taps. Uniform is optional."

"How can it be scheduled if it's spontaneous?"

"Get with the program, Mouse. You didn't really want to sleep,
did you?"

"Look, Howie, I don't call you 'Weird.' I don't think it's right my
own classmates should call me 'Mouse.'"

"It doesn't mean anything. Look at the nicknames the firsties have. Whimp—Snatch—Time Warp—"

"Well, I don't like it."

"Better get hot," said Rollo. "It's almost time."

With only a couple of minutes to get ready Philo contented himself with changing his class shoes for his running slicks and pulling on a black watch cap. He was just finishing when the taps bell rang and suddenly, like a flash flood in an arroyo, the corridor was wall to wall with roaring plebes. He followed the current at full tilt through the sixth, fourth, and second wings and down into T-court, pausing only long enough to grab some toilet paper from a head on 2–1.

Tecumseh Court, lit by floods and by the headlights of three of the big football team buses the mids called "milk cartons," was a solid mass of people, screaming and shouting, rushing about in eddies of twenty or fifty. He stood at the edge of it for a moment, hearing the cries of "Beat Army! Beat Army!" coming back from the enclosing granite arms of Mother Bancroft, and then someone shoved him forward from behind and he was one with the rest.

Some time later, initial hoarseness and a repetitive bellowing from the PA system set up on the Rotunda steps combined to quiet things enough that an address was possible. First to the mike was the Supe, a notorious football fan. They heard the old man out in near silence, interrupted only by the wheezing coughs of the goat, which stood tightly reined off to the side. When he stepped down up popped the Brigade cheerleader, a peppy little guy in a gold and blue blazer, who led the plebes (and there were upperclass there too, and more of them hanging out of the windows that surrounded the court) in the 3-N cheer. The band struck into the derisive strains of "The Old Gray Mare" and then, after they had roared that out and gotten somewhat in tune, "The Goat is Old and Gnarly."

> *The goat is old and gnarly, And he's never been to school*
> *But he can take the bacon from the worn-out Army mule;*
> *He's had no education But he's brimmin' full of fight,*
> *And Bill will feed on Army mule tonight*
>
> *Army, Army, call the doctor,*
> *Army, Army, call the doctor,*

Army, Army, call the doctor,
You're all in, down and
                    —Whoa! Any oats today, lady? No?
                         Giddyap!
Army, Army, call the doctor,
You're all in, down and OUT!

Looking up from the old uneven bricks of the court, Philo, short as he was, could see everything. It was suddenly an amphitheatre, a vast *son et lumière:* the lights cutting the dark to glow brilliantly on the stage, the steps, flanked by cannon; the gray vertical cliffs of the first and second wings, lit and streaming with giant posters painted by the first and second batts; the immense sense of expectancy, of heightened life, of inexorability inherent in mass and spirit. The air was chill and gritty in his lungs but from being pressed among warm bodies, from screaming and jumping in the cheers and singing he did not feel the cold, was in fact sweating as the next man up mounted the stairs. George Mason—the coach! And after he spoke and their voices were hoarse again someone even better—Major Thayer, the West Point exchange officer. He looked harried; this had been a bad week for him. His car was ruined, and each morning he came in there was something novel in his office—a torpedo, two hundred cans of foamed shaving cream, a drawerful of goat manure. Even as he tried to speak twelve second class on 5–2 were bricking up his door so that in the morning, unless he climbed up to the window from outside, there would to all intents and purposes be no office there at all. When he opened his mouth against the lights not a word he said was audible; seconds later he was only rescued from destruction by the watch squad, who linked arms and shielded him as the Supe dragged him back into the Rotunda, still waving the little "Beat Navy" flag he must have hidden for months, God alone knew where.

Then the band again—"Anchors Aweigh." And the doors of the buses opened and the Team came out of them, in full ball gear, carrying their helmets, and were caught up by nine hundred crazed plebes. This was the moment and Philo cocked his arm and sent roll after roll of paper spinning out over the Court, unrolling as they flew, drifting down on the struggling cheering hundreds in long twisting arches of white tissue. And then suddenly he was in motion, they were all in motion, they were running, it didn't matter where, up the Rotunda steps and through 1–1 into the Hall, shouting and screaming, knocking one of the second string guards silly against a low overhead as they ran him bodily toward the seventh wing.

The night was young. At 2300 the Brigade streamed out to Farragut, plebes, upperclass, everyone, to the bonfire. For weeks waste wood and trash, old desks, driftwood, pallets, sheathing, had been saved for a heap that was now at least forty feet high, with an effigy of the Black Knight staked on top. There was utter quiet on the field as it was torched by the team captain. The flames ran up the side slowly, despite pails of diesel oil from the YPs, but then they bit in and the whole pile began to steam and then glow and then roar. The flame pushed them back and the mass of men pushed them forward, the screaming beginning again, and the heat began to blast their skin, lighting up the seawall and the thousands of faces and the crowd pushed at his back, he was at the front, the whitehot heart of the flames only feet away, his hands could not protect his face, he couldn't breathe, he was too close, but he was screaming with the rest and *he did not care.* . . .

Struggling back to his room later, tired and hoarse as a wolf after full moon, he felt something crackle as he crawled into his pad. He took it to the door, read it, and cursed, but half-heartedly, as if he had expected this or something like it. Darrin was SIR, sick in room, and he was next on window closing detail. He looked at the corridor clock. One A.M. Too early to do it yet, but not enough time to make it worth while going to sleep, either. He sat instead at his desk in the dark room, listening to his roommates snoring, and looked out of the window for a while at the stars.

Maybe, he thought, maybe the simplest thing to do is just to put in my chit.

He wouldn't be the first. He knew a hungry plebe on the second batt tennis team, pretty good man, but he'd made the mistake of lying to an upperclass about a doughnut; said he was taking it out of the mess hall for a firstie, and the upperclass called his bluff and he was out, canned in a midnight meeting of the Honor Committee in the warren of windowless rooms over the Rotunda. There were the gays, the druggies, and the guy who wouldn't carry a rifle plebe summer; there were lots gone by now; one of them, in their own company, who hadn't been able to pass the mile run, going slower and slower in each of six tries until they took him to sick bay and found he had something wrong with his blood.

But those were different. They hadn't resigned; they'd been forced out, for reasons honorable or dishonorable; but they hadn't quit; they'd been dropped. Come end of first semester and grades and there would be a lot more joining them, and not only plebes, either. Attrition was high at the Boat School.

But voluntary resignations . . . they happened; but not many of them. For some reason, hell though it was, most Annapolis men wanted to stay.

He thought about that for a while, and then thought about old Philo Norton, about what it took to write a give-a-shit note when you were going blind and ready to cash in; and about turning around and going back to fight a war when you knew the captains were cowards and the supply system so crooked none of your shells would explode because they were filled with sand instead of a bursting charge. He shook his head. Philo N. had been a nut, that was all. A nut . . . but one with undeniable style.

He stuck his head out into the corridor again to check the clock, and was startled to see three men in black walking down the darkened hall. They saw him, too, and stopped. "Who's that?" the lead one whispered.

"McGiffin. Sir."

"Oh, Mouse. It's me. Cross."

Philo examined the plebe ball player. He was all in black; the dark blue class uniform, black wool sweater, watch cap. Black gloves. There was something dark over his face, too. "Hey, Truck. What's going on?"

"We're going over the Wall."

"Frenching out? Really?"

"Sure. Want to come?"

"Who is it?" whispered one of the others, who had stopped behind Cross, listening.

"McGiffin. Okay if he comes with us?"

"McGiffin? Shit!" whispered one of the others. Philo recognized
Wiebels, the youngster who had seconded Dubus in the fight at
Macdonough Hall, and then realized, with a flash of surprise and
instant fear, that the one who was speaking was no other than Dirty
Dan himself. *"Christ,* be serious, Cross. When you're going over the
wall you want somebody you can depend on. Somebody with balls.
This guy's the max pussy of the whole Brigade. Not only no, *hell*
no!"

"I can hack it if you can, fat man," hissed Philo, surprising himself and all of them.

Dubus laughed nastily. "You want to come? Cross, you really
want to take this scumbag along? Okay. It's your ass, McGiffin,
remember that. We can't carry you along if you whimp out,
though."

"Here," whispered Cross, coming up to him. "Smear this stuff
over your face. It's Marine camouflage. Get dressed quick. And
bring some cash."

"Where we going?" he whispered, not looking at the fat youngster, hating him more than he had ever hated anyone in his life.

"Buzzy's."

Fifteen minutes later the four of them, after a swift and silent
transit from shadow to shadow across the moonlit Yard, were crouching in the shrubbery between the Supe's house and the Chapel. The
lights of the dome were on and Philo, looking up at its towering bulk,
remembered the story that Philo N. had climbed it, had set his cap at
the very top, and then at the request of the Superintendent had
climbed it again and taken it down . . . but no, that was before this
chapel was even built, so it had to be legend, not fact . . . though
there was fact to every legend, and therefore, legend to every fact . . .
once you had the Idea for it all to coalesce round. . . .

"Ready?" whispered Cross. He seemed to be the leader, though
he was only a plebe. Maybe it was his size, or just the fact that he
had the kind of easy confidence that Philo envied above everything,

the kind that made men follow you without thought. The two third class nodded. Cross looked from left to right along the wall. An upper window in the Supe's house was lighted, but no one was visible. He stepped out from the bushes and leaned himself head first against the wall. "Dan, you first. You're the heaviest."

Dubus blundered out of the bushes, climbed up the plebe ball-player's broad back, and disappeared. They waited for a moment, listening, and then Wiebels went up, skinny and fast as a spider monkey. Philo hesitated, looking at Cross, who stood head bent, waiting, like Atlas. "Truck?"

"Yeah."

"How will you get over?"

"Stand on top and pull me up."

"Jesus, Truck, you weigh twice what I do."

"Then you stand here and I'll go first."

To his surprise it worked, though his shoulders felt as if they'd been crushed. The big plebe balanced like a cat atop the wall, sil-houetted plainly in the streetlight from the other side. He stretched an arm down. "Here," he whispered. "Jump up."

Philo straightened and looked up, at the night over the top of the wall that had restricted, enclosed, protected him for so long; and felt suddenly faint. Up till now it had been fruit, a lark; recon paint like a Marine, sneaking through the Yard at night. Now, seeing his class-mate balancing up there, between Yard and Outside, he realized suddenly just how non-reg this was. Not just "non-reg;" *big*, a Class A offense if they were caught. He felt his legs weaken, and took a step back from Cross's outstretched hand. "I—"

"Come on, Phil. Quick."

"I'm . . . afraid of heights."

"Jump, damn it!"

"I can't!"

"Come on, you pussy," hissed Cross. "Last chance—or you go back alone."

"Oh, Christ," said Philo, almost aloud. He wanted to go back to the Hall, back to his rack. He wanted to crawl back, to pussy out, whimp out, but from somewhere back in his head he remembered a word, a faded photograph: *jauntily* . . .

He put up his hand and jumped.

Cross caught him at the top of his spring and lifted him. It was as easy and smooth as an elevator, but the height was terrific in the darkness. He crouched on the narrow top of the wall, eyes squeezed tight, unable to look down ten feet to the pavement. He tried not to think about the enormity of his wrongdoing.

"What's the holdup, Cross?"

"It's Mouse. He's froze up."

"I knew it. Come on. We can't hang around here too long."

"Jesus, Philo. Come on, jump," said Cross.

"Jump, dammit," the youngsters muttered.

"I can't."

"Okay," said Cross. "Ready below." He pushed him off the wall. Philo gave a short scream as he fell and then Dubus and Wiebels caught him and dumped him on the cold bricks. Somewhere not far away, near the jimmylegs' station at Gate Three, a whistle shrilled. Cross swore and swung himself down. "Run!" he said. "Run like hell!"

Philo, lying at their feet, had a moment of panic. *Caught*—that was all he could think of. He grabbed at Wiebels, who shook him off. Cross pulled him up and shoved him into motion. They all began to run, but the brick walks were frozen slippery and Dubus, in front, went down and the rest of them tripped and flew over him like a team of drunken tumblers. The whistle blew again, nearer, echoing along the empty alleys, and Philo was up and free then, sprinting out desperately. Running like hell, he thought, is *something* at least I can do. The dark houses flew by, the mouths of narrow streets . . . he ducked into one and flattened himself behind a porch, panting.

Only then, in the sudden quiet, the yowl of a cat several houses off, did he realize that he was alone, outside the Wall. He stiffened with dread and stared around the empty street, the blank dead windows. The houses were full of sleeping civilians. If they found him here in the morning, would they turn him in? What would he say then?

"McGiffin," someone called hoarsely.

A rattle of footsteps, loud breathing, from the next street up. He peered over a trash can. It was Cross and Wiebels, with Dubus bringing up the rear. There was no one else with them. When they had passed he looked around once more, then took a deep breath, stepped out, and broke into a run again.

He found himself in front when they all fetched up, wheezing like a pack of sick dogs, in a blind alley somewhere between Maryland and Prince George Streets. "Christ, guys," panted Philo, "Now they know we're out here."

"They wouldn't have if you hadn't clutched, dickhead."

"Lay off him, Dan," said Wiebels. "We're all in this together now. Here. We might as well change clothes here."

"Civvies? *Jeez*—if they catch us in civvies, out here—"

"What's the matter with you, puke?" said Dubus, turning on him. "You afraid of starring on the Form One? It don't hurt. I knew it was a mistake to bring this whimp."

"You turd," said Philo. For some reason being here beyond the Wall, already a major violation of regulations, made him less afraid of Dubus, as if what he was doing was so enormous that lesser things did not matter at all. "I'll make it. Gimme a shirt."

"Here's a washcloth, too," said Wiebels. "Wipe that guck off your face."

Buzzy's was a dive, a basement bar not far from St. John's College. It was dim, noisy, and crowded with nodding long-haired guys and spaced-out, greasy-looking girls. The four mids, in civvy shirts and with their black stocking caps pulled low on their foreheads, got a table in the darkest corner, near the back door. A waiter brought them a pitcher of rather flat draft Pabst and four scuzzy glasses. Philo gulped his down. His throat was as dry as Worden Field in July. "Take it easy," said Wiebels, looking at him.

"Aye aye, sir."

"Hey . . . and can that shit, man. Hell, if we can french out together, I guess I can spoon you." They shook hands. "My first name's Pete. Friends call me Muff."

"*Muff?*"

"'Fraid so. My firstie stuck me with it during Hundredth Night buildup and I guess I'll be living with it forever."

Dubus looked disgusted. He demanded pretzels loudly from the waiter and when they came began stoking himself with them.

"You know . . . you're the first upperclass who's spooned me."

"Well, don't let it go to your head."

"What's the drill now . . . Muff?"

"This is it. Trouble isn't getting over the wall. It's what to do in Crabtown once you're out. It might be a little hairy gettin' back tonight, though. We better wait a while, let the jimmylegs go back to sleep."

Philo refilled his glass from the rapidly emptying pitcher, drank half of it, and leaned back. *Leaned back*. It felt great, just to sit here, no one looking at you, expecting things of you . . . he looked slowly around the room. Civilians. People his own age, but how different. They looked like another life form; unshaven, dressed in ragged jeans and parkas and fatigue jackets stencilled with studied obscenities. He glanced furtively at Dubus. He hated the fat youngster, but he was a mid, at least. He daydreamed briefly about a brunette, somewhat cleaner than the rest, who sat in a corner with three guys not far from them. To wake up in the morning with her. . . .

"Oh, Christ," he said suddenly.

"What?" said Cross.

"I just remembered. I got window-closing detail."

"Haw haw," said Dubus.

"You're kidding."

"Wish I was."

"Well, we'll get you back in time."

"Maybe," said Dubus. He belched, then produced an echo from the seat of his chair. "Ready for another pitcher, turkeys?"

"Sure," said Philo. He put a bill, his last money, on the table. He was feeling better than he had all that day. Looking again around the smoky interior of the bar, he decided that even the brunette made him queasy. He yearned for a flash of flame-bright hair.

"We'll be closin' soon, gennulmen."

"Another pitcher."

"You better take it easy," said the waiter. "Hear tell that there wall is hard to climb when you is drunk."

"What do you mean?"

"What wall?"

"One more pitcher, comin' up, gennulmen."

"All right," said Philo later, as they walked unsteadily, four abreast, down Prince George Street. It was extremely dark. "Where do we go back over?"

"Guy from the wrestling team recommends back of Porter Road. Rear of the officers' houses, there. Says the team uses it all the time."

"It isn't lit too good, that's right," said Dubus. "Okay, we'll try it there. McGiffin, we'll put you up first. Take a look around when you get up top."

The beer, Philo found, tended to displace his fear of heights, at least temporarily, though it was making him dizzy too. Lying flat along the foot-wide top of the wall, he examined the yard beyond. As Dubus had said, it was badly lit; great pools of shadow lay all around, and the deepest of them was between the side of the house and the wall. He leaned back over the Crabtown side.

"All clear. Come on over."

Dubus, again, came up first; then Wiebels. Then Cross. Philo, still lying flat along its top, feeling dizzier and dizzier, could hear their boonies scuffing against the concrete. Then they were all three over, and looking back up at him, when a light came on and a short, familiar figure stepped out from the shadows next to the house.

"Hello, gentlemen," said Major Bartranger. "What are you doing over Christmas leave? No travel plans, I hope?"

Above them all, flattened woozily on the top of the wall, Philo could see the three mids on the ground freeze. The flashlight held steady on them as Bartranger, and a shadowy figure that could only be the mate, came up to the wall. "Good evening, sir," he heard Muff Wiebels say. "Caught us fair and square."

"The only way I operate," said the Marine. "Mate, take their names."

Philo suddenly felt sick, and the dizziness began to spin the yard, the house, the men below in widening circles, centered on his stomach. He gave a despairing cry and let go of the wall. There was a moment of terror as he dropped and then a burst of stars as he hit something soft and then it was dark and he felt the flashlight under his hand. He threw it as hard as he could and heard it shatter on the far side of the wall. "Grab him!" came Cross' voice. The mate began to shout for help. Simultaneously the Mouse felt himself lifted by

both arms, felt himself rushing through the whirling darkness at an
enormous velocity. "Jesus!" said Wiebels, from somewhere behind
him. "Jesus! He took out Black Bart!"

"Let me down," said Philo.

"Screw that," said Dubus. "I'm carrying you all the way to the
Hall. What a maneuver."

"I hope I didn't hurt him."

"Are you kidding? You can't hurt a Marine by falling on his
head."

They paused for breath just inside the doors of 5–0. "Hear anything?" said Dubus, wheezing slightly, leaning against the coke
machine.

"Just the mate, yelling his head off."

"Let's hit the pad. Black Bart'll call a bed check for this."

"What time is it?"

"Four."

"Just time to close windows," said Philo. He shook off their supporting hands and took a couple of unsteady steps. "See you, guys."

"Hey," said Dubus. "You forgot something."

He was holding out his hand. This time, half-smiling, Philo took
it.

"Dirty Dan, to my friends," said Dubus.

"The Mouse," said Philo.

Once in his room again he felt safer. He changed his clothes for a
b-robe and klax and turned on the sink light to wash the last traces
of paint off his face. What the hell, he said to himself, swaying a
little. What the hell. For the first time, he realized, he had *delib-
erately* broken a regulation, and it was an experience in its own way
as enlightening and as much a rite of passage as his first redheaded
woman. He was sore in spots, now that the numbness of the beer
was wearing off, but he felt great. In the corridor he paused by a
window to look out and down over the lot. He was rewarded to see,
far below, the limping figure of a small Marine, with the mate, two
steps behind, carrying his hat.

Windows, he reminded himself.

He closed all the windows. He was as careful as ever, but he felt
different. He no longer trembled when he made a small noise. The

upperclass slumbered on. In the last room, Breen's room, he paused
on the way back to the door. The faint light from outside lay across
something glittering on the desk. A can of Brasso stood beside it.
McGiffin looked at the sword for a long time and then picked it up,
holding it by the rings of the harness so that it would not jingle, and
took it down the corridor to his own room.

"Wha'sa?" muttered Zeard, as Philo shook his rack.

"Howie. Got any chewing gum?"

"Huh? Wha' for you—"

"Lemme have some."

"In my drawer. Le'me g'some sleep, damn it."

"Go to hell, Howie," he whispered. He stood in front of the sink,
chewing Double Bubble ferociously, looking at himself in the
mirror.

I fell off the wall, he thought. I didn't "take out" Black Bart. I was
dizzy and I fell. Right?

That was right.

But Cross and Dubus and Wiebels thought he had, and respected
him for it. It looked like bravery; but it was not. But still it worked.

What did that mean? Was it only a matter of acting?

It was too deep for him. He was too sleepy and too drunk. But
still he stared at his eyes in the dark mirror, and still he chewed.
There was *something* there he had to figure out. And something that
had changed.

Yes. He even looked different.

He looked like Philo McGiffin.

CHAPTER EIGHT

Don't ask how far you're going to get in this
organization; ask how you got as far as you did.
— The Log

"You were supposed to get a haircut prior to this evolution, Mister," said Lieutenant Portley. "A haircut—not a bowling-ball polish. It's not funny."

"No, sir," said Zeard, dead-pan.

"Unless you plan to go Marine Corps, and even then. . . ." The company officer trailed off and bent closer. "Mister, uh, Zeard . . . where are your eyebrows?"

"Shaved them off, sir."

Portley stared up at Zeard. His nose lofty, the plebe was looking out past them all, past the Hall, out over the bay. Beside them Breen stood attentively, only the rapid noiseless tap of his fingers on the scabbard of his sword revealing impatience. It was the final inspection before the company boarded the buses for Philadelphia and the Army–Navy game.

"Shaved them off! Why?"

"Regulations, sir."

"What regulation says you shave your eyebrows?"

"Reg book, sir, article 1416, paragraph three. 'Hair and beards. Moustaches, beards, or other forms of facial hair shall not be permitted.'"

"This is the man I told you about, Lieutenant," said Breen. "The one I asked at the tables, which way sub props revolved."

"And?"

"'Round and round,' he said."

"I see," said Portley. Giving Zeard a last glance, he moved on along the rank. "Ah, McGiffin. Been thinking over our conversation?"

"Yes sir."

"What happened to the side of your face?"

"Uh . . . I fell, sir, after taps. It was dark."

"I see. Better get those shoelaces changed soon, they look frayed . . . All right. They look adequate, Mister Breen, not outstanding, but they'll do. I want strict accountability on the buses, now. No skylarking, no horseplay."

"Aye aye, sir . . . Thirty-fourth Company! Fall in at the LA area, buses thirteen through fifteen. Dismissed!"

Philo got a place on the single broad seat that stretched across the stern of the bus. Zeard wedged himself in beside him. Under them the diesel rumbled, like the engine of a YP, and they stared out the windows at the officers' wives walking by. "Hurry up and wait," said Philo, absently. "Say, Howie, why *did* you get a recon like that? You look like a water tower."

"I couldn't afford to flunk this inspection. Mary Jo's going to meet me in Philly."

"Oh."

"It was wild down there, man. The barber shop was full. Firsties, second class . . . even Dodo was there, sleeping on a pile of hair in the corner."

"Dodo?"

"Yeah. Tracy says he likes to hang around there. Says sometimes the barbers will snip off a little bit of ear for him."

Philo opened his mouth to laugh, but something else occurred to him. "Hey—I thought you were through with Mary Jo. After she ditched you at the tea fight."

"That's right. But we made up. She wrote me that he was only after one thing, and when he got it, he dropped her. So I asked her to Army."

"Jeez. You forgave her?"

"You got to forgive people sometimes. And I guess I love her, too."

"You're quite a man, Howie," said Philo, but privately he thought, you're quite a fool.

"Who are you seeing? You ever catch up with that redhead again?"

"No, dammit—I forgot to get her number. There must be sixty Doyles in Crabtown and I called them all. None of them seemed to know her."

"That's funny."

"Oh well. And I don't know anybody else I'd care to take. So me and Dan and some of the other guys are just going over to the Sheraton afterward."

Zeard nodded.

He enjoyed the ride to Philly. As the milk cartons rolled along, nearly a hundred of them strung out on the highway, the plebes sang fight songs till the upperclass told them to can it, save it for the game. So they had four hours with nothing to do except pull the shades down when they went past B-more. It was great. Sitting there, Zeard's bald head on his shoulder and his snore in Philo's ear, he realized that never, before the Boat School, had he appreciated the luxury of sitting still and thinking what he wanted. Or even napping a little. It was the height of ease. It was even better, in its way, than having a non-reg hotplate in your room.

Outside of Wilmington the buses made a rest stop and he got a cup of hot coffee out of a machine and drank it. It was good. Nobody interrupted him, shouted at him, or clamped him on.

And if we win, he thought with a little thrill of hope, there'll be two weeks of this . . . carry-on till Christmas.

They finally reached Kennedy Stadium, in bitter cold, just in time to stand around in the parking lot for two and a half hours. Some old grads came by and told the mids boring stories of what it was like when they were plebes. Philo eyed them uncertainly. In civvies they looked like anyone; old, getting heavy, all of them loudly drunk. But they had all been through plebe year too. Worse than his, if the stories were true. He wondered what it had done to them, what it had meant. While he was thinking Dubus talked one of them out of a fifth of vodka and passed it around till Breen saw it and poured it out. Presently it began to snow.

At last the guidon went up and they drifted over to form up. There was another delay after that, then finally, hearing the band strike up somewhere ahead, they fell in line of companies and went trucking through a maze of parked cars and hot dog wagons and then down a long shabby ramp with garbage cans along both sides of it, which the outside rank kicked in cadence as they marched along.

And then a gate and suddenly they—the one and only Brigade of Midshipmen—were on display before the country, the world. As they stumbled onto the field, in pretty good though not perfect order, the cold sort of froze your knees up standing around, the whole immense human reef of the stadium rose in a cheer. "Ladies and gentlemen," the PA thundered over it, "the Brigade of Midshipmen."

"I wiped my greasers out on those damn trash cans," someone complained behind him.

"Pipe down back there. They got TV on us."

"Hi mom! Hi grammaw! Hi, you sweet little honey-tongued—"

"*Shut up*, you nerds. You'll get the whole company in hack. The Supe watches films of these march-ons."

The voice from the back subsided. Philo tracked the guidon. When it dipped . . . there. Right, left, *halt*.

At attention, he stared straight ahead, at Wiebels' pimply neck. Breen and the company commander and the CPO went marching off to report. He watched them striding proudly forward over the field, their backs straight, their heads high.

A murmur spread through the company. Breen, to the left of the company commander, seemed to be having a sort of fit. His right shoulder jerked as he paced along. He seemed to be pulling at his . . . yes, at his sword.

"What's with Brad?"

"Why doesn't his. . . ?"

Philo began to sweat. Why did I do that? he asked himself. Why did. . . ? I was drunk. Sure. But it's too late now to. . . .

The three first class came to a crisp halt before the battalion commander. Breen was still spasmodically tugging at his sword hilt, trying his best to be unobtrusive, but it seemed to have grown to the scabbard. More murmurs came from the ranks. Then the batt commander nodded and the company staffs executed the flashy sword salute, bringing the hilt to their faces, thrusting the blades skyward, then sweeping them to the ground in unison in a glittering rainbow of steel.

Except Breen. Breen did a hand salute. When they about-faced to come back Philo saw that his face was as white as his gloves.

When they broke ranks and headed for the stands he made sure he was far away from the assistant company commander. They milled about for a while, then settled into their sections. Meanwhile the Woops were marching onto the field, wearing their gray overcoats and the silly capes that made them look like Victorian cabdrivers.

"Ladies and gentlemen—the Corps of Cadets!"

The Navy stands broke into loud cries of ridicule and reproach, but the gray ranks stood unmoved. Philo had to admit they looked pretty good. But then, the Army was *supposed* to march.

West Point won the toss, and the game started. The stands quickly became a howling jungle. For the first quarter Navy was unstoppable and the plebes yelled themselves dizzy. The sheer volume of sound they were putting out seemed to them sufficient to topple the players, to sweep the compact heavy Army line off the field. Only when they stopped could they hear the equal volume of sound from across the stadium, from the Hudson High stands.

At the half the score was 14–0 Navy.

"We're gonna do it," said Castigliano, standing in front of the long communal trough in the head under the stands at halftime.

"Looks like it," said Philo.

"But our defense isn't so good," said a young guy in civvies behind them. They both looked at him, thinking, who the hell is this?

"They'll hold them," said Philo confidently.

"I hope. I could sure use two weeks of carry-on."

"You and eight hundred other guys."

Dubus pushed through the line to Philo's side. "There you are," he said. "Want a shot of brandy?"

"Put that away, dammit, Dan. There's a full captain in the stalls there."

"He's the one gave it to me."

"Mouse," said Castigliano. "You going to the Sheraton? To the hop?"

"Maybe. Hey, aren't you done yet? You'll have other chances in your life to piss."

"Take it easy. What was wrong with Breen?"

"His sword stuck."

"Huh?"

"Serves him right," said Dubus. "The tit."

"Let's move it up a little, guys. We got some serious beer drinkers back here."

"Use your pocket. Oh, sorry, Colonel."

The third quarter was a series of vicious rushes and stubborn defenses. Army, playing a stubborn ground game, gained enough yardage for a touchdown, and then missed the kick. The Navy stands laughed themselves sick for about a minute before the graylegs intercepted a fumble at their own forty and ran it all the way back. This time they made the extra point.

"Anyway, we still got one point on 'em."

"It's anybody's game now."

"Shut up. They're coming out of the huddle."

Philo was hoarse. They all were, able hardly to croak, from plebe to Brigade Commander, but they sent up a 4-N cheer all the same as the Big Blue jogged to their positions on the line. Far below, the goat pranced angrily under his blue and gold N-star blanket, pulling his husky herders around the sidelines. Dodo had gotten loose and was running up and down, his "Bite Army" blanket flapping, his breath white as he barked, with two lieutenant-commanders and a string of photographers on his tail. The cadets sang "On, Brave Old Army Team," and the mids roared back their parody:

> *We don't play Notre Dame*
> *We don't play Tulane*
> *We just play Davidson*
> *'Cause that's the brave old Army way!*

And then two minutes into the final quarter Army scored again, making it 20–14. The Navy stands were gripped with apprehension.

Behind! How could it happen! But they responded again to the cheerleaders as the Navy offense went in. Unnaturally large men, so heavy every movement hurt their legs, bulked up like cattle for the slaughter, the cynosure of millions of eyes, they trotted wearily onto the torn-up sod, sweating in the cold.

The bar at the Sheraton, like a raft after a shipwreck, was three deep with shattered men in blue.

"Somebody had to lose, guys," the bartender said reasonably, putting fresh drinks down and then slowly withdrawing his hands from the surface of the bar.

"It could of been a tie, coont it?" said the plebe next to Philo. He had no lapel anchors and his face was bruised.

"What happened to you, classmate?"

"Met a Woop outside the stadium. He passed an unsportsmanlike remark. So I decked him."

"He got you back."

"Not him. Three of his buddies."

"Another drink here for my friend," called Philo.

"Goodbye carry-on," said the bruised one. "Two full weeks of slack. I'd of given anything to win this game."

"You'll win next year, guys," said the bartender.

"Next year somebody else'll be plebes," said Philo.

"Yeah," said the bruised one, an expression of nostalgic rapture coming into his eyes. "Think of 'em right now—loafin' in high school, parking with a six pack and some hot little chick Friday nights down by the river—"

"Drinking coffee whenever they want."

"Sleeping till zero-eight-hundred."

"Eating those homemade pies and cakes and brownies."

"When I think," said the bruised one, "Of—thanks, bourbon's okay—of the fact that I had carry-on for eighteen years before I got here, and I never appreciated it—never knew I had it—it makes me want to cry. I wish my mama had braced me up once in a while, or my old daddy gave me leaning rest, just so's I could have *appreciated* what a sweet bag-it deal I had going."

"It's sad," said Philo, blinking back tears. The bartender brought them more drinks. Trying to focus on his wallet, Philo thought how bittersweet it all was, how translucent the world was with regret and missed chances and might have beens. "Keep the change, friend," he said to the bartender softly.

Then sometime later it seemed he was sitting in another place, and it was the same, only there were more plebes, and some upper-class too, and they were all around a big table instead of at the bar; or maybe it *was* the Sheraton; but he had had many drinks and things were not too clear (in one way; in another they were much clearer, much more luminous and true). They were all talking and he looked from one gloom-laden face to another.

"Did you bet a b-robe?"

"Uh huh."

"Lost our *asses*. I can't believe it."

"It wasn't a bad season. Five and five."

"We lost the one that mattered."

"What time is it?"

"Ten. I mean twenty-two-hundred."

"Four bells. Ding ding, ding ding."

"Shut up, assholes. You have to take Mother B on liberty with you, too?"

"Don't say that about my mother," said Philo.

"When do the buses leave?"

"Oh-one-hundred. We got all the time in the world."

"I can't walk. I'm paralyzed."

"More beer."

"I thought there were supposed to be girls here?"

"Philadelphia girls."

"Well, they can't be worse than crabs."

"What's wrong with crabs?" said Philo.

"Don't pop your safeties, shorty."

And sometime much later that night he came to again, briefly, and stared slowly around him at the waiting buses, the snow-slicked street, the staggering groups of mids; upperclass retching into the gutters, pissing against the tires; a flurry of shouting and wild punches as a group of unsteady plebes encountered a sodden third class. For all the drink, he saw only one emotion on his classmates' faces: fear. They had lost Army, and their lives at the Hall, they all knew, would not be worth a fart in a hurricane for weeks. He turned his numb face upward, into the glow of the streetlights, watching the snow whirl downward; and then the clarity dimmed and he staggered into a lamppost head first. Disappointment and alcohol rose in his throat, and he bent to the icy bricks of Philadelphia, vomiting as though his heart would break.

At noon the next day—it was Sunday, but for once in the year Chapel was voluntary—he was standing in the shower, and it was on full, and he was just beginning to grasp the meaning of life after death—when the door banged open.

"Attention on deck!" he heard Gray scream.

"Out of that rack! All you bastards! On deck!"

It was Breen's voice. Philo stiffened in the shower, listening. A nasty feeling began to recur in him. It was his memory.

"Who's in the shower?"

"McGiffin, sir."

"Get your ass out here, mister."

"Aye aye, sir."

He stood dripping naked in front of a white-faced, shaking Breen. Gray, Zeard, Kaufman were against the bulkheads, braced tight, the fear of God already in their eyes.

"What's this, assholes?"

"Your sword, sir?" said Gray.

"That's right, maggots. It's my sword. Zeard, I've caught you chewing gum before. Did you put it in my scabbard?"

"No sir," said Howie, looking completely blank.

"Kaufman!"

"No, sir."

"Gray?"

"No, sir!"

Breen looked at them all, rage and frustration working in his face. "I know one of you plebes did it," he said. "And when I find out who, remember this: one of you is going down for lying, and the rest of you are going down for covering for him. This was no prank.

We were on national television. I'm going to see you all out of this institution."

"Sir," said Philo.

"Resume shower, McGiffin."

"Sir. I did it, sir."

Breen almost smiled, in a terrible way. "Don't try to save your classmates, Mouse. If they'll lie they aren't worth it."

"They're not lying, sir." He swallowed. "They didn't know. I did it on window closing detail the other night."

There, he thought, it's told. The terrible fear was gone and now all he had was numbness. God, it was cold.

"You're serious," said Breen. "You really think you did it."

"I *did* do it, sir."

"Well, I don't believe you, Mouse. I don't think you've got the balls. But don't worry. I'll get him—whoever it was."

"Jesus," said Zeard, when he was gone. They shook themselves and looked at each other. "So that's it. I wondered what the drill was up there. So somebody put gum in his scabbard."

"I love it," said Rollo, not very loud.

"I did it."

"Come off it, Philo. It isn't funny. Somebody's ass is doomed."

"I did do it, damn it. Howie—don't you remember me getting the gum from you?"

"What? When?"

"You were asleep."

"How would I remember it then? I don't keep a log when I'm in the rack."

"Plebe ho! Thirty-fourth! Plebe ho!" came from the corridor.

"Oh, God," said Zeard. "And fourteen shopping days until Christmas."

"Go Christmas, Beat Navy," said the windtattered banner trailing lone, forlorn, from the corner of the first wing. Philo cast a weary eye up at it as he trudged through the slush toward the Hall. He shivered as he walked, clutching the armload of books to his chest like a lover. It was late afternoon; the light was dimming toward ι... .ght; and he, like every other plebe in the Ghetto, was wending his way back with reluctance and dread.

Somewhere in the Hall the sun was, if not bright, at least visible; *vide* the banner; but it did not shine on 8–4. The double purge of losing the Army game, plus Breen's anger, was making the weeks before Christmas leave, normally a time of anticipation, a throwback to the first screaming days of the Brigade's return. There were plebe ho's every night, generally ending with every article the fourth class owned dumped in a pile in the corridor and trampled as they sallied ship back and forth from wall to wall. There were formal room inspections daily and forms 2 and 3 flew like the snow. Ind was out of action, at Hospital Point with a concussion; running a relay race in the hall, exhausted beyond vision or balance, he'd slipped in a pool of sweat and skidded head-first into the mate's desk. Lieutenant Portley had the firsties in for a talk after that, and the physical punishment went underground; but the moral, the mental pressure, got steadily worse in a kind of degenerating loop.

Only the thought of Christmas leave, creeping toward them day by day like the sure delivery of death, kept any of the plebes sane.

And tomorrow, Philo thought wearily, is punch-out day. He walked slowly along the pavement between Dahlgren and the fourth wing. It would be warmer to go through the Hall, but he felt like freezing rather than brace up. Terror was a familiar lump in his stomach, part of his uniform, part of him. Chopping up the ladder to the fourth deck, he felt utterly weary. As he came out onto the company area Kim dropped him for forty pushups, screamed at him in Korean, made him sweat a dime to the bulkhead. He did it automatically, not caring, and ran on. Another of the first class dropped him again, for fifty, and he did those too and endured another minute of screaming and then zigged into the head and squatted in a stall, whimpering softly, like a hunted hamster.

"Jesus, it's freezing in here," he said, as he entered the room.

"You always notice things, Philo," said Zeard. He was sitting at his desk, bundled in sweater and reefer; their breaths were white smoke. "The youngsters say its like this a lot on 8–4. Anytime the pressure drops in the Hall, we get to sweat ice cubes."

"What's the latest flap?" he said, looking in the shower.

"Cleaning out the soap scum inside the drain." Kaufman held up his toothbrush. "Breen was by. He wants this room *clean*."

"Crap . . . what else is new?"

"Nothing."

"Who we going around to tonight?"

"I forget. Does it matter?"

"I guess not," he said. He sat at his desk and began going over his packing list for leave. He'd decided to go back to Raymondsville for the two weeks off. Not for anybody at the Home, but to see his uncle and his track buddies. He was packing his B-4 and his AWOL bag both. Looking at the list, he decided to take his full dress; a couple sets of white works, for hacking around; blue parka and WUBA, to wear around town; sweatgear, to show the guys how he spent most of his time. . . .

"Hey, Phil."

"Mmf."

"You were sleeping on your desk."

"Sorry. Thanks. What time is it?"

"Comearound's in five minutes."

"Okay."

The last comearound before leave, the last meal . . . he would get through it somehow. It was vicious but at last it, too, was over. When they fell in for meal he was too tired to notice that some of the upperclass were carrying their rain gear.

When they entered the mess hall, though, even he could tell that something was imminent. The air was charged with it. There was tension, expectancy, in the way the upperclass stood around the table.

"What's the menu, Mouse?" said Stamper lazily. He had that same old ball-fondling look in his eye they remembered from plebe summer.

"Sir, the menu for evening meal is: peanut butter and jelly sandwiches: brussels sprouts; shoestring potatoes; kaiser rolls; chocolate milk, coffee; dessert is shiverin' Liz and fruit, sir."

"Oh good," said Wiebels. "Jello is just right for this."

"That's kind of a skimpy meal, isn't it, Mister Kaufman?"

"I'll find out, sir."

"You sure will, Rollo."

"Brigade . . . *seats!*"

"Weird," said Keyes, "See if anyone has any rolls for Mister Singleterry."

Howie leapt to the top of his chair. *"Attention world! Attention world! Does anyone have any rolls for Mister Singleterry?"*

Abruptly the air was filled with kaiser rolls from all over the company's tables, and from the 33rd's too. Singleterry had a bare second to duck before the barrage of dough hit him.

"Down boy," said Keyes. "Now. Watch him. He'll try something sneaky, the prissy bastard."

"Here comes the chow," said Breen. "Don . . . rain gear."

"Damn. Forgot mine."

"Use my cape."

"Thanks, Brad."

The carts were indeed coming in, but in an odd manner. The stewards wheeled them forward like medieval siege engines, crouching behind the aluminum racks of food and vats of milk and coffee. They passed the trays out quickly, ducking back under cover.

"Praise the Lord," said Stamper, "and pass the ammunition."

There was a quick movement behind the first class, and Philo had time to say nothing before it happened: Castigliano, both hands full of green jello, had clapped them together on either side of Keyes' head. "Wild man! Wild man!" he screamed, capering like a monkey, rubbing the stuff in Keyes' hair and ears as the two firsties tried to fight him off. The second class buttoned their rain gear. "I'll get you for this!" Keyes screamed. "Fourth class—with one brussels sprout—load! Your target, Mister Singleterry! Main battery—*fire!*"

"Hit the deck!" said Dubus. The youngsters disappeared under the table just as an answering barrage whistled into their midst. The sprouts were overcooked as usual and the one that hit Philo spattered onto his messmates too. "Rapid continuous fire! Get those rounds out!"

"Drop one hundred!" Singleterry was telling his table. "You're overshooting. Now! Fire for effect!"

Now the neighboring tables were joining in, on one side or the other, and it was happening up and down the messhall: a table would go to general quarters, fire a few spotting rounds, and then the battle would begin.

"Food fight!" screamed Breen, just before the decks were swept clear by a barrage of grape. "Sling that peanut butter! Make every potato count!"

Over the tables, just under the ceiling, a solid mist of food took form, crossing and recrossing in a thousand low arcs, splattering and skittering across tables and mids. The stewards were gone, the carts skewed and abandoned in the middle of the aisles, where presently they were raided for more food. Philo, ducking under flying dishes, got several boxes of milk to add to the magazines. Upperclass began to stream out, holding plates and tablecloths to ward off jello and more dangerous missiles. And at last, hungry still but happy, the mess hall a complete shambles, he and the other plebes tore out, forgetting their braces, forgetting their rates, to pack for the big trip home.

Thirty hours later he looked out of the bus window at Raymondsville. It hadn't changed much.

"This your stop, soldier?"

"Yes, sir." You dope, he thought. You don't say "sir" to a bus driver.

Leaning sleepily against the tinted window of the Scenicruiser, he watched the familiar houses, the familiar streets slide by. Raymondsville was not very big, a fact that had made his childhood harder than it might have been in city anonymity. Main Street, the library, Rezk's Bar and Grill, the corner of School Street where he had waited with his secondhand suitcase to go off to the glorious life of a midshipman at Annapolis. . . .

He decided he would stay at the Hotel Gerroy. The rooms were cheap.

That evening he got together at Rezk's with Joe De Freeze and Tony Stitz, who had been on the high school track team with him. Joe had almost been state high jump champ. The bartender carded Joe and Tony; he didn't say a word to Philo. "It's the uniform," said

Joe enviously. "What'd'ya call that anyway? What you're wearing?"

"This is working uniform blue alpha. We call it WUBA. It's our class uniform in the winter."

"Wooba. That's a cool hat, too. You mean you wear that to class? I guess you wear uniforms all the time, though—to parties and everything."

"We don't go to many parties," said Philo.

"Yeah, I heard you can't do lots of stuff there at West Point," said Tony Stitz. He flipped his hair back out of his eyes. He was working at Thunder Oil now, overhauling pumps out on the leases. "Like drink, or have girls in your rooms, or smoke. Sounds real dull."

"We have some fun down at West Kittanning," said Joe.

"Annapolis," said Philo.

"Huh?"

"It's not West Point. That's Army. I'm at Annapolis."

"Oh, I thought you was up to the *academy*. You know."

"Gee, you look different, Phil," said Stitz. "You lost weight?"

"Some."

"I bet it's rough," said De Freeze. "But I guess if you like it . . . funny, I never thought of you as a military kind of guy. Figured you had to be tough, a real he-man, you know. But you're getting along okay, huh?"

Philo fingered his glass. "I don't know," he said at last. "I guess I'm doing all right."

"You like it there?"

He pondered this. "I don't know," he said again. "It's too big to say you like it or you don't like it, like it was a piece of pie or something. It's pretty complicated."

"Yeah, at West Kittanning State it's real rough sometimes, too," said De Freeze. "Like, they got separate dorms for the guys and the girls, see, and if they catch you in the girl's dorm after ten o'clock, you get busted."

"What do they do to you?" said Philo. "If they bust you?"

"I don't know . . . nobody ever checks on it. You know. It's just a rule."

"Jeez, that's rough. You guys need somebody like Black Bart, or Lieutenant Loose."

"Who's that, man?"

"Just some guys with swords."

"Swords, yeah. That's neat. Like the musketeers, huh? You got a sword, Phil?"

"Not yet."

"They give you a gun, though, huh?"

"They issue you an M-one."

"Yeah, I got a new thirty-thirty," said Stitz. "Got it off old Halvorsen, out on the leases. Too bad you missed the season this year, Phil. Maybe you ought to take your vacation earlier next year, we'll go out get us a couple buck."

"Yeah, maybe," said Philo. "You want to get some more beer?"

"Okay," said De Freeze. "Hey, Phil—how long you gonna stay in town?"

"Just a couple days, I guess," said Phil. "Maybe I'll go back early and study."

As it turned out, he left the next day. There was nothing left for him in Raymondsville.

CHAPTER NINE

*As you might expect from the Academy's high academic
reputation, your studies can be rough sailing. They
need not be, however, if you study hard and efficiently,
and utilize every spare moment. The academic
department will always give you a fair break, and if
you . . . put forth all your effort you should not have
any trouble.*

—Reef Points

*Fifty thousand dollars' worth of education, shoved up
your ass a nickel at a time.*

—Heard at an all-night poker game
in Stalag Fifteen

"Would you care for some pancakes, sir?"
He held the heavy tray level without effort, his eyes
straight ahead. By now he didn't even feel a brace. It was natural.
He could sit for hours on two inches of a hard chair and swallow
anything with two chews first.

"Nope," grunted Breen.

"No, thank you," said Keyes. "Just eggs for me. I ate one of those
collision mats plebe year and I can still feel it when I run."

The first classmen ate silently. So did the second class and even
the youngsters. The mess hall was deadly quiet these mornings.
Outside the windows it was still dark. Few of the upperclass had
bothered to shave yet and they chewed slowly with their ties loose
and collars open and eyes on their plates. The whole Brigade was
glum, listless, and slovenly.

The Dark Ages had come.

Their black apathy lay over the Hall, over the Yard. The Severn was frozen solid. A bitter wind came off it in the mornings, bringing tears to the eyes of mids ploughing through snow to class, freezing their bare ears under the uniform caps. There was nothing to look forward to for a vast white stretch of January and February; and between them and spring leave, like barbed wire before a prisoner, stood finals. Depression and boredom and fear lay like a gray pall over the academic buildings. Too many had bagged studying for too long. "A USNA grad may not know anything, but he can out-memorize anybody else," they told one another, and in true Academy tradition it was time now to trust to all-nighters, pony sheets, and a lemming-desperate search for the Gouge.

"Wop," said one of the youngsters suddenly, breaking the silence, "Who are you asking around for Hundredth Night?"

"Haven't thought about it yet, sir."

"You've got to start early or it's too fruit."

"Yes sir."

"You'll like it," said another of the third class. "Good clean fun. Don't you think you'd enjoy sleeping in a laundry bag?"

"That sounds good, sir."

"It does?"

"I could enjoy sleeping anywhere, sir," said Castigliano. "I could enjoy sleeping under this table even."

"Don't pull that briar-patch routine on me, Wop," said Stamper. "We can see right through you. McGiffin, who you asking around?"

"I'll find out, sir."

"Not me," said Keyes, belching moodily. "I'm too easy for a hard-ass like the Mouse. He wants somebody he can get his teeth into."

"Sure," said the first youngster. "You got to ask somebody you hate. That's part of the tradition. Hundredth Night buildup's the best part of plebe year."

"You guys better decide. And fast."

"Yes sir."

"Pipe down, you jerks," said Breen. "I can't hear myself chew."

Philo thought about it as he stowed away pancakes. He knew what Hundredth Night was. It was the Academy version of Saturnalia—the night, exactly one hundred days before Graduation, when the first class came around to the plebes, when the highest dropped and the mighty were humbled. Basically, what you did was to ask a firstie around. There was a separate web of custom about that. But to ask him around for Hundredth Night meant that you spent the weeks before it going around to *him*.

And for those comearounds all the plebe indoctrination guidelines were off—especially here in the Ghetto.

Engel jogged his arm and he turned back to the conversation at the table to hear the youngsters telling stories of their Hundredth Night buildups. One of them knew (or said he knew) of a plebe who had been ordered to sleep in a different place every night for three weeks. The fifth night he had tied himself to the gutter on 5-4, outside the company office, and had nearly frozen, losing several toes to frostbite. Another had been caught by Lieutenant Loose sleeping in the Midshipman Sample Room; still another found a secure niche in the cart the mokes used to pick up laundry bags, but had found it so comfortable he woke up at ten A.M., at the Laundry, and drew 120 demos for missing morning meal formation and two classes. Another man told about the plebe who had been ordered to wear sweat gear everywhere, under his regular uniforms, and who had fainted from heat exhaustion while singing in the National Cathedral with the Catholic choir.

"That's nothin'," said Stamper. "Our plebe year—now that was when being a plebe still meant something. I remember Mike Nodels—old Raingear—told Fred Smirk to be a duck sandwich. He did it so good the company officer sent him over to Hospital Point for observation. They had him there for a week, him quacking and wearing slices of bread under his cap and in his back pockets—and with total hundred percent carry-on the whole time—till finally Raingear said he could tell the medics it was a prank."

"Do you believe that story, McGiffin?" said Keyes.

"Yes sir," said Philo.

"Do you believe that, Engel?"

"Yes sir."

"Wop?"

"I don't doubt Mister Stamper's word, sir. But he may be . . . exaggerating a little for effect."

"I never exaggerate," said Stamper, looking dangerous.

"That's right," said one of the youngsters. "You will find, young ploobs, that we older heads are underestimating, if anything, the rigors and demands of a true Hundredth Night buildup. Have we youngsters ever misled you? Ever?"

"Once, sir," said Castigliano.

"When?"

"You said we would get a charge out of fall YPs, sir."

"That's professional advice. That doesn't count."

"Mister Wop," said Keyes. "You're smiling. Wipe it off."

"Aye sir." Castigliano wiped the smile off his face, threw it down, and stamped on it. "Hell on the Hudson; hell on the Hudson; damn the class of '17."

"Why seventeen?"

"Because there are seventeen letters in Johnson and Johnson, sir, and that describes you, sir; cotton balls, one-hundred-percent sterile."

"Not bad . . . Mouse, what do you owe me this morning?"

"A report, sir."

"On what?"

"Aircraft carrier development, sir."

"Go."

"Sir. During and after the Second World War the Royal Navy pioneered three advances in seaborne air power. One: the steam catapult. Two: the angled deck. Three: the use of lights in the approach system. The steam catapult was developed as an improvement. . . ."

As he kept talking Philo held up the tray for more eggs, and then the pitcher, in his other hand, for more coffee. ". . . which were incorporated in postwar classes of U.S. aircraft carriers, continuing till the present day," he concluded. "Sir."

"Good. Where'd you find that out?"

"Article in the Naval Institute *Proceedings*, sir."

"You know," said Keyes, "I'm beginning to think you studs might actually make naval officers someday."

"*Attention world, attention world,*" bellowed a plebe from Singleterry's table. "*I think a pelorus is a bird that lives at the south pole sir.*"

"Belay my last," said Keyes.

"It's too early in the morning for 'attention worlds,'" said Breen. "Whose table was that, McGiffin?"

"Mister Singleterry's, sir."

"You feel like wild manning him, Mouse?"

"Uh, not really, sir."

"Don't be such a whimp, McGiffin. You're turning my stomach."

"Sir—"

"That's an order. Go wild man his ass, and make it good."

With a heavy heart, Philo got up. The only food left on the table was the scrambled eggs that had just come in. He took two handfuls, screamed "Wild man! Wild man!" and funneled them into Singleterry's ears from behind. He spent the rest of the meal at leaning rest under his old squad leader's table. One of his classmates passed him down half a piece of toast without being seen.

The room was in darkness, and the windows were open wide, letting a frigid wind roar in off the bay. One red bulb glowed in a Tensor lamp over the desk, on which were scattered maneuvering boards, parallel rules, dividers, and a speed/distance calculator.

"Okay," said Zeard. "Signal in the air. Guide is at one-three-zero true at sixteen knots. Four DDs are stationed in a bent-line screen at the following stations: six-AD-eight; six-DH-eight; twelve-FK-eighteen; twelve-MP-eighteen. At zero-one-hundred the screen commander signals reorientation to screen axis two-seven-zero by method RUM. Calculate course, speed, and time to station for each unit."

"You got any more of these Wolf Brothers', Howie?" asked El Rollo.

"Here."

Reefer collars up, caps on, cigars tucked into their mouths and glowing red in the darkness, they toiled over the maneuvering boards. "Just like being at sea," said Philo. "Only thing's missing is getting the room to roll."

"Spare me," said Zeard. "I already seen dinner once tonight."

"S-sub-one, eleven point four knots at three-one-zero true," muttered Kaufman. "Hell."

"Gonna wear stars this semester, Rollo?"

"I'll be happy if I'm wearing a uniform after finals, Phil."

"Done!" said Zeard, clicking his parallel rules shut. He read off the solutions and they checked theirs with his. One of Rollo's was six knots slower than Philo's and Zeard's. They checked his work. "Here it is," said Rollo at last. "I must of used the wrong distance scale. Yeah. I had three to one instead of five to one. No problem."

"No problem," Zeard repeated sarcastically. "Only you were crossing in front of a carrier at ten knots. Look—he'd of cut you in half. Remind me to wear a life jacket to bed when you've got the conn."

"Take it easy, Howie. It's only a problem."

"Problem hell. How would you like to have a bucket like Rollo in charge of your formation?"

"I don't see you wearing stars."

"I will."

"You know, Howie, you're not only weird, you're a geek."

"And you're a gungy FUBAR who's scared of his own shadow, Mouse."

They stared at each other in the red light as the wind rattled the blinds. "Hey, guys," said Kaufman anxiously, "Let's not argue. We're roomies, huh?"

Philo felt his own eyes drop first. "Ah hell," he said. "What do you guys want to hit next? Dago?"

"I'm sick of dago. What about some integrals?"

"I heard a good one. The youngsters told me they had it on a p-work this semester. You ready? Given that a squirrel sticks his head out of a hole in an oak tree. Five seconds later he sticks his head out of another hole ten meters from the first. He then takes four seconds to get back to the first hole. Solve for the number of seconds before the squirrel is sticking his head out of both holes at the same time."

"That's like the one I read in the *Log*. The International Diplomacy course. 'Analyze the effect of Descartes' rationalistic philosophy upon German rearmament after World War One and its relationship to the stabilization of the Swiss franc. Utilize the three-minute rule and the second law of thermodynamics.'"

"In five hundred words or less."

"Time limit—ten minutes."

"Illustrate with a three-plane view."

The door knocked and opened. "Carry on, guys," said a tow-headed, furtive-looking second class. "Hey, look. I got some of these 'Beat Army' panties left over. Only a buck apiece. What do you say?"

"We're broke, sir."

"Sorry sir. My girl doesn't wear panties."

"Okay," said the second class agreeably. He took several foil-wrapped cylinders out of a bulge in his b-robe. "Hot dogs?"

"Got redeye, sir?"

"You bet. Nickel extra."

"I'll take one," said Zeard. When the second class was gone they divided it into three precisely equal pieces with the edge of the parallel rule.

At evening comearound the next day Singleterry had him compose a poem about Breen's fiancée, Gwen. Philo recited it at evening meal, at an "attention world." He got a full meal for once, of sliced onions covered with A-1 sauce, and an order to come around at noon the next day for something, in Breen's words, "extra special."

The next morning, capping the breathless days of waiting, grades came out. They were posted in long lists on the bulkheads. The plebes read them at parade rest, braced up.

Philo read his with a feeling of vertigo, as if he was looking down again from the water entry platform. B in English Comp, C in P.E., D in mechanical drawing, B in language. So far, not bad—but he had two more lists to go. It was when he stood before the lists for the heavyweight courses—math, chemistry, and engineering—that he saw that he was safe, safe home, for he had a rock-solid D in all three. The pennies thrown at Tecumseh on the way to finals had been well invested. For his first semester he had a solid 2.1 QPR, a full tenth of a point of gravy.

He got to his room to find Gray already wearing the two gold stars above his lapel anchors that meant Dean's list. Zeard had a 3.2 and the Supe's List. But Kaufman sat crushed at the desk, his shoulders telling the story. He was unsat, a 1.8, and Philo immediately felt shabby at his own elation. But there was no time to try to cheer the Rollo up. He had to change for comearound. He spun to a halt, sweating already, in front of Breen's door at 1800 exact, knocked, and pushed the door open.

"Midshipman fourth class McGiffin, sir, reporting as ordered."

"McGiffin, McGiffin," Breen sighed, turning away from the window, beyond which, in the half-darkness of winter noon, he seemed to have been contemplating the falling snow. "Every time there's a fuckup in my company, I hear that name again. What the hell am I going to do with you, boy?"

"I'll find out, sir." Thank God, there was a response for everything.

"Got your grades?"

"Yes, sir."

"QPR?"

"Two-point-one, sir."

"Damn." The assistant company commander shook his head sadly. "I'd hoped the Navy might get lucky for a change."

Philo said nothing. The first class crossed to his desk and sat down. On it was a picture of Gwen, a pair of freshly shined shoes— Breen, Philo reflected, must be the only firstie in the Brigade who spit-shined during the Dark Ages—and a half-written letter. Breen regarded him moodily, his strong chin squared and firm, deepset eyes as dark as the windows. "Mouse," he said, "You don't like me a hell of a lot, do you?"

"I respect you, sir. I mean that."

"I wonder. You seem to go out of your way to pull me down on your ears, McMuffin. A little guy like you, you'd get through here easy with a low profile. But you've got to screw up, stand out. Why can't you conform, Mouse? Square away, behave yourself? The upperclass don't like you, your classmates hate you for balling up on them. The Snorkel's longing for an excuse to boot you out. What's the story on you, anyway, man?"

"Sir, permission to make statement, sir."

"I wish you would."

"I'm sorry about the poem, sir. About Gwen. Mister Singleterry told me to make it up and recite it."

"You don't understand, do you? I admit, you pissed me off with that one. But I'm talking about your whole attitude. See, McGiffin"—Breen leaned back in his chair—"You're a mystery to me. You're a disgrace to my company. You're about as unlike the real Philo McGiffin as you could be. You're a mouse—but without that undistinguished air of mediocrity that lets a mouse blend in. I can't decide if you're worth my time, worth the effort it would take to shape you up, or whether I should just let the system go ahead and shitcan you."

"Yes sir."

"'Yes, sir.' What's *that* expression for, McGiffin?"

"Sir?"

"This hangdog whimpering expression of yours. I don't like it in my room. Goddamn it, McGiffin, we're supposed to be producing people with some backbone here!"

Philo did not think he had been looking especially hangdog; but only a sea lawyer argued. "Aye aye, sir," he snapped, trying to look cheerful and aggressive.

"And another thing. I'm tired of telling you to *brace up!* Chins, boy! I want to see chins!"

"Chin chin, sir."

"Oh, wise ass time, huh? Maybe you better sit on the green bench for awhile."

He assumed the position, sitting on air with his back against the bulkhead, his arms hanging down. Immediately his knees protested at the outward thrust.

"Permission to make statement, sir."

"*Now* what?"

"I'm having trouble with my knees, sir."

"I'm having trouble with my *temper*, McGiffin. What's wrong with your knees?"

"I don't—I'll find out, sir."

"Have you got a light duty chit?"

"No sir."

"Have you been to sick bay?"

"No sir."

"You're just whimping out again, McGiffin."

"No sir."

"Shut up, you damn pussy. I'm sick of your whining."

"Aye aye, sir."

His knees were hurting in earnest now. The position was held with his thighs and upper legs; as they weakened, you tended to slide down the bulkhead. He locked his back teeth together, re-solved, now, not to let a sound escape him. At the corner of his vision he saw Breen pick up a book and begin to study.

"McGiffin."

"Sir."

"Let's hear the Laws of the Navy. Maybe they'll inspire you or something. You can secure as soon as you're done."

"Aye aye, sir. Sir, the Laws of the Navy, dedicated to his com-rades in the service by the author, Ronald A. Hopwood. Now—"

"He spoon you, Mouse?"

"Sir?"

"Admiral Hopwood. Did he spoon you?"

"No, sir. By the author, Rear Admiral Ronald A. Hopwood, Royal Navy, sir."

"Okay. Go on."

"Now, these are the Laws of the Navy," Philo began, talking through his locked back teeth.

> Now these are the Laws of the Navy,
> Unwritten and varied they be;
> And he who is wise will observe them,
> Going down in his ship to the sea.

"Not so loud," said Breen.

"Aye aye, sir."

> As naught may outrun the destroyer,
> Even so with the Law and its grip.
> For the strength of the ship is the Service,
> And the strength of the Service, the ship.
>
> Take heed what ye say of your rulers,

Be your words spoken softly or plain.
Lest a bird of the air tell the matter,
And so ye shall hear it again.

"That includes filthy poetry, McGiffin."
"Yes sir."
He spoke faster, praying that he wouldn't clutch. So far, though,
the words were flowing easily.

If ye labor from morn until even,
And meet with reproof for your toil,
It is well—that the gun may be humbled,
The compressor must check the recoil.

On the strength of one link in the cable
Dependeth the might of the chain;
Who knows when thou mayest be tested?
So live that thou bearest the strain!

Five stanzas; there were fourteen more. He plunged on, his eyes
fixed and bugged, feeling sweat leaking through his eyebrows. From
his position near the door he could see out Breen's window, watch
the snow falling through the navy blue of evening. It fell on the little
decorative balcony, and he remembered the story of Breen and his
toothbrush, scrubbing it . . . it did look clean out there, and if anyone in Slack 34th did such a thing it would be the assistant company
commander . . . he called his mind back from its tenth-of-a-second
of wandering and bit at his lip. His legs were molten masses of pain,
fighting to keep him up.
"Having trouble, McGiffin?"
"No sir." He'd be damned if he'd whine any more, even if he
passed out here in Breen's room. Maybe that would show him, the
bastard. No. He'd say I was faking it, he thought.
"Then knock 'em together, damn it!"

. . . Canst follow the track of the dolphin
Or tell where the sea swallows roam?

Where leviathan taketh his pastime?
What ocean he calleth his home?

Even so with the words of thy Rulers,
And the orders those words shall convey.
Every law is as nought beside this one—
"Thou shalt not criticise, but obey!"

Saith the wise, "How may I know their purpose?"
Then acts without wherefore or why;
Stays the fool but one moment to question,
And the chance of his life passeth by.

The next stanza he forgot. But he doubted if Breen remembered it through. The important thing—he had learned this long ago, doing chow calls—was to go on, to keep up the steady flow of words, for a dead halt always caught attention, while a finesse often got by. The important thing was to go on, to get done, to get out of this unnatural position. He skipped to the next one he knew, and went on.

—Lest ye strive and in anger be parted
And lessen the might of the ship.

Dost deem that thy vessel needs gilding,
And the dockyard forebear to supply?
Place thy hand in thy pocket and gild her:
There be those who have risen thereby.

"McGiffin."

"Sir."

"Stop grunting. You know the Boat School version of that stanza?"

"N-no, sir."

"It goes like this: 'Dost deem that thy dick needs a workout, and thy girl forebears to supply? Place thy hand in thy pocket and stroke her: there be those who have risen thereby.'"

"Yes sir." He tried to laugh a little, but it came out a sickly croak.

"Don't *grunt*, damn it."

"Aye aye, sir," he grunted.

"Go on."

He went on. His hands, scrabbling involuntarily across the surface of the bulkhead behind him, found a small ridge; he hooked his fingernails into it and pressed upward, taking perhaps a pound of weight off his thighs. It felt like a month's vacation. Now, though, he felt the cloth of his uniform sliding centimeter by centimeter down the wall. He went on reciting, faster and faster, and then his legs gave suddenly and he fell.

"Come on, you pussy. Try putting out for a change, McGiffin. Only a couple more stanzas."

> *So thou, when thou nearest promotion,*
> *And the peak that is gilded is nigh,*
> *Give heed to thy words and thine actions,*
> *Lest others be wearied thereby.*

> *It is ill for the winners to worry,*
> *Take thy fate as it comes with a smile,*
> *And when thou art safe in the harbour*
> *They will envy, but may not revile.*

"Slow down, McGiffin. Enunciate. Don't mumble."

"Aye aye, sir."

His whole body was shaking now, breaking out in great shudders of the major muscles, the legs, the diaphragm. But he went on, past caring much now, hardly listening to his own words. The last stanza, thank God:

> *As the wave rises clear to the hawse pipe,*
> *Washes aft, and is lost in the wake,*
> *So shall ye drop astern, all unheeded,*
> *Such time as the law ye forsake.*

"Permission to come aboard sir."

"Come aboard, Mouse."

As he struggled up, using his arms for the lack of feeling in his legs, he slipped in a puddle of sweat where it had run down his back, dripped from his face, onto the floor tiles. Breen saw it too. "Get some paper out of the head and clean that up before you go . . . not bad. You know your rates anyway. But I don't know. Am I wasting my time on you, McGiffin?"

"I'll find out, sir."

Breen wiped his shoes moodily, smiling at himself in them. "Well, I don't know . . . I don't know. There's *something* there. He's not just a whimp. That sword bit . . . but I'm not sure how to find it." He glanced up at Philo, who was standing, showing chins, beside the locker. "Do you understand what I'm talking about, Mouse?"

"No, sir."

"Well, maybe it's all a forlorn hope . . . see what time it is."

Philo stuck his head out into the corridor, but at that moment the ten-minute call went. Zeard, at his station in the hall, was screaming his lungs out. Down the hall from him a group of plebes were throwing themselves on a mattress, propelled by slaps in the ass by a second class. Carrier Landings.

And suddenly he felt weary. Numb. He did not know what Breen was mumbling about and he didn't care. Would it never end? It seemed that all of his life he had been coming around, rigging food, memorizing things that made no sense, abandoning and masking his feelings just to get by.

If only there was some way to get back at them, he thought hopelessly. It wouldn't change things. But if only there was something he could *do*—

"Mouse. I asked you, *what time is it!*"

"Ten minutes till formation, sir," he said, turning back into the room.

"Chins, dammit! I said *chins!*"

That night there were poppyseed buns for evening meal. They were hard and the upperclass loathed them so the plebes got four each. Breen, Keyes, and most of the other upperclass left early to get in half an hour making love to their pads before Study Hour began. Only one of the youngsters, a Mister Norfon (called "Norforms" by his classmates) was left at the table. As soon as the others

had left, Norfon looked around cautiously and then, as the senior
man, flashed them two fingers for carry-on. Now the tray of buns
lay in the center of the table. Fourth class dismissal bell rang at last.

"Mister Norfon, sir?"

"Yeah."

"Sir, could I—request permission, sir, to take some buns out of
the mess hall."

"That's against regs, guy. I can't give you permission." He
glanced around the almost empty mess hall. "But I guess if you stuff
a couple in your hat you could get 'em out okay."

"Aye aye, sir."

"But I didn't give you permission, remember."

"Yes sir."

"I heard Lieutenant Loose caught a firstie carrying a cherry pie
out of the mess hall. He made him put it inside his service dress blue
blouse and then hit him on the chest."

The plebes laughed dutifully.

"But around here you rate what you can get away with. So don't
get caught."

"No sir."

Philo got back to his room safely, sweating all the way, with two
poppyseed buns in his combo hat and four more inside his blouse (it
had been a good idea, after all). He drew the curtain in the shower,
while Zeard and Gray talked, and started to gnaw at one. You never
could tell when an upperclass might come in, or worse yet, the
OOD. Then, suddenly, he stopped, and looked carefully at the hard
bun.

"What are you doing in there, Philo?" said Gray.

"Picking the seeds off these buns."

"Oh. Okay."

When he had all the seeds off them there was about a handful.
They were big buns. He put them in a pile on his desk, opened the
window, returned to the desk to pick up the seeds, and crawled out
on to the long gutter that ran the length of the roof outside. As he
balanced there, half in and half out of the room, Zeard came over to
the sill.

"Hey, Phil."

"Yeah."

"What's the drill?"

"Never mind."

"Going to end it all?"

"Maybe."

"Say, can I have your clean skivvy shorts, after? I think we take the same size."

"Go put yourself on report, Howie," said Philo. "Heart, failure to own. Close the window. Cover for me if the study hour inspector comes by while I'm out."

"What do you want me to tell him? That you went out the window?"

"I don't care. Pitch him the usual line of bull."

Zeard secured the window; a moment later, faintly, Philo heard the rattle of the blinds as they dropped to the regulation half-mast. Suddenly it was dark, cold, and windy; and suddenly he realized that he, the Mouse, was a hundred feet up from the pavement, on a yard-wide copper-sheathed gutter; safe and solid enough, despite its corroded green color, but over its open edges was . . . space. He crouched down, pressing his belly to the metal as his stomach flew free, and cowered there in the dark for some minutes. His eyes were closed and his fingernails dented the copper he gripped.

Over several minutes, with an immense effort of will and apathy, he forced his mind back from the edge of panic. He opened his eyes again. He was shivering; had only the woollen trou and thin white dress shirt on. He discovered that he still held the poppy seeds in one clenched fist.

Come on, you damn pussy. He forced one knee ahead and then the other forward for a few feet, staying away from the edge. There were three rooms to go past. Schochet and Reefer's, a second class room, and then a youngster room. He crawled slowly past the brightly lit upperclass windows, feeling as conspicuous as an actor in limelight; but none of the men he looked in at, sitting at their desks talking, reading, smoking, seemed to see him pass, like an errant vampire seeking virgins.

Mirror effect in the windows, he thought. It was so much brighter inside than out here in the night that he was completely safe.

Crawl on; crawl on; hands growing numb, shivering, and then
. . . there. The balcony. Scraped and brushed clean of the last
snowfall, he could see it clearly in the light from Breen's window.
He hauled himself over the low railing and crouched there. It was
better with the railing between him and space, though the balcony,
only about two feet across, had him right up against the window.
Yes, the balcony was better. As long as he didn't have to *look* over
the edge, he could talk his mind into believing he was on the
ground. He looked around the edge of the window, and froze.

Breen was in there, facing the window, puffing on a pipe. He was
wearing a non-reg T-shirt and a pair of boxer shorts decorated with
little red hearts. A maroon bound copy of the *Manual for Courts-
Martial* lay open on his lap. He was staring straight out the window,
though, pipe in his mouth, his eyes right on the motionless plebe's.

Then he blinked and looked back down at the book. He was
studying; he had seen nothing beyond the black mirror that was his
window.

Good thing there's no wind, Philo thought.

He pried his left hand open with his right and scattered the poppy
seeds around the scrubbed stone deck of the little balcony, and shivered. Jeez, he thought, it's cold. I better get back before I freeze.

Over the little edge of the balcony, back into the gutter. Now for
the long crawl back. He hugged the roof, as far from the beckoning,
intoxicating edge of the night as he could get, and swallowed as he
crawled, not looking toward it. He was intensely anxious; yet inside
him something bright and free was growing against the cold, the
dark, the bleakness of the winter and of the Dark Ages.

The rest, he thought, I can leave to the seagulls.

"You back?" said Zeard faintly, through the glass.

"Open the window, goddamn it. I'm freezing my ass off out
here."

He was halfway through when a knock came at the door. Zeard
and Gray each took an arm and jerked him in and Kaufman
slammed the window shut and dropped the blinds. There was just
time to brush the green stain off his trou before the door swung
open and Dubus came in. "Greetings, fellow turkeys," he said. "Hi,
Phil. Rest of you guys carry on."

"Hi, Dan. What's the occasion? You don't come in here very often."

The fat youngster jerked his mouth to one side. "Nothin' big," he said. "Just saying so long."

"What d'you mean?"

"You haven't heard?" The fat youngster sat down on Gray's bed; Gray writhed a little in his chair, but said nothing. "Thermo and Weps won at last. My best semester at USNA, final QPR one-point-eight out of four-point-oh."

"Oh, shit, Dan."

"I'm not even going to wait for another Ac Board. This is it. They won't have Dirty Dan to kick around any more. No more Exec Department bananas. No more getting fried for holes in your shoes while you're lying in sick bay giving blood." He sighed. "No more sub races along Lover's Lane; no more over the walls; no more p-rades. Actually I'll miss it."

"That sucks, Dan," said Philo.

"Say, what size shorts you wear, sir?" said Zeard. "The laundry seems to have it in for me. Last time I sent out ten, and—"

"Go to hell, Zeard," said Dubus, not unkindly. "I guess I can let you have a few, if you think you can get into a forty-four. Gray, I've got a can of Brasso left over from plebe summer you can have. It's good; never been opened . . . Mouse, for you, something special." He took a weird assemblage of wires and colored parts from his pocket. A flesh-colored earphone dangled down.

"A radio?"

"Goes right in the magazine. Connect this clip to the barrel; it's your antenna. Add two AA batteries and you've got the only M-one wired for sound in the Brigade. Takes the boredom out of marching extra duty. A wires slash made it for me."

"What did you give him?"

"A shackup for June Week with the hottest Irish broad in Crabtown."

"Jeez, thanks Dan—but hell—they can't throw you out of here!"

"*That's* a big negat," said Dubus. "Anyway—I'll be thinking of you guys when I see Mother Bannapolis in the old rear-view. I hope you all have fun Hundredth Night, and June Week—Graduation—

being officers—ah, shit." He got up and left, not looking at them.

The room was quiet for a couple of minutes. Gray got up and smoothed out the wrinkles on his rack, and it was suddenly as if, Philo thought, there had never been a Dirty Dan Dubus at all. "Shit," he said at last. "That's rough. I remember when I would have been happy to see him bilge out. Now—it's Shaft Alley, I think."

"He couldn't hack it," said Gray, frowning over his cap; he was scrubbing the stitching with toothpaste. "He was here for three semesters and was never sat for a day. He never got a grade above a D. You wouldn't want a bucket like that on the bridge at night, or flying wingman, or as your skipper on a sub, would you?"

"I'm not pointing fingers. I just said it was tough, that's all."

"Yeah," said Gray, touching his stars absently with one finger. "It's tough all right."

The depression he felt over Dan's demise lingered the next day, through all the comearounds and petty detail of the morning and afternoon. He felt shoddy even as he stood in line in Dahlgren Hall for the third and final event of the fourth class's social Brassoing: the last tea fight of the year.

"What's with you, man?" said Jack Ash. "You been drinking cokes and aspirin?"

"Nope."

"You look pretty down."

"Sorry," he said. He tried to smile. Conform, he thought. Smile. Act confident and cheerful. Wasn't that what they were always telling him?

"That's better," said Ash.

The jostling line was quiet this time, resigned. Tired, too. There was no mooing, no pushing. The strain was visible on the faces around him. There was little of the ebullient spirits young men about to meet girls should display. No, they all seemed beaten; tired; worried.

It's not just me, he thought. It's the whole class. We've got to get some spirit—something to grab hold of. Something other than what passed for girls at pig pushes. Something less tangible, but more real. Something to give them heart . . . a *symbol.* . . .

"You. The short guy. Get up here, stud."

He was paired with a chub. His height, but she must have weighed forty pounds more than he did. He pressed her wet hand, looked into her wet blue eyes, blonde, fluffed hair, stiff and movementless as dead grass in winter. He smiled and dutifully put his arm around her waist—Louise, she said—but his arm was too short, it was like trying to palm a basketball. He was steering her out onto the dance floor when he saw something that stood his heart still and then, with a labored double thump, started it again at max rpm.

It was the flash—real or imagined, remembered?—between dark uniforms and bright dresses, bare shoulders, of a red-gold flood of hair—

"Hey. Where are you going?"

"I got an allergy," he called over his shoulder. Her porcine form faded from his mind even faster than it did from his vision as he headed after the elusive flash. Like a fish after a lure, he thought for a moment to himself; but when he saw freckled shoulders, rounded cheeks, saw that it was really her, he forgot to think any more; his mind went blank. Only when a long arm came between him and Tawdry Doyle did he blink and begin again to function, like a battery-operated toy with an intermittent short. "Hey," said the arm. "Back off. This is my partner."

"Tawdry!"

"Hi, Phil. Long time, huh?"

The rest of the arm came into view. It owned a large body, a knuckle-nosed six feet of it with hair like the fuzz on a used tennis ball.

"Hi," said Philo.

"Get lost," said the arm. "Classmate."

"It's all right—Hermie?"

"Hymie."

"It's all right. He's my cousin."

"You didn't tell me you had a cousin here."

"I haven't told you a lot of other shit, too, Hymie. Say—I got an idea."

"What?"

"Why don't *you* get lost? I think you're a loudmouth and no gentleman. Shove off, turkey."

The arm put a two-second glare on both of them, strong enough to sunburn, and then stalked away. Philo forgot him instantly as Tawdry pulled him closer. There were upperclass watching from the balcony above; but he did not care any more; he could smell her . . . she was here . . . the same wide mouth, the way her upper lip wrinkled as she smiled, the overwhelming physical *hereness* of her. . . .

"Let's go in the coatroom," he suggested.

"You want to talk, huh?"

"No. I mean, yeah." He took her arm. "Jeez, Tawdry—where've you been? I looked in the phone book—I called every Doyle in Anne Arundel County."

"Let's go out the side door here. No, you couldn't reach me that way. My mom's name is O'Connor now. And I don't live with them anyway."

"You have an apartment?"

"Sort of . . . but no phone. Christ," she said, hugging herself as they emerged into the open air. "It's cold out here."

"Yeah," said Philo. They stood in the shadow of the terrace, between Bancroft and Dahlgren, in a little park filled with quaint old-fashioned machine guns. It was fairly dark and he suddenly found that it was well worth risking fifteen and three to kiss her.

"I like the way you kiss, Phil."

"Uh," he said. "More."

"Hey. You know what?"

"What?"

"I kind of missed you after that dance."

"Yeah? Well, why didn't you call me? At the main office—"

"I started to. Then I couldn't remember your last name. I'm such a dummy sometimes. I remember it was kind of an ordinary name—"

"You're about the only person around here who thinks so. I looked for you at the last tea fight too."

"I couldn't make it. I don't make them all. Just when I get lonely."

"Oh."

"But I made this one. And I'm real glad to see you, Phil."

They kissed again, he not trusting himself to speak. He held her against the stone and it seemed less cold outside. Through her dress he could feel the sharp bones of her pelvis. He wondered if she could feel. . . .

"Boy," she said, "are you hard up. Hey, I've got a car now. Let's go someplace private."

"What? I can't ride in a car. They throw guys out for that."

"Okay," she said. She was breathing as fast as he was and her eyes were half-closed. "Let's just get in back then."

The car was a battered Ford, so old the paint was turning leprous, and there were holes through the side panels. The back seat folded down. There was a blanket, smelling like dogs. Even as he pulled it over them he knew he shouldn't be doing this. They were parked less than a hundred yards from Commander's Row, where the officers and their families lived in big, white, awninged houses. Public Display of Affection, he thought. They would zap you big for just holding hands in the Yard; imagine if he got caught doing *this*—

"Oh, Tawdry."

"Oh. Oh. Harder. Oh!"

When they were done she held him hard under the blanket. It was over both their heads and it was utterly dark and completely warm and the smell of both of them was mixed with the animal smell until you could not tell which was what. Voices came by the car and went on by, dwindling back into the world that existed, somewhere, outside the world they had there, with each other. He smiled blindly, feeling against his face and body the curve of her cheek, her shoulder, her hip, all quiet and quiescent and intimate and close and warm and for the first time he realized how hungry he had been for months just to *touch* someone.

"What is it?" she whispered.

"I was just smiling."

"I'm glad. You feeling good?"

"Oh, *yeah*."

"Want to do it again?"

"Do you want to?"

"Sure."

"Okay."

After that they lay close again and let the warmth creep back between them. Outside the metal shell of the car it was quiet. Faintly, through the night and the old stone of the walls and the slowly rusting steel, they could hear the dance band. For a while it was nice but then it began to annoy him, the sound, and he tried to ignore it then, tried and failed, and at last lifted up a corner of the blanket so that the street light fell on the steamed-over face of his watch.

"What is it?"

"It's okay. Just checking the time."

"You got to go?"

"Not yet."

"What a way to mess around."

"Yeah."

They lay close again for a while, but he could feel that something had changed in her. He felt her take a breath a couple of times, as if to talk, but nothing came out. Then she took a third breath, a deeper one. "Hey," she said.

"What?"

"You think I'm cheap, don't you?"

"What? No, I don't." The thought had really not occurred to him. To him she was simply unquestioned wonder, a stroke of luck too grand and lovely to be thought about at all. "I don't."

"Going into the coatroom with you the first time we met. Then here in the car. That's the way I am, Phil. I don't ask for anything from the mids I go with. So you all think I'm cheap."

"I don't think you're cheap, Tawdry."

"That's nice. But I don't believe you."

"Then why do you do it? If you think what you do makes people think you're cheap? Which I don't think."

"Why do I do it? Because I like to mess around."

"So does everybody."

"Let me tell you something," she said, wriggling closer to him under the doggy blanket. "It's like when I was a little girl. I just loved my body . . . playing with it, everything. When my mom told me about what it would do, about sex and all, I thought it sounded really neat. Like it was something that would really be fun to do. So I found a guy to do it with me. I was about eleven. But very developed."

"Uh huh," said Philo. "You are. Pretty too."

"You think so? All these damn freckles."

"I like freckles. Makes you look like an apple."

"I even have them on my butt."

"I'd like to see that."

"You're sweet. Hey, want to. . . ?"

"I don't think I can."

"If I do this. . . ?"

"Hey!"

Half an hour later he stood in front of the mirror in the Dahlgren head combing his hair—or anyway running a comb through the stubble. Tawdry had left, chugging off through Gate One, and this time he had her number, at a glass-repair place where she worked. He felt dry, empty; there was a hollow cavernous feeling in his stomach; he felt fantastic.

There's no thrill like not getting caught, he thought. And this had been far better than going over the wall. Even Do-Dirty Dan had probably never done *it* right in the Yard. On Commander's Row. Maybe no mid in history had . . . though a lot could happen in a century and a half.

When he reentered the Hall and broke into the automatic brace, double-timing up the winding ladder and across the fourth and sixth wings toward the Ghetto, he was still smiling, not on his face—no plebe smiled in Bancroft unless ordered to—but somewhere in his heart.

There are still, he was thinking, some beautiful things in the world.

CHAPTER TEN

Pick out the biggest and commence firing.
—Captain Mike Moran, USS *Boise,* at Cape
Esperance

Plebe year is dead.
No it's not—it's alive and well in Mexico City.
—Found in head, 31st Company area

*I*t was like old times, almost. He, in a soft stuffed chair, trying to look relaxed, but actually scared as hell. The office, bigger than Portley's, more officially luxurious, but with a curious utilitarian spartanness imposed over the standard Navy desk and carpet and furnishings. On a polished table near the door lay several issues of *Leatherneck,* their edges carefully aligned. On the other side of the desk, sitting with a framed photo of Chesty Puller glaring over his shoulder, two pairs of U.S. Marine Corps eyes aimed at the Mouse, was Major T. T. Bartranger. The file folder marked *McGiffin* lay neatly squared on his desk, held down by an ash tray lathe-turned from the base of a brass 155-mm shell.

"Yes sir," said Philo, wiping his palms surreptitiously on his trousers.

"What's that?"

"I said 'yes, sir.'"

"I haven't said anything yet," said Bartranger.

"Yes sir. I was just . . . saying, yes sir. Sir."

He could see the little major's eyes sharpen. So, behind him, did Puller's. The old man had never liked wise-asses. Then, after a moment, Bartranger shrugged slightly, as if he was used to hearing mids, on the carpet, produce statements that did not always make exquisite Cartesian sense. Philo tried to keep his own look steady, though it was rough. He remembered the stories about Black Bart: how he had a smile in the back of his neck, how he bench-pressed small cars, how his hobby at USNA was frying a mid for each reg in the book, as another man might collect stamps.

And there was still the memory of coming back over the wall that night . . . though he was sure Bartranger would never suspect that *he* was one of—

"I've been asked by Lieutenant (jg) Portley to have a talk with you," the major began. "I don't generally interview aptitude cases. I leave that to my company officers. This seems to be a special case, or so Portley says. So I decided I'd make an exception."

Philo waited, then decided this was the time. "Yes, sir," he said.

"I see the latest entry is a fifty-four A," the major went on, opening the folder, "A special aptitude report. It's from one of the upper-class in your company. I won't mention his name, but he's one of the men whose judgment I respect in the day-to-day running of the Thirty-Fourth."

This time when he paused Philo said nothing, merely sat there and sweated, and got sharp looks from both Bartranger and Puller.

"Mister McGiffin."

"Major?"

"Are you still . . . serious about a career in the Navy–Marine Corps team?"

"Yes sir, I am."

"Really sure?"

"Yes sir."

"I'm not so certain you should be. Neither is your company officer. He states here that he has discussed with you your aptitude for the service, as evidenced by your peer evaluations. Now, granted peer evaluations are sometimes wrong. Especially in the first semester of fourth class year. You could improve. But this special fitness report . . . it disturbs me."

Philo sat back in the chair and wished he could wipe his face. He had a pretty good idea who had submitted the 54-A, and what it said.

"Your first semester grades are sat," Bartranger went on. "Not good—just sat. Two-point-one isn't the sort of thing to impress a retention board with."

"No sir."

"I see especially you're having trouble with math. And placed on report twice for sleeping in that class. This institution is primarily an engineering school, Mister McGiffin. That's probably your most important class, aside from leadership training, of course."

"Yes sir," said Philo. "I'll try harder in class, sir. I really will."

"Well, that's what we like to hear," said Bartranger, his face relaxing just a bit. "Everybody here has faults, shortcomings. The idea of the Academy is to put you under enough pressure so that they come out . . . and then to help you correct them. In the end we have a trustworthy, competent, self-confident man, far above the average input from OCS or the ROTC programs, not just in academics but in the leadership area—bearing, initiative, manliness, ability to make tough decisions under intense physical and mental pressure— everything you need to take men into combat and win."

"Yes sir," said Philo.

"And what worries me," the major went on, tapping the opened folder, "is that it's just in this area that you fall short, according to both your peers and your seniors."

Philo nodded; against all his will, his throat was closing up, just as it had with Portley. But I'm not going to bawl this time, he thought. What can they do to me, anyway, that hasn't been done already?

"In a way it's a shame," said the major, seeming suddenly to soften just a bit; he swivelled back in his chair and tilted it back toward the photograph. "I do know part of the reason you're having a tough time here, and I want to take that into account, believe me. Your name is an honor in one way; but a big handicap in another."

"Yes sir."

"You know, McGiffin, when I was a plebe here—some years ago—I had a classmate named Elmo Fudd. God only knows what his parents were thinking about. But he used to go around all over the Brigade because the firsties wanted to see if he was short, bald, and had a big nose."

"Did he, sir?"

"Not then," said Bartranger. "At our last reunion, though . . . but look, I didn't ask you in here to tell sea stories. Living in the Hall with the name you have is a problem, I know. But it might help if you thought of it as an honor. Something to live up to. An inspiration, rather than a handicap."

"Sir?" said Philo.

"After all, old Philo Norton was a brave man. Good officer. Leader of men, even if they were Chinese."

"Yes sir."

"That's about it," the major said, flipping the file closed and tossing it into his out basket. "You've been counseled. You've got to work on your aptitude, McGiffin. And that equals attitude, for you. It'll be rough to do. But if you're serious about a military career, you've got to buckle down right now. The end of this semester, even, will be too late. You'll be out. Understand me?"

"Yes, sir."

"Dismissed."

Outside the battalion office, chopping down the hall, he carefully wiped his face clear of anger and apprehension. If any upperclass saw him in this mood it would be curtains. Bartranger had made it abundantly clear that any further evidence of lousy aptitude would be the end. But he could not contain it, his stomach began to quiver, and then he saw the door of a head out of the corner of his eye and cut a sharp corner into it and closed the door of the stall and sat there. It was the only place he could be alone with his feelings. He sat there blankly and looked at the veinings in the marble stall dividers.

It was Breen, of course, who had submitted the special fitness report. He was not in Philo's direct chain of command in the company, did not write his regular evaluations, so he'd taken the chance to slip it to him with a special dirt sheet. He could imagine the kinds of things Bartranger had read from the folder while Philo sat in front of him. He'd heard most of them from the upperclass already, a hundred times over; hangdog look, poor attitude, can't take it physically, excessively timorous, conducts himself in an unaggressive way, lacks self-confidence.

Damn, he thought wonderingly. Am I really like that? A puke, a rabbit? He was small, sure. Maybe he clutched up sometimes when he wasn't sure of himself. Guns and heights scared him. But everybody was afraid . . . sometimes . . . weren't they?

But nobody else in the company seemed to have the problems he did.

Oh, hell, he thought, and then did not know what to think next. He hugged his knees, staring at the inside of the stall. A graffito caught his eye, a long one, pencilled on the door.

MONSTERS EXIST

They hide in forests, at construction sites, in swamps, at rocky beaches. Why I bet there's even one hiding over at Isherwood Hall waiting to kill somebody. All monsters know how to do is kill people. They're trained for it. They're too dumb to do anything constructive. They'll just be walking through the woods or something and see a bum cooking some mulligan stew. The monster will kill the poor bum. Not to eat. Just for nothing.
I do, I do, I do believe in monsters.
Monsters have to exist. How else could people take
pictures of them to put in the movies???

He put his head down. His free period was almost over. He had to be seated in Room 310, Maury Hall, for European History since 1814 in fourteen minutes. And here I am, he thought blindly, crying onto the trousers of my working uniform blue alpha; weeping for the homelessness of monsters, doomed to live in a world to which they can never belong.

"McGiffin! Where in the hell do you think you're going?"

It was Breen's voice. Again. Everlastingly. Philo stopped dead in the corridor, composed his face, and then did a neat little squared corner and chopped back to him, stopped again, and came to attention. "Sir. I have a comearound to Mister Reefer tonight, sir."

"Since when does a second class take precedence over a first class?"

"This is a squad comearound, for professional topics, sir. I thought—"

"No," interrupted Breen. He stood leaning against the jamb of his room, tall, solid, square-jawed, somber, impeccable. "You *didn't* think. Go tell Mister Reefer to excuse you. You're coming around to me tonight."

Philo clamped his teeth shut, but couldn't stop his thoughts. Why is it always me? I'm not even in this guy's squad. And that special report chit to Bartranger—what has he got against me?

"Well, McGiffin?"

"Sorry, sir. Aye aye, sir."

When he got back to the assistant company commander's room Breen was standing in front of his mirror. Philo remembered to pull his chin in extra tight. "Midshipman Fourth Class McGiffin, sir," he shouted, popping to.

"Ah, McMouse. Here, brush me off."

"Aye, sir." He flicked the whisk broom over Breen's back, reaching up to get his shoulders. They were immaculate as far as he could see. But that made no difference, nor did the rule against using plebes for personal services. As he brushed, seeing Breen's eyes on his own image in the mirror, he risked a glance at the window. His mood lightened a little as he saw that several gulls had left their calling cards during the night.

"Hey, Mouse. You asked anybody around yet?"

"No sir."

"You know," said Breen, frowning into the glass as he crimped the dimple into his tie, "There might not *be* a Hundredth Night this year. Seems the Brigade staff decided to leave it up to individual companies. What do you think of that?"

"Ah . . . I'll find out, sir."

"Still don't know what you think, huh, Mouse?"

I know what I think of you, you bastard, he thought, but aloud he only said, "No sir."

"Maybe you'll figure it out some day."

"Yes, sir."

"We'll decide some time this week, I guess," said Breen. "The other stripers and I. I don't know. Seems hardly worthwhile to have

Hundredth Night with the plebes we got this year. No spirit, no spark—I don't know. There's something missing there, and we can't quite figure out how to get it back. Maybe we can't."

Philo finished brushing his trousers and came to attention again. Breen turned to him, then backed off a step, his nose wrinkling. "My God, McGiffin. Don't you believe in the USNA laundry?"

"Yes sir."

"When'd you send that set of sweat gear out last?"

"One—no, two weeks ago, sir."

"Good God. You smell like the inside of a stable. Get over there by the window. Might's well sit on the green bench."

"Aye aye, sir." He went to the window and dropped into the by now familiar posture. His knees began to hurt, but not as sharply as before. On Kaufman's advice he was taking two aspirin half an hour before comearounds now.

"You know, Mouse, that worries me about your classmates. You're just the worst case of it, that's all. They're whimps, most of them. Those that aren't don't seem to be interested in anything except academics. They're apathetic. Except Gray—he might turn out okay. But what's with the rest of you guys?"

"I'll find out, sir."

"I doubt it."

"Yes sir."

"That's why I concentrate on you, McGiffin. Maybe if I can figure you I can figure them. And if I can't I'll at least spare the Navy one mistake."

"Sir?"

"You don't belong here, Mouse. I've got nothing against you personally. But you belong at some pussy civilian college, where you can sit up front of the class and learn accounting. You just aren't an Academy man. I think you ought to realize that and put in your chit."

"I belong here, sir," said the Mouse, through locked teeth.

"I think you're wrong," said Breen, giving himself one last self-satisfied look in the mirror and pulling out the tab of his sword belt to hook onto his scabbard. Evidently he had main office watch tonight. "I think you're dead wrong and too stubborn to admit it.

And that's why, McGiffin, I've decided to run you out of here."

Philo shuffled his feet quickly, swallowing a groan.

"Mister Breen, sir?" said Cross, at the door. His eyes met his classmate's and they exchanged a wink. "Lieutenant Portley's compliments, and he would like to see you for a moment before you go on watch, sir."

Breen left. Philo, alone now in the room, braced himself more fiercely. It would be just like Breen to come in suddenly and fry him for slacking off. He held himself tight against the wall, sitting on air. Minutes crept by. His gym shoes kept slipping in sweat and everything from his chest down was turning numb. Worse than that, the ten-minute call came and went, plebes screaming in the corridor about chicken tetracycline and the days till June Week. Then there was a long pause. He watched the door, sweating steadily. He left me in here without orders, the Mouse thought. He's probably standing right outside the door, ready to write me up for securing myself without permission. . . .

"Sir you now have five minutes till evening meal formation. Formation is inside. The officers of the watch are—"

Sweat and pain and growing fear.

"Sir you now have *four* minutes—"

I can't secure myself, he thought.

But if he's forgotten about me, and I miss formation—

As the three-minute call came and finished without a sign of the first class, Philo decided. He stayed shoved out, but waddled to the door, still in the position, to see if he could spot him somewhere in the corridor.

Breen was nowhere in sight, but Stamper was, walking down the corridor rapidly and humming to himself. As he saw Philo he stopped dead. "Mouse! What the hell are you doing in sweat gear?"

"Mister Breen left without securing me, sir. I guess he forgot."

"I guess so," said Stamper. "I think he went down to early meal already. Why don't you secure." As he caught Philo's hesitation he added, "Yeah, I know—I'm a second class, he's a firstie. Forget that shit, Mouse. Come on, I'll help you dress. Hey, Time Warp—tell 'em that McGiffin and I'll be a little bit late."

They both ran into Philo's room. With Stamper alternately curs-

ing and dressing him, they skidded into formation ninety seconds
later with Philo missing a tie clip, cufflinks, one sock, and with one
shirt button fastened. As he stood in ranks, panting, his legs trembling from the green bench so that he could hardly stand, he saw the
upperclass glancing back toward him with little smiles, pitying
shakes of the head, as if to say: what a whimp. Too scared to secure
himself. As he took a breath and brought his chin up he heard
Breen's words again, echoing in the corridors of his mind as if spoken aloud.
No spirit. No spirit. No spirit.

With Breen gone from the table, and Keyes deep in talk with the
second class about service selection, Philo got a little to eat. He
bolted it without chewing, and the chicken compound, a close second to fried liver as the Brigade's least favored meal, congealed in a
lump just forward of his kidneys. When the mess hall emptied he
chopped back toward the eighth wing, moodily pondering the shov-
ing-out incident, reviewing his whole relationship with Breen.
    There was something funny about it, all right. It all had started
when he'd bad-lucked onto the striper's table. Breen really seemed
to have it in for him. He thinks I'm fucking up his company, Philo
thought, squaring a corner. That's why he sent that 54-A up to
Bartranger.
    But there was more to it than that. Every once in a while, when I
do something right, I can see that—the way he sort of smiles, kind
of surprised. And at times Philo would catch Breen studying him,
catch the firstie's air of puzzlement, almost of concern. It's as if
sometimes he wants me to make it, and sometimes he wants me out.
    He headed upward, knees hurting as he hit each step, his breath
echoing in the concrete stairwell. There was no one else in it, but he
was as obliviously braced up as ever. And how do I feel about him?
    Hate his guts, said the quick flip-smart mid within him.
    True? False? Pick one. No multiple choices. But there were times
and places and feelings where life was neither true nor false. You
could hate a man and respect him, want to be like him and yearn to
smash in his face, to get even, to show him what you were made of.
Only here it was all on one side. The firsties dished it out and you

just gritted, grunted and gave. No other option, except signing your chit—the option Breen, in fact, had recommended that evening, just before he left for watch squad inspection—

Watch squad inspection. He emerged from the stairwell onto 6–2, an unconscious frown making a passing youngster do a double-take. Why had his mind stopped suddenly on that phrase, reached far back to summer, to someone telling a tale. . . .

And suddenly he remembered. It took only a fraction of a second to set itself up in his mind. In the middle of the corridor he spun on his heel, nearly wiping out the plebe running along behind him, and doubled back toward the Rotunda area, climbing one ladder per wing until he was on 2–3. The upperclass were unfamiliar and no one bothered him as he ducked into the head there and opened the cleaning gear locker, where the moke kept his swabs and buckets. Wax . . . polish . . . ah, here it was. He turned the can over in his hands, looking at it closely. Cleanser, Detergent, Scrubbing, Type II.

It wasn't flour, but it would do.

He tore open three of the cans and dumped them into a paper towel. There was string in the locker too and he cut a thirty-foot piece and wrapped one end around the bundle, holding it closed with a slip knot. He ducked his head out to check the corridor clock. Yes; first section should be forming up just about now.

Wait a minute, Philo, he thought then. Are you really sure you want to do this? A noise in the corridor startled him and he stepped into one of the stalls and drew the bolt and stood there, holding the heavy string-wrapped paper, staring at the polished commode. It was not too late to back out. He wasn't the right guy for this anyway. Untie the packet, dump it into the bowl, flush once, forget it. Right? That was the smart, the safe thing to do.

Hell, he thought, then his mind was empty for a while. Safe? You were never safe. There was always something ahead to face. There always would be. He felt afraid at that for a moment, at all the future, and then he frowned again.

Someone inside him had just laughed. Someone who sounded a little like old Dirty Dan . . . and a little like himself . . . and then there was someone who was a stranger, but familiar; someone who sounded devil-may-care, happy-go-lucky, not at all scared, no matter what.

Philo N.? he thought.

Ah, to hell with it anyway, he thought then, turning from the open commode. They're going to bilge me no matter what I do. Portley . . . Breen . . . some anonymous aptitude board.

Besides, if he was going to do it at all he had no more time to think about it. It had to be done *now*.

He rolled out of the head and squared the corner, package tucked tight under his arm. God, he thought, I hope it doesn't leak. "Any attempt to commit an offense will be treated as if the offense was actually committed." He hesitated at the double doors to the Rotunda, then stepped out and closed them firmly behind him.

He stood on an ornate wrought-iron balcony, sixty feet above the great domed court that was the heart of the Academy. Above him, enclosed by pendentives and arches, was an enormous mural of the battle of the Philippine Sea, picked out with spotlights.

He lowered his eyes. Far below was the marble-mosaiced floor of the Holy of Holies of Bancroft Hall, the open area just behind the immense bronze doors that opened on to Tecumseh Court.

On it, the watch squad was forming up. White cap covers, the glitter of swords, the spotless blue uniforms and polished brass of some thirty men, brushed and gleaming for the tightest spit-and-polish inspection at Annapolis—probably in the whole Navy. Often the Admiral himself would come down for a look, and there was always a lieutenant commander or a Marine major or lieutenant colonel as inspecting officer. There was no sound from below; the whole ceremony of inspection and relief of the offgoing watch took place in sacerdotal silence.

A familiar pace drew his eyes. Yes, it was Breen, looking oddly foreshortened from this far up. He took his position at the front of the forming ranks and a whisper of his voice floated upward in the hushed air.

Philo measured off nine yards of the light line and tied the bitter end to the center of the railing. He worked fast. A kind of passion was coming over him. He felt no longer the same—he was no longer, or anyway was not for a moment, the Mouse—

"Watch squad." The order, in Breen's crisp-ringing command tone, echoed amid marble and bronze. "Atten-*hut*."

Philo hefted the package. The dizziness increased. His forehead was breaking out in prickles. There was no more time to think, it was too late already—

It wasn't poppy seeds or chewing gum any more. Or even going over the wall. If he was caught now it would be *big*. A hundred demerits—dismissal—

"Ah, shit," he said, and threw it.

The parcel went out overhand, as hard as he could throw. It spun a little as it reached the end of the line, beginning to drop, and then the knot slipped and it exploded soundlessly in an unraveling fall of white smoke, many yards above the motionless ranks of the oncoming watch, waiting patiently for inspection.

Barely in time, he remembered to turn and run.

"Cripes, guys—did you hear what happened?" said Zeard, bursting into the room. The shoulders of his service dress blues still bore a distinct wash of white, driven deep into the felty wool by vigorous brushing.

"What?" said Gray. "Hey—aren't you supposed to be down at the Main Office?"

Zeard made wild motions with his long arms as he described how they, the oncoming watch, had been standing there spic and span, polished and brushed to the last perfection, but still sweating because Lieutenant-Commander Joynes was the inspecting officer, when down on them had come a vast cloud of white stuff. The gritty powder had drenched the formation, wiping out uniforms, shoes, the works. No one had yet figured out what it was, or who had dumped it. He propped one of his feet on the edge of the desk. "Look at that," he said, half bitterly, half in elation. "I tried to brush it off with a rag. The stuff is like sandpaper. They sent us all back to change. Christ! What an idiot!"

"The guy who did it?" asked Rollo.

"Hell, no—he had balls by the bushel. I mean Breen. He lost the bubble—started running up the ladder, screaming and waving his sword. Joynes called him back down and chewed his ass right in front of everybody. It was great." Zeard took his shoe down, rubbed his hands, and grinned. "So relieve the watch won't go till twenty-one hundred tonight. What a scene! What a douche-out!"

Philo composed his face over the book he had been reading as his roommate began to change uniforms. After a few minutes he got up. Turned to his locker, he permitted himself a grin. There was a sound in the corridor and he sobered instantly. He took out his SDB blouse and held it to the light. A few grains of white powder clung to the inside of the left sleeve. He brushed them off very carefully and hung the jacket behind a fresh one.

After study hour Wiebels came in. He dropped into the chair Gray offered him, his face alight. "Hi, Mouse. Carry on, you two. Say, did you hear—"

"Yeah, Zeard told us. What do you think?"

"Think?" repeated the youngster. "I think it's four-oh. Wish I'd of been there. Dan would have loved it." He rubbed his head, a little of the glee going at the mention of Dubus. "Damn . . . I been cramming all night. Literature! Why do we got to take *that* horseshit? Give me Weapons. Next week we get to build little model warheads with plastic explosive and set 'em off over in Ward. Now, that's what I came here to study."

"Sounds like fun. Boy . . . that could be nice stuff to have."

"I'll try to abscond with some, if you really want it."

"Thanks," said Philo, getting up; it was too hard to keep his face straight. "Well, Muff, I'm gonna hit the head before lights out."

"Good luck."

After study hour, just before taps, the seaward head was the fourth class wardroom. "The one thing all the youngsters say about it," Ash was saying as he came in, "is, don't take their hand. They'll try to get you to spoon them. Don't fall for it. It's considered cowardly, or something."

"I don't think we'll have to worry about Hundredth Night at all," said Ind. "Kim says we're all such pussies, he's against having one this year."

"I'd just as soon skip it," said Castigliano. "I mean, it sounds like a gigantic red-ass. Fun is fun, but I got to study at least one night this semester."

"I heard we're going to have it."

"Well, I heard not."

"They're going to vote on it, *I* heard."

"Who?"

"The firsties, dumbass. Who else?"

"Firsties," said Kaufman. "Did you hear how Breen got wiped out tonight?"

"Yeah."

"The hardass. He rated it."

A segundo came into the head. "Well . . . so long," said Ash to them all.

"Night."

"G'night."

Lying in his rack an hour or so later, listening to the ticking of his clock, Philo McGiffin was still awake, and still thinking.

He was reliving for the dozenth time how he had felt that afternoon, looking over the balcony on 2–3, the Ajax bomb heavy in his right hand. Looking down, as he had from the top of the water entry platform. Only now was he remembering that he had felt no fear of the height. Apprehension, yes; but of a different sort; a less personal, less squalid and shameful kind. In fact, now that he had time to analyze it, perhaps it had not been apprehension at all, but excitement.

What can they do to me? he asked himself, there in the dark. They could throw him out. That was the worst thing they could do. And it didn't look as if he would make it through anyway. So why not, he asked himself silently, why not go out like somebody—like a man—like Philo McGiffin?

He smiled at the image Zeard's description had called up. Of Breen, powdered half an inch deep in scrubbing cleanser, running screaming up the ladder, and being reamed in front of everybody by a lieutenant commander.

Yes—and further back, trying to get his sword out at the Army game march-on.

Scrubbing the seagull shit off his balcony with his nailbrush.

Philo giggled, then stopped, a little scared; but Zeard's high snore whined on, and Gray breathed away in his remote dreams of high stripes, and there was complete silence from Rollo's rack. And outside the wind sighed and howled over the hollow clanking of the Ghetto's faulty radiators.

A new worry occurred to him. Would there be a Hundredth Night? Would the firsties approve it—deign to give the plebes the opportunity to be run for a month?

Hell, he thought suddenly. Why should *they* decide? Hundredth Night is when *we* have *them* around. *We're* the ones who ought to be deciding. Not them.

He lay and thought about it for a long time; and then, feeling the fear familiar and hollow in his stomach, but knowing it now for what it really was, he reached out to set his clock.

0430 found Mouse McGiffin standing shivering in the seaward head filling a five-gallon galvanized pail from the moke's shack with cold water. The pressure was low here on the fifth deck and the icy water rose slowly. He yawned. It was cold and the corridors were dark. He tucked his hands inside the pockets of his sweat gear and waited for the pail to fill. Under his arms, despite the cold, he could feel sweat begin to trickle.

Ten minutes before reveille he hit the door screaming and douched Breen out in his rack with five gallons of ice-cold water. "Can't decide about Hundredth Night, huh?" he screamed. "Well, chew on this! *Come around, asshole!*"

Somehow, all through the next ten minutes—each minute as long, it seemed, as all the time consumed in building the pyramids—he somehow forgot what he was doing there; where he was; even who he was. He forgot Breen coming out of his wet rack, silent and fast as a tiger. He forgot the look on his face as he wiped off water and saw for the first time who had done it. Then, quite suddenly, he began to remember again; yet still he could not place the time, the occasion.

It was very strange. He perceived quite clearly that he was hanging by both arms from a shower bar in sopping-wet clothes, breathing hard. The shower was on full, cold. But he did not know what he was doing there. When a hand came through the shower curtains he stared at it stupidly. Over the roar of the water a voice—he couldn't identify it, but it seemed familiar—was offering persuasively to spoon him, to knock off this ridiculous business and take things on a first-name basis from here on.

Hanging there, panting, he had no idea what business the voice was referring to, and was unclear as to what the hand meant; nor had he yet figured out, pastless, memoryless, who he was. He seemed to be hanging from a shower bar in wet sweat clothes, but that was obviously unlikely. A dream, perhaps? But in dreams you remembered *something* of your waking identity. . . .

"Come on, Mouse. What do you say? You got what you wanted. Here. Call it off and shake hands."

It was eerie, but not as yet actively frightening. He hung on the bar and watched the hand curiously. If he really were hanging by his arms in a shower, there must be a reason why; but he could dredge up from blankness no clues to work on. He did seem to recall that there was something wrong with these repeated offers to shake hands, and he refused several times in as picturesque and forceful language as he could muster.

That day was the longest of his life. He was run till the morning meal bell and spent all of morning meal clamped on like an opossum. He reported ten minutes before noon meal formation and spent them all shoved out, rigging two M-ones. Noon meal he sat shoved out at the table, chopping in place, while Breen and Keyes shouted abuse and questions. He had one free period in the afternoon that coincided with Breen's and he spent that running and duck-walking up and down the hall, stopping only to throw up twice. Evening comearound started half an hour early and continued right through the meal. The chow was nonexistent, or worse—olive oil and Tabasco, or mustard sandwiches.

But there was an odd thing about it too. His memory snapped back on the way to morning meal and he was totally his suffering self again as he c-clamped the edge of Keyes' table. The second and third class looked at his wet hair and pop eyes, and then looked at Breen. "Hey," said the firstie. "Know what the Mouse pulled this morning at reveille?"

"What, Brad?"

"Hit me with a pail of ice water. Asked me around for Hundredth Night."

"No shit!"

"The Mouse did that?"

"Our Mouse?"

"Mister Meek?"

There was an odd tone both in their voices and in Breen's. Almost a note of . . . pride?

The Mouse hung on grimly, cursing. After a while he stopped cursing—it took too much energy—and just hung on, while puddles of sweat collected on his empty dish. Breen shouted at him, and offered, in front of the whole table, to spoon him again. But he hung on, shaking his head stubbornly, even when Keyes said he was getting too much sweat in his eyes and ordered Kaufman to peanut-butter his forehead. In fact, he was grinning fiercely as Rollo Skippied his eyebrows.

"You think this is funny, McGiffin? A real party?"

"Yes sir, you whale turd sir, I do."

"Well, I'll tell you something that's not so funny, then," said Breen. "Because asking me around this morning, McGiffin, was the biggest mistake you've ever made. Here it is. I've been holding back on you, trying to get you to wise up. Now I'm through. I give you eight days to crack. That's all you'll last, McMouse. You had your chance to spoon me. The only way you're going to live to Hundredth Night now is to put in your chit." He looked around the now-silent table, smiling slightly. "You think I don't know who pulled that flour bomb routine? I don't know what's come over you all of a sudden, but you've gone too far. Eight days, and you'll either be a civilian or dead.

"Still think it's funny, McGiffin?"

The Mouse was no longer grinning. Breen meant it. He could see that. He was at his best. Cool, impressive, in command, and utterly convincing. Not for the first time, he knew he admired this firstie. Admired . . . envied . . . hated . . . respected. And now it was out in the open. Head to head. Breen versus the Mouse.

"Is that your nose, sir," he said, "Or did your suspenders break?"

And from there the day ground on downhill, inch by inch, like a glacier; and in the course of it Tony Castigliano asked Kim around with a full bowl of chow mein; Len Ind asked Mister Baylor, the Georgia boy, around with a note scrawled in Magic Marker across the Rebel flag in his room; and Howie Zeard asked Singleterry around by drenching his uniform locker with a bottle of what he called "Cochon de Paris 12-day Cologne."

By the time taps sounded that evening every plebe in Slack 34th had asked his least favorite firstie around; and throughout Bancroft, but most balefully in the high fastness of the Ghetto, Hundredth Night Buildup ruled in red-eyed rage.

CHAPTER ELEVEN

Every year on the hundredth night before First Class graduation, there comes a time appropriately called "Hundredth Night" which is held dear to every Plebe. Plebes enjoy this night so much because the Fourth Class reigns supreme. Because they do, the Fourth Class can take "revenge" on the First Class by making them become plebes for the evening. This night, besides being a lot of fun for everyone, shows the First Class that they will soon be at the bottom of the ladder again as Ensigns in the fleet.

—Reef Points

IHTFP—Jimmy '47
—Found scrawled in soap on a mirror in the Fencing Loft

"All hands listen up to word," came the bored voice of a youngster mate from the hallway. "Heating service has been temporarily interrupted to the sixth and eighth wings. All personnel are cautioned not to adjust, play with, or disassemble the heating systems."

"What's going on?" said Philo.

"I heard about it in Chem," said Kaufman. His eyes were bleary from lack of sleep. "Some thermo slash in Thirty-first decided his radiator wasn't puttin' out. He tried to open his valve wider and it broke. Vented all the steam in the system through his room in about two-point-two seconds. Instant enthalpy."

"Great," said Zeard. He yawned. "It's been freezing all week anyway, it's time for a breakdown . . . all last night I could hear them in the walls."

"Hear who, Howie?"

"Our cockroaches. They're killing the mice for their pelts."

"Funny," said Philo. "Hey, Dick—you got any of that chow package left?"

"You all said you didn't like oatmeal cookies."

"They're okay if you soak them in the sink. Can I have a couple? Please?"

Gray hestitated long enough to let them know it was a favor, then nodded. "Sure, Phil. Roomies—after all." He checked the corridor, then stood on his desk to lift a ceiling tile. "Here. Close the foil up again and I'll put it back. Rollo, Howie—you want any?"

"Okay."

"Thanks, pal."

With the tile replaced, the food hidden from predators, the four roommates settled in again to study, slumped in their chairs. Their eyes, swollen and heavy, kept drifting closed, and often they would reach a leg under the desk to kick whoever seemed closest to unconsciousness.

They had spent the night before in novel ways. Philo had slept in full dress inside a knotted laundry bag. Zeard had "gotten his clothes pressed" by spending the night between two mattresses. Gray had crammed himself into the tiny shelf at the top of their lockers, next to the overhead, and Rollo Kaufman had spent the night on the smooth, cold tiles of the head.

"What's for tonight?" Zeard asked suddenly. Philo jerked awake. "What?"

"We're not going to get any sleep anyway. Why don't we get something going? Phil, that was great, what you did the other day to his rack. Breen was pissed blind."

"Couldn't have done it without help. Rolling the snowball was easy—it was getting it into the elevator, dragging it down the hall, and lifting it into his rack that was rough."

"He didn't wake up?" said Gray.

"Nope. When we left he had his arms around it and was murmuring, 'Gwen, Gwen, how can you be so cruel.'"

The four of them were laughing raucously when there was a sound from the corridor, a sort of soft detonation and then a yell.

"Fire in the hole!"

The four plebes jumped up as the door slammed against its stops, there was a hollow *thwock*, and a ball of flame came flying through the doorway. Philo ducked under the desk. Zeard threw himself backward as the ball hit the bulkhead, spattering yellow fire, and rebounded onto the desk and then the ceiling. At each bounce it left a patch of smoking flame. At its third ricochet Kaufman fielded it into the shower with his dixie cup, tossed the hat in too as it caught fire, and twisted the water on.

"Tennis ball," said Dick Gray. "And lighter fluid. Real smart. Who was that?"

"They're gone," said Zeard, from the door.

Philo came out from underneath the desk. They looked at him. "Where'd you go, man?" said Zeard.

"I'm afraid of fire."

"I wouldn't say that so they can hear," said Zeard, "or you'll wake up with napalm in your rack."

The study hour bell rang without further interruptions. When the lights dimmed Philo made for the head. The corridor was chilly. Tonight, Breen had told him at evening meal, he had to sleep somewhere in the Snorkel's office. That wouldn't be too bad, he thought. Even the floor of an office was better than that damn laundry bag. He'd stood it, almost insane with claustrophobia and near-suffocation, until about 0300, and then cut himself out from the inside with his utility knife and gotten Zeard up and gone down to the parking lot to roll Breen's snowball.

Ind and Fayaway were in the head. "Hi, Len, J.J."

"Hey, Phil."

"Hi, Mouse. What's the drill?"

Philo checked under each of the stalls; they were empty. He felt in his b-robe pockets for the pill bottle, flashed it to them, then hid it again.

"What are those?" asked Fayaway.

"Disclosure tablets?" said Ind. "The things you chew, and they stain your gums, show you where to floss?"

"Right."

"What are those for?"

"I got some ideas," said Philo. "But you got to wait till tomorrow morning to see if they work out. What are you fellows doing tonight?"

"Sleeping around, that's all."

"Where?"

"Snork's office."

"What? Me too."

They looked at each other for a long second, then turned and raced out of the head. Philo beat Ind this time, by a meter or more, but still he was the tenth man into the office, and more were arriving every moment. The firsties had ganged them up. Philo shared the top of the desk with Darrin and Hartford. It was not an entirely bad night though. Zeard found Portley's confidential safe unlocked and they had all the Trix they could eat.

And that was the second day.

The next morning, back in his room, he opened his locker to find his grease shoes frosted with half an inch of liver paté. Two maraschino cherries dotted the toes. "They're shot, Phil," said Gray, peering over his shoulder. "They'll never take polish again with the oil in the leather. He must have snuck in while we were in Snorkel's last night."

"That sucks," said Zeard, punching his arm.

"It's okay," said Philo, staring at the shoes. "I was in his room too." But he finished dressing very carefully. His caution was rewarded when he found a cup of stale beer under his cap on the top shelf; if he had snatched it down as usual he would have caught it on the head. He carried it quickly to the sink and chased it with tap water till not even the smell of it remained. Beer in the Hall was a Class A offense. Breen was escalating, upping the stakes. He's getting mad, the Mouse thought. Maybe I should slack off and just let him run me for a while.

And then he remembered, and thought, Philo McGiffin never slacked off.

Breen showed up late for morning meal formation. When he took his place at the front of formation there was a slight snicker in the ranks. His face was bright scarlet, extending down below the collar; so were his hands, where they showed at the ends of his sleeves. When they fell out to go down to meal he called Philo over. "All right, McGiffin," he said, speaking with difficulty. "What did you put in my shower head?"

"Me, sir?"

Breen came closer, sniffing suspiciously. "Say, is that alcohol I smell, McGiffin?"

"Not on me, sir."

"Are those your grease shoes?"

"No, sir. I'm saving them for a snack, sir."

Breen looked around then, seeing the smiles on the faces of the second class. "This dye better come off, Mouse, or you're screwed."

"Twelve or thirteen showers should do it, sir. Unless you haven't been flossing regularly."

He spent morning meal rigging a ten-pound bowl of ice cream at arm's length. The youngsters tried to talk him into putting it on Breen's head. He resisted the temptation. The assistant company commander had a dangerous look on his face, and the scarlet dye made him look uncommonly savage. But he kept quiet through the meal and so did Philo. An undercurrent of tension seemed to run through every utensil and bite of food on the table, as if it all were charged to several thousand volts' potential. He was glad when the bell rang and both first classmen jumped up and walked out of the mess hall, carrying jury-rigged egg sandwiches with them. As soon as they were out Stamper flashed the plebes two and they relaxed warily. "Damn," he said. "What was wrong with Brad? I was afraid to ask him about his face."

"I put disclosure tablets inside his shower head, sir."

"You're asking for it, Mouse. You press him too close and you'll be sorry."

"I have not yet begun to fight." Philo reached for toast and sausages.

"Better have some of that battery acid, Mouse."

"Yeah. You're sweating too much. Put some salt on those sausages."

"At least it's warm in here," Philo said, wolfing the toast.

"Yeah. I think they're trying adiabatic heating in the Ghetto now."

The second class talked among themselves, about the new cars that, in a few weeks, they might be allowed to bring into the Yard; the third class talked about women; the plebes ate. It was all very cozy and low key.

When they got back to their room the door was slightly ajar. Philo eased it open slowly, and looked up just in time to see the bucket start to tip. Zeard reached it down. "Pretty dumb," he said, looking into it.

"No imagination," Philo agreed. They poured the water in the sink, and it came out in a rush on their shoes, flooding the deck. They looked under the sink. The drain elbow had been removed.

"We better check this room out," said Howie, looking at his sopping feet. "*Good*. They must have had all of ten minutes in here while we were feeding our faces."

"Only twenty-one more days," said Gray.

"Great," said Rollo, sounding defeated. "Well, good-bye QPR. I never enjoyed studying anyway."

They checked the room thoroughly, moving like sappers entering an occupied town, but found nothing else. Only when Philo thrust his arms into his reefer did he sense something odd. When he took them out of the sleeves his blue uniform shirt was covered with talcum powder.

It was almost as cold on Stribling Walk as it was in the Ghetto. The wind, straight off the Severn, was like bayonets laid against his cheeks. All the upperclass had the collars of their reefers up. Philo and Len Ind walked along with theirs down. The uniform of the day was "collars down."

"Cold enough to freeze the balls off a Christmas tree," said Ind.

"Cold enough to freeze the skis off a Polack," said Philo.

"Hey," said Ind, "Did you hear about Baylor's latest invention? Cottontail races."

"What's a cottontail race?"

"Listen up and I'll tell you. Lunchbags gets these chow packages

from his folks down in Georgia. Mostly it's that southern crap—
pecans and that sweet shit they make. Well, this last one, he finds a
bag of little marshmallows. 'Whee-*ew!*' he screams, like he's remembered this great thrill. 'We goin' to have us some bunny races!'"

"You said cottontail races."

"Same-same. So here's the drill. He lines this other guy and me
up on the starting line in Service Dress Jockstrap. The marshmallows, one each, go in the crack of your ass. 'Five laps,' says
Lunchbags. 'End of the corridor and back. The guy who wins
doesn't have to eat the marshmallows. Ready—go!'"

"I hope Breen doesn't hear about that one," said Philo, concentrating on the frost smoke his breath made, the lazy way it rose drifting
in the direction of the Chapel. "Hey—what's going on over there?"

They stopped for a moment by the Mexican monument and
shaded their eyes. Something was going on high up on the dome;
men, scaffolding, ropes, tackle. "Oh, yeah," said the black mid at
last. "That cracked sheathing. They're putting on new copper."

They walked on. "But anyway," the Mouse continued, "Breen
gave me eight days before I broke. Six more to go. I figure if I can
last that long he might cut me some slack."

"I hope he does," said Ind. "But I don't think I'll see it."

"What do you mean?"

Ind had to go to Sampson, Philo to Melville; they paused in front
of the Macedonian monument, the figurehead with its big hooked
nose that always reminded him of Zeard. "Keep it to yourself, Phil,"
said Ind, "but I turned in my chit to the Snorkel yesterday."

"But we're almost through, Len! After Hundredth Night, the
youngsters all say it's practically over."

"Yeah. They were saying that before Army. And then after
Christmas leave. No, man, this bullshit gonna go on right up till we
climb Herndon. And even after that. Look at the upperclass. Study
your ass off to get a two-point-five so you can have Wednesday afternoon off to walk around Crabtown, where all the ladies look at
you weird 'cause you're a squid, and black besides. Where you can't
hold your woman's hand, where you can't go upstairs with her even
if one of the drag houses'll take a 'cullud boy'." Catching Philo's
stare, Ind shrugged, looking a little embarrassed. "It isn't you guys.

The mids are okay. Even that redneck Baylor—I think we could make out all right once we got a few things squared away. But look. My test scores, I can get into G.W. this semester, full scholarship. The white liberal world wants my ass. I can take poli sci—none of this engineering. And I don't really need five years of obligated service."

"And Debra's at George Washington."

"Uh huh. She's got an apartment on K Street. Invited me to move in." Ind stamped his feet in the fine remnants of snow, shivered, and looked back along the tree-arched length of Stribling, crowded with mids on their way between classes. "It wasn't an easy choice, Phil. I kind of liked the Academy. I'll miss you guys. But blue's just not my color."

Philo nodded. He felt pretty down; he liked Ind.

"I'm sorry I started all the Hundredth Night stuff, Len."

"Forget it. That's not what made up my mind. But you'll make it, Phil. Just hang on." Ind slapped his arm. "Keep it under your hat, now. I just want to leave quiet and not give Baylor time to crow about how he drove me out."

"Right, Len. See you later."

"Bye."

Calculus was vague and dull as usual. Philo came to a couple of times during the period. He got yanked for a recitation; at the board he looked hopelessly at the symbology and moved the chalk around; he had no idea what he was doing. Grades were coming up. But there was just no time to study. He took the prof's tired ass-chewing in silence and sat down. Have to get the gouge, he thought vaguely. He opened his three-ring and wrote three words in it for the day's lesson: Get gouge. Memorize.

"Ten," said Fayaway, who had come over to the room to help suit Philo up. "Ain't that enough? He isn't going to count them, is he?"

"He might ask. And if there aren't a dozen, like he ordered, he'll want twenty tomorrow morning."

"Your funeral."

Blinking sweat out of his eyes, Philo stared straight ahead. It was all he could do. Gray and Fayaway worked the eleventh pair of sweat pants over his elephantiasitical legs, tied them, and reached for the twelfth. A few minutes later they tilted him gingerly forward from his propped position against the bulkhead. "You look like a gray blimp," said Gray. "Can you walk?"

"I'll try."

"Look out! He's falling!"

"Let him go."

He rocked gently to a halt, face down on the deck. He wriggled a little inside six inches of cotton, then gave it up. He was helpless as a flipped turtle, a swaddled infant, a beached and gas-bloated whale. All he could move were his eyelids and the tips of his fingers.

"At least he won't get hurt," said Fayaway.

"Come on. We'll tow him over."

His two classmates each took a foot and double-timed out of the room. Behind them the Mouse slid smoothly along, face down, skidding outward as they squared corners in the hall. They set him on his feet outside Breen's door, waited for the clock to click over to 1800, and knocked.

"Get in here, McGiffin."

Gray pushed the door open and they ran as Philo toppled inward. Breen screamed and ranted, trying to run him, make him do pushups, ordered him to get up, but all he could do in his cocoon was flex the tips of his fingers obediently.

That night, while Breen slept, the Mouse and Rollo unrolled the hose from the 8–4 fire station. Leading it into his room, they sealed the bottom of his door with towels and turned the valve on low. At 0300, when the water reached the top of his mattress, Breen's scream of "plebe ho!" brought every fourth class in the company into the corridor. Everything they owned had to come out of their rooms and into a chest-high pile in the middle of the passageway; then for an hour they ran relay races through it. At 0400 he secured them with the promise of formal room inspections the next afternoon—with white gloves.

By the end of the week McGiffin and Breen had developed a routine. Each comearound began with the Mouse chopping in and spending some time "hanging around," from the top of the door, until his fingers went dead. Then he sat on the green bench or shoved out until his legs died. After a few days of conditioning this took ten or even fifteen minutes. Next, he did pushups to exhaustion, recovered his breath at dead horse or leaning rest, and then joined some of the other plebes in the hall for relay races. When he could run no more, not a staggering step, he went back to the door or the shower bar to get his wind. This continued till the five-minute call, when Breen secured him and he sprinted to his room and showered and changed and made formation. At tables, morning, noon, and night, he spent most of the time clamped on. Sometimes, to the upperclass' astonishment, he was even able to eat that way; but then, he was light and strong.

In the course of the routine he ceased, largely, to think. The very conviction that he couldn't take it for long helped. At some point, he knew, he would run out of rope. Lack of sleep, of food, physical exhaustion, mental fatigue—at some point he would collapse, be carted off unconsious to sick bay. Then at last there would be food and sleep, a day or two of rest, and then—why, he would come back, and it would all begin again.

And that was the only way he could see out. He didn't let himself consider the alternative, even when Breen made him fill out a special request chit for his resignation and made him carry it in his cap along with his Form Two and the sweat-stained picture of the girl from the magazine.

"Mouse!" Breen would shout—as he in fact did at evening meal that Friday night. "How many days you got left?"

"Four, sir."

"You sure? Isn't it only three?"

"No, sir. Four, sir."

"Get that chin in. You call that clamped on?"

"Yes sir," he grunted, moving his chin back another millimeter or so, then letting it slide forward again. That always made Breen scream, he knew.

Over the murmurs and shouts, screamed commands, clash of crockery and metal that filled the long, corridored tables of the mess hall, music began. The NA-10 was playing, up near the anchor. Philo's heart sank. That was it. He wouldn't get a bite for the rest of the meal.

"*McGiffin!*"

"Sir."

"What's that song?"

"I'll find out, sir."

"You don't know what that song is? They played that last week and I asked you what it was and you didn't know then. And you still don't know?"

"That's about the size of it, sir."

"What's the story on you, McGiffin? Where've you lived all your life? In a hole?"

"Yes sir, and I'm still here, sir."

Breen bent suddenly and looked under the table. Phil tried to haul his legs up from the supports of the table, but it was too late. "Damn you, Mouse! You're bagging out on me again. *Rig those knees!* There—what are they playing now?"

"Uh . . . "Dreams of Desire," sir?"

"What?"

"Don't guess, Mouse," Keyes contributed kindly. "You'll only make our assistant company commander pop his safeties."

A short period of silence. Clamped on, hanging from the table by elbows and knees pressed together, Philo made a groping motion toward the food that Gray had served out on his plate for him. A lobster tail, hot, thick with melted butter, steamed there just under his dripping nose. Straining, he got his hands on it, managed to break it open, had a clawed-out piece of the white flesh halfway to his already opened mouth—

"McGiffin."

"Sir." He let it drop, despairing. It missed the plate and fell in his lap.

"Feel like favoring us with some basic rates?"

"Any time, sir."

"What's a stadimeter?"

"Sir, a-stadimeter-is-a-visual-instrument-used-to-find-distance-between-your-ship-and-an-observed-object-of-a-known-height-above-the-water."

"What's the most famous monument in the cemetery?"

"The-most-famous-monument-in-the-Academy-cemetery-is-the-tall-icicled-granite-cross-which-is-a-replica-of-a-similar-cross-erected-in-the-wastes-of-Siberia-by-Chief-Engineer-Melville-honoring-his-lost-shipmates-on-the-*Jeannette*. The-original-wooden-cross-stands-over-the-body-of-Lieutenant-Commander-DeLong-who-was-officer-in-command-of-the-illfated-northern-polar-expedition."

"Tell me something about conditions of readiness."

"Material conditions of readiness, sir?"

"Right."

"Sir. 'Material conditions of readiness. To-assure-maximum-watertight-firetight-and-fumetight-integrity-of-a-ship-material-conditions-are-set-according-to-the-tactical-situation-as-follows. . . .'"

He droned on. When he was done Keyes popped in with a question. "McGiffin. What's the sixth largest sub fleet in the world?"

"Disneyland, sir."

"Oh, shoot. He's heard it."

"He seems to know his rates," said Breen. "Gray, was that all right? What he was spouting off?"

"Word perfect, sir."

"So explain to me, McGiffin, how it is that you can get all that happy horseshit stowed in your gourd and you can't remember a simple thing like a pop song?"

"No excuse, sir."

"No, go ahead, Mouse. You've always got an excuse. Let's hear this one."

"I guess I don't remember songs too well, sir."

"There's a lot you guess you don't remember too well, McGiffin, isn't there? Tell me again how many days you got left."

"Sir, I got four days till you said I would break, a hundred and twenty days till June Week, one thousand two hundred and fifteen days till I graduate from this turkey farm, and ten thousand, three hundred and forty days till I make flag rank and retire, sir."

Breen laughed with the others at the table. "Only the first one was right, McGiff. You got four days left in blue and then it's CIVLANT for you. But you get a break this weekend. I'm taking White Lightning into B-more to see Gwen. Just one thing. Stay out of my room."

"Sir? Why would I—"

"You know why. Just stay out. That's an order. In fact, I think I'll lock it."

"Lock your room?" said Keyes. "I've never heard of anybody doing that around here. Who has the keys?"

"Batt office, I think . . . you got that, Mouse? Just stay out of it. Get some sleep this weekend, and bring your chit in signed when you come around Monday morning." Breen got up as first class dismissal sounded. "See you guys."

"Have a good time, Brad."

"Fly low."

"Don't put it anywhere I wouldn't put it."

When one of the second class gave them carry-on Philo slumped into his chair, his stomach cramping and quivering. He stared at the lobster. At last he gave it to Gray.

He was thinking about it all that night. It was like a mystery story: a locked room you couldn't enter, how had the murder been committed . . . it wasn't until third period the next morning that he got the idea. The prof was talking about organic molecules—about carbon. About how carbon would bond to anything, practically. Bond, he thought. Stick. . . .

As soon as he got out of class he headed for the mid store and got two tubes of plastic glue, the kind some of the upperclass used for ship and aircraft models. Saturday night, when the last restriction muster was over and all the upperclass were on libs, he squeezed it out onto a piece of foil from one of Gray's chow packages, worked it under the crack in Breen's door until only one corner remained in the corridor, and then touched a match to it. As soon as it flamed he shoved it the rest of the way into the room, waited for about fifteen minutes, until the yellow flicker ceased, and pulled it back out, cursing as the foil burned his fingers.

When he went around Monday morning, his chit still in his hat unsigned, he found Breen waiting in his room. He looked hung over; his head was on his arms in a little patch of the desk he had wiped off with a towel. Except for that patch every horizontal surface in the room, including his rack, was covered with a thick coat of rich, black, greasy soot. Worse yet, Breen must have left his locker open when he left, and all his uniforms right down to his skivvies lay under a soft layer of lamp black. It looked as if Pompeii had gone off over the weekend.

"Clean it up," grunted Breen, not lifting his head.

He spent two full days at comearounds cleaning it up, and then the fun resumed.

The eighth day was something he did not really feel that he was involved in.

It was strange, he thought, trembling that evening at leaning rest, how detached you could become from your own body. All that day he had eaten nothing; he had been run like a dog; he had braced up even in his room, by Breen's orders—strictly interpreted, he would have had to brace up even in class, but they both knew doing that would bring the Academic Department down like an avalanche. He had done it all like a machine, without resentment or enthusiasm; running till his vision flickered on and off like a loose light bulb, clamping on till his elbows gave way and he fell on his back on the deck. He ran the corridor races, wheelbarrows, inchworms, crabs, toboggan races, seeing in a curious haze, as if there were bay fog in Bancroft Hall, or as if all the solid walls and decks were insubstantial, circumstantial, and there were times that day when he too felt light, immaterial, and only in tenuous connection with what he had always thought of as life. He did not, through all that day, even crack wise, the way tradition demanded a plebe occasionally bullshit the firstie he had asked around.

"Well, Mouse?" came Breen's voice, through the fog. "Gonna sign it?"

At leaning rest there he watched another drop detach itself from his nose, gather speed at thirty-two feet per second per second, and impact the opened piece of paper under his face with a soft *plop*. He tried to remember the equation for velocity. . . . *The undersigned hereby tenders his resignation as a member of the Brigade of Midshipmen and respectfully requests. . . .*

"No, sir."

"Pen's right here. Sign it and you get instant carry-on. *Permanent* carry-on. What do you say?"

He didn't say anything. He felt himself sliding off to sleep.

"McGiffin! Answer up!"

"Sir?"

"You gonna sign this chit, or not?"

He did fall asleep then and his arms buckled and he fell heavily, sagging down into the deck, rapping his chin. He lay there for several seconds watching the colors before Breen noticed that he had gone down and shouted him up again. His arms shook. The chit was wet now, the ink seeping and dissolving into the neat printed lines and boxes.

"You going to sign?"

"Negative, sir."

"You really think you belong here?"

"Affirmative, sir."

"You're making a big mistake, Mouse. You think you get through plebe year that's it. Bull roar. There's lots of upperclassmen get fired out of here on grades."

"I can hack that too sir."

The door came open, and Breen looked up. It was Wiebels, with the mate's brassard on his arm. "Red alert," he said, before the first class could speak. "Bogey incoming. Black Bart's reported en route."

"Thanks. Come aboard, McGiffin."

"Aye sir." He stood up wearily. His legs shook. Breen got up to open the door, then sat down at the desk again.

"Wipe off your forehead, Mouse. We don't want the battalion officer to get the idea we're imposing physical strain on our freshmen."

Wearily, they looked at one another. As they did so Philo thought suddenly, How seldom our eyes meet. The plebe, eyes in the boat, hardly ever got to look an upperclass directly in the face. You didn't stare. You were a mechanism, operating according to the programming of some voice emanating from the air near your head; not a human being, someone to be looked at or spoken to. You were not conversed with. You were commanded. Now, across Breen's freshly waxed desk, they looked straight at each other, and second by second Philo's chronic fatigue and fear dropped away and something fresh and defiant steadied him.

He could hold Breen's eyes, full on, and not drop his own.

At last, as if realizing it, Breen looked down at the deck. He sighed. "Mouse," he said, "you're a stubborn son of a bitch."

"No, sir."

"What is it then?"

"I just want to stay, sir."

"Is that all?"

He considered it seriously. It was a good question. "No—no, sir. I'd like to stand out, too."

"Now *that* you'll never do." Breen smiled, leaned back in his chair. With his solid chin and with his arms locked behind his head he looked the very picture of the rock-steady William Chandler Christy midshipman, a turn-of-the-century leader of men. "That you'll never do. But I'm beginning to think you might make it through here—just on stubbornness, of course."

"All secure in here?" said Major Bartranger, appearing suddenly in the door like a prestidigitator's illusion.

"Yes sir," said Philo.

"Yes, sir," said Breen, dropping his chair to the deck and standing up, although the Marine was not, strictly speaking, inside the room.

"Hundredth Night buildup?" said Black Bart, glancing keenly at both of them. Philo saw that he was no taller than himself. Odd—he had looked pretty impressive that night in the garden.

"Just some routine plebe indoctrination, sir."

"Keep to the regs, Mister Breen."

"Aye aye, sir."

"He treating you okay, Mister McGiffin?"

"He's not giving me much slack, sir. But I've got nothing to complain about."

"Enough to eat? Sleep? You look a little ragged."

He felt Breen's look shift for a moment from the major to him. He felt annoyed that the firstie should even worry. "I get all I need, sir," he said.

"Good," said Bartranger. He looked around the room once more, still not coming in, and moved away down the corridor. They heard

his footsteps fade. After a minute more Breen stuck his head out for
a recon.

"Okay, McGiffin. Our conscience is gone."

Obediently, Philo dropped to leaning rest again.

But somehow he made it through that day, the eighth day, without collapsing quite, and without signing the chit either. After the
battalion officer's visit the Snorkel started eating lunch with the
company, instead of drinking it at the O club, and the fourth class
got one meal at least every twenty-four hours. After having his room
wiped out Breen seemed unwilling to go head to head any more with
the practical jokes. Or maybe he was just growing tired of the game.
It was true that he spent every evening he could in Baltimore,
wheeling the white Porsche out from its space in the first class lot
and sending it whining along Brownson Road, sounding his horn as
he turned for Gate One so they could all, even on 8–4, listen for the
roar as he accelerated in the direction of Route 50. Some of the
second class spoke knowingly of arched swords and miniature rings
and the Chapel after graduation, the first legal opportunity the
newly commissioned ensigns and second lieutenants had to marry.

Philo didn't listen all that closely. He was still concentrating on
hanging on, and looking forward to noon meal every day.

On the ninth day he burned the still unsigned chit in his shitcan.
The flames were yellow from the salt in the paper.

On the tenth, Zeard, to his surprise, flipped a letter on his blotter
as he came in. "What's the matter? Don't you check your mail slot,
boy?"

"I never get anything."

"You got something today. Smells good, too."

The handwriting was unfamiliar. He tore the envelope open
hastily.

Dear Phil,

Haven't heard from you for a while. I know you're busy,
plebe year and all, but how about taking some time out for fun.
I can pick you up some night and get you back before revellee.

We can drink some wine and mess around at a place I have. What do you say?

Tawdry

PS—You can call me at work. I still don't have a phone.

"What is it?" asked Zeard, turning on his study light.
"Nothing big."
Call—or not to call? He had enough to worry about. Breen, Bart-ranger, his grades. There would be time for girls later. Tawdry—she was nice, but he couldn't have her flitting in and out of his life. Could he? He writhed a little on the chair. It was her perfume on the letter, all right.
He was suddenly conscious that not all hunger is for food.

CHAPTER TWELVE

The Superintendent is charged by Title 10, U.S. Code 6962, with reporting to the Secretary of the Navy any midshipman who possesses insufficient aptitude for commissioned service. Aptitude for the service will be measured and judged by evaluating demonstrated performance utilizing the procedures established by this Instruction. Procedures for separation of midshipmen for insufficient aptitude are explained in Chapter VI.
      —COMDTMIDN INST. 1610.6D, paragraph I-1.b

"I'm going crazy here."
"Well, join the friggin' crowd, Jack."
            —Overheard between two first class waiting
               to commence the Two Hour Swim

*H*undredth Night, they all had ascertained in their Trident calendars, fell on a Wednesday, the last day of February. Day by day, pushup by pushup, they all, plebes and firsties, worked their way toward it through the flaccid days of the Dark Ages. On this side of it, the fourth class saw plebehood. On the other side was ease and plenty—for, after running your firstie all evening, it was traditional to end it with a shake of the hand and part friends, often for life.

Somehow, thought the Mouse, I don't think it's working out that way.

After the eighth day of the buildup things had cooled. To some extent, he supposed, it had to happen. You couldn't keep things at white heat but for so long, and there were a lot of days left to go. In the course of the second week they had evolved a deal, not expressed but tacit, de facto. They left each other's rooms alone. They left each other's uniforms alone. Aside from running him like a sled dog thrice a day, Breen pretty much began leaving him alone, too. He even got to eat some at meals. The youngsters said that the slackoff was because the firsties were thinking of their own hides; that as the Night got closer, they would try to bribe the plebes into going easy on them.

Somehow Philo, with mingled hatred and respect, did not think that was true of his firstie.

He lost his other battle. He called Tawdry a couple of days after her note arrived. Huddled in the phone booth in the basement of the sixth wing, he'd listened to the telephone's distant *brrrr*.

"Hewson's Glass and Mirror Company Incorporated, Auto Work Our Specialty, How May I Serve You?"

"Tawdry?"

"Who's this? Tom?"

"Phil. McGiffin."

"Oh, *Philo!* I never heard you on the phone before. You sound different."

"So do you. I got your note."

"Oh yeah? What about it—want to have that party? We've never partied together, have we?"

"No. I mean, yes, I'd like to. I can't this week though. They keep pretty close tabs on us at night, and there's no liberty."

"Next week?"

"Well, no. Hundredth Night—"

"I know all about that stuff. So when *can* you come?"

"I guess around the first of March."

"I can't wait that long for you."

"Oh, come on, Tawdry . . . I got to wait too."

The line hummed for a moment. In the background he heard the sound of glass shattering, a lot of glass. "Look. I got to work, Philo. Tell you what. You call me when you can spare the time. Maybe I'll

be free. But I can't just sit on the shelf, you know that. I'm not that
kind of girl."

"Wait," he said. "Wait. Okay, look, Tawdry—how about if I
come meet you the night of the twenty-sixth? That's Hundredth
Night. I've got something I want to pull that night, but afterward
. . . after taps things should be pretty quiet, everybody'll be
exhausted."

"I hope *you* won't be exhausted."

"Uh, yeah, well. . . ."

"G'bye, then."

"Wait," he said again, but she had already hung up. He put the
phone down and stared at it, counting days in his mind.

Damn, he thought. Sixteen days.

Her image, her smell, came up sweet and sharp and clear, and he
wondered how he could ever last that long.

The next morning he was assigned to drag a swim team from
Purdue around the Yard, and he got a full meal sitting with them.
He put in three hours of extra duty, pounding the Red Beach in the
freezing wind with rifle at his shoulder and chin rigged in. Checking
the Form One, he saw he had only fifteen hours to go for a clear
record.

On the fourteenth, Valentine's Day, he tried to call Tawdry, but
she wasn't at the glass company; they would say only that she
"hadn't come in." He mailed her a soppy valentine from the mid
store. He read three books for his government course. Stamper
spooned him and told him to call him Snatch.

On the twenty-second, Washington's Birthday, he slept all morning. It was lovely. In the afternoon he studied for the upcoming
four-weeks tests. Breen spent the weekend in B-more and came in
looking sick.

"Tonight," said Zeard, rolling the word in his mouth like a cherry
cough drop, relishing it like the punch line of a dirty joke. "Tonight!
They say they'll really run us, just like Day One, right up to eigh-

teen-hundred. Then the firsties drop for *us*."

"In sweat gear."

"Braced up."

Philo tightened his chin and drew the razor quickly over his face. It took him a timed eleven seconds to shave. He buttoned his shirt with one hand as he combed his hair with the other, flipped his already tied tie over his head and two-blocked it as he stepped into his shoes, and set the spiffy into the cloth of his collar. Breen wanted him around that morning in WUBA. "Time?" he asked.

"Three more minutes."

"Brush me off?"

"Me too."

He and Zeard brushed each other off simultaneously, moving with complete coordination, like dancers. "Ready? Check us."

"You look good."

"Center your belt buckle, Rollo."

"Got it. Dick? Phil?"

"Ready."

"Let's hit it."

At the door of his room Breen was waiting, a stop watch in his hand. He barely looked up as McGiffin skidded to a halt. "You up for this, Mouse?"

"You bet, sir."

"Okay. Service Dress White. Three minutes. Go."

Seven seconds flat-out sprint back to his room. Cap off, spiffy off, tie off. He banged his locker door open. Clothes flew around the room as the others raced into the changes. Now: SDW. White socks, stiff starched white trou, white blouse—thank God he'd put all the buttons in his ready blouse beforehand—white shoes, white gloves. "Hey, Dick. Hook my collar?"

"Yo."

Grease cap on, a check in front of the mirror—you had to be ready for inspection, not just in the proper clothing—and out he went. Seven seconds back to Breen's room. He banged the door. "Midshipman Fourth Class McGiffin, sir."

"Yeah? You're late. Fifteen seconds slow. Let's try Infantry Uniform, Blue Bravo. Two and a half minutes. Ready? Go."

Seven seconds back, and whites began to fly into his locker, piled in a heap at the bottom. He should have hung them, in case Breen pulled a trick, asked for the same uniform twice, but with 150 seconds there was no time for that. Blue trou, blue shirt, tie, white web belt; then the interminable lacing of leggings. He sweated through this, feeling time leaking away through the pores of the universe, then panted back. Breen glanced him up and down.

"What's that uniform supposed to be, Mouse?"

"ID 'B', sir."

"Then what are those on your trou?"

"Sir?"

"*Pockets*, McGiffin. You've got your service dress trou on, you airhead."

"Yes sir. Sorry, sir."

"*That's* right, anyway—you're about the sorriest ploob I know. Ready for a hard one?"

"Yes sir."

"Half and half! Four minutes . . . *go!*"

He bolted. Clothes flew as he crossed the room's threshold. Half and half in four minutes was impossible. He fumbled at his uniforms. Each set of trou had to be folded inside itself, one leg inside the other, one pair white, one pair blue. Same with the blouses. One foot had a white shoe and sock and the other a black sock and shoe. The finished half and half, if done correctly, had you in blues to port and whites to starboard, with the point of congruence right up the centerline.

"Rollo! Got a safety pin?"

"Common pin."

"Lemme have it."

His tie had to be pinned half under the blouse, since the white uniform had no tie at all. Cap on, out the door. He staggered in the passageway, almost hitting another plebe proceeding west at high speed in Trop Khaki Long.

Will it never end? came one clear thought through the sweat and exhaustion.

"Athletic gear! One and a half minutes! Go!"

*   *   *

At around 1730 that night the corridor began to crowd with people. Youngsters carried cameras; second class stood around reminisc-
ing about their own Hundredth Night, when plebes had really been
plebes. The fourth class lurked in their rooms, plotting strategies.
All of them felt the mounting air of tension. Philo found himself
pacing, unable to keep still. "What are you going to do, Howie?" he
asked Zeard.

"To Singleterry? Drop him for about fifty first; then get him in
full dress and start doing salamander races. Dirty him up a little.
After that we'll practice hanging around, maybe some record
races—"

"Record races?"

"Carry a forty-five disc between your cheeks. Great fun. He introduced me to it, in fact." Zeard folded a wolfish grin around his
nose.

"Rollo?"

"I got some things planned for Keyes," said Kaufman quietly.
"What you gonna do to Breen?"

"Run his ass off," said Philo. "If he can move after evening meal
it'll only be on a cart, to sick bay. He'll be a dead man. He better
not try to bag it, either."

"Four minutes," said Gray.

At 1800 their door slammed open. Singleterry, Keyes, and Kim
crowded in, dressed in a weird miscellany of sweat gear, pink jocks,
Hawaiian T-shirts, high black sneakers.

"Midshipman Singleterry, Fourth Class, sir!"

"Midshipman Kim, Fourth Class, sir!"

"Midshipman Keyes, Fourth Class, sir!"

"Drop," screamed Zeard, Gray, and Kaufman in one voice, coming out of their chairs in a bound. "Out in the corridor. Get that
back straight! All the way down! Hit it, you frigging hot dog!"

Philo, grinning, waited another ten seconds, then went out.
Where the hell was Breen? The corridor was swarming with screaming plebes and red-faced running firsties. Flash bulbs painted the air
with red afterimages. Somebody slammed into him. "You cracker
ape!" yelled Ind. "You good for nothing po-buckra piece of hog shit!
Apologize to Mister McGiffin for touching him."

"I'm sorry, Mister McGiffin," said Baylor, braced tight till his neck was wrinkled. His face was running sweat. "Indeed I'm sorry, sir."

"That's no apology! Kiss his ass, boy."

"Aye aye, sir."

Grinning, Philo accepted the salute, then went on. Where the hell was Breen? Was he sick? The door of his room was closed. He headed for it, a knot of second class gathering after him, and banged it open. Breen, in white shirt and blue service dress trou, looked up from the wires text he was reading.

"Breen. I told you to come around."

Breen just looked up at him, an expression of faint interest on his face. Philo shifted uncertainly. "Hit the deck!" he ordered nonetheless, pointing to it.

"Get out of here, Mouse," said Breen, going back to his book.

The upperclass behind Philo gave a collective gasp—horror at the defiance of tradition, perhaps. Hearing it, Breen looked up again.

"You're supposed to come around to me," said Philo, stammering a little.

"Don't stutter, McGiffin. I'm not coming around to you. You showed me nothing during buildup, so you get nothing tonight. Copy? Now shove." He opened the book again.

Philo stood in the doorway, hearing the snickers behind him. "Sir—"

"Get out!"

And the Mouse felt himself breaking, felt himself break; hating Breen and the others behind him; but he could not impose his will, and he couldn't even take Breen's eyes. He turned and went out. The second and third class barely moved for him now. He walked between ranks of sweating firsties, among whom his own classmates, wearing the firsties' blouses, moved, shouting commands. The flashbulbs stabbed. He went into his room and shut the door firmly behind him.

Late that night he got up, and twirled the dial of his con locker and took out the lump of puttylike material that Muff Wiebels had given him. He stared down at it. He had planned to rig the cannons

with it, like old P.N. had. *Hell*, he thought. Why? Why keep trying
to be something I'm not? He put it back in the locker, resolving to
give it back to the third class.

There was no reason to rig cannons now; there was no reason to
care about jokes, about doing anything. Nothing he did was going to
bring Breen around, and nothing he did was ever going to get him
respect or even acceptance.

I'm not him, he thought, squatting there alone in the dark, in the
cold. I'm not the great Philo Norton, class of '82. I'm just the
Mouse.

In that moment he decided to resign. There was no point any
longer. He had done everything they asked, done the best he could,
and it wasn't good enough. He could get through the year. He could
probably graduate. But he would never *be* anybody; only a curiosity,
an object of pity or fun.

He decided to type his chit up in the morning.

Sighing, he took out the puttylike stuff again and fondled it, ooz-
ing it back and forth between his hands. There was quite a bit of it.
Muff said it was powerful. He'd gotten it out of the explosives safe
when the prof's back was turned. Even managed a length of fuze.
Philo molded it with his hands and allowed himself to brood darkly
on blowing himself up. No . . . hell, that was infantile.

Still, he couldn't imagine what would come after; what happened
when you walked out of Gate Three. There was still nowhere to go
for him and no one at all he knew . . . unless you counted Tawdry.
She was fun. He knew he loved her, but he didn't really know how
much of a future they had together.

"Shit," he whispered at last, "I'll do it anyway."

He dressed quickly and slipped out. Tawdry would be waiting in
another fifteen minutes. The two big French cannons in front of the
Rotunda, the Virgin Guns, were his best bet. A salute from those,
confined and amplified by the enclosing wings of T-court, would
wake up all the first and second wings, and probably the third and
fourth as well. Philo N. had used black powder in the old Mexican
guns to fire his salute. I'll do the best I can, he promised himself
again.

Outside, he breathed deep of the cold air and flipped his reefer collar up. The stars glittered hard and cold and very far away. He stared up at them for a moment, feeling the pavement of the parking lot numb his toes, and then started toward T-court and the cannons.

After six or seven steps he stopped. Breen's Porsche, White Lightning, was parked there in the lot, not twenty yards from him.

He stood there for a full five minutes, shifting his feet, looking up at Breen's window and around the lot, before he decided. He slid in among the autos and squatted at the rear of the sports car. The muffler—that would be the best place to put it. He molded a little of the doughy stuff, now growing stiff with the cold, and pressed it to the rough metal. It stuck easily. Not too much, now, he thought. Just enough to make a good bang and scare him. He grinned, half-sprawled under the car, and led the fuze cord from the plastic around to the end of the tailpipe. That would light it. Wiebels hadn't told him how long it would burn, but that didn't really matter. There; all done. Looking at the finished job, though, he felt some doubt. There really wasn't much of it, and the metal of the muffler was pretty thick. He added a little more of the dough to the wad on the muffler, then put it all on. He'd hear that, sure enough. It might even blow the muffler clean off. That would be fun. Too bad about the cannons—there wasn't enough to rig both the car and the guns. He would have to do without that last salute to old Philo N.

He crawled out from under the car, flipped up his collar again, dusted himself off, and headed for the Wall.

Tawdry had said she'd be waiting on Hanover, near where he and Dubus, Cross, and Wiebels went over the first time. That seemed long ago. He grinned at the memory. Dirty Dan. He was out in the Fleet somewhere now, a white hat, making life hell for his division officer, probably. If I had a tenth of Dan's balls, he thought wistfully, they'd be begging me to stay.

The Chapel was quiet, and the lights that usually set it off against the night were dark. He wondered why, then remembered the repairs to the dome. As he paused in the shrubbery by the Supe's house he could see scaffolding dim against the sky, where the sheathing was being replaced, and a jumble of lines and stages and ladders. Have to be careful, he thought. If I fall over any of that there's going to be a hell of a racket.

Without help it was harder to negotiate the wall, but he got a running start and kicked himself up. He hung there for a moment, not caring any more if he fell or not, till he saw the ancient Ford and then swung his legs over and dropped to the bricks.

"Hi, babe."

"Hello, Tawdry. Jeez, you look great."

"Yeah? I'm tired as hell. Worked all day."

"They said at the office—"

"I'm not there any more. Got a better job, dancing. Say . . . you going to get in or just stand there?"

He got in. She started the car and headed south, toward Compromise Street, over Spa Creek. The streets were dead; the single headlight, the other was out, gleamed on empty windows, empty roads.

"Want a drink? I got a six-pack in back."

"Thanks." He reached back, cracked a Schlitz, and drank it almost without stopping. This was going to be a great night. He could tell. She looked great. Different, though; her hair was shorter, and she had lost weight—lost some of that youthful roundness, chubbiness. It made her look more glamorous but he was not sure he liked that. She had lipstick on, too red for her hair.

"What you been doin', Phil?"

"The usual."

"How was Hundredth Night?"

"Oh—all right."

"Did you run that guy who was running you? What's his name—"

"Breen."

"Uh huh. You get him?"

"I got him," said Philo, justifying the half-lie by imagining Breen's face when he lost his muffler. "Yep."

"Here we are." She pulled the car up a driveway. "Eastport." Philo got out, a little awed. When she unlocked the door to the big stone house he was even more so.

"This isn't yours, is it, Tawdry?"

"No. I got thrown out of my apartment. A friend of mine lives here. He lets me use it when he's out of town."

"That's nice of him."

"He's a good guy. He said help myself to the liquor. What'll you take?"

He took bourbon, and a little later on she showed him the bedroom.

He woke in the dark, with a pain between his eyes and the taste of burnt cork sticking to his tongue. Beside him someone was snoring.

"Tawdry. Get up. It's oh-five-thirty. I got half an hour to get back before reveille!"

"Uh."

He shook her. She pushed her hair back from her face with her fingers and ground herself deeper into the sheets.

"You said you were quitting."

"I haven't quit yet."

"These habits really get to you, huh? You squids are all like that. Even the fun ones." She rolled over and got up, yawning. She was naked and her lipstick was smeared over her cheeks. "Sometimes I wonder why I bother. But you're all so cute. Boy . . . I don't feel so good."

"You drank a lot."

"So did you."

"I remember." He shrugged on his reefer—he'd dressed without thinking, in about thirty seconds—and held out her panties for her.

Outside, by the Ford, they could see a red glow out on the bay. She handed him the keys, her eyes closed. "You drive."

"Me? I can't drive. Even being in a car is—"

"You better, if you want to get there so bad. I feel like I'm going to call Ralph any minute." She huddled herself on the passenger's side and cranked the window down.

"But I don't have a license."

"For Christ's sake, Phil, just *drive* it and stop whining."

It was the word "whining" that did it. Even from her, he thought, enraged. Somehow he got out of the driveway and headed toward town. Cars were on the street now, most of them headed toward the Academy: faculty, staff. It was easier for him to steer once they were out of the narrow streets of Eastport. It was only the second or third time he'd been in a car. He turned north on Compromise and crept along, glancing at Tawdry. She looked bad. The rush of air in her window was freezing. He turned at Main and went around the circle and down Randall toward Gate One. He was only a hundred yards from it on the narrow street when he realized he couldn't just drive through, not in uniform, the jimmylegs would stop him sure, and he hit the brakes a bit too hard. She gave a little shriek as the car behind, a gray Chevy, hit them. The Ford bucked forward a few feet and stalled.

"Ah, Christ," said Philo. He slumped in the seat, holding his aching head, and watched in the rear view as the door of the car behind opened and a short man in civvies came up to them. As he came abreast of the door Philo slammed it open. "Jeez, man," he said angrily. "Why don't you pay a little attention to the road, huh?"

"What?"

"You heard me, dummy. You hit us. What have you got to say?"

"Well," said the man. He was short and middleaged and looked slightly familiar. Then he bent closer to look into the car. "Say— don't I know you, son?"

Philo looked up at him and nodded miserably once. Yeah. It would have to be. The short guy in civvies was Major Bartranger.

He got to sit in the Superintendent's outer office for most of the morning. When he came out it was noon, too late to go down to the mess hall even if he'd felt hungry, and he went back to his room instead and took three aspirin and showered and got into a fresh set of blues. When Dick Gray came in, humming "Hands Across The Sea," he was sitting by the window, looking out at the light-filled square of gray stone below.

"Hey, buds," said Gray, putting his hand on Philo's shoulder. "Been hearing some scuttlebutt about you. What happened"

"I was over the wall."

"Go on."

"Black Bart caught me."

"How big you down?"

"I don't know yet. I had to see the Supe. It's not just unauthorized absence. It's also driving a car, drinking, disrespectful language, and conduct unbecoming an officer."

"Is that all?"

"And I busted in one of his headlights."

Gray dignified the list with complete silence for a moment. "Wow," he stated at last, dropping into his chair. "So you got to see the Admiral."

"For about four minutes."

"What's your current status?"

"I'm in hack, of course—suspended. Don't know how many demerits yet. I kind of doubt Bartranger can count that high." Philo sighed. "I guess I'll be out of here sometime this week. Low grease, low grades, and lousy conduct—hard to see why they'd keep me. I was thinking of resigning last night, but I guess I don't even get to go out on my own. Me and Len will go out together."

"Len?"

"He's resigning. I guess it's okay to tell you."

"Like hell he is. He and Lunchbags were joking down at the tables. Len says he's going for Trident Scholar."

"That's great," said Philo, honestly happy for Ind.

Zeard and Kaufman came in. They too had to know all about his "bust-out night," as Rollo called it. "Mouse," said Zeard, sounding awed for the first time since Philo had known him, "I take back everything I thought about you. You got more balls than the Yankees. Did you really chase Black Bart for three blocks before you rammed him?"

"Hell, no. It was accidental."

"That's what they were saying down at the tables . . . what happened to the girl?"

"Left her out there by the gate. The Major more or less dragged me in by the neck. He's pretty strong."

"Bummer," said Zeard.

"No gentleman," said Kaufman.

"So, you going to class this afternoon?"

Philo shrugged.

"You ought to. Come on."

"I'm out."

"Well, keep us company."

He felt like saying, to hell with it and you too, but habit was too strong; he got up and shuffled his books together. His eyelids felt gritty. At least, he thought, I can get a nap in Calculus.

*   *   *

He had forgotten all about it, was walking back toward Bancroft from the academic buildings about 1600, when he heard the dull boom from out near the Field House. Even then he kept walking, his head down; the diggers and the fillers, the Academy grounds people, were always doing odd things around the Yard, most of them noisy. It was only when he saw the column of dirty smoke rising beyond Luce Hall that he remembered suddenly, and began to run. The smoke drifted downward as he neared the gate shack, and blew toward him, smelling of oil and burning rubber.

White Lightning sat skewed across the intersection of King George and East Streets, about fifty feet outside the gate. From the windshield forward, he saw as he neared, it was untouched; from midships back it was opened up like a gutted chicken, and on fire. A crowd of townspeople, officers, and first class on their way out on Wednesday afternoon liberty was gathering, an empty radius of respect between them and the burning vehicle. Philo stared, then sprinted forward through the smoke. A fat jimmylegs in a Smoky Bear hat grabbed him and swung him back. "Get away from there," he said over the roar of the flames. "She might go up. We got the foam truck on the way."

"The guy—the driver—"

The jimmylegs gestured over his shoulder, and Philo turned.

Yes, it was Breen, though his face was sooty and his liberty civvies were covered with smut. He squatted alone on the curb near the gatehouse and watched the new Porsche burn.

"Mister Breen?"

No answer. He moved his hands in front of the firstie's wide-open, motionless eyes.

"It wasn't even paid for," Breen mumbled.

"Sir, I'm sorry. I figured to blow the muffler off, that's all. Scare you some. I didn't think—"

"What?" said Breen. "I can't hear too good, McGiffin. It was awful loud."

"I said, '*I'm sorry. I only figured to blow your muffler off.*'"

Heads turned toward them in the crowd. The fire snapped and roared now, gasoline-fed, and the circle widened. From somewhere inside the Yard a siren sawed at the sky. Philo shut up and squatted beside Breen.

"You mean," said the firstie.

"Sir?"

"You mean"—he made a little gesture at the wreck—"you had something to do with this, Mouse?"

"Yes, sir. I'm sorry. I'm glad you weren't hurt."

Breen stared at him. He seemed to try to say something twice, and only on the third try did it come out.

"Well, you showed me, Mouse. You really showed me. Something—at last."

"I'm sorry," Philo said again.

Breen got up, a little shakily; Philo could see him bear down, take a deep breath, and let it out. He lifted his head, looking away from the smoking wreck. The crash truck shouldered forward through the gate.

"Sir?"

"Nothing," said Breen. He looked at Philo once, a long, measuring look, shook his head, and walked away, back toward the Yard.

CHAPTER THIRTEEN

He who will not risk cannot win.

—John Paul Jones

The Lord giveth
And the Lord taketh away;
The Lord is an Indian giver.

—Found engraved on one of the
long tables at Buzzy's

*H*e expected all that week to leave within a day or two; but each
day his mail slot was empty, the mate came not by, he found
no 3790/2K Midshipman Message Forms on his desk when he came
back from class. "They're trying to make me sweat," he told
Stamper, "and they're doing it, too."

"Just hang in there, Mouse. You made it this far. Don't scuttle
before you get the word."

"Yeah," said Philo, saying nothing more to good advice like that
but thinking. *Now that I can't stay, now that they're ready to fire
me, I'd give anything to hang on. It's funny. I'm funny, I guess.*

And that was true; but at any rate, he told himself, he was a little
wiser now. *If I can keep on learning at this rate,* he thought, *by the
time I get to be eighty I might have something figured out.*

After their conversation at the gate, he and Breen had hardly
talked to each other. Philo knew, though, he hadn't turned him in.
The fact that White Lightning had effected explosive disassembly
outside the Yard made it no business of the Academy's, and Breen
apparently was just going to order a new Porsche with his insurance

money. Or so the firsties, several of whom had stopped in to spoon
Philo, told him.

That was some consolation. The firsties left him alone. In fact
almost everyone left him alone. Even his classmates seemed wary,
fearful of giving offense. Seldom anymore did he even hear his
nickname.

He wondered what was happening.

At the end of the week he was called out of the ranks of the extra
duty marchers to see the battalion officer. He dragged himself in
from the terrace, signed out in the batt office, and left his M-one
with a mate. "Midshipman Fourth Class McGiffin, sir," he said, not
even bracing up.

"Marching E.D., Mister McGiffin?"

"Yes sir, major."

"You may be doing a lot of that . . . better sit down."

He sat in the same armchair, faced the same table, the same por-
trait, the same Bartranger. He wondered what the little Marine
meant. "Maybe." But there was no room at the Naval Academy for
the conditional. Everything not forbidden was compulsory here.
What was this "maybe?"

"McGiffin, I've been talking with the people over in the Executive
Department about your case. It's pretty involved . . . a hairline deci-
sion. Whether to discharge you for conduct or not."

"Yes sir."

"You know, it's damn strange." Bartranger drummed rapidly with
his fingers on the shell casing. "Last time I had you in here it was to
counsel you on your problems with self-confidence, aggressiveness.
Patton, I think it was, said 'the most vital quality a soldier can
possess is self-confidence, utter, complete, and bumptious.' Every
report I had on you questioned your fitness for command, described you as a . . . noncompetitive individual. I thought you
were myself, from our first interview. More than that. I thought you
were weak."

Philo, resting in the chair, his right shoulder aching from two
hours of the rifle, was beginning to feel bored. Why doesn't he just
hand me my papers and wave good-bye? I don't need this song and

dance. But he tried to look interested out of politeness.

"Now all this." Bartranger waved the sheaf of Form Twos in front of Chesty Puller's face. "Don't get the idea I'm encouraging this sort of behavior, McGiffin. I condemn it in the strongest terms. But at the same time it makes me think you've got a little more of the devil in you than the rest of us thought."

Philo felt a faint flicker of hope. "What do you mean, sir?"

"I mean this," said the major, putting the papers down and leaning over the table. "As of last Monday you had a hundred and fifty-five demerits. Nickel and dime stuff, but still that's a C-minus in conduct. The maximum number of demerits a fourth class is allowed before dismissal is two hundred and fifty. Now, I added these charges up before I went to see the Admiral. Unauthorized absence, consumption of alcoholic beverages within seven-mile limit, riding in private automobile, driving private automobile, conduct unbecoming an officer, disrespectful language to a senior, and good judgment, failure to use—they just happen, by my count, to total ninety-five demerits."

"That's, uh—two hundred and forty-five, sir."

"Good, Mr. McGiffin. You can add."

"But sir—you left out the damage to your car."

Bartranger made a little rejecting motion with his fingers. "I talked to a patrolman friend of mine about that. Seems I was in the wrong. Probably following you too closely to stop in time. And it wasn't that expensive to repair. So we'll just leave that out."

"Jeez," said Philo.

"What's that?"

"Nothing, sir. So—what does that mean, sir? Two hundred and forty-five demerits?"

"It means you get a D– in conduct. Hack from now till June Week. No liberty. No privileges. Extra duty and restriction every weekend and over Spring leave. And one screwup, *anything*—one missed formation or flunking a room inspection, forgetting to tie your shoelaces, and you're out."

Bartranger paused; he toyed with the shell case. "Actually—"

"Sir?"

"I had to fight to get you that. Your head is on the block, McGiffin. I understand there have been some other things going on you weren't caught at. You're getting yourself quite a reputation in the Brigade."

"Yes sir."

"But you screw up once more in the next two months"—the major pointed his finger like a .45—"and you're out Bilger's Gate six hours later, in civvies. Understand?"

"Yes, sir. I understand."

"Dismissed, then."

He walked out and stood for a moment in the battalion office, thinking. It wasn't much of a chance Bartranger was offering; but it was a chance.

The mate came up with his rifle. "Hey, classmate," he murmured. "You really Philo McGiffin? The one they call the Mouse?"

"No, I just wear this name tag for laughs," said Philo. "What about it?"

"Nothing, nothing. Here's your piece back."

"Thanks."

"That's kind of a nice rifle." The mate glanced in the BOOW's direction and lowered his voice even more. "What's that inside the chamber? A radio?"

"You've got to be kidding," said Philo. "A radio inside your rifle? That's against regulations."

There was something uncomfortably close to admiration in the eyes of the mate. Philo looked away; then brought the gun to port arms and trotted out to the terrace to begin again.

At the end of March the Brigade settled down to mid-terms. After that, they knew, came Spring leave, and then, only nine short kick-it-in weeks later, June Week. The Dark Ages were drawing to a close; the weather warmed, the days lengthened, the Yard grew green again. One fine April morning the knockabouts returned to Dewey Basin, like white waterfowl returning from the south.

And all that time, Philo McGiffin was riding, as Mister Keyes put it, with his balls over the edge of a razor.

He spent every minute of every day alert. There was no margin for error: none. He could no longer half-doze in chemistry class, could no longer hope for a couple of seconds' grace getting to formation; couldn't bag inspections with a brushoff and a cottonball-and-water instead of a fresh press and a shoeshine. You did things like that and maybe 90 percent of the time you got away with it but the tenth time you went down. He could no longer afford to play percentages like that.

But as the long alert days went by he became aware that there were factors operating in his favor, too. His classmates, for example. They knew who he was now in Calculus, in Skinny, in Bull. They kept him awake, fed him answers when the risk wasn't too great, and told him when his spiffy popped out. His roommates. Rollo and Weird and Care Package—as they had begun to call Dick Gray, dignifying him at last with a nickname—checked his uniform and shave before formations, reminded him about DQ and TSP and when it was time to get ready for his classes. Fayaway came by and brought his class shoes up to a NAPS gloss and boiled enough oil out of the others on Kim's hot plate so that he could wear them to class. Len Ind, who it seemed had really changed his mind about resigning, gouged him on Math during study hours, and Darrin did the same for Chemistry. Even the upperclass unbent a little. Mister Norfon, who'd worn stars every semester since plebe year, gave him all his notes and copies of old tests for wires and steam, a treasure of gouge roughly equivalent to half a point on his QPR over four years.

Over Spring leave things eased off a bit. With the Brigade gone for five days there were no formations; all he had to do was drop down to the Main Office every hour from 0800 to 2200 and sign in; other than that, his time was his own, as long as he stayed in his room. Nobody braced up over leave and upperclass and plebes ate almost like equals at two tables in the cavernously empty mess hall.

When classes started again he was startled to find that everyone in the Brigade, and all the profs, knew who he was, and knew about the 245 demerits. He was a marked man, but it seemed to be to his advantage at times. He was late for P.E. class once and the coach didn't seem to notice it. Singleterry found a fingerful of dirt behind his rack at a formal room inspection and contented himself with smearing it on Philo's tie; he gave them a 3.0, the highest grade their room had ever seen.

Breen still didn't talk to him much, but there was no evidence of enmity; White Lightning II, with a bigger engine than the one that had burned, crouched in the firsties' parking lot outside 8–0.

What, he wondered, was going on? Were they all taking care of him? Most likely it was simply that no one, whether officer or upperclass, professor or one of his own classmates, wanted to be singled out as the instrument, the lightning rod, to bring down the last demerit and the ultimate disgrace of dismissal to a personage so dubiously famous as Philo T. McGiffin. He was wryly aware of it. Before, he had been nobody, and the obscure no one cared about; they were fried or overlooked, they screwed up or BZ'd in obscure ways, greased up to their seniors in shadow, probably unnoticed even by them. But now he was no longer of their ranks. He was *known.* The news of his fatal misstep, and the name of the person who called him down, would echo around Bancroft Hall like a fire alarm.

He began to think of himself in the third person.

Three weeks went by without trouble, right to the end of April. Another two days and it would be May; another month and it would be finals, and June; and another few bright, gay days after that and there would be no more plebes. Herndon would be conquered, the long grind would be over and plebe year would be, for all of them in the Class, history at last.

He sat at his desk in his track clothes and looked at the chit. Slowly he bent and slipped off the running shoes, tapped them on the deck to loosen the dirt, and tossed them into the closet. The spikes rattled against the rifle rack.

"Hey, look at this," said Howie, looking up at the sound. He pulled a piece of paper out of his three-ring. "Saw it in Maury; Professor Alati had it on the wall of his office there. He's the Masquerader faculty adviser. I think I'll join up next year. I'd like to act."

"Yeah, Howie, you should be on the stage," mumbled Rollo feverishly from his rack. He had a Sick In Room chit for the flu.

"He's a good head though. For a civvie. They say the only way you can flunk youngster bull is to die on the way to the final."

"I bet I could do it easier," muttered Rollo.

Philo was too stunned, too shattered, to say anything. Perhaps he hadn't even heard. He had picked up Zeard's paper automatically as it came over the desk toward him and laid it alongside the book overdue chit from the Brigade Library. The paper, image faded by too many photocopyings, showed a smiling Donald Duck in Service Dress Blue, one finger raised in an obscene salute. Under it in broken letters was a twelve-line poem.

> *When things go wrong*
> *As they usually will*
> *And your daily road*
> *Seems all uphill,*
> *When funds are low*
> *And debts are high,*
> *When you try to smile*
> *But can only cry*
> *And you really feel*
> *That you'd like to quit,*
> *Don't run to me;*
> *I don't give a shit.*

"Oh, jeez," he said, half-aloud.

"What?"

"Nothing. Nothing." He pushed the paper back to Zeard across the table, but Howie had reached out already, and he got his fingers on the wrong sheet. His long nose traced down the chit to the bottom. Philo, not noticing, sat looking at the clods of dirt his spikes had left on the deck.

"Hey, Dick."

"Huh?"

"Take a look at this." Zeard passed him the chit with a jerk of his face toward the oblivious McGiffin.

Gray read it and passed it on to Kaufman. Rollo was a little light-headed from the cough syrup, though, and he muttered the last line aloud, ". . . unless subject book or publication is returned within four days disciplinary action will be automatically taken."

"Hey. Gimme that," said Philo, slamming his chair down. He snatched the paper from Kaufman's hand. The three of them looked at him for a long moment. From outside the open window they all heard a screech of trumpets as the Dumb and Bungle Corps practiced for the June Week parades.

"Phil," said Gray, "What was the date on that chit?"

"March eighth."

"You turned it in, didn't you?"

For answer he slid open his desk and held up a book. It was the book he'd checked out to read about Philo N., *Real Soldiers of Fortune*. All four of them looked at it as they would have at a large tarantula, had one suddenly appeared in Philo's hand.

"I just found the chit," he said.

"Found it? Where was it?"

"In my Tactics book."

"What was it doing there?"

"I must of stuck it in there for a bookmark after I got it. Then the buildup started and I forgot."

"Shit," said Rollo weakly. They turned to look at him. "There's just no other word for it," he said unhappily.

"He's out of it," said Gray.

"He's right," said Zeard. "Look, guys: we got to get that book back, right now, and get the librarian to cancel the pap. She's a good kid. She winks at me."

"She's sixty years old. I think it's a tic," said Kaufman.

"It's too late," said Philo, kicking at the dirt, grinding it into the tiles. "I saw the new Form One up on first deck. I got five for it. First offense. I just came up here to see if I could find the chit, remember what I did with the book." He sighed, a deep half-groan, and they watched him grind the last clod of dirt into powder. "Nope. I'm out."

They sat around. Kaufman hiccoughed. It was a somber sound.

"What are you going to do, Phil?" said Gray.

He shrugged. Now that he knew it was over he just felt tired.

*   *   *

That evening they all got carry-on. Since Hundredth Night there was generally carry-on at the tables, unless somebody had forgotten to deliver an upperclass' laundry, dropped a pie at the table, that sort of gratuitous screwup. Otherwise things were pretty loose. About half of the upperclass had spooned any given plebe anyway, and the second class referred to them openly as "youngsters j.g." At most of the 360 tables in the Mess Hall plebes and upperclass were laughing together, trading jokes and banter.

Not so in Slack 34th. There only the clank of tableware marred a brittle silence. No one commiserated with Philo. No one told him they were sorry the blade had fallen. He knew they were sorry, if they were, and if they didn't care, then he didn't either. It went too deep to talk about. And then too, he knew, he was only a plebe. Lots of plebes left; most of the one in three were attrited during the first nine months. It was different when an upperclass left. You'd put in the sweat and the work, taken the grind, been beside the guys you were leaving for three or four years. Then there might be a party out at the Beehive, a gift, invitations to come back and see the class graduate.

But he had only been a plebe.

Lying in his pad that night, hearing the long cool music of taps faint from Smoke Park, he realized that he could not go home. He *was* home. Raymondsville was like a bad dream from which he had awakened into a larger and more glorious life. He would go anywhere rather than back there again, ever. But where else was there? Nowhere. He knew of nowhere else in the world to go; and there was nowhere else, in the entire world, that he wanted to be. Only here, with his friends.

And now he was out.

He stared at the overhead, at the same parallel ranks of light the blinds cast every night from the lamps down in the Yard.

The Naval Academy was no party. No pleasure cruise. He knew now that they'd been right from the start. He wasn't suited. Couldn't hack the program. Didn't have what it took to lead men. He was a whimp and a bagger. There was nowhere for him, pretend how he might, in the hard-charging, tightly self-disciplined man's world of Annapolis. The others had adapted: Fayaway, Kaufman,

Gray, even Weird Zeard was changing, conforming, outwardly at least.

Why can't I not care? he cried inside himself, eyes open to the night. Why can't I go and not care? Apathy, apathy, that's my cry; they don't care, so why should I? Wisdom from stall partitions. Why couldn't he walk out, leave it behind and go on to something else—a job, enlisted service, study hard and apply for a loan to go to some two-year college—better, worse, but something else, and let his Academy life-that-never-was drop astern, all unheeded?

It would have been easier, he had to admit, if he'd gone earlier, and not hung on so long and stubbornly. And the cause of that was purely and only the coincidence of his name.

Damn, he thought hopelessly, *Oh, damn.*

His hands curled into the sheets, pulled halfway up his body as per regulations, and over the blank stare of his opened eyes flickered the memories, the scenes . . . Philo N.'s face, wrapped in bloody bandages after the Japanese destroyed his fleet. Kaufman slipping him a slice of rye toast under the table. The Virgin Guns. The Supe taking the salute during the pass in review. Falling free through sunlit space, fear clutched to him like a life preserver, waiting for the shock of the water. Diesel fumes and the crackle of PRITAC on YP-667. Dodo trotting along after the CMOOW, his tongue out, at watch squad inspection. Seagulls outside Breen's window. The slow deformation of a steel bar under a destructive-stress test. Salamander races for Singleterry down 8–4 in double sweat gear. Tearing down the goal posts after the Air Farce game.

Tawdry. . . .

And here in the room with him, asleep, the best friends he'd ever had, would ever have, in his life. . . .

He got up quietly and sat at his desk. There was enough moonlight to see by. Zeard snored quick and high, Kaufman cleared his throat in his sleep, Gray breathed slow.

He couldn't just pack the next morning and leave, like Portley said he'd have to do. Not after all that.

Not with his name.

There had to be the gesture.

He took a sheet of note paper out of his drawer and began to write. The first note went into an envelope addressed to St. Audrey Doyle.

Dear Tawdry,

I found out today that I'll be leaving the Academy. I don't know where I'll go, but I guess I won't see you again. I'm going to do a final trick before I leave, and it could be kind of dangerous. But whatever happens I guess this is goodbye. I loved you for a while, anyway, and it was pretty good.

Philo
(McGiffin)

The second note was to Breen. His pen scratched in the quiet. It was mainly an apology. The third and last note was to his classmates and friends in the 34th. He didn't put it that way to himself, but it was pretty much in the nature of a lighthearted give-a-shit note. When it was done he left the three letters on his desk and began to get dressed. WUBA, gym shoes, dark gloves. He had the wool watch cap in hand and then remembered and put it back and settled his combination cap on his head, his best one, out of its cocoon of plastic wrap so that the gold band wouldn't tarnish.

When he was dressed he took a look at each of his roommates. Rollo was zonked; the pint bottle of issue cough syrup was nearly empty; he was high as a kite, deep as shark shit. He was tempted to take a pull himself, but decided not to. Tonight he would need all his coordination. Zeard had stopped snoring but both he and Gray were motionless, soundly out, breathing with their mouths open, drinking the cool air from the window.

Philo opened the door and slipped out into the passageway. He went down the ladder to 8–0 without looking back.

The moon was a discarded toenail. The night was warm and smelled of new grass and bay fog. It was only midnight. He plodded across the Yard, past Dahlgren and Luce, up the slight rise toward the Supe's house. At its corner a camouflaged gun barrel jutted suddenly in the streetlights, the moonlight. It was a relic of the Spanish American War, or the First World War—he wasn't quite sure.

The first hint of fear stirred in his chest. He ignored it and went on past the hedge of the big house, where he had crouched before on the night of the Wall. He paused there for a moment and checked the walks and yards ahead. Nothing moved. The open lawn between the elms and oaks was still and dark, crossed by the curves of the upperclass walks.

At last he moved on, crouching a bit, and fetched up against the south wall of the Chapel. To his right were the stone steps leading down to the crypt, the veined black marble of John Paul Jones' sarcophagus, supported on the backs of bronze dolphins; his sword.

He winched his mind back and looked upward.

The vast curve of the dome was hardly visible from this close to the building. In any case, his upward view was cluttered by a confused webwork of planks, scaffolding, ropes. Near him he gradually made out big, curved sheets leaning against the building. He touched a piece. Smooth metal. The new sheathing, solid copper, surprisingly thick.

The climb divided itself in his mind. First would be the side of the building, up to where the dome began. Except for the height, the scaffolding would make this fairly easy. Second—he craned his neck back in the darkness—would be the dome itself. Steep, long, and possibly slippery. But there would probably be scaffolding there, too, though he couldn't see it from down here.

Three: to the top of the bell tower.

Four, and last: up the gilt spire, the twelve-foot gold needle that capped the dome, rising far above the tallest trees in the Yard.

He had no idea at all how to do *that*. But you've got to get up there first, he reminded himself.

Okay, Philo. Let's go. He jammed his cap tight on his head, found the ladder at the base of the scaffolding, its first stage, and began to climb. He got about three rungs off the grass before there was a scuffle of feet behind him and he felt himself being pulled off backward. Falling, he punched out wildly, and was rewarded by a muffled grunt before long arms wrapped themselves around his shoulders.

"Hey, calm down, Mouse," somebody whispered. "It's us."

"Dick? Who else is that?"

"Howie."

"What the hell is this? You guys following me around now?"

"Sort of," said Gray.

"What's the story, anyway?"

They were all three talking in whispers, watching a light that had come on upstairs in the Supe's house.

"Well, you know," said Gray, sounding a little ashamed of himself. "The bad news—we knew how much you figured on sticking it out. Figured we'd sort of watch out for you. Then you snuck out tonight, after writing something at your desk—"

"So you figured what?"

He could feel them shrug. "You know," said Gray again.

"Anyway, what *are* you doing?" whispered Zeard.

"What's it to you?"

"We're your wives, Phil. After all."

He grinned suddenly in the dark. He punched Gray lightly. "Hey. Sorry I swung at you. You surprised me. You hurt?"

"Naw." But he could see Care Package rubbing his cheek.

"What are you doing out here?" Zeard asked again.

"Climbing the Chapel."

"Yes, but why?"

"Why would anybody want to climb the Chapel?"

"I can think of a couple of reasons," said Zeard.

"See this combo cap?" Philo asked him.

"Uh huh."

"What's my name?"

"Mouse."

"My full name, Howie."

"I forget."

"Come on, cooperate a little. Philo McGiffin. Right?"

"Wait a minute," said Gray. "You're not going to. . . ?"

"Gonna try," said Philo. "Carry-on for the whole class if I do. Right?"

They both backed off from him and looked upward. "Pretty good climb," said Gray, after a minute or so.

"There's the scaffolding. Then maybe a Jacob's ladder up on the dome."

"You got a rope?"

"No. But the yardbirds must have some way to get up there. To attach the sheathing."

He could feel them weighing it. He looked across the Yard while he waited. There was plenty of time. It was only a little after midnight.

"You serious about this, Phil?" asked Howie.

"Affirmative."

"You wouldn't be planning on . . . taking a dive or anything?"

"I wasn't, no, Howie. And believe me, I wouldn't now that you guys are here." He paused, then took a step toward the ladder again. Their hands were still on him. "You gonna let me go?"

"Let you go, hell," said Zeard. "We're going up with you. Right, Dick?"

"Right, Howie."

"Oh, no, you're not. This is my job."

"We either go with you," said Gray, "or we blow the whistle for the jimmylegs."

"You'd bilge me?"

"'When you've got a buddy, tried and true,'" quoted Zeard from the Laws of the Salt Mines, "'screw him before he screws you.' We're coming."

"Okay. If that's the only way. But me first."

He turned again to the ladder and this time their hands dropped away. He went up the first stage fast but careful, his hands on the side bars like they showed you on the obstacle course on Hospital Point. The steel was night cool. Behind him he heard them coming up too. About twenty feet up the first ladder ended and there was a little platform on the scaffolding and then another ladder.

"Comin'?"

"On your tail."

The second ladder, then. Up he went. Now he could see over the hedge into the Supe's yard, the pale blurs of lawn furniture. To his right, the rough granite and white brick of the Chapel, the corner of a stained glass window; Philo remembered it, though it was dark now, as the figure of a white-robed, avenging angel, holding a sword and the dove of peace; he had nodded beneath it many times in Sleepy Hollow. There was quite a way yet to go even to get to the dome. He waited at the top of the second ladder.

"You guys don't have to do this."

"Neither do you."

"Yes I do."

"Then we're in it together, boy."

Again he was smiling in the dark, climbing toward the third platform. They were his friends, they were with him, no matter what happened. He felt a sudden thrill of courage—not apathy, but something bright and strong, something he had never felt before.

But this was no time to examine it. One more long stage of climbing brought them out at the top of the scaffolding. There was no railing at the top; only a line, strung around a platform of planks about four feet narrow, clinging to the side of the building a little below where the base of the dome ran. Philo kept his eyes upward, away from the ground. Up close like this you could see how immense, high, it really was. The whole Chapel was over 190 feet high, from base to the tip of its needle, and they had only covered about half of that.

Around him on the platform, as he lowered his look, lay tools, coils of line, twisted sheets of metal. He picked one up. Old, thin, corroded copper. It felt green even in the dark. As he fingered it Gray came over the edge of the platform, and then Zeard. They were breathing hard. So, he realized, was he.

"Let's grab five," said Zeard.

They sat and squatted and looked out over the Yard. From a hundred feet up, they could see out over the roof of the Supe's house, over Bancroft, all the way out to the boat basin. A green light out there winked on and off. Four . . . three. Four . . . three. Philo moved so that his back was to the granite, and reached back to grip it, hard. They were a lot higher than he had expected, and there seemed to be more wind up here; the structure of the scaffolding swayed slightly under their feet.

"Now what?" said Care Package.

They turned and looked up at the convexity of the dome. The moonlight silvered it, making it seem to lean out over them. It was big. At the very top they could see the cylindrical bellroom, and then above that the obelisk that tapered to a point 192 feet above the ground. The whole curved surface of the dome was smooth. There were no handholds, nowhere to grip, and the pitch was far too steep even to think of walking or crawling up it.

"What's that?" said Zeard.

"Where?"

They all three peered upward. Philo wished he had a light. Yes, there was something there—a line, darker than the shadow of the dome, leading down from the central tower to a point not too far to his right . . . he edged over toward it. It was beyond the platform, and when he leaned out toward it there was nothing, a great gulf under him, and he jerked back, feeling his legs go weak.

"Here," said Gray. "Maybe you can reach it with this."

With the crowbar he was just able to scrape it toward him along the edge of the dome's base.

"It's a line. Feels like manila."

"One line?"

"Yeah. Just one." He hauled on it. The line dragged a bit as it came in and then tautened.

"What is it, Phil?"

"A rope. Seems to be fast up topside somewhere."

"*Seems* to be?"

"Yep."

"We better go back down," said Zeard. "I thought the scaffolding might go all the way up. We can't go up the dome."

"That's right, Phil. C'mon, let's go back and get some sleep."

Philo pulled again at the line. It was rough in his hands even through the black leather dress gloves. He didn't like to think about the next step, about going up over the curve of the dome. In fact he didn't like it so much he felt his knees weaken again. He licked his lips, but there was no moisture there.

"I'm going up," he said.

"What? Like hell you are."

But already as Zeard twisted around to stop him he had stood, his throat closing as he did so, wrapped his arms around the line, and started to haul himself up the almost vertical curve of the dome. The rope vibrated as it came taut, and in a kind of Neanderthal crouch he began to crab-walk upward. He was glad he'd worn the gym shoes.

"Phil!"

"Mouse!"

He hardly heard them calling behind him, below. He hauled himself rapidly upward, hand over hand. Here, where the dome was steepest, it was all arm work. The dome was big, all right. It was like climbing a cliff, or the curve of the earth. The new copper sounded tinny under his kicking feet. His arms pulled taut against the line. He'd done pretty well on the obstacle course on the rope climb . . . until, once, he had looked down.

This time he wouldn't look down.

After a while the curve gentled . . . just in time; his arms were about gone. He was about halfway up the ogive of the dome. It was getting easier to stand up. The rope held, rough under the gloves. He locked himself in the line for a few minutes, like they showed you in P.E., and then moved on upward. Now he could almost walk. At last, around the dark curve, he saw the vertical upthrust of the bell tower ahead. He pulled-walked himself up to it, it was almost level here at the crest, and hooked an arm over the little decorative railing and hauled himself in. He was at the top.

"Whew," he said, and let go of the rope.

The bell tower—he looked around it from inside, letting his heart pound and pound, waiting for it to slow—was small, a little decorative structure plumb on the crest of the dome. As far as he could see with the moonlight there was no bell in it. He forgot his resolution, lowered his eyes for a minute, and found himself looking across the Yard.

And the Severn . . . and the bay. . . .

He could see for miles. The river was a black band beyond Maury and the old laundry building. Beyond that and behind him he could look out over a carpet of lights that was Crabtown, and far away, level with him, the single white colonial tower of the state capitol, lit by floods. The Superintendent's home was tiny now, half-eclipsed by the edge of the dome at whose apex he crouched. He could look beyond it down on all of Bancroft Hall now, could see all eight wings at once, as if from an aircraft. Out beyond it, beyond Faggot and the basin, he could see the bay, a dark irregular emptiness, and far out on it—on the other side?—a distant salting of lights.

Jeez, he thought, I'm really up here. With the little banister around him, the utter Earthlike solidity of the dome beneath, he didn't feel all that bad.

Behind him there was a scrape and a scuffle and he started, almost sending himself over the railing, and Zeard hauled himself into the tower, puffing like a sprinter. He lay inside and moved feebly, waving his arms. "Howie," said Philo, "you didn't have to come up *here.*"

"Let's . . . not go into that again."

"Is Dick coming too?"

"Here."

Gray came into view several yards below, coming up sure and quick on the rope. As he came over the railing Philo saw by the moonlight that he had a couple of coils of rope slung around his shoulder. He saw Philo's look. "Like they said plebe summer, a sailor can't ever have too much line. We got a way to go yet. The hardest part, too."

Philo leaned back, holding tightly to a stanchion of the tower, looking upward. Gray was right. From here on—say twelve more feet to the top of the bell tower, and another ten or twelve after that up the narrow needle that topped it, sparkling with gilt in the daytime—there was no scaffolding, no ladder, and no line. In fact, as far as he could see, there was no way up at all.

"Dick . . . how much line you got there?"

"I think I got ten, eleven fathoms in this big coil here. Nine-thread."

"Let's see it. Howie, hold my belt, will you?"

Leaning backward over the low rail, carefully looking away from the ground, he coiled the line for a heave. Twelve feet above them a slight cornice jutted at the corner of the roof. If he could get a loop over that—

"What are you doing?" said Zeard.

"Just hold on to me, Howie. Gonna try a toss now . . . *uh!*"

The line missed, by quite a bit, and banged loudly in coils back onto the dome below. He coiled it again, tossed, missed again.

"You're nuts, Mouse," said Zeard.

"*Uh!*"

"Get it?"

"Almost."

On his seventh shot the uncoiling line arched over the cornice and came down near him. He evened up the ends and thought for a moment and then put a figure eight knot on it as a stopper and then tied a travelling slip knot and sent it up. When it hit the cornice he jammed it as tight as he could. There. Now—hand over hand; never mind the knot tightening in his stomach, tighter than the one he'd just tied. "Let go," he said quietly to Zeard.

"What?"

"I'm going up."

"Wait, wait," said Gray. "He's nuts. He can't climb any higher than this."

"It's got to be at the *top*," Philo said.

"Who says? Nobody's ever done this before. You think McGiffin got up here a hundred years ago?"

"That was the old chapel he climbed," said Philo. "Not this one. This one's a lot higher."

"It can't be dood, fella."

"I'm going to try," said Philo. "And I don't care if Philo N. did or didn't. *I'm* going to."

"What if you slip? Or clutch?"

"I won't slip. I'm good at rope climbs." The other possibility, he had to admit, was more likely. But he just had to see if he could do it.

Gray, meanwhile, had been doing something inside the tower. Now Philo felt his arms around his waist. "Here . . . just a sec . . . bowline. For safety."

"You'll break his back if he falls."

"Better than spreading him all over the Yard."

With Zeard distracted by Gray, Philo saw his chance; he leaned forward and bit Howie's hand. There was a shockingly loud yell, and at that moment he felt himself swung outward. His arms cramped tight on the line for a moment, and then he began going up, twisting his feet in and locking automatically at each slide upward. The line pendulumed uneasily. He hoped it wasn't working toward the edge. Six feet—ten—there above him was the dark loom of the cornice. He reached for it with one hand, hauled at it, and almost fell as a big chunk of rotten stone or tile came off under his weight and hit his shoulder. It went rattling and bonging down the dome. Fortunately he had his left arm locked in the line and he dangled there for a few seconds, pawing with his right until he found the cornice again. When he was balanced he punched what was left of the cornice a couple of times with his fist. It held. He offered a desperate kind of prayer, got both arms around the cornice, and hauled his body up over it from under in a kip. The lights of the Yard reeled below him. He struggled with his weight, inching it away from the edge, from space, feeling with his left hand till it brushed the base of the spire. He got his arm around it then in one lunge and lay on the little cupola that would shine gold in daytime, hugging the spire tighter than he'd ever held anybody but Tawdry, and closed his eyes for a while.

Howie and Care Package are down below, he thought. They wouldn't come up any farther. He was in the really dangerous part now. All he had to do was clutch and—

He opened his eyes, and clutched.

He knew it the instant it happened. His fingers clamped shut on what they held and his breathing stopped. The Yard, Crabtown, the Severn all began to lift and tilt and revolve slowly around him. The already distant ground fell away a hundred miles more. He was weightless, falling, going to hit any second now. The whimper was locked in his throat but it was too strong for him and he heard it cry out in the night.

He half-crouched, half-lay there for a long time. The wind's getting louder, he thought, some time later. His fingers were hurting. Then he recognized Gray's voice. "Philo! Philo!"

"I'm up here."

"You okay? Where are you?"

"Up top."

"D'ye do it?"

"No."

"What's the matter? You clutch?"

The phrase, the arrogant assumption even from his friends that he couldn't hack it even now, made something happen in his chest. He actually heard himself snarl, like an animal.

"What?"

"Nothing, I said. Just wait. Give me some slack on that line."

"Yo."

In the dark, in the moonlight, a hundred and ninety feet above the Yard, Philo T. McGiffin made himself stand up. His legs were pretty shaky, he noted, and his hands were numb. He could see the tears in the gloves where his fingers were coming through. He looked upward along the shining shaft. I've got to save something for getting down, he thought. Even if I make it to the top, I've got it all to do over; get down. Can't cut it too fine, or else. . . .

Or else what?

Or I won't be around any more, right? he answered. But I won't be around the Academy anymore anyway, and so what's it matter?

Anyway, he still wasn't at the top.

He wrapped his arms around the spire—it was just narrow enough here at the base, about the diameter of a telephone pole— and then his legs.

He began to shinny his way up it.

Under his arms and against his face, pressed to it, its rough surface flaked and scraped and chipped. Cheap gilt, he thought. Or maybe expensive gold leaf. They didn't bother about saving money when they built this place. He tried to occupy his mind with the question as he worked upward. With each foot he gained now the world dripped away another mile, a dark semicircle below him, dotted with light, inked with vast spaces of black water. Damn— damn—a gust grabbed at his hat and nearly took it and he had to hang on with one arm and screw it back on with the other. Why hadn't he thought to rig the chinstrap? No way to do it now . . . he inched upward, humping himself up little by little, his chin scraping the cold stone . . . how high *was* this damned thing . . . it was pretty windy up here. . . .

His groping glove found suddenly nothing but space; then, cupping downward, felt a blunt pyramidal point about six inches across. Above it, above him, there was nothing but air. It was awful dark. He realized that part of the reason was that his eyes were squeezed shut. He opened one.

Yep. This was it. He hauled himself up another six inches and actually looked down at it, the little square moongilded weather-chipped pyramid top of the spire, the very highest point of the U.S. Naval Academy. It looked like it needed a good Keyes-type field day with nailbrush and Ajax.

With great care, he took off his cap and laid it over the point. It settled slightly, pushing a bulge up in the middle of the white cap cover. He pushed it down, making sure it was set solid. A stray gust after all this work . . . he didn't like to think of it.

"Okay, Mouse," he said aloud. "Back down."

He relaxed his hold and slid downward several feet. His wrists scraped but he hung on, feeling his face abrading too. He slid a few more feet, thinking about it. His friends were waiting below. Once he was with them he was as good as on the ground, as good as back in his rack. To reach them he had to halt at the bottom of the spire; swing around, facing the Yard, and still not freeze up; drop to his stomach on the cupola; feel with his feet for the rope down. As the procedure organized itself in his mind his feet hit the roof of the bell tower. He unwrapped his thighs from the spire with difficulty. *Jeez,* he thought, I'm numb. He was cold. His hands were raw.

Just to get back down, now, was all he wanted out of life.

Holding to the spire with one arm, he turned to face the cornice. Which one was it? That one—he saw the bulge of the knotted line around it. There. Now to let go and—

It all happened at once, and very quickly, though it took long to complete in his mind. He let go from the spire with his other arm. At the same time, though, he saw spread out below him like a temptation, but already lost to him, the whole Yard, all of Annapolis; the tree tops puffs of silver like shell-bursts; the old brick walks, threading lawns and fields like the wakes of circling ships; the spartan rectilinearities of Bancroft, Dahlgren, Luce; the winding dark of the Severn; the great shadow of the bay. And all of it, all so small, so distant, so far down.

At the same instant that he clutched, knowing that he could now never take the step to the edge of the cupola, to the line down, he felt the gritty snap of old tiles breaking underneath his feet.

His last thought as he went over the edge—it was clear, calm, not at all scared, and he had a flash of satisfaction, pride, that he, Philo T., could go out with such a give-a-shit thought—was that, whatever happened, he would never have to brace up again.

POSTSCRIPT

*I*n front of the two middle-aged men the polished wood of the table, shadowed in the dim light, was layered now with slowly drying, interlocking rings. At the civilian's elbow the square glass ashtray, engraved with the USNA seal, was heaped with the charred remains of several loads of latakia. The last of it smoldered in his pipe now, and through its haze the two men, civilian and officer, looked at each other as in the nearly empty taproom a clock sounded three bells.

"Yeah," drawled the commander. He rattled the last chips of ice in his glass and raised it, catching the eye of a sleepy Filipino. "Yeah. The Mouse. We never knew what he had until that night. And when the sun came up next morning—"

"It was just after reveille," said the civilian. "The whole Hall seemed to know something. Remember? We never said anything. But the Brigade all went out to T-court to see it. Way up there against the light, the top of the spire, a little small white dot—his old size 6½ cap."

"What ever happened to it, anyway?"

"J.J. got it. It was pretty raunchy when it finally blew down. Half rotted, and with bird shit all over the visor. He said he was going to keep it forever as a symbol of pure brass-assed balls. Probably went down with him on that cruiser."

"Uh huh," said the captain musingly. "But by that time—when it fell, finally—the Mouse was gone."

"Long gone. He was only around for a couple of weeks after that—long enough for his arm to knit, and his ribs. And all that ropeburn. The Executive Department wanted him out, out, out. Even Black Bart couldn't save him after that."

They sat for a while quiet, not speaking. The taproom was emptying, but a little eddy of alertness swept the stewards; they were looking toward the entrance. "Yes," said the commander, "old Philo had nerve, all right."

"More than you and me put together."

"I thought we'd lost him there for a minute, when we heard those tiles go. You tie a good bowline, Dick."

"Out of practice now. But thanks, Howie."

Their fresh drinks came. They sipped at them and glanced around the room. Only a few old grads were left. The younger officers, ensigns and second lieutenants, had left for the glossier more lively bars of the waterfront, where secretaries and blue-blazered executives out of D.C. and Baltimore packed themselves elbow to elbow. "Yeah," said Gray again, at last. "It's damn funny, how things turn out."

"I guess you're right." Commander H. J. Zeard, USN, lifted his gaunt arm, admiring the three slightly tarnished stripes as if they belonged to someone else. "You can't tell. We couldn't tell about the Mouse. Just like, back then, we couldn't tell, deep down, about ourselves; what we might become; what we might be like in his place, facing his challenges with our guts. Facing his fear—no matter how he learned to conceal it at first and then use it, turn it into his own kind of strength."

"You still go off on those flights, I see."

"So?"

"So, nothing." Gray sucked on his pipe, discovered it was out, and knocked the bowl empty in the ashtray. "Anyway, the room was sure quiet after he was gone, wasn't it? All that June Week— eight hundred guys fighting to climb Herndon, going up sheer greased granite on each other's shoulders, churning the Yard into mud—I was thinking about him. It was something he wanted so goddamned much, to make it through."

"And he did," said Zeard.

"Yeah. Enlisting as a sailor, and then that fight over his reappointment. Hell! Two plebe years—and boot camp too! He must have wanted it bad. But when he came back he had a reputation. And we were there to help out, as second class."

There was a stir at the door as he finished. The stewards stood more alertly. The murmur, the clink of glasses stopped, and the two men turned.

At the entrance a small man in uniform was hanging up his cap. He was slightly heavy and getting bald, with a tired, lined face. But the tiredness did not disguise sharp eyes, shaggy graying eyebrows, a hint of wrought iron in the set of his back that in some men would have looked pompous, but in him was calm and self-confident. As he shrugged his bridge coat off, helped by a tall aide, the broad gold bands of an admiral flashed forth.

"He's here," said Zeard.

The man looked out over the room for a moment, then saw them, waved, and made his way in their direction, pausing at several tables to shake hands. As he reached them both the civilian and the commander rose to their feet.

"Jeez, sit down, guys. Howie, Care Package—where'd you draw the chin whiskers? Figured I'd find some of the old class over here sucking up cheap booze."

"Hi, Mouse."

"Siddown, Phil. How's duty with the Joint Chiefs?"

"Scotch for me," said Philo McGiffin to four hovering stewards. "The Pentagon? In a state of panic, as usual. Wish I could have gotten over earlier. What have you two been doing all evening?"

"Just telling sea stories."

The admiral grinned. "Nothing about me, I hope?"

"Hell, no," said Zeard. "Why should we talk about you? No, I was just sitting here listening to the Care Package blow smoke."

And in the emptying taproom, late at night, the three old grads smiled at one another.

The Naval Institute Press is the book-publishing arm of the U.S. Naval Institute, a private, nonprofit, membership society for sea service professionals and others who share an interest in naval and maritime affairs. Established in 1873 at the U.S. Naval Academy in Annapolis, Maryland, where its offices remain today, the Naval Institute has members worldwide.

Members of the Naval Institute support the education programs of the society and receive the influential monthly magazine *Proceedings* and discounts on fine nautical prints and on ship and aircraft photos. They also have access to the transcripts of the Institute's Oral History Program and get discounted admission to any of the Institute-sponsored seminars offered around the country. Discounts are also available to the colorful bimonthly magazine *Naval History*.

The Naval Institute's book-publishing program, begun in 1898 with basic guides to naval practices, has broadened its scope in recent years to include books of more general interest. Now the Naval Institute Press publishes about one hundred titles each year, ranging from how-to books on boating and navigation to battle histories, biographies, ship and aircraft guides, and novels. Institute members receive discounts of 20 to 50 percent on the Press's more than eight hundred books in print.

Full-time students are eligible for special half-price membership rates. Life memberships are also available.

For a free catalog describing Naval Institute Press books currently available, and for further information about joining the U.S. Naval Institute, please write to:

Membership Department
U.S. Naval Institute
291 Wood Road
Annapolis, MD 21402-5034
Telephone: (800) 233-8764
Fax: (410) 269-7940
Web address: www.usni.org

Printed in the United States
33727LVS00004B/121-297

9 781557 506894